D1566150

THE FINDING

Nicky Charles

The Finding
Copyright © 2018, 2016, 2011 by Nicky Charles
Ingram Paperback Edition

All rights reserved. This book may not be reproduced or used in any form whatsoever without permission from the author, except in the case of brief quotations embodied in reviews. Please do not participate in or encourage piracy of copyrighted materials in violation of the author's rights. All characters and storylines are the property of the author. Your support and respect are appreciated.

This book is a work of fiction. Names, places, characters and incidents are drawn from the author's imagination and are used fictitiously. Any resemblance to actual events, locales, organizations, or persons either living or dead is entirely coincidental.

This book contains mature content and is intended for mature readers.

Edited by Jan Gordon
Line edits by Moody Edits

Cover Design by Jazer Designs
Cover images used under license from Shutterstock.com
Paw print and wolf head logo Copyright © Doron Goldstein, Designer

ISBN: 978-1-989058-15-2

THE FINDING

Prologue

Las Vegas, Nevada, USA...

Cassie stood at the edge of an alleyway, staring out at the breaking dawn. A few cars drove past but none of the drivers turned their heads in her direction. Just to be sure, she stepped back a bit. The street was lined with stores and small businesses, and in the distance there appeared to be a number of flashing, lighted signs. If she didn't know better, she'd think it looked like Las Vegas. No, the bus she'd been on couldn't have travelled that far! She tucked her hair behind her ears and furrowed her brow, wondering where she might be, and how she'd ended up in an alley.

The last thing she remembered was lying on a bed in a motel, having spent half the night fleeing from the sight of her uncle's death and the wolf attack. She'd taken her medication and tried to calm down by thinking of happier places. That was the last thing she could recall until waking up here a few minutes ago.

Blearily, she'd opened her eyes, at first too groggy to even wonder why her body was wedged between a brick wall and a dumpster, her muscles cramped and aching. Then she'd become aware of what had stirred her from her sleep; a tickling sensation on her hand. Rolling her head to the side, she'd discovered a mouse was crawling over her palm. Screaming, she'd snatched her hand back to her chest and skittered a few feet away, watching in a combination of horror and disgust as the tiny creature ran into a hole under the metal bin.

She'd been wiping her hand on her shirt, trying to erase the feeling of small feet and quivering whiskers when another shock hit her. Frantically, she'd looked around, her brain suddenly acknowledging she wasn't in her motel room. Her heart had been pounding, panic wrapping around her like an iron fist as she took in the fact that there was no bed, no TV, no faded curtains; just brick walls, utility meters, bits of garbage and graffiti.

The strap of her bag had been clenched in her hand; amazingly enough, when she checked, there still money inside it, so she hadn't been robbed. And her clothing, while filthy and wrinkled, was intact which probably meant she hadn't been assaulted. Her skin crawled as she thought of all the things that could have happened to her while she'd been unconscious. Obviously something *had* occurred though, otherwise how had she arrived in this place?

Wracking her brain, she had no recollection of the events that led to her being here. She glanced fearfully at the shadowed areas around her, wondering if the werewolf had something to do with this; if he was lurking, waiting to attack. There was no sign of the creature, but she couldn't relax. It might still be following her, ready to end her life as easily as it had ended Mr. Aldrich's.

The memory of the large black wolf and its blood-drenched muzzle had her shivering, despite the relative warmth of the air. She stepped back into the alleyway and, wrapping her arms around her waist, hunkered down by the dumpster where she'd awoken. The smell of garbage and stale cooking grease assaulted her nose and she made a face. Striving to ignore the unpleasant odour, she leaned her head back against the brick wall and stared at the graffiti-covered sign that graced the steel door straight across from her; Chinese and Thai Restaurant, Deliveries Only. She furrowed her brow; apparently she was in a back alley behind a number of businesses. Glancing to either side, she noted other similar doors giving support to her assumption.

Okay. A back alley, a restaurant, but where...?

At that moment a white delivery truck turned down the narrow passageway, roaring towards her. She pressed herself closer to the wall, feeling a moment of panic before realizing the dumpster provided her with some protection. She exhaled in relief and adjusted her position so she could observe the vehicle as it stopped a good distance from her hiding place.

Eventually, a man got out whistling tunelessly. She watched him go about his business, taking cartons out of the truck and balancing them carefully as he pounded on a door. The door swung open and he handed the containers to someone who stood inside. A few words were exchanged but she was too far away to make out what they were.

The man never once glanced in her direction, solely focused on his early morning duties, but she knew she had to move. No doubt other trucks would be through there in the near future and she didn't want to be found crouched by a dumpster. People would ask questions; questions to which she wouldn't have any answers.

Her mind racing, she searched for a possible course of action. She'd never been alone before; there'd always been someone with her; guiding her, smoothing the way. Knowing she needed to do something—to go somewhere—but being solely responsible for the decisions and the consequences was so overwhelming. How she longed to be back in the security of her uncle's home. To hear him blustering away; to see Franklin, the butler, pulling faces behind the old man's back. To have Cook fussing and making her favourite meals. Her chin quivered. Oh God, how could her world have been destroyed so quickly?

A lone tear trickled down her face and she quickly wiped it away. Crying wouldn't help or change facts. Her uncle was dead and she was alone now with a crazed werewolf chasing her. There was no one to lean on, no one to come to her rescue. She had to handle this situation on her own and that meant finding safe shelter and food. She needed to hide, perhaps even establish a new identity.

A short, wry, laugh escaped her. Her private tutors had never covered topics related to running for your life while being chased by a werewolf. How remiss of them. She'd really have to bring that point to their attention, if she lived long enough to see them again!

Her brief moment of levity quickly died at the sound of the delivery truck's engine starting. It roared past her leaving a cloud of exhaust and dust in its wake. Coughing, she forced herself to her feet, wiping her eyes and giving an inelegant sniff. Action was better than staying in one place. At least it gave the impression that she had a plan. Still holding tightly to her bag, she walked back to the end of the alley, resuming her earlier position in the shadows.

The sun was higher in the sky now and people seemed intent on getting to their work or appointments, hurrying past her hiding place. No one glanced towards the shadowed alley entrance. The relative anonymity of her position gave her some modicum of comfort as she considered her options.

There were a variety of businesses lining the street. Her gaze skimmed over dress shops and nail salons before finally focusing on two; a restaurant on the corner and the variety store beside it. She squared her shoulders in preparation of leaving the relative safety of the alley.

"Hey there, girly! What're you doing?" A voice spoke from nearby and she jumped, backing away until her spine was against the opposite brick wall. Her vision blurred for a moment as fear washed over her. Had the werewolf found her? No, it couldn't be the creature; it wouldn't give her warning by calling out.

Blinking rapidly, she forced her eyes to focus on the speaker. It was a young man, probably in his early twenties. He had brown hair, blue eyes, and was dressed in a respectable looking shirt and pair of pants.

She clutched her bag to her chest and stared at him warily.

"Are you okay?" The man looked concerned but didn't attempt to approach her. "Are you in trouble? A runaway?"

She shook her head and licked her dry lips. "No."

"Funny, 'cause you sort of look like life's been treating you pretty bad." He studied her for a minute, then smiled and held out his hand. "My name's Kellen. Kellen Anderson."

Hesitantly, she extended her own hand. "I'm...er...Sandra." She heeded the voice inside that told her not to reveal too much, so she switched to another derivative of her full name.

The Finding

"Pleased to meet you, er...Sandra. Strange name, with the 'er' in front of it." Kellen grinned and winked. "Never mind. I'll call you Sandy, okay?"

She nodded not sure if she trusted this jovial person.

"You look like you could use something to eat and maybe a place to stay? I've been down on my luck before, so I know what it's like. Actually, I'm sort of on the downslide right now since I just lost a poker game up the road. Come on. Misery loves company. I'll buy you breakfast, no strings attached." He gestured towards the restaurant.

"I...I have money." Immediately after she spoke, she chastised herself. Telling a complete stranger—one she'd met at the edge of an alleyway, no less—that she had money was not a good idea. Trying for some damage control, she qualified her answer. "Not much, but enough to buy my own food."

Kellen shrugged. "Sure. No skin off my nose. At least we can sit together, right? Eating alone is no fun."

Her stomach chose that moment to growl and he laughed, holding his hands out at his side. "Hey, I'm completely harmless and you're obviously starving. There's usually a crowd in the restaurant, so you don't need to worry. You won't be alone with me."

She paused, then gave a brief nod. The idea of being by herself was daunting, the werewolf could be anywhere, but surely it wouldn't attack in front of witnesses. Having someone with her, even a stranger, seemed like a good idea. Besides, she needed information and right now Kellen was her only source.

"Not much of a talker, are you?" Kellen quipped as he led her across the street. "That's okay, though. It doesn't bother me. Listen, no offense but you might want to get cleaned up. There's a ladies' room right inside the door. I'll get us a table while you use the facilities." He held the restaurant door open for her.

She gave him a brief smile. "Thanks, I wouldn't mind washing up." As she headed to the washroom, she glanced back. Kellen was already sitting down, perusing the menu. She allowed herself to relax. He seemed nice enough.

Three years later, in Stump River, Ontario, Canada...

Bryan sat in front of the computer, frowning at the screen. He drummed his fingers on the desk and sighed then ran his hands through his hair, flexing his shoulders and arching his back.

Ryne looked up from the papers he was working on. "Let me guess; you're still brooding over that girl, right?"

"Yeah, I keep thinking I'll find something if I look long enough." The Cassandra Greyson case had become an obsession for him. Every time he vowed to forget her, something called him back to take one more look. It was as if his inner wolf, having had a brief yet tantalizing scent of the girl, couldn't relinquish the hunt for her.

"You've been working on it for the past three years. What makes you think today will be any different?" Ryne could be annoyingly practical at times.

"I don't know. For some reason I can't let her go. Maybe it's the Beta in me, needing to protect the pack; you know the danger a rogue wolf could put us all in." He swivelled his chair until he faced his Alpha.

"But the fact is, she *hasn't* gone rogue or we would have heard something. Though how a young kid like that is keeping her wolf under control all by herself, is beyond me." Ryne narrowed his eyes and reiterated what they both already knew. "You traced her to that motel in Kansas—"

"And then she just disappeared." Bryan finished the sentence. It was a story they'd gone over many times. "I realize almost two weeks had passed before I arrived at her last known location, but there should have been a residual scent leading away. Instead, there was nothing; no scent, no trail, no one saw her leave town. There was nothing on the surveillance cameras at the bus stop. She stepped off the bus, found a room at the motel across the street, and vanished. All I found was a trace scent on the pillows and that pill wedged between the nightstand and the headboard."

"A prescription strength sedative."

The Finding

"Yeah. Very hard to get hold of and used only under strict medical supervision. Definitely suitable for a Lycan, but heavy duty stuff for a human. Whoever gave it to her knew something about Lycans."

"That would have been her guardian, Anthony Greyson. I'm sure that's how he kept her under control during the full moon, though how he knew..." Ryne let his voice trail off.

"Well, that pill was the only concrete clue I found in Kansas. Two days later all her bank accounts were emptied from an instant teller inside a casino in Las Vegas and her credit cards were maxed out. From there, it's a dead end."

"Except for that anonymous personal ad someone tried to place in the Stump River Gazette. It's a good thing Melody was working there the day it came in."

Bryan flipped open a file and took out a piece of paper. Unfolding it he read, "To whom it may concern. Cassandra Greyson was last seen in Las Vegas. She accessed her bank accounts at a casino ATM, then withdrew the maximum amount allowed on all her credit cards." He shook his head. "Who places a personal ad like that?"

"Someone who's trying to lead us around by the nose."

"Right." Bryan rubbed his chin. "All I was able to determine was that the person who sent this had to be elderly. It was written on an old manual typewriter. I didn't think anyone used those things anymore." He stared at the paper for a moment longer before carefully folding it and tucking it back in the file.

"Someone still does and it gives me the creeps to think they know enough about us to send the note to Stump River." Ryne growled softly, his fingers clenching. "It's kept us in a constant state of alert waiting for the other shoe to drop."

"It's been nerve wracking." Bryan agreed, easing back in his chair. "We could move, start over where we aren't known."

"But where? Finding a new territory isn't easy. Stump River was a once in a lifetime chance. No, until we know the source of the letter, we aren't doing anything."

Bryan nodded. "The sender might have been trying to flush us out, watching for any sudden movement in the area."

"And it's too vague to enact the Keeping." Ryne sighed heavily. "So we sit tight and keep our eyes and ears open."

Bryan rubbed the back of his neck and frowned. "Yeah, I guess. This whole situation has me frustrated. After all this time, I've made no real progress."

"Not true. You confirmed the Greyson girl was in Vegas at one point in time. Getting the hotel to let you look at their surveillance footage was no easy task."

Bryan laughed softly at the memory. "Thank heaven the head of security was female and she liked my eyes."

"From the story you told when you got back home, I don't think it was just your eyes she was interested in."

"There might have been a few other features that drew her attention." He grinned for a few moments thinking of the sexual romp he'd had while in the city. For some reason, his libido had been in overdrive that weekend. He laughed softly, then leaned forward to study the screen again. "I was looking at this footage that shows someone using the ATM machine at the time Cassandra Greyson's account was emptied."

Ryne stood up and moved to the computer, peering over Bryan's shoulder. "Do you see something new?"

"Not really. It's the same thing as always. Average sized individual, wearing jeans and a hoodie pulled up over his or her head and low across the forehead. Unisex sunglasses. Chin tucked into the collar."

"They knew what they were doing; knew there'd be cameras recording the transaction."

"Yeah, there's nothing here except... See that bit of a shadow?" He turned his chair back to the computer and pointed to a spot on the screen. "I think someone was standing there, watching."

"Could be." Ryne stood up straight and shrugged. "It doesn't really help us much, though."

"Maybe not. But it means she might not be on her own. I think she met up with someone and went with them to Vegas, possibly realizing it was a perfect place to get lost in a crowd."

"So where did she go after that?"

Bryan shook his head. "Damned if I know. I checked every bus, train, and plane out of there from the day of this footage and for two weeks afterwards. There was no one matching her description."

"So she must have left by car or stayed in the area."

"Uh-huh. I searched all over that city and there was no sign of her. And I put alerts out to packs all over the country to contact me if they see her, but no one has ever reported anything."

"You'd think after three years someone would have noticed a lone wolf; an inexperienced lone wolf at that. How has she stayed hidden and managed the lunar changes? Those pills must be used up by now. Someone must know something."

At that moment, Melody called from the kitchen. "Ryne, did you buy chocolate ice cream when you were in town?"

Ryne grimaced. "Since she's been pregnant and can't have her coffee, she's switched to chocolate, but it's not mellowing her mood."

"Isn't chocolate just as bad?"

"Are you volunteering to tell her? I survived the no-coffee rants. I'm not inciting another one!" Both men winced as they recalled Melody's reaction when Nadia, the nurse practitioner, e-mailed her to cut back on coffee until the baby was born.

"Hey, she's your mate and you're the Alpha. Go do your duty."

"Thanks, Bryan. You're a real pal."

Bryan shook his head, amused at his Alpha's predicament, then returned to studying the image on the computer screen. Narrowing his eyes, he searched for clues, his inner wolf stirring restlessly over the long delayed hunt. Somewhere out there Cassandra Greyson was a lone Lycan and he was determined to bring her in.

Chapter 1

Las Vegas, Nevada, USA…

The air felt cool and damp against her face as she moved through the trees, the greyish-brown trunks rising high on either side of her. Pine needles littered the forest floor, deadening the sound of her feet as she padded along. Twice she stopped and searched the shadowy depths of the forest, before lifting her muzzle and sniffing, nostrils flaring as she took in the myriad of scents that drifted by on the breeze.

Suddenly, instinct had her hackles rising. Another presence was nearby. Cocking her ears, she searched for a sign of the other one. As always, his scent eluded her. His paws made no sound. Inexplicably, he was just—there!

Like a ghost, he appeared out of nowhere, standing in front of her, blocking her way. Thick light brown fur covered his massive body, muscles rippling as he shifted his stance and raised his head in challenge. His beauty took her breath away each time she saw him and on each occasion she wondered what his name was.

Part of her wanted to submit, to expose her throat and belly. Her tail dipped between her legs, even as she fought the urge to roll over. His hazel eyes narrowed and she quivered until, finally breaking away from his gaze, she turned quickly and began to run.

Where she was running to, she didn't know, but the need to escape was strong. She flattened her ears and ran as if her life depended on it, her body low to the ground. The sound of him following her was easy to detect. He made no effort to hide his pursuit.

He was breathing hard, she could hear it. His bigger frame was at a disadvantage when it came to speed, yet with every stride his longer legs brought him closer and closer.

Panic began to well within her and she dug deep inside putting on a burst of speed, twisting around trees, jumping over logs. It was all in vain. Without warning, his body slammed into hers and they both fell to the ground. She rolled, attempting to get to her feet, but even as she tried to stand, he was on top of her.

Hot breath fanned across the side of her face. Her peripheral vision caught a glimpse of shiny white teeth, before she felt those same teeth penetrating her fur, biting her neck.

"No!" Part of her was screaming in protest even as another voice, one deeper inside her, cried out *yes*, craving his domination, his possession. She pushed that part of her aside and struggled. This beast was like the one that had killed that man, Mr. Aldrich. It was an unnatural creature known as a werewolf.

Her uncle had said she was one as well, just before he died. But she wasn't; she couldn't be. She wasn't a wild animal. She couldn't kill anyone. Could she? Even as she fought against the wolf that loomed over her, a part of her mind was acknowledging her four legs, her tail, and the brown fur covering her body. Closing her eyes against the hot tears that threatened to spill down her face, she screamed her denial of the truth.

"No! Please, no! I can't be a werewolf. I don't want this!" Pushing and struggling, she flailed against the beast that seemed to surround her. She couldn't get away. Her breathing became rapid and shallow; everything was growing dark and she felt herself slipping into unconsciousness, falling and then…

Cassie's eyes flew open as her body landed against something hard, the breath whooshing from her lungs. She looked at her surroundings and relief washed through her as she realized it had only been another nightmare.

Shaking in the aftermath of her nocturnal imagination, she disentangled herself from the blanket and pushed her hair from her face. She was in her bedroom, having laid down for a nap while waiting for Kellen to get home. The dream had been just that, a dream.

Well, not exactly. As she stood and picked up the blanket, she acknowledged that the woods and the other wolf were non-existent, but her being a wolf—a werewolf to be exact—was all too real. She hid from the grim reality as much as possible, however her subconscious mind wouldn't let the notion rest. It was in the dark recesses of her mind that the beast inside her roamed free and sought out others of its kind.

It wouldn't happen in reality. She jutted her chin in resolve as she folded the blanket and clutched it to her chest. She'd never seek out others of her kind. The filthy animals were interested only in killing and dominating and…sex. Her mind shied away from that last idea. Her dreams were always erotic, usually involving a lusty male who was intent on tracking her down and taking her.

The memory had her shifting uncomfortably as arousal stirred inside her. She curled her lip at the irony of the situation; her nightmares were hotter than Hades while her real life was…

No. She didn't want to think about that right now. Setting down the blanket, she went to the dresser to check her appearance. The turquoise top she wore went well with her Mediterranean colouring, even though she was still pale as a result of her dream. After applying a swipe of blush, she studied her eyes and decided the thick lashes and deep green irises needed no enhancement. A touch of gloss on her full lips completed her makeup.

Grabbing a comb, she set to work on her hair, not for the first time wishing it shimmered with highlights instead of being a solid dark brown. The colour reminded her too much of the animal in her dream. Yes, she could try dyeing it, but she always wondered how the colour would take, given her unusual genetic makeup.

Glancing at the clock, she realized it was time to start dinner. Kellen would be home soon and she wanted to surprise him. Setting the comb down, she headed to the kitchen, resolutely pushing all thoughts of wolves from her mind. Tonight it would be all about her and Kellen.

Stump River, Ontario, Canada...

Bryan grunted and firmed his jaw, ignoring his protesting muscles. Sweat trickled down his face as he lifted the weight, counting in his head, before giving a sigh of relief and lowering the heavy disks. They clanged against the metal stand, the sound echoing off the walls of the exercise room. He relaxed against the bench, breathing heavily and feeling pleasantly spent.

"Done for the day?" A towel landed in his face as the speaker walked past.

Wearily, he reached up and wiped the sweat from his face and chest while eyeing the room's other occupant. Daniel was chugging back a bottle of water, his body glistening from an intense workout.

Bryan sat up, giving his arms a shake and then stretching. His muscles ached from the strain they'd been under; not tired, just well used. "No. I think I'll go for a run. Want to join me?"

"Nah. I'm whipped. You Beta-types can exercise until you barf, but not me. I'm the intellectual in the pack, remember?"

Snorting, Bryan studied his young friend. At twenty-two, Daniel might claim to be an intellectual, but his lean frame was still packed with muscle and had all the local ladies swooning. Make that most of the local ladies, he amended, noting that Daniel was staring out the window with a look of longing in his eyes.

The object of the younger man's attention was Tessa, a doe-eyed, dark haired Spanish beauty who had joined the pack three years ago. Not that Tessa ever gave Daniel any encouragement, but that hadn't stopped the man from wanting her.

Shaking his head at the follies of young love, he stood up and clapped Daniel on the shoulder. "Why don't you make a move on her?"

Daniel firmed his mouth and shoved his hands in his pockets. "She's not ready yet."

The Finding

"Ready? She's nineteen; definitely time for her to choose a mate."

"You know her history." Anger washed over Daniel's face and Bryan gripped his shoulder.

"I do. But she can't live in the past forever. Someone needs to help her move on. Why not you?"

Shrugging, Daniel threw his water bottle in the recycling bin and picked up his discarded t-shirt. "I don't know. The time never seems right."

"If you wait too long, you might lose your chance." Bryan threw out the warning and headed for the door, knowing he'd pushed all he could. Daniel had to be the one to make the move.

Once outside, he debated about turning into his wolf form, but decided to finish his workout as he'd started. His human body needed the exercise more than his wolf did.

Bending to tighten his laces, he heard giggling coming from the nearby gazebo and glanced that way. An exasperated sigh escaped his lips as he saw two young girls peering at him. Becky and Emily were the daughters of the newest family to join Ryne's pack. At fifteen and thirteen respectively, they were harmless enough, but the crush they'd developed on him was both annoying and embarrassing.

As Beta, he was the second in command, the Alpha's bodyguard, and the pack's enforcer. Being followed by giggling teenagers did nothing for his image, nor did he know how to deal with them. He didn't want to hurt their feelings, but subtle hints weren't having much effect in dissuading them.

Knowing if he delayed any longer, they'd actually work up the nerve to approach him, he got to his feet and prepared to walk past them.

"Hi Bryan!" The girls spoke at the same time. One was attempting an exaggerated model stance while the other settled for tossing her long blond hair over her shoulder.

"'Evening, girls." He kept his eyes focused straight ahead and didn't slow his pace in case they thought it was an invitation to join him. It wouldn't be the first time it had happened. As he continued on his way, he caught parts of their conversation.

"Did you see how his muscles rippled? And his butt is so tight."

"Mmm. And his voice. It's so deep it makes me shiver."

"I like his hair best. Dark blond is so cool."

"No. I think it's more of a light brown."

"Whatever. His eyes are dreamy."

"Oh yeah, hazel eyes."

He winced. Geez, it was like he was some pin-up poster boy. It was nice when the ladies in town were all over him, but these two were just kids. It made him feel creepy, like he was some kind of pervert. He broke into a slow jog and headed around the curve in the driveway, catching a glimpse of the girls still staring his way.

He wondered when he'd quit being a kid himself and why he felt he was so much older now. After all, he was only twenty-four. That was young, wasn't it? Maybe it was the responsibilities of being Beta that weighed him down and made him feel older. The pack was growing. Ryne was going to be a father. He chuckled at the thought of his bad-ass Alpha changing diapers. He could never imagine himself in such a position.

Breaking into a run, he veered off the driveway and headed deeper into the woods. Nope, a Beta had to be tough and ready to defend the pack or deal with trouble makers. Settling down to family life wasn't part of his plan. Right now, he was a no-strings attached kind of guy. That's how he liked it and that's how things would remain.

Las Vegas, Nevada, USA...

"Hey, Kellen! It's almost supper time." Cassie called out from the stove where she was stirring a pot of pasta sauce. She hummed a Latin tune under her breath as she worked, swaying to the beat. Her singing was off key, but it didn't matter. Her plans had gone off without a hitch so far and she was feeling extremely pleased with herself.

Executing a fancy step, she paused and listened carefully. Kellen hadn't answered yet. Opening her mouth to call out again, she heard a board creak near the front door. She frowned. Now what was he doing? He'd only arrived home a few minutes ago.

Perhaps he was playing a joke on her as he sometimes did. A mischievous grin spread across her face and she decided to turn the tables on him. She set the spoon down and tiptoed to the archway that separated the kitchen from the living room. Peeking around the corner, she saw Kellen was almost at the front door.

Stepping out, she cleared her throat loudly, planted her hands on her hips and spoke in a mock serious tone. "And where do you think you're going?"

Kellen froze, then slowly turned around to face her. Something about his posture gave her the feeling he'd been trying to sneak away unnoticed rather than planning to trick her. His expression, a combination of guilt and exasperation at being caught, confirmed the fact. "Out."

Her playful mood rapidly evaporated at his evasive answer. She leaned against the doorway, suddenly feeling weary as she took in his appearance.

His lithe body was dressed for a night out with the boys. Nothing special of course but not his usual at home gear of sweats and a comfortable old t-shirt. Well-fitting denim encased his hips, a band t-shirt showed off his broad shoulders and a brown leather jacket was clutched in his hand. The jacket was the same shade as his hair, which was one of the reasons she'd bought it for him last Christmas. Since he often worked the night shift, and evening temperatures could be quite cool in the desert, she'd deemed it to be a practical extravagance. He'd been duly appreciative of the gift, but those had been happier times.

"Out where?" She knew the answer already, yet some devil inside prodded her onward even as she questioned her own actions. Why did she do this to herself? Why did she set herself up to be hurt by asking stupid questions? She should just let him go, turn the proverbial blind eye to his behaviour; but hiding from the problem wouldn't solve anything.

Really? A voice inside her taunted. *You hide every day; keeping me locked up, denying my existence. Your own secret is a living thing, struggling to get out and make itself known.*

Never mind, she hissed to herself. That's not the issue right now. She pushed the voice firmly away, focusing on Kellen. What excuse would he use this time?

Kellen's mouth was drawn into a straight line. She watched the blue of his eyes deepen before he lowered his lashes as if trying to hide his expression. "Out with friends. It's no big deal." Giving a shrug, he pulled on the leather jacket and adjusted the collar.

"I know the kind of friends you mean and—"

"You're not my mother, okay? So lay off!" The angry words were flung at her and she fought not to respond in kind. Both of them shouting wouldn't solve anything. Someone needed to keep a cool head. As usual, it would be her.

Taking a deep breath, she steadied herself. "Kellen," she stepped forward, her hand held out beseechingly. "Stay home. Please. Keep me company like you promised."

He winced at the word *promised*.

She paused until he met her gaze, then smiled tentatively, gently. "I...I made your favourite meal."

The words hung between them, the bubble of hope like a palpable entity while she waited for him to comment. She'd never been taught to cook, but had mastered the basics over the past few years. Her lack of ability was a standing joke between them; Kellen gently teasing her about her culinary disasters then helping her turn them into something edible. Spaghetti and meat sauce was one of her few successful, independent meals and he frequently claimed it was the best he'd ever tasted. He could be so sweet sometimes.

Silence stretched between them and his lack of response forced the smile to fade from her face. She let her hand fall to her side and swallowed. Kellen shifted his weight before exhaling slowly. His eyes flicked towards her before lowering to stare at the floor. "I'll only be a little while. When I get back, I'll heat some up."

The Finding

Clenching her hands, she concentrated on the feeling of her nails digging into her palms. Better to feel physical pain than to let the hurt settle in her heart. He was lying. He wouldn't be a while; he just said that to assuage his guilt.

Bitterness crept into her voice. "No you won't. I know you're gambling again." She watched his shoulders hunch as if to protect himself from her words. "I'll not pay off your debts again." The words were tossed out like a challenge.

"It's a few measly bets. You know, me and the guys playing poker. No big stakes." He brushed his hair from his eyes and gave a light laugh. "Besides, it's not like you don't have money—"

She was angry and let him know it. *"My money*, not yours. And I'm saving it in case of an emergency." Kellen knew that—oh, not the exact kind of emergency she was worried about—but he knew she didn't want to spend it foolishly. "We live on what we make from our jobs." She lifted her chin and glared at him.

"Yeah, right." He was using his snarky attitude now, his hands shoved in his back pockets, a sneer twisting his lips. God, she hated that tone. "Like the money you earn as a cashier at a grocery store will ever make us rich."

"We don't need to be rich!" The volume of her voice rose, despite the fact she knew she shouldn't respond to his words. It was the same old argument. Kellen always wanted more.

Correspondingly, he spoke louder as well. "Maybe you don't, but I have no intention of stocking shelves and mopping floors for the rest of my life. I want more than this!" He swept his arm out to encompass the living room of their small, rented home.

She knew what he saw. Worn furniture and an older style TV; tables she'd purchased at a second-hand shop and draped with colourful fabric. It wasn't much, but it was clean and it was theirs. They owed no one. She refused to acknowledge the stinging hurt of his derisive words. While she was proud of how they'd managed thus far, Kellen wasn't content with the life they'd forged together. He was always seeking that mythical pot of gold.

She brushed an imaginary speck from the small table beside her, then looked at him out of the corner of her eye. Exhaling slowly, she tried to keep her voice calm and reasonable. "Gambling is a bad habit. You told me you'd quit."

"Just like you quit the drugs?" He fired the words back at her.

She folded her arms defensively and looked away from his accusing stare. How typical of him to try to twist the conversation around. "I never promised you I'd quit. Besides, it's not the same thing."

"No? I've gone for months at a time without placing a single bet. Can you say the same thing?"

She was silent. She needed her monthly 'fix' as he called it, though for far different reasons than he suspected.

Kellen continued, heaping blame on her. "Who else has a once a month habit like yours? You lock yourself up for three days every month. You won't let me see you or talk to you. Hell, you even tried to ban me from the house while you're off on some freaky drug induced trip."

She knew he was trying to draw attention away from his own shortcomings, but the truth of his words left her with no defence, or at least not one she could share. Even after all this time, he knew nothing about the three days from hell she suffered every month. Days filled with fear; fighting the raging voice inside, struggling not to convert into a monster capable of killing any person who got in her way. Hating herself and what she was. He had no idea of her self-loathing.

"I've heard you when I'm home; the crying, thrashing around, babbling to yourself. And you look like shit afterwards."

"It's not your concern." She hugged herself even more tightly, trying to forget what it was like; how with each month the struggle grew harder, how the beast was becoming stronger.

"Sorry sweetheart, but it *is* my concern. I'm the one you call when you wake up God knows where with no idea of how you even got out of the house. I'm the one who covers for you at work. I'm the one risking my neck and possible arrest every time

I buy your illegal drugs." His face was ruddy with emotion by time he finished speaking.

She shifted uncomfortably, knowing the dicey situation her need placed him in. "I never said you had to. I can buy them myself."

Kellen snorted. "Yeah. Right. In case you've forgotten, the dealers don't know you. You don't know how to talk to them, and a pretty, naive girl like you wandering the streets is asking for trouble."

Giving a half shrug, she knew he was right, but didn't want to admit the fact. When she'd first run out of her migraine medication—well by then she'd known it wasn't for migraines, but that was what she still called it—she'd gone to a clinic in the hopes of getting more. Her request had been met with stunned silence and then a flurry of activity as the staff had started to make arrangements for blood work, urine samples, and a plethora of other tests. Realizing that something she'd said must have made the nurse wary, she'd slipped out of the small clinic when no one was looking, fearful that her secret might be discovered.

Once she was home, she began researching the medication on-line, only to find that it was a heavy sedative rarely used and only under strict medical supervision. It had come as a shock to discover what her uncle had been pumping into her month after month, yet fear of the consequences, should she not take the drugs, drove her to find more.

Her previously sheltered existence as the ward of a multimillionaire had left her exceptionally ill-prepared to deal with real life, let alone the seamier side of it. The first time she'd tried to buy her medication on the street, Kellen had watched from a distance and narrowly saved her from approaching an undercover narcotics officer. After that near debacle, he'd taken over the task.

"And do you know how hard it is for me to get that stuff?" He ran his hand through his hair. "The dealers think I'm crazy. No one takes that junk for fun."

"That's my business." The weight of her guilt made her snap at him.

"Just like the occasional night of gambling is mine." Kellen growled back before striding to the door.

"Kellen!" His name ripped from her throat as she called after him, not caring that her voice betrayed her emotional pain. She hated parting this way, hated how their relationship was falling apart.

He grabbed the handle, but paused before opening the door. Seconds ticked past as she watched him standing there, his head bowed down. His shoulders rose and fell once, then he turned and looked at her, his eyes reflecting his internal grief. "Sandy, I...I'm sorry."

He half turned to her and her heart beat faster, hoping he would choose to stay home, that he'd choose her over the thrill of gaming. She tried to put her heart in her gaze, begging him wordlessly, promising, pleading.

A car horn sounded from the street. He gave a start and darted a glance out the window. "That'll be Greg." For a moment, he seemed torn and she thought she might stand a chance, but his friend beeped the horn again, obviously impatient. His hand flexed on the door knob. "I...I have to go. I'll talk to you tomorrow." Quickly, he pulled the door open and stepped onto the front porch. There was a miniscule pause in his stride and he spoke without turning around. "We'll talk later. I...I love you."

"I love you, too." She whispered the words, wondering if they were even true. It didn't matter though; he hadn't waited to hear her reply. The door shut quietly and she allowed her shoulders to slump. She leaned her head against the wall; the smooth, coolness of the painted surface felt good against her flushed face. A single snort of sardonic laughter escaped her. The fact that he called her Sandy—a fake name she'd given him three years ago—epitomized their relationship. Secrets and deceit were interwoven into their lives; he didn't even know her real name was Cassandra or that her family had called her Cassie.

Pushing off from the wall, she crossed the room. She hadn't really expected to make him stay, but she'd hoped. Insanely, ridiculously, she hoped that this time... With a roll of her eyes, she cut off her own thinking. Who was she trying to fool? The gambling was a sickness within him. For periods of time it went into remission, but it always came back; rearing its ugly head and destroying the happiness and peace that had developed between them. Sure it was his pay cheque to waste, but it put an added burden on her to cover household expenses and she resented the fact.

She pulled aside the curtain to stare out the window at the car parked out front. Kellen was walking towards it, laughing at something one of his cronies had called out to him. Even at this distance she could sense the change in him. There was a bounce in his step; his voice indistinct yet full of excitement. Energy seemed to radiate from him as adrenaline pumped through his system.

He might berate her for her supposed habit, but gambling was his drug. She'd seen the effects up close. His eyes dilated and became overly bright as he scanned the gaming table; the trembling of his hands, the way he'd lick his lips and his breathing would quicken.

Kellen climbed into the car, his friend barely giving him time to shut the door before pulling away from the curb and speeding down the street. Letting the curtain fall into place, she turned and wandered back to the kitchen, her steps echoing in the quiet, lonely house. The meal she'd prepared earlier no longer seemed appetizing, but she forced herself to eat a small portion. When she was finished, she put away the leftovers. Why did she even bother? Maybe she should be spiteful and throw Kellen's portion in the garbage. No, this wasn't a silly, childish game and she wouldn't stoop to such petty revenge. Besides, she couldn't afford to be that wasteful.

As she prepared to leave the room, she took a moment to do a quick survey, checking the stove was off and the tap wasn't dripping. Her gaze passed over the table and the small bouquet she'd arranged. It was flanked by two candles, all ready to celebrate the anniversary of the day they'd met.

Three years ago today, she'd first set eyes on Kellen. At the time, she'd been scared out of her wits, not knowing which way to turn. He'd been her knight in shining armour, showing her how to survive. She sighed. Now she wasn't sure what he was anymore.

For some reason she decided to light one of the candles. The flickering flame cast shadows across the wall and table surface, creating mysterious images. She squinted trying to determine what the shapes looked like, but they shifted too quickly. She smiled a little crookedly. It was like her own life. Mysterious shadows and secrets seemed to dance around her and she, well, she was the lone candle; her supposed partner was decidedly absent.

Reaching out, she let her hand hover around the warmth of the flame, feeling its heat, mesmerized by its brightness. Then, firming her chin, she blew it out and headed to bed.

Chapter 2

The first tentative fingers of dawn were streaking the sky as Kellen unlocked the front door and let himself into the small house he shared with Sandy. He closed the door as quietly as possible, the sound of the lock snicking into place making him wince. Standing in the entryway, he listened carefully, and gave a slow sigh of relief when, hearing nothing but silence, he realized Sandy must still be sleeping. There was still an hour left before her alarm was due to go off, but sometimes she was up before then and he really didn't feel like he could face her yet.

He placed his jacket on the hook by the door, and took off his shoes before padding into the kitchen in search of some water and pain killers. His head was throbbing and his body felt worn out, no doubt let-down from the adrenaline rush he'd been on for most of the night. A small smile graced his face as he relived the excitement of the winning streak he'd been on recently. Up twenty thousand dollars, he'd been hard pressed to contain his excitement believing his mother-load was finally coming in. Of course, lady luck was as fickle as ever. Just when it seemed he couldn't lose, his good fortune turned and despite his best efforts, he ended up deeper in debt.

Rubbing his hand over his face, he wondered if he really was recalling events clearly. Greg had found a new group to play with and the stakes had been higher than normal. Scott, one of Greg's friends, had a liberal hand when it came to mixing drinks; and the women... God, he couldn't believe the women that had been there. Gorgeous, miles of legs and scantily clad, they'd fawned all over him when he was winning. Even after the tide had turned, they'd been there; encouraging him, sharing his frustration over his losing streak, consoling him.

"Sure." Sandy shrugged but didn't meet his eyes. "Dinner and a movie fixes everything, doesn't it?"

He suspected her words were more sarcastic than an attempt at humour but he chose to believe the latter and chuckled briefly.

Sandy flicked an unreadable look at him then turned and headed down the hallway calling over her shoulder. "I have to get ready for work. I'll talk to you later."

As she walked away, he watched her slight form outlined in a tank top and sleeping shorts. A familiar stirring in his groin compounded his guilt over the missed dinner. Could he sink much lower than this? Lusting for her, after last night's events? He could still smell the other women's perfume on his clothes; still recall the feel of their fingers teasing his hair, their hot breath on his cheek as they whispered encouragement to him.

Disgusted with himself, he stomped down the hallway, pulling his shirt off and throwing it into the hamper. Shucking his jeans, he tossed them in the basket as well, then fell onto his bed and stared at the ceiling.

God, why did he always screw up everything? Sandy deserved better than him. He rubbed the heels of his hands into his eyes. Letting his arms drop lifelessly at his side, he sighed heavily. Damn, he was tired. His eyes felt dry and scratchy so he let them drift shut as he contemplated the day to come, and how he could make amends for his mistake. Maybe he'd clean the house and do some laundry; that usually made her happy. Then he'd fix dinner and have it ready when she got home.

A yawn escaped him and he rolled onto his side, listening to the hissing of the shower and the faint sounds Sandy made as she prepared for the day. He'd rest for a few minutes and when she came out, he'd get up.

Smythston, Oregon, USA...

Kane paced their private sitting room, reading the latest report from Chicago before crumpling the paper and throwing it to the ground. "Damn!"

The Finding

Elise looked up from the child she was nursing and frowned. "Language, Kane. Little ears are in the room."

He stopped in his tracks and looked down at the toddler who was sitting on the floor playing with a truck. The boy was the image of himself with dark hair and amber eyes.

Possibly feeling his father's gaze on him, Jacob looked up at him solemnly before switching to an impish grin. "Damn, Daddy. Damn!"

Guiltily, Kane shot a glance at Elise. Her eyebrows shot up almost to her hairline before lowering in disapproval. "Sorry!" He mouthed the word before hunkering down to talk to his son.

"Jacob, you can't say that word when Mommy is around."

"Or even when I'm not around." Elise added from her chair by the window.

"Right." He looked at his mate and then back at his son. "Damn is a grown-up word and I don't want you using it."

Jacob scowled. "Why?"

"Because..." Kane paused and sighed, knowing where this was heading; an interminable conversation that featured him trying to explain and the boy questioning his reasoning. Deciding on a new tactic, he spoke sternly. "You cannot use that word, because I am your Alpha and whatever I say is law." He sat back on his heels and stared at his son.

For a moment, Jacob scowled back, his small chin lifting, his brow slightly lowered, but after a few seconds the look faltered and his lower lip trembled. Ducking his head, the child conceded. "Okay, Daddy."

For a moment Kane was pleased, both that his son had shown some spirit and that he was learning the ways of the pack so quickly. But then, he looked at the bowed head and the dark curls resting against the nape of the tiny neck. He swallowed hard, a pang of guilt washing over him. Memories of his own father flashed before his eyes; the bastard raging at him, hand raised to strike. Kane shook his head to erase the image. Maybe he'd been too harsh. Jacob *was* just a little boy.

Reaching over, he scooped the child into his arms, stood up and tipped him upside down. Jacob squealed with delight apparently forgetting the confrontation. Kane blew raspberries against his belly making him laugh all the louder. The happy sound filled his heart; he never wanted his children to be afraid of him.

Tipping the boy back upright, Kane lifted him over his head. "I love you, Jacob, but you must listen to me and not always question my orders." He looked at Elise then continued. "Or your mother's."

Jacob nodded, still giggling.

Setting his son down, Kane whispered in his ear. The boy grinned and trotted off.

"Kane, what did you promise him?" Elise gave him a knowing look.

"Just a cookie. Helen's baking—"

"You know it's almost dinner time." Elise lifted the baby from her breast and held it against her shoulder, gently patting its back.

"One cookie won't hurt him."

"Jacob has Helen wrapped around his finger, just like he has everyone else. It won't stop with one cookie."

He winced, knowing Elise was right. Helen, the previous Alpha's widow, had stayed on after the man's death, eventually taking on the role of housekeeper and cook for those living in the Alpha house. She was also a substitute grandmother for many of the pups and had no qualms about spoiling them.

"Perhaps you're right. Oh well, too late now." Shrugging philosophically, he wandered over to where Elise sat. He crouched behind her, making faces at his daughter. She chortled and then burped loudly. Laughing, he tapped the infant's nose. "You're just like your mother."

"Kane, I do not burp loudly like that!"

"I meant in looks!" He tried to explain his comment.

"Oh, so I'm almost bald and have no teeth?" He could hear the faint trace of laughter in her voice.

Circling around the chair until he faced his mate, he knelt in front of her and ran a finger down the slope of her still exposed breast. "Of course not." He leaned forward and kissed her gently before murmuring against her lips. "But even if you were, I'd still love you."

"Mmm..." Elise leaned into the kiss and swept her tongue over his, before easing back and shifting the child in her arms. She started to rock the little girl to sleep. "So what was making you swear?"

He stood and began pacing again. "The damn...er...the disappointing report from Chicago. There's still no progress on that fellow Aldrich. It was a simple enough assignment. I asked the Chicago pack to deal with him and they still don't have the job done. I can't believe how inefficient they are. They have a stake in this as well. None of us want to be exposed to the human population. Maybe I should take care of the man myself."

Elise rolled her eyes at him. "Kane Sinclair, you know perfectly well that you can't go traipsing into another pack's territory like that. Besides, I've read the reports and you couldn't do any better. Leon Aldrich keeps himself locked up like Fort Knox. He never leaves his penthouse unless he's surrounded by guards and there's a careful screening process for all his employees. The Chicago pack has tried to get someone on the inside but they can't make it through the screening process. Face it, he knows you're after him and he's not taking any chances."

Kane growled at her matter of fact restating of what he already knew. Aldrich's continued existence was a thorn in his side. Three years ago, the man had stumbled upon the fact that Lycans actually existed and had planned on abducting one of their kind, namely Melody Greene, and selling her as living proof of his discovery.

An ancient Lycan law known as the Keeping dictated that any human who discovered their secret existence faced possible extermination. Kane's brother, Ryne, had attempted to kill Aldrich but desperate circumstances dealing with Melody's safety meant he'd had to leave before finishing the man off. Since that time, Aldrich had been at the top of their 'most wanted' list. "The Chicago pack claims they have a new plan, but I'm not holding my breath. As long as Aldrich is alive, we aren't safe."

"There's no guarantee on safety, Kane. You kept most of the pack in hiding for four months when this whole thing first blew up, but nothing happened. It's been almost three years now. Aldrich has never made a move against us or given any indication that he plans to. Maybe he's too afraid to do anything; maybe it's time to let it go."

He braced his arms against the window frame and stared outside, considering his mate's words. Idly, he noted the signs of spring appearing in the forest that grew around the homestead. "Perhaps you have a point. It's just..." Pausing, he tried to find the words to express himself. "I have this feeling in my gut that trouble is still brewing and it has something to do with Aldrich."

Elise stood and laid the now sleeping baby down in her crib, before walking over to where he stood. She began to rub his back.

He rumbled appreciatively at the feel of her hands soothing the tight muscles in his shoulders, then sliding down his side. She wrapped her arms around his waist and laid her head against him.

"You know, Kane, I have a feeling in my gut too, though actually it's a bit lower. You could fix it, if you wanted to."

His breath caught in his chest as she accompanied her suggestive words by shifting her hand lower and using her finger to trace over his zipper. Immediately, his flesh responded, growing harder and straining against the material of his pants. He placed his hand over hers and pressed her palm to the aching bulge. When she squeezed lightly, he groaned in appreciation. "I might be able to accommodate you."

"Might?" Elise circled around him and nipped at his chin, then pulled his head down so she could tease his earlobe.

Kane ran his hands up her back and then down, cupping her enticingly rounded rear, pulling her closer. "Uh-huh. I'm Alpha, you know; a very busy man. But I suppose I could try to work you in."

Giggling, Elise took his hand and led him from the sitting room towards the adjoining bedroom. "Actually, from the feel of things, I think I'll be trying to work *you* in, big boy."

The Finding

Chicago, Illinois, USA...

Marla stood in the office of the late Anthony Greyson, eyeing the contents. Gold pens, two silver letter trays, and an ivory letter opener were on the desk that dominated the room. Beside it, floor to ceiling shelves housed a collection of books; many were rare first editions, autographed and in mint condition. She trailed her fingers over the leather spines and then across the wooden surface of a nearby table, her mind ticking off its salient features; mahogany, cabriole leg, hand carved detailing, eighteenth century design, probably an original Chippendale. It would fetch a tidy sum at auction. A picture arrangement caught her attention next. Each one was a much sought after original oil painting, meticulously maintained. Her eyes gleamed; she knew exactly where she could get the best price for them.

A regretful sigh escaped her. They were much too big and certainly would be missed should one or two of them suddenly disappear. A single silver letter tray however... A smile curled the corner of her lips and she drifted over to the desk. Yes, the tray was lovely and, thankfully, large purses were in style this year. Casually looking around the room to ensure no one was watching, she lifted one tray and examined it carefully, noting the elegant etching. It would do the trick nicely.

Setting her purse down, she began to unzip it, when someone cleared their throat behind her. Her hand barely paused before she continued the task of opening her purse, reaching in and pulling out a tissue as if that had been her goal all along. Turning, she leaned a hip against the desk top and surveyed the elderly man who stood in the doorway.

"Yes, Franklin?" She kept her tone even and pleasant, her expression one of bland inquiry. Nothing about her gave any indication that her actions were anything but respectable.

"Do you need any help, ma'am?"

"No, thank you, Franklin. I'm inspecting the Estate as per Mr. Aldrich's orders. As usual, you and Mrs. Teasdale are doing a splendid job."

"Thank you, ma'am." While Franklin's voice was polite, she was sure she detected a flash of loathing in the man's eyes.

That was fine. It was a game they'd been playing now for almost three years. On the surface they were so cordial, butter wouldn't melt in their mouths, but underneath the polite façade, that's where the truth was found.

She narrowed her eyes in annoyance at the man. He was always appearing at inopportune moments, always watching her. As he stepped further into the room, she hastily rearranged her features into a pleasant but mildly bored expression.

Franklin walked over to the desk, his stride purposeful. She observed as he picked up the tray she'd had in her hand moments before. He flicked a glance at her, then took a polishing rag out of his pocket and cleaned the surface before placing it back on the desk in its original position.

"Such a lovely piece," he murmured. "It would be a shame if it went missing like some of the other small items have." She knew he was watching her out of the corner of his eye, but remained calm and cool. If the butler thought he could rattle her, he couldn't be more wrong.

"Indeed." She raised one eyebrow. "Any progress yet on finding the supposedly misplaced items?"

"Stolen, ma'am. Not misplaced."

She waved her hand negligently. "Semantics, Franklin. Stolen, misplaced. It's all the same in the end. The items are no longer where you claim they used to be." Pausing, she feigned a concerned expression. "You know, Franklin, this really is a large house to manage. I'm sure you've done your best, but you must be getting tired. Three years with hardly a break, supervising the hired help, assisting with the inventory."

Shaking her head, she made a little moue. "I know I've mentioned it before, but it is possible that the inventory you conducted wasn't entirely accurate. I don't think the courts took your age into consideration when they gave you the job." Reaching over, she patted his arm lightly. "No one would think any the less of you, if you decided—"

The Finding

"I'm not in my dotage yet, Ms. Matthews, though I thank you for your concern. The inventory was accurate, the items *are* missing, and the police have been notified. Everyone has been questioned as to the objects' whereabouts and the local pawn shops have been alerted." He pulled his arm out from under her hand, his voice reflecting his affront. "Of course, you know that already, seeing as how we had this same conversation during your last visit."

Laughing lightly, she gave him a condescending look. "Of course we did, Franklin." Ignoring his glare, she patted his arm again before wandering over to the window and inspecting the glass. "Hmm... These windows are rather dusty and streaked. It's important to keep the house in top condition at all times, you realize. Perhaps, if you put me in charge of hiring the cleaning staff, these problems could be avoided."

"Perhaps. But the courts appointed Cook—Mrs. Teasdale—and myself as caretakers until such time as Miss Cassie returns. That includes the cleaning and maintenance of the Estate."

"*If* she returns." Qualifying the answer, she turned to face the man and then reached for her purse in preparation for leaving, resisting the urge to take one last look at the silver tray on the desk.

"She *will* come back, Ms. Matthews. Cook and I are sure of it."

Marla moved her lips into the semblance of a smile, but made no effort to hide the coldness in her eyes. It wasn't worth the effort trying to sway the old man over to her side. She'd attempted that during the first year, but he was annoyingly loyal to his dead master and the truant young girl. "Your Miss Cassie's return is what we all hope and pray for, Franklin. Mr. Aldrich and I think of her often, speculating whatever became of the poor thing."

"She's out there somewhere, biding her time until the right opportunity arises for her return." The man spoke with confidence and, not for the first time, Marla wondered if he knew more about Cassandra Greyson than he let on.

No, she quickly dismissed the idea. It wasn't possible. There was no way a simple cook and an aging butler could accomplish what she and Leon Aldrich had been unable to do. For three years, they'd sifted through reports, followed up on leads, and hired private investigators in an effort to find the missing young heiress. If all their experts couldn't find Cassandra Greyson, then the old man wouldn't have been able to either.

Nodding at Franklin, she left the library and exited the house. It was a sunny day and she paused on the front step, squinting at the brightness and making a show of donning a pair of fashionable sunglasses.

While she was at it, she slyly scanned the area around the home, even sniffing the air surreptitiously. She played the various scents through her mind, finally focusing on one. Damn! A Lycan had been in the area again. Not recently, but still it gave her human half cause for concern. The wolf within her pricked up its ears in interest, but she ignored it. Absentmindedly rubbing her side where an old injury still twinged on occasion, she moved briskly to the waiting limousine.

As the door shut behind her, Marla breathed a sigh of relief; the thought of encountering one of her own kind made her edgy. The chauffeur-driven car was reinforced to withstand an assault and not for the first time, did she thank her employer, Leon Aldrich, for his paranoia.

For some reason, which he never explained to her, the man was obsessed with his personal safety, sure it was only a matter of time before an attack was launched against him. Exactly what the nature of the attack might be, he didn't say, but his paranoia resulted in personal guards, alarms around his penthouse, security cameras, and a ridiculously intense screening process for anyone he came in contact with.

"Where to, Ms. Matthews?" Jeffries, the chauffeur, looked back at her through the rear-view mirror.

"Back to the penthouse. I'll complete my other errands tomorrow." She barely met his gaze before staring out the window, searching the massive gardens and the woods beyond for any sign of movement. Conflicted feelings stirred within her as she considered what it would be like to encounter a wolf again after all these years. The idea excited the animal inside her, but she paid the silly creature no mind. Life in a wolf pack was no bed of roses, despite what the creature might say.

Jeffries cleared his throat as if to speak, drawing her attention back to him. He looked disappointed and it brought her mind back to another matter; a more personal one just between the two of them.

"I'm sorry, Jeffries. I'm no longer in the mood this afternoon."

He pouted briefly and she sighed. The chauffeur was good-looking, in a boy-toy sort of way. His white blond hair, perfect features, and well-toned body were drool-worthy but he was more high maintenance than she preferred. Still, he was a relatively good lover and always available when she needed him, so some pandering was warranted. Leaning forward, she reached over the seat and stroked his jaw. He hummed in appreciation, leaning back towards her. She whispered in his ear. "Perhaps tomorrow? By the Jacuzzi?"

A slow grin revealed perfect teeth and his baby blue eyes heated with obvious lust. "Sure. Whenever you need me."

"Anticipation sweetens the real thing." She tickled his ear before leaning back, the soft leather seats moulding around her body. Jeffries shifted in his own seat before starting the vehicle, but by then Marla had lost interest in him and barely noted the action.

The constant presence of Lycans was unnerving her. When she'd first come to this area, she rarely scented one, but in the past few years, there always seemed to be some about. She was almost certain they weren't aware of her presence. Aldrich's screen of security ensured people were kept at a distance and she was employing an old trick to mask her scent; a rare perfume that she'd perfected years ago which allowed her to remain undetected by the keen noses of other Lycans.

Yet despite reassuring herself that it was all a coincidence, a niggle of doubt remained. A falling out with her old pack had made her a fugitive and she didn't doubt for a minute that they would kill her, if she was ever found. The question was, had they discovered she was here and sent assassins to deal with her?

For months after parting ways with her old pack, she'd lived in a constant state of fear, but with the passage of time, she'd slowly started to relax. Her logical mind believed an active search for her was over, but she wasn't taking any chances.

Her cell phone rang and she glanced at the number before answering. "Hello, Mr. Aldrich. What can I do for you?" She furrowed her brow and pressed the phone closer to her ear. The man's vocal chords had been severely damaged during a wild dog attack three years ago and as a result, he could be difficult to understand.

"Yes, the Estate appears to be in good order ... No, Franklin had no news about the missing items. Of course, given his age, I still suspect the inventory was faulty. Perhaps we should reconsider my suggestion of conducting another? ... All right, we'll discuss it when I get back ... Yes, you'll be with the nurse. I'll see you after your session with her."

She ended the call and gave a self-satisfied smile. Perhaps Aldrich was finally going to start listening to her suggestions. It gave her hope that she might actually be able to snag the fussy old goat. Jeffries served his purpose on a purely carnal level, but Aldrich had what she really wanted. The lawyer was well on his way to gaining control of the Greyson estate and there was no way she was letting him, and all that money, slip through her hands.

All that was needed was to ensure that Cassandra Greyson didn't reappear too soon. The waiting period for missing heirs was almost half over. Through some skilful snooping, she'd learned that Aldrich had a plan in the works to ensure that significant portions of the estate ended up in his own coffers.

She stretched sinuously, taking a moment to appreciate the fine leather interior of the vehicle, the small bar and entertainment centre. She was enjoying the perks that came with being Aldrich's personal assistant. Once she convinced him to marry her, she'd be able to gain access to even more. Then her life would be perfect.

The Finding

Not really, her inner wolf murmured. *We're alone, without a pack.*

She scowled at the faint discontent that filled her. Having a pack didn't matter. She was independent and soon to be wealthy. So what if there was no one to curl up with at night, no one to go running with? She didn't even enjoy those activities. Sniffing, she wrapped her arms around herself and lifted her chin only to stare sightlessly at the passing scenery as memories of youthful frolics with packmates danced before her eyes.

Chapter 3

Las Vegas, Nevada, USA...

Cassie sat down in the employees' lunch room, ready to enjoy the relative peace and calm the small space provided. It wasn't much to look at; some old furniture, a refrigerator, and an array of notices posted on the wall, but at least it was a place to rest away from the constant beeping of the price scanner and the rattle of grocery carts. She'd awoken with a headache, after spending a restless night listening for Kellen to come home, and was finding it hard to maintain a pleasant facade for the customers.

Exactly why she had wasted time listening for Kellen, she didn't know. Her feelings towards him ranged from anger to disappointment to sorrow; none of them suitable for sharing in the middle of the night without inviting a fight. Yet, underneath it all, she still cared for him. So, she'd tried to stay awake, wanting to know he was home and safe. Some of his gambling friends were more than a little disreputable and she worried about him, despite his failings.

When sleep had finally claimed her, strange dreams had dominated her rest. Kellen had been there, but when she tried to reach his outstretched hand, he'd backed away; his figure slowly fading into a cool, grey mist. Frustrated, she'd run towards him, but strong arms appeared out of nowhere, and held her tight despite her struggles to free herself. Slowly, inexorably, she'd been drawn backwards farther and farther from where Kellen had disappeared. The arms around her waist loosened and then eased her around until she was facing a broad, muscular chest.

For some reason she had been more curious than panicked, sensing this person meant her no harm. But who was it that held her? And why was he keeping her away from Kellen? When she'd looked up, the man's features were lost in the shadows. He didn't speak, but his hands began to stroke her, calloused fingers trailing over her skin in a hypnotizing rhythm that had her eyes drifting shut.

As she'd relaxed against him, his lips feathered over her forehead, across her cheek and finally brushed her lips. Over and over again, he'd teased her with butterfly kisses and soft touches that brought every nerve ending to aching awareness. Need built inside her and she'd pressed closer to him; straining to wrap her arms around him, to pull his head down for a deeper kiss. Yet, even as she'd reached out, he began to fade away leaving her achingly alone.

She'd turned round in a circle searching for the man, then calling out for Kellen. No one had come. Despondently she'd sunk down on the ground and curled up in a ball feeling lost and abandoned in the cool grey fog. Tears had dampened her cheeks as she wondered why she'd been abandoned. Everyone she loved was gone. Kellen, her uncle, the mother she never knew, even Franklin and Cook.

We aren't meant to be alone, the creature inside her had whimpered. *We have to find him.*

But she'd stayed where she was, too afraid of the unknown to go searching. Danger lurked in the shadows that surrounded her. It was best to stay where she was. Yet even as she'd pressed her forehead to her drawn up knees, the illusion of safety slipped away. The greyness darkened to black, the fog thickened and pressed down on her, threatening to crush her with its oppressive weight. Too late she realized staying curled up was more dangerous than moving. She'd tried to crawl away, but the darkness invaded her body, choking her with its evil. Opening her mouth, she'd tried to call out, but the sound stuck in her throat. Her vision blurred, she'd fought to breathe, and then finally, mercifully, she'd passed out.

When morning came, she'd awoken feeling spent and disinclined to face the day. Unfortunately, hiding under the covers wasn't an option. Work awaited and she'd had to face

The Finding

Kellen as well; she'd heard him moving around in the kitchen and decided to get the initial meeting over with. The encounter had been purposely low key. There'd be time enough for talk and recriminations later. Scheduled to work the early shift, she had no time to waste listening to his explanations and excuses.

With a sigh, she decided that she needed to think of something else. Replaying earlier events over and over in her head wouldn't change what had happened. She rolled her shoulders, trying to ease the tension that had settled there, then kicked off her shoes and propped her feet up on a nearby chair. Giving her toes a wiggle, she closed her eyes and rested her head in her hand. For just a moment she'd rest.

Forcing her body to relax, she kept her breathing deep and rhythmic. Randomly, the image of soft grass popped into her head. Lush vegetation, tall trees, a gentle breeze ruffling her fur as she lapped cool water from a stream. It was so peaceful. A contented smile spread over her lips, before she gave a start and scowled at her wayward thoughts.

Darn! The full moon was approaching and the beast inside her was growing stronger, pushing to come out, to gain control. She sat up straight and took a juice box out of her lunch bag. She sipped the contents with forced enjoyment, ignoring the chemical taste of artificial colours and flavours. This was what she drank, not stream water. She wasn't an animal, no matter what the troublesome creature inside her might believe.

And it wasn't as if she didn't have enough *real* trouble to deal with. Her thoughts returned to Kellen, his gambling and the pile of unpaid bills on the kitchen counter. What should she do about it? If she asked for advice, people would likely say to cut her losses and move on. But move on to what?

Kellen was all she had. And he'd been there for her, helping her when she had nowhere else to turn. She couldn't walk away, could she? As she tried to imagine such a scenario, her heart ached. Despite his faults, Kellen had her loyalty. He was her pack...er...family. She grimaced at the animalistic term that had inadvertently slipped out.

temptation of gambling, but Kellen had connections in the area and, if the man chasing her ever found her, there were people here he could turn to for help. It made sense at the time, so they'd stayed. Kellen had spent the next year teaching her how to function in the 'real' world.

She had been amazed at how sheltered her upbringing had actually been. Cleaning, doing laundry, cooking, even buying groceries, or using city transit. Kellen had laughed himself silly over some of her mistakes and she had joined him in it. She smiled thinking of the laundry incident with suds pouring from the washing machine, and the time she'd nearly asphyxiated herself by mixing cleaners. And then there were the ruined dinners Kellen had bravely tried to eat.

Kellen said it was like the story Pygmalion only in reverse; bringing her down to the common level, rather than elevating her to the status of refined lady. His Professor Higgins accent had been hilarious.

"Earth to Sandy! Where'd you go, girl?" Debra's voice interrupted her reverie and Cassie jerked herself back to the present.

"Sorry, what did you say?" She blinked at the other girl.

"I said that from the look on your face, your anniversary was more than 'okay.' Your eyes got all dreamy and—"

The door swung open and the manager walked in. "Isn't break-time over, girls?"

Cassie looked at the clock, gasped, and shoved her shoes back on. Jumping to her feet, she started to apologize. "Sorry, Mr. Bartlett. We were talking."

"Don't worry. You're a hard worker. I can cut you some slack. Unlike other people who work here." He looked meaningfully at Debra who laughed. Shaking his head, he put out a hand to stop Cassie from leaving the room. "Before you go back to work, I wanted to talk to you about something." Mr. Bartlett paused and stared meaningfully at Debra who sighed and got up.

"I know. I know. I'll leave the room. Geez, you'd think I was a big gossip or something," Debra grumbled. Gulping down the rest of her iced tea, she dropped the can in the recycling bin and left the room. As the door shut behind her, Mr. Bartlett turned to Cassie and stroked his greying beard.

"I hate to ask you this, but... Is Kellen gambling again?"

A flash of fear shot down her spine and around into her gut. What kind of a mess was her partner in now? Mr. Bartlett was aware that Kellen gambled, but had been willing to give him a chance. She clenched her fingers and forced the tightness from her throat before speaking. "Umm... Why do you ask?"

The manager avoided looking at her for a moment. It appeared he was regretting starting the conversation, but then drew a deep breath and continued. "Kellen's been missing work, not showing up for his shift or arriving late. It isn't fair to the other employees who have to do his share of the work."

"I'll talk to him tonight." Her mind was already racing. If Kellen lost this job, they'd be in big trouble financially. Yes, she had a large amount tucked away, but that was her emergency fund, in case the werewolves ever found them and they needed to run.

Mr. Bartlett was still speaking and she forced herself to focus on his words. "A man's also been around, asking about you."

"Me?" She squeaked in surprise.

"Uh-huh. The fellow wanted to know your name and where you lived, but of course we didn't say anything. He showed up a week ago and the other employees have noticed him hanging around the store. He tries to act like he's shopping, but mostly he watches for you. MaryAnn asked him his name, but he wouldn't say. Just paid for his things and left."

She shivered and wrapped her arms around herself at the thought of someone actually stalking her; watching her as she worked. Who was this man and why was he interested in her? A horrid thought popped into her mind. What if it was the werewolf? The memory of the huge black beast with its snarling bloody teeth, made her feel faint and she grasped the back of a nearby chair to steady herself. Surely it couldn't be. Not after all these years.

"I thought I should warn you, in case Kellen's in debt and someone is thinking of using you as leverage."

That statement grabbed her attention and swung her thoughts in an entirely different direction. Maybe it wasn't the werewolf like she feared, but something to do with Kellen's gambling. She gulped. Talk about out of the frying pan and into the fire!

Fear continued to writhe in her belly as she contemplated this new scenario. Pressing her hands to her stomach, she swallowed hoping to keep her lunch in place. She'd heard about loan sharks and what they would do if you didn't pay up. Her skin prickled at the very idea. Oh God, who did Kellen owe money to and what would they do to her or him, if he didn't pay?

This had never happened before. At least not since the first time she'd paid off his debts; that had been when they'd initially got together. Since then, Kellen kept his gambling associates away from her, only taking her with him a few times in the early days and it had never been to anything high stake. He'd assured her he was done with gambling except for occasional small games at a friend's home and that he never mentioned her around the gaming tables, knowing she wasn't comfortable with it. Apparently that was no longer the case, or someone had followed him and made the connection.

"Listen Sandy, I'm sorry to have upset you. Would you like to go home? I can get someone to cover the rest of your shift." The older man looked at her with kind eyes, his bushy grey brows lowered in concern. A wave of gratitude washed over her. Mr. Bartlett was so nice to her, hiring her when she'd had no skills and then with only her recommendation, taking on Kellen.

She forced a smile. "No, I'll stay." Sitting at home, she'd worry all the more. It was better to keep busy. Besides, if she saw Kellen right now, she might be tempted to kill him! Squaring her shoulders, she tried to look unconcerned. "It might be nothing, but I'll talk to Kellen tonight about missing work and see what's going on."

The Finding

The manager gave her shoulder a friendly squeeze before opening the door. As she stepped back into the store, she mentally berated Kellen. What the hell had he done now?

Chicago, Illinois, USA...

"Anything else to report, Swanson?" Leon Aldrich rasped out the words to the security guard that stood before him.

"I've changed the access codes for the elevator and notified authorized personnel. The surveillance cameras have also been repositioned near the parking garage, and I've completed the weekly report." Swanson set the folder on Aldrich's desk and then folded his hands behind his back.

Picking up the report, Aldrich quickly flipped through it before setting it aside for closer scrutiny later. He nodded in approval at Swanson's stance; shoulders back, eyes straight ahead, quietly awaiting instructions. The man was built like a tank—sturdy, all muscle, no neck—and with his military buzz cut and blank expression he was intimidating as hell. Perfect for the job.

Swanson was former military. His record while in the service was less than pristine, but the man was effective. He also wasn't above turning a blind eye to certain activities if the price was right. Aldrich could appreciate that in a man. It was a quality he himself possessed and had used to his advantage throughout his life.

As a matter of fact, it'd got him where he was today. As executor of the Greyson estate and the respected lawyer of the late Anthony Greyson, he had power and wealth; those two combined to open doors that led to the exalted realms of the socially elite. He'd learned that from Anthony Greyson. True, society's blue bloods might not approve totally, but they didn't want him as an enemy so they fawned and simpered while turning a deaf ear to any of his less socially acceptable dealings.

Swanson was still waiting patiently and Aldrich smiled inwardly, keeping his face blank. It wouldn't do to let Swanson know of his approval. Employees functioned most effectively when they weren't completely sure of the employer's opinion of repute would normally have scoffed at the old man's preposterous idea if it wasn't for one simple fact. He, Leon Aldrich, had observed a young woman named Melody Greene actually turn into a wolf just hours before.

So yes, *he* knew werewolves existed, but he had no proof to substantiate his claim; the one picture that might have added some veracity to his story had mysteriously disappeared, much to his ire. Therefore, keeping his own counsel was the best course at this point in time. That wasn't to say he was willing to forget the whole incident. In fact, he was actively conducting research on the supposedly mythical creatures; a thorough knowledge of an opponent always made for the best defence.

That the wolves would attack again, he had no doubt. Greyson had been babbling about some werewolf law called the Keeping just before he died. Since then, carefully sifting fact from fiction had revealed such a law did exist and called for the elimination of any human who discovered the truth. With this in mind, Aldrich took every precaution to keep the beasts at bay. If he now had to live the life of a recluse, so be it. One day he would triumph over them; he had plans in place.

A flashing light caught his eye; he'd had all calls held while he talked to Swanson. Activating his voice mail, he picked up a pen in preparation for taking any salient notes.

"Hey, Aldrich! This is Nate Graham."

Aldrich grimaced when he heard the voice, despising the casual manner in which the man addressed him, but willing to overlook the fact since the fellow was making some progress in straightening out the mess in Nevada. Narrowing his eyes, he listened to what the man had to say.

Once the basic information had been delivered, Nate began his usual whining for more money. "I'll get back to you in a few days and let you know how the situation develops. If you want me to keep working out here, then you need to finance it. I'm not sitting on a pile of money like you are. Talk to you later, Aldie."

"Talk to you later, Aldie—indeed!" Aldrich shuddered at the over-familiarity of the phrase, but made a notation to have Ms.

The Finding

Matthews take care of the financial matter. He'd known Nate back when they were both little better than street rats. He'd risen above his lowly beginnings, but Nate continued to swim in the sewer. Oh well, it took contacts in all kinds of places to keep things running smoothly, and Nate was good at leg work.

Turning his chair, he accessed his computer and pulled up the Nevada file. It was a leftover business venture from his early days. Several times, he'd considered letting the business go as it no longer suited his present image, but some quixotic bit of nostalgia had him hanging on to it. Dollar Niche *had* been operating successfully up until Greyson's death and his own hospitalization. Unfortunately, about that time, he'd let things slide, thinking the company was in competent hands. He'd been wrong. A steady drop in the profit margin had come to light during the last audit and Nate was investigating the source of the problem. Aldrich had his suspicions, but knew better than to act without cold hard facts.

After scanning the file, he turned to the electronic chess game he was playing. Steepling his fingers, he narrowed his eyes and played out the possible moves and countermoves he could take. He curled his lip as he sent out a pawn, knowing he was sacrificing it to save a more important piece.

Life was rather like a large chess game, he reflected, only the stakes were higher. In real life, the pawns were people rather than playing pieces, but they served the same purpose; eventually being forfeited in order to gain the main prize. And he would gain the main prize, no matter how many pawns he had to sacrifice.

Stump River, Ontario, Canada...

Bryan sat in the pack house office completely unaware of the bright sunshine that streamed in through the window heralding the start of spring. Nor was he aware of the piles of paperwork stacked on the side of his desk, the half-eaten sandwich and now cold cup of coffee. Instead, he was transfixed by the e-mail displayed before him on his computer screen. A mixture of excitement and disbelief washed over him as he finished scanning the text.

"Hey Ryne! Come look at this!" He called over his shoulder, knowing the Alpha was in the house somewhere.

A minute later, Ryne strolled into the room with Mel, his arm wrapped possessively around her thickening waist. He was nuzzling her neck. "What's up?"

Bryan looked at the two of them; watching as Ryne nipped Mel's neck and she made an appreciative noise in her throat.

"Did I interrupt something?"

"Not yet." Mel grinned and ran her fingers through Ryne's thick black hair, then trailed them down his chest towards his belt buckle.

The Alpha growled and clamped his hand over hers. "Behave."

Tugging at her hand, Mel tried unsuccessfully to free it. "I can't help myself; raging hormones, you know. Besides, it's your own fault for getting me pregnant."

"It had better be my fault." Ryne rubbed the swell of her belly. "If I ever found out you'd—"

"Me? You're the one who had women draped all over him when we went to that show in Toronto a few weeks ago!"

"What can I say? I'm a chick magnet." Ryne waggled his eyebrows and smirked.

"A chick magnet? Conceited is more like it." Mel finally freed her hand and stepped away, looking at him with narrowed eyes.

"Hey! I'm just aware of my strong points and as Alpha—"

Mel rolled her eyes. "Oh, right. How could I forget that whole 'you're my supreme leader' bit?"

Ryne pulled her closer and patted her on the head, then spoke in a condescending tone. "That's all right, Melody. From what I've heard, becoming forgetful is all part of making baby-brains."

Bryan groaned inwardly sensing another one of their infamous arguments. The two really loved each other, but sometimes the bickering could cause one to wonder.

The Finding

"So what's up?" Ryne quirked an eyebrow at him as Mel sputtered at his side, no doubt trying to think of a suitable retort.

"It's about this e-mail that came in. I might have some information on Cassandra Greyson."

"Really?" Mel looked at him with interest, apparently forgetting her spat with her mate. Then just as suddenly, she winced.

Ever vigilant where his mate was concerned, Ryne immediately reacted concerned. "Are you okay, Melody?"

"I'm fine. The baby kicked, I think." She blushed and then began backing closer to the door. "I...I think I need to go to the bathroom." With that she turned and scurried away.

Ryne watched her, shaking his head. "Pregnant women live in the bathroom, and the strangest things upset them." He frowned as if trying to fathom the problem, then shrugged and turned back to Bryan. "So what did you discover about the Greyson girl?"

Bryan gestured to the computer screen. "Look at this. A Lycan named Robert Walker was on vacation in Vegas and thinks he's found Cassandra Greyson. He wasn't able to get any information on her, but he did take a picture using his cell phone. Does this look like her?"

Ryne leaned over, bracing his arm on the desk to examine the photo displayed on the computer screen. "Hey, I think that's her! Zoom in a bit... Uh-huh... Uh-huh..." A slow smile spread over his face. "Yeah. I only saw her for a moment, but it looks like the same girl." Straightening, he shook his head. "If it is her, we're damned lucky. After all this time, and only having a description to post rather than an actual picture, it's amazing anyone made the connection." He paused and rubbed his neck. "This was taken in Las Vegas, you said?"

"Yep, and in a grocery store of all places."

"That could work to our advantage." Crossing the room, Ryne rifled through some papers on a shelf, then pulled out a map and spread it out on his desk. Bryan followed, leaning his hip casually against the corner of the desk as he stared at a map of North America. It showed all the packs and their respective territories.

Tapping the map with his finger, Ryne indicated the area in question. "There are other packs in the area, but as you can see, Las Vegas is considered neutral territory. Being a major tourist destination, it would be too difficult to constantly have wolves reporting in and signing out. If Cassandra is there, it will be a lot easier for you to bring her home; no Alphas making you wait while they contact me for confirmation, and no paperwork to be processed either."

"And we all know how efficient you are when it comes to paperwork." Bryan quipped, trying to keep a straight face.

"I get the work done. Eventually." Ryne scowled at him before relenting under Bryan's steady gaze. He gave a self-deprecating laugh. Everyone knew his strength was in leading, not administrative paper-pushing. "Anyway, paperwork aside; it was a clever place for her to hide. With visiting wolves leaving their scent everywhere, no one would pay any attention to one more being in the area."

"When I went there to check out the ATM security footage three years ago, I searched everywhere except the suburbs. I never pictured a rich girl choosing that as her hideout." Bryan chuckled softly. "If this guy hadn't become lost while sightseeing and his mate hadn't made him stop to ask for directions, we'd probably never have found her."

Ryne sat down and propped his feet on the desk, folding his arms behind his head. "It's probably one for the record books; an heiress worth millions of dollars working as a grocery store clerk." He paused and quirked one eyebrow. "You know what this means, of course."

Bryan could feel his wolf rising inside him, anticipation surging as the beast strained to be set free. He couldn't totally suppress the grin that threatened to spread across his face. "I get to go hunting?"

"Uh-huh. Find the girl in the picture, determine if she really is Cassandra Greyson, and if it is her bring her back here. Once we're sure of our facts, I'll get on the internet and contact the

Lycan Link network. They'll make arrangements to slip her through Customs." He gave a satisfied sigh. "It will be good to get this wrapped up before the pup is born. A rogue wolf can be dangerous."

"She's not exactly a rogue." He felt the need to qualify his Alpha's statement. Rogues were loners with no packs, out for themselves and possessing no sense of duty towards the well-being of others of their kind. Some even teetered on the border of sanity, having no pack to keep them grounded. They could be unpredictable and often became a menace to those around them. Originally, that's how he had viewed the Greyson girl, but the longer he'd searched for her, the more his opinion had softened. He frowned inwardly, not sure why that was.

Ryne shook his head. "Cassandra Greyson might not be a rogue yet, but I'm sure it's pure luck. From what we've been able to determine, she was raised human. What does she know of our ways? What type of control does she have over her wolf? You know as well as I do she's a recipe for disaster. The girl is like a time bomb waiting to explode. And, since we're the ones who discovered her, she's our responsibility. The Finding clause is quite specific on that. It's definitely a case of 'finders keepers', whether you want to or not."

Bryan nodded. He'd studied that particular part of the law several times over the past few years, knowing he would eventually be responsible for dealing with the young, untutored wolf. If a pack found a rogue or a lone wolf, it was their duty to deal with them in whatever way was deemed most appropriate; integration, relocation or, at worst, eliminating those who refused to comply.

Usually, when a wolf wandered into a pack's territory the newcomer automatically fell under that pack's jurisdiction, but Cassandra Greyson was a special case. They'd found her in the Chicago pack's district and it could have been a dicey situation since Ryne hadn't exactly asked permission of the local Alpha. Thankfully, the elderly Alpha of the other pack had been cooperative and willing to abide by the Finding, not wanting to deal with the problem himself. It had been decided that the

Greyson girl, if ever located, would come to live with Ryne's pack.

Bryan looked at the map and eyed the distance between Las Vegas and Stump River with trepidation. It was a long way to travel with an uncooperative Lycan, and something was telling him she wasn't going to be happy to see him. He scrunched up his face. "If it is her, do you think there's any chance she'll agree to come along quietly?"

Ryne snorted. "She's a female, what do you think? Do they ever do anything the easy way?"

"I heard that!" Mel's voice drifted into the room. It had a teasing quality to it and a gleam of interest sparkled in Ryne's eye.

Standing, the Alpha stretched. "I think it's time for a chat with my mate." He folded the map they'd been looking at and casually tossed it at Bryan, grinning. "Another thing about pregnant women; their libido goes way up."

Bryan rolled his eyes, but chuckled none the less. "I'll start to make arrangements to head to Vegas."

"Do whatever you need to do. I'm putting you in charge of checking the girl out, and if it is Greyson, bringing her home." Ryne started to leave, then paused and tossed out one more comment. "Oh, and Bryan? From what I recall, the girl's quite a looker. Remember, it's business before pleasure."

Bryan snorted, then listened to the retreating sound of his Alpha's footsteps. Wandering back to the computer, he stared at the grainy photograph. Yep, even in a sub-quality picture, her beauty couldn't be denied. He reached out and traced the curve of the girl's face with his finger. "Hello, Cassandra Greyson. You and I are going to become very good friends."

Chapter 4

The next morning, Bryan ambled down the stairs from his suite of rooms in the Alpha house, eyes only half open, and rubbing his bare chest. The carpeted stairs were soft beneath his bare feet and he trailed one hand down the polished wooden railing, idly noting it was a far cry from the rickety structure that had been there when they'd first walked into the house almost four years ago. The whole place had been falling down around their ears, but Ryne hadn't cared. The man had been more interested in the land that went with it, than the building itself.

Still, they'd needed suitable housing and over time the rambling monstrosity had been refurbished. Work remained to be done on two of the wings, but the main living areas were habitable and provided enough room for all the pack members.

In a way, Bryan wished there was a big construction project underway at the moment. Wielding a hammer or tearing down walls would have gone a long way in helping to work off some of the frustration in his body right now.

As it was, he'd have to settle for coffee and paperwork to help shake the unsettled feeling that had been with him ever since he awoke. It had nothing to do with the fact he was leaving for Las Vegas in a few hours to capture the elusive Cassandra Greyson. No, that would be too sensible a reason. Instead, he was off kilter because of a dream, the same damned dream that had plagued him at least once a month for the last three years. It was a recurring scenario involving him chasing a female wolf through the woods.

She was chocolate brown with green eyes, petite yet fast as the wind. Each time he had to strain the limits of his endurance in order to catch her, but a part of him knew she would prove to be well worth the effort. He'd raced after her, inhaling her scent and quivering with the need to possess, to mate. In the end, he always caught her, gripping the ruff of her neck and forcing her to submit. The urge to claim her was strong; he'd nipped and licked her fur, rubbing against her to ensure his scent was on her and then they would both shift to human form.

Last night had been more vivid than usual. There in the forest, on a patch of soft green moss, he'd made slow, exquisite love to her. Kissing her softly, trailing his lips down her golden body, inhaling her unique scent, tasting her. Her moans of delight filled his ears and she caressed him as he worshipped her. Gently, she'd teased his skin until every nerve ending was alert, until his body was aching with arousal. Then—his breath caught at the memory alone—she'd taken him in her hands and stroked his turgid flesh.

He'd almost come undone. His body had trembled with the need to possess her, to feel her hot wet warmth squeezing him, yet he'd forced himself to hold back. He had to see her face first; to know who this elusive goddess was that teased him with promises of pleasure beyond telling.

Kneeling between her knees, he worked his way up her body, taking in her curved hips and slim waist. For a moment his eyes hesitated at her lush breasts with their dusky tips begging for his attention. She reached out and took his hand, guiding it up to her face. Her tongue darted out and licked at his palm, before drawing his thumb into her mouth. He dragged his gaze upward, then, just as his eyes reached her chin, her image dissolved and he was left staring at the mossy green forest floor.

Bryan growled at the memory. As always, when things were getting interesting, the dream would end leaving him aching with desire. This morning, he'd awoken more unsatisfied than ever and burning with the need to search out the mystery female. It was ridiculous. She didn't even exist, but his inner wolf wasn't receptive to that line of thinking and demanded action on his part.

He reached the bottom of the stairs and gave his pyjama pants a hitch from where they were sagging on his lean hips and turned down the short hallway that led to the kitchen. That room too had been redone and sported gleaming hardwood, marble counters and stainless steel appliances.

"Bryan?" Marco called his name from the kitchen and Bryan bit back a snarl. He didn't want to talk to the friendly Spaniard today. His wolf was restless and on edge, looking for a reason to snap at someone.

Forcing himself to be calm, he entered the kitchen with what he hoped was a polite expression and leaned on the counter, arms folded across his chest. "What can I do for you, Marco?"

"I just wanted to tell you that Levi and I switched shifts. Levi is doing patrols today so I can take Olivia out for her birthday."

"That's fine with me. Give Olivia my best." Levi was new to the pack, but reliable. Bryan nodded curtly and started to turn away, intent on grabbing a coffee and leaving, when a thought occurred to him. He'd never shared his dream with anyone. He was a Beta for heaven sake; foolish dreams weren't part of his image. Still... Marco was a sensible sort and somewhat of an expert on Lycan phenomena.

He poured himself a cup of the dark brew and considered his next step. It couldn't hurt to ask, could it? He sipped the coffee and walked over to the table, sitting down across from where Marco was reading the newspaper.

"Can I ask you something?" He cradled the warm cup in his hand, staring at the steaming liquid rather than the other man.

"What's on your mind?"

He heard Marco fold the paper. He looked up, meeting the man's gaze then looked away, already regretting his decision to talk about his dream. However, he'd started so he might as well continue. Taking a deep breath, he began. "I've...er...been having this dream over and over again and..." He rubbed his neck not sure how to continue, then glanced up sheepishly.

"Ah. And you wonder what it might mean?" Marco's eyes twinkled with amusement. "Let me guess. There's a female."

Feeling his cheeks start to flush, Bryan forced down his embarrassment. "Yeah. Always the same one. I chase her, catch her and then..." He let his voice trail off. Clearing his throat, he started again. "The next day, I feel half there, as if a part of me is missing."

"Hmm..." Marco settled back in his chair. "Have you heard about the concept of predestined mates? Or how for some the inner wolf already knows its soul mate in some other dimension?"

"I've heard of it, but figured it's a bunch of crap. Sure some wolves meet and click right away, but that's random chance. Most just meet and gradually fall in love. Anything else is folklore left over from the old days when the magick of Lycans was still pure."

"To some extent you are right, but there are few 'blue-blooded' Lycans left who possess this ability. For most of us, the magick has been diluted through careless breeding, not that it really matters. We are content to have increased sensory acuity, strength and, of course, the ability to shift into a clothed state. Naturally, those of mixed parentage can seldom magick their clothes back on, but that is another matter altogether."

Bryan chuckled. "Poor souls have to keep a stash of clothes around somewhere or risk being arrested for public nudity. Mel's always griping about how unfair it is that she's only half and ends up naked after a run, scrambling to get dressed in the bushes while the rest of us simply *think* the word clothes and we're ready."

Marco smiled softly, sharing his amusement. "In the ancient days, they say that a wolf could mentally find and connect with a mate years before they physically met. In addition, they could appear and disappear at will, move objects with their minds." He shrugged. "A fascinating array of rather unusual skills existed. It is rumoured that some royal families in Europe still practise selective breeding in an effort to preserve these abilities, though it's all kept hush-hush."

"So, you're saying that maybe my perfect mate is some blue-blooded Lycan who seeks me out in her dreams?" Bryan screwed up his face, trying to wrap his brain around the concept.

"Perhaps. Or maybe you have a very strange and vivid fantasy life." He stood and slapped Bryan on the back. "Either way, there is nothing you can do about it. If your mate is out there, you will find each other eventually. In the meantime, enjoy the dreams."

"Yeah, right." He muttered under his breath as Marco left the room. He'd had a raging hard-on when he awoke, just like he did each time he had the dream. There was no relief to be had with the nebulous female.

He took a sip of coffee and grimaced. Damn. It was cold, and with Mel on a no-caffeine diet, Ryne was only allowing them to make one pot a day, fearing Mel would go off the wagon. Well, there was no wasting of coffee around this house. Using the microwave, he reheated it and headed for the office, intent on getting some work done before it was time to leave. Income tax season was almost upon them and Ryne had no skill when it came to numbers.

As he approached the office he noticed the door was open, and winced. Hopefully Ryne hadn't taken it into his head to try to deal with the accounts. He shuddered, recalling the mess his Alpha had made the last time he tried to help. Pushing the door open, he was ready to chastise Ryne when he noticed that it was Mel in the office, not her mate. She was hunched over the computer frowning at whatever was on the screen.

Thinking she was writing an article for the local newspaper where she worked, he had just stepped back, deciding to leave her alone, when she gave a cry.

"No! Dammit, no!" She hit the desk top. "I don't believe it!" Her voice sounded distressed; not the usual frustration she showed when an article wouldn't flow properly. There was actual anguish in her voice. "This can't be happening. Not now!"

Concerned, he turned back. Was something wrong with the baby? No. She wasn't clutching her belly, but she was definitely troubled. His protective instincts came to the fore and he stepped into the room.

"Mel? What's wrong?"

Her hand flew to the computer mouse and she quickly closed whatever program she'd been working on. His senses immediately went on alert. What was she hiding?

"Oh! Hi, Bryan. What are you doing here?" Her face bore a smile, but he could still see the lines of worry around her eyes, hear the strain in her voice.

"I was going to work on the books." He knew she was trying to avoid his question, but the Beta in him wasn't allowing that. "I asked you a question. What's wrong?"

"Nothing." She pushed her hair back from her face and he noted the tremor of her hands.

He stepped closer, his gaze steady and she lowered her eyes. If she wasn't the Alpha's mate, he'd force a response from her. As Beta, it was his job to protect the pack and he couldn't do that if he didn't know what the problems were. But since she was the Alpha female, he took a gentler approach.

Sitting casually on the edge of the desk, one leg swinging freely, he studied her for a moment sipping his coffee before speaking. "You look upset. Are you sure you don't want to tell me? I'm a good listener."

"I'm fine." She shrugged, still not looking at him. "It's something I was researching. Um…childbirth. It sounds painful."

He was sure she was lying, but didn't want to overstep his bounds. The Alpha female technically outranked him, but Mel had never really acted on that fact, if she was even aware of it. He made a mental note to ask Ryne how much she knew about Lycan hierarchy and history. Ryne had a bad habit of neglecting to share certain bits of information.

For a few moments he didn't speak. Silence was a great way of forcing people to talk. Unfortunately, she didn't fall for his gambit, playing instead with a loose thread on her shirt. He exhaled slowly and decided if something was really wrong, she'd tell Ryne. He rose to his feet. "All right, I'll let it go this time, but remember if you ever need anything, just ask. As Beta, that's my job."

Mel smiled up at him, then stood. Pressing a light kiss to his cheek, she laid her hand on his arm. "Thanks, Bryan. I'll keep that in mind." She paused and looked down at the floor before glancing up at him again. "Um...you don't need to tell Ryne about this, okay? He's already worked up enough about impending fatherhood." She gave a nervous laugh and looked at him, her big brown eyes wide. Framed with incredibly long lashes, they still had the ability to make his heart thump faster.

At one point in time, he had half fancied her for himself, but once Ryne made his interest in Mel known, he'd backed off. As a matter of fact, falling for the wrong woman was the story of his life. First it was Elise, but she ended up with Kane. Then Mel with Ryne. He cleared his throat.

"I won't mention it to Ryne, for now. But if I thought something was seriously wrong…"

"I know," she interrupted. "You'd have to do your duty. Trust me, nothing is seriously wrong." Mel patted his arm again and stepped away. "I'll leave and let you get to work."

He sighed as he watched her walk out of the room and then moved to the desk with its stack of paper work that awaited his attention.

Las Vegas, Nevada, USA...

Kellen looked around the house one last time, pleased with his efforts. Everything was spotless. Papers put away, floors swept, furniture dusted, pillows plumped. He'd even lit one of those scented candles Sandy liked so much. Dinner was warming in the oven and he had dessert in the fridge. He rubbed his hands together in gleeful expectation. Sandy was due home any minute and he couldn't wait to see her reaction when she walked in.

Checking the clock, he positioned himself near the window so he could watch for her. The bus should be letting her off about now, then a quick walk from the corner to their place. Yep, there she was.

He frowned as she came closer. She looked out of sorts. His stomach gave a nervous quiver; maybe her mood had worsened from this morning as she contemplated his sins. He took a deep breath and exhaled slowly, flicking a glance over his shoulder at the welcoming ambiance of the room. All the work he'd done around the house should fix that, shouldn't it?

Stepping away from the window, he positioned himself just inside the door. His palms suddenly felt damp and he rubbed them against the legs of his jeans. He hated it when they argued or when she was mad at him; not that she ever really yelled, but the hurt in her eyes was hard to handle. Hopefully he could cajole her into a better mood.

The door swung open and Sandy entered, head down as she bent and set her purse on the floor, then turned to slide the deadbolt into place.

"Hi." He spoke softly as he slipped up behind her and snaked his arms around her waist to give her a hug.

"Oh!" She gave a start, then looked at him over her shoulder, her eyes filled with suspicion. "What's this all about?"

"Nothing. I just wanted to give my girly a friendly greeting at the door."

She gave him a funny look and then twisted to break free of his grasp. He took her by the shoulders and turned her so she was looking into the room. "What do you think?" He couldn't keep the pride out of his voice.

"It looks nice." She shoved her hands in her pockets, sounding less impressed than he'd hoped. "You cleaned, right?"

"Yep. Made dinner *and* dessert." He ducked his head so he could see her expression better. For a minute she just looked at him and he felt the smile slipping from his face. Had he forgotten something? His mind raced. Cleaning, dinner, dessert. Ah-ha! He knew what the problem was! "I...uh...cleaned the bathroom, too. Even the toilet."

For a heartbeat there was silence then she gave a snort of laughter, closing her eyes, and shaking her head. Opening them again, she looked at him and he was relieved to see the familiar fondness in her eyes. "Oh, Kellen. That was sweet of you. I've never gotten the hang of actually *liking* cleaning the bathroom."

He flicked a finger over the end of her nose. "No one does and, since you never had to do that sort of stuff growing up, I understand why it grosses you out."

She raised her brows, a teasing note creeping into her voice. "Then why do you usually leave it for me?"

Pleased that she was getting into the spirit of the evening, he adopted a superior tone. "Practice, my dear. Practice. I'm way ahead of you in experience when it comes to cleaning, so that's why I usually leave it for you. I want you to get caught up to me."

"Kellen, I think after almost three years of cleaning up after you, my experience is on par with yours."

"Technically the first year we were together doesn't count, since I had to show you how to do most of the stuff."

Sandy rolled her eyes and stepped further into the room. "Mmm... What's that I smell?"

"Chicken stir-fry. It's in the oven keeping warm. You go change and I'll put the food on the table."

"All right." She hesitated and then leaned up to kiss him on the cheek. "Thanks for the surprise."

"It's the least I could do after messing up last night."

"Yeah." She grew silent for a moment, almost pensive, but then smiled again, though it wasn't as bright as before. "We'll talk later. Right now, I'm starving. I'll change my clothes and be right out."

He watched as she walked down the hall towards the bedrooms. He shoved his hands in his pockets and rocked back and forth on his heels. All in all, that had gone well. For a few minutes they'd even been joking back and forth like they used to do. God, but he missed that. They used to have so much fun. Now... He lowered his eyes to the floor and sighed. Like Sandy said, they could always talk about it later. Right now things were good between them again and he didn't want to spoil the mood.

Sandy stood in front of her bedroom mirror, combing her hair into a ponytail. She could hear Kellen working in the kitchen. It was obvious what he was up to; trying to ease back into her good graces after totally screwing up last night. She should be angry with him, especially after what Mr. Bartlett had told her.

But then, he'd called her 'girly'—a silly word he'd used when they first met. It was his term of endearment for her and it always found a soft spot in her heart. And he'd even cleaned the toilet! She gave an amused sigh and shook her head, thinking of how much fun it had been to joke with him a few minutes ago. They didn't do that often enough anymore. Perhaps now wasn't the time to mention what she'd learned at work. The matter could wait an hour until dinner was over. Ruining the mood right now wouldn't serve any purpose other than to waste a perfectly good meal.

"Sandy? Are you almost ready? Food's on the table!" Kellen's voice drifted down the hall.

"Just a minute! Don't start without me!" She set down the comb and hurriedly pulled on a clean top and sweat pants before making her way to the kitchen.

Kellen really was a nice guy. Generous to a fault, funny, always looking for the positive. He was even willing to admit when he made a mistake...eventually. Sometimes his conscience was a bit slow, but he usually came around; like tonight, making amends by cleaning and cooking.

Yep, they'd have a nice normal evening together and then they'd talk.

By the time dinner was over, a faint hope stirred in her again. Everything was going so well. The creature inside her had been silent for a change; the restlessness blessedly absent. Perhaps, this was all that was needed; for her and Kellen to spend more time together like a real couple. She hummed happily to herself as she carried two cups of coffee into the living room and set them on the table in front of the sofa. Kellen was sprawled out and taking up most of the seating area. "Dinner was delicious."

The Finding

"But of course. I am a chef extraordinaire." Kellen grinned at her while flourishing his hand. He shifted as she prodded him with her foot, giving a mock groan of annoyance. Once there was room, she sat beside him. As was his habit, he draped his arm casually across the back of the sofa and began to absentmindedly stroke her ponytail, tugging at the strands, and sliding them through his fingers. It was a comforting gesture that lulled her into a half trance-like state.

"I've put one of your chick-flicks in for you, girly." He worked the remote with his other hand.

She smiled at the term *girly*. It wrapped around her like a soft blanket and made her feel warm and comfortable. "Good. And remember, no rude comments allowed." She cast a fierce look of warning his way before picking up her coffee.

"I promise to behave." He followed the statement with a Scouts' honour sign. She narrowed her eyes, knowing full well he'd never been a Scout; it was one of the few tidbits of information she knew concerning his past. Kellen wasn't one to share much about his background and that suited her fine. She wasn't keen on sharing her past either. There had been some type of falling out with his family, she knew that much and she'd told him her mother was dead and her uncle murdered. It was enough. The past was just that, the past.

For a while they watched the movie in companionable silence. She relaxed thinking how nice it was to spend time together again, like a real pack...er...family.

"Here comes the mushy stuff." Kellen whispered teasingly in her ear and she hit him lightly across the stomach. He clutched at his belly as if in pain and doubled over only stopping when she rolled her eyes at him.

"Remember, you promised to behave."

He sobered and sat back to watch again, his arms crossed casually behind his head.

On the screen, the female lead was studying her secret love interest, enumerating all his good qualities to a friend. She glanced at Kellen out of the corner of her eye, trying to see him as the actress on the screen might. Kellen *was* good looking, there was no denying that. His brown hair was stylishly long and fell appealingly over his brow. Laughter sparkled in his blue eyes and often curved his mouth into a mischievous grin. Good shoulders, a few muscles, trim waist.

Biting her lip, she sighed and Kellen murmured softly, pulling her closer so his chin rested on top of her head. She inhaled his familiar scent, felt the warmth of his body creeping into hers, and waited expectantly for some sign, some stirring of excitement within her.

Of course, it didn't happen. Nothing ever happened. The only thing to occur was a low rumble of discontent from the beast inside her.

No. He isn't for us.

She curled her fingers into fists, frustrated at the trap she found herself in. The beast inside was anxious and needy, pushing her to find something or someone, but it wouldn't consider the human she was living with. She'd learned that lesson two years ago...

The first time she and Kellen had been intimate was about a year after they first met. In all the months they'd been together, Kellen had never pressured her for sex. That he was interested, there was no doubt, but he'd never pushed her.

"You can stay with me as long as you need to," he'd offered generously that first day.

She'd entered his small apartment warily, not sure if he really was just a nice guy or if he had an ulterior motive. Her uncle might have kept her sheltered, but she'd read enough to know what could happen to young girls who were alone on the street.

"I won't sleep with you." She'd made the statement boldly, throwing it out like a gauntlet and then watching his reaction carefully.

"It's polite to wait to be asked." He'd responded mildly and she'd felt her face flush in embarrassment. Kellen had studied her for a moment then put her out of her misery. "Listen, you're a pretty girl and maybe I will sleep with you one day, but not tonight, not until you're ready."

The Finding

When she'd folded her arms and given him a disbelieving look, he'd flopped down on the sofa and laughed. "Look, you're wise to be wary of me. There are a lot of creeps out there, but I'm not one of them. I know what it's like to find yourself on the street with nowhere to go and I made a promise that I'd never let anyone else go through something like that if I could help it." He'd given her a sheepish grin. "You're my way of making amends for some of the stuff I've done in my life, okay?"

Eventually she'd realized that Kellen was speaking the truth, and as the months passed he never made any demands on her. Naturally, there had been hugs and brief caresses, even a few kisses, but he never expected more than she was willing to give. It was one of the things that made her love him; the way he'd gently kiss her as if testing the waters and then drawback to study her expression. When there'd been no answering passion in her eyes, he'd smile softly and squeeze her hand or shoulder before moving away.

He was so patient with her and at times she had despaired of herself wondering why she didn't respond. She wanted to; she wanted to give him something back after all he'd done for her. That probably explained why, when a sudden rush of need inexplicably developed in her, she hadn't questioned the abrupt change too deeply.

It had been near a full moon, a time she always dreaded for fear the wolf inside her would break through the drug induced cage it was in. Her supply of 'migraine' pills was almost gone and she was trying to make them last by stretching the interval between each dose.

Looking back now, and given what she'd learned through her internet research, she knew what had happened. She'd let the medication get too low in her blood stream and her wolf had come to the fore, in full heat. At the time, however, that possibility hadn't occurred to her. Waking from a vague, but incredibly erotic dream involving a well-endowed man, she'd been sweating and restless. Tension had coiled low in her belly and an aching need was growing between her legs.

Unsure as to what was going on, she'd thrown back the covers and crept down the hall, intent on getting a glass of water. Her skin felt as if it was crawling and she'd rubbed her hands up and down her arms, trying to ease the sensation. As she passed by Kellen's room, a pain had stabbed her belly and she'd gasped, inhaling deeply. That was when it hit her; Kellen's enticing scent had drifted by tickling her nostrils and sending her senses into overdrive.

Instinct took over and she found herself in Kellen's bed, crouched beside him, nuzzling his neck, kissing his jaw, easing the covers off his sleeping body.

"Kellen?"

"Wha..?" He'd groggily opened his eyes, raising his hands to her shoulders.

"Kiss me."

"Sandy?" He'd blinked at her owlishly, obviously confused.

She'd stopped any further comments with a kiss, for once enjoying the wet slide of his lips against hers. He'd responded briefly, before breaking the embrace and capturing her face in his hands and holding her away even as she struggled to get closer. "Sandy, what's going on?"

"I need you, Kellen." Unable to break from his grasp, she'd run her hands over his chest and his muscles twitched in response. Her palms revelled in the smooth warmth of his skin and her body ached even more, wanting to feel him pressed against her full length.

"This is awfully sudden. Did you have a bad dream or something?" God bless him, Kellen had done his best to try and figure out her sudden about-face, but she hadn't relented. Need had driven her to straddle him, to grind against him. She recalled how excited she felt to be finally responding to him like he deserved.

Turning her face in his grasp, she managed to nip then lick his wrist. "I...I just want you, Kellen. I can't explain it, but I need you, now. Please? I...I hurt."

"Sandy..." Her name was a groan on his lips. She wiggled against him, feeling his body responding despite the material

72

separating them. Slowly, he'd loosened his grip on her face, sliding his fingers through her hair and bringing her face closer to his. He'd searched her eyes for an explanation, but then gave in and crushed her to him.

A cry of relief had escaped her and then it had been all frantic hands and lips, gasps and groans. Clothing disappeared, and their positions became reversed. She'd felt his manhood pressing hot and firm against her thigh. At that moment, a warning had sounded in her brain; something wasn't right, but she couldn't focus on the thought. Part of her was craving his possession while another part was protesting that he wasn't the right one for her.

Need had won out and she'd spread her legs, guiding him to her aching core. He'd paused, breathing heavily, his forehead pressed to hers.

"Are you sure?" She could hear the strain in his voice.

"Yes, yes, please!" She'd arched her hips and felt his tip press into her. Need clawed at her, she couldn't believe how empty she felt. Kellen could give her relief.

He resisted a moment longer. "It's your first time. It'll hurt. I'll try to go slow."

"I don't care. Take me." Grasping his buttocks, she'd pulled him closer, whimpering at the feel of her flesh parting to accommodate him, at the slight burning sensation as her barrier stretched. She didn't care though. Shifting, she had dug her nails into him, her body craving more.

Kellen relented then and had driven himself into her. The sudden pain had shocked her into stillness for a moment and a voice howled within her. *He isn't the one!* She'd stiffened, part of her rejecting the act, but then he moved inside her and the need returned.

After that it was a blur of shifting bodies and panting breaths. Kellen whispered nonsensically to her, but she could never recall what he said. A soft wave of feeling swept over her, a tightening of her body, though nothing spectacular like she'd heard would occur. At least the intense craving inside her eased.

Chapter 5

Cassie awoke the next morning, once again filled with an all too familiar feeling of discontent. Her sleep had been punctuated with strange dreams where she'd kept trying to talk to Kellen about his gambling, but when she'd reached out to touch him, he'd morphed into some other man. A man who took her to bed and brought her to unbelievable heights of ecstasy, no less! She squirmed at the memory. Why did her subconscious keep conjuring up this fellow?

It certainly wasn't some version of Kellen. Their first time having sex had been their last. She recalled the morning after clearly. Getting up early, she'd scrubbed her skin in the shower, trying to remove the memory of what had happened. Then realizing the phase of the moon, she'd grabbed her pills and locked herself in her room afraid of what she might do next. Kellen had been concerned, knocking on her door, asking to talk to her, but when she'd mumbled migraine; he'd left her alone truly believing she was ill.

Days later, as gently as she could, she'd explained their night together had been a mistake. Kellen had tried to talk her out of it, claiming he'd been too rough and had scared her. She'd even gone so far as to let him kiss and caress her, a part of her hoping he was right, that they could have a normal relationship together.

Of course it hadn't worked. His touch didn't excite her, his kisses didn't arouse. In fact, the harder he'd tried, the stiffer she became as she fought to suppress the snarling protests of the fickle creature inside her. Eventually, he'd agreed it wasn't working between them, but she could tell he was hurt. And how could she blame him? She'd come on to him one minute and rejected him the next. Feeling guilty she'd offered to leave, but he wouldn't hear of it.

And so they continued living together, but it was a strange platonic relationship. She loved Kellen and was sure he loved her. There were moments of fun and laughter, companionable time watching movies, grocery shopping or painting a room, but there was a certain hollowness as well; a sense of despair that grew ever larger. Lately, the creature inside her had started pacing and panting; searching, as if it knew something important was coming. She raked her hands through her hair, wishing she knew what was going on inside her and how to fix it.

Her most recent attempt—the anniversary dinner—certainly hadn't worked. The animal within was no closer to accepting Kellen. Sadly, she suspected it would never accept any human and she mourned the loss of her dream. There'd be no family, no 'happily-ever-after' for her. Her fate was sealed; she was destined to live her life alone.

She tried to look at the fact philosophically, to see that perhaps it was for the best. In reality, who could she burden with her strange lifestyle? Even Kellen questioned her monthly seclusion, no longer believing the 'migraine' story. He too had done some research on her pills once she had to start buying them on the street. His conclusion was that she was a closet drug addict, but, at least beyond a few initial speeches, he left her to make her own decisions on the matter. She doubted others would be as tolerant.

Poor guy. He'd put up with so much from her, and here she was planning on chastising him about his gambling. Of course, his addiction was real while hers wasn't, but Kellen didn't know that.

Climbing out of bed, she wandered through the silent house and prepared the coffee pot before stepping out back. Leaning on the deck railing, she absorbed the new day. Dawn was breaking, streaks of yellow showing through the purple and pink clouds. The darkness slowly seeped away revealing the outline of buildings and shrubs. There was a chill to the desert air that would soon disappear as the sun rose to its zenith. Faint sounds of birds and insect life mixed with the stirring of the human inhabitants of the neighbourhood; a door slammed, a car started, a baby cried. Normal life.

The beast inside raised its head, whining and prancing like a puppy wanting to go for a walk. *Morning is the perfect time to run, to hunt.*

She frowned. Normal people didn't have animals talking to them inside their heads. She tried to ignore it, but found herself shifting back and forth on her feet, fighting the urge to step into the backyard, to give in to the call of nature.

Just for a while. To feel the wind against our face, our muscles stretching and straining, the ground racing by. The creature quivered in excitement. *It would be such fun to answer the call, to be what we truly are just this once.*

No! She jerked herself back into her human mind, realizing she was actually standing in the middle of the yard and... Oh God, her fingernails! The air around them shimmered and for a moment they appeared longer, thicker, almost like claws. Then the air quivered again and they were back to normal. That had never happened before!

Horrified, she glanced around, fearful someone had observed what had happened. Thankfully, at such an early hour, no one was around. Relieved, she stumbled back into the house ignoring the smell of freshly made coffee and rushing to the calendar. Frantically she searched the date and slumped in relief when she realized it was still almost a week until the full moon.

Then she stiffened again. If that was the case, then why...? She pushed down the panic that tightened her throat. The creature within her was getting so much stronger. What was she going to do? What would happen when she could no longer keep the animal suppressed? She wrapped her arms tightly around herself as possible scenarios played out in her head.

Horrifying Images filled her mind. Images of herself as a snarling, snapping animal, attacking everyone in sight. There was blood dripping from her jaws as she left a path of destruction in her wake. First Kellen, then the neighbourhood children.

Clamping a hand to her mouth, she held back the cry that threatened to burst from her. How long until that fateful day came? Until she became an uncontrollable beast? And what could she do about it?

She braced herself against the kitchen counter, her gaze flashing around the room. She couldn't stay here. It was too dangerous to those around her, but where could she go? Was there any place far enough away from other humans where she wouldn't be a threat? Shivers wracked her as she contemplated her future; alone, always running and hiding, fearful of what she might do.

A tear slid down her face at the bleak life she saw ahead of her. She'd never be able to have a home or a family, never fall in love, never be able to relax or let her guard down. God, what had she done to have such a fate thrust upon her? First she lost her mother before she was even able to remember her, then her uncle was shot in front of her and now she lived in constant fear of discovery. All she wanted was a simple, ordinary life! Was that really too much to ask?

The beast inside whined pitifully, but she didn't care. She hated the creature. Hated herself! Turning, she caught sight of her reflection in the glass door of the microwave. Her face looked distorted. Gasping, she touched her cheeks, her nose. Had the change already started?

She hurried to the bathroom and looked in the mirror, then slumped in relief. No. It was her usual image that greeted her, though her eyes were wide and her nose was pink. Lines of tension bracketed her mouth and even her hair was sticking out all over. She did look rather wild; a short dry laugh escaped her.

Smoothing her hair with her hands, she tried to force herself to relax, to think rationally rather than panicking. She inhaled deeply, and then exhaled slowly. Once she felt calmer, she headed back to the kitchen and poured a cup of coffee.

All right. Perhaps she was over-reacting. This morning was one slip; a...a warning that she needed to be more cautious. Yes, that was it! She had to guard her thoughts more, and not get too caught up in the creature's thinking. There was still time to find a solution rather than running away. Maybe if she played with her medication; increased the dosage. It might only put off the inevitable, but it would buy her some time at least.

She held onto the idea like a drowning woman. She wasn't ready to leave her present life. Staring around her tiny kitchen, she took in the crocheted potholder one of her customers had made her, the lace curtains she'd bought a month ago, the ugly picture on the wall that Kellen had given her.

Ah, Kellen. What would happen to him once she left? They had their rough patches, but there were good times too and really, they only had each other. She didn't dare let anyone else get too close, and Kellen only had his gambling buddies who came and went with the tides of fortune, leading him into scrapes and then walking away. She would battle the beast within as long as possible so she could stick around and take care of Kellen. He was her family now and that's what family did.

A queasy feeling stirred in her stomach. How long would she be able to keep control? Another month? Another year? She pushed the thought aside, and wiped the dampness from her cheeks. Enough of the melancholy. It wouldn't help anything and besides, it was time to get dressed for work. "Like a normal person." She spoke the words firmly to the empty room as if saying them out loud would make them true.

The garbled sound of flight announcements washed over the buzz of hundreds of voices and the distant drone of jets landing at the McCarren International Airport in Las Vegas. Throngs of people pushed and shoved, children cried, happy vacationers enthused. Bryan did his best to ignore them as he made his way to the car rental agency. It had been two days since he'd received the e-mail about a supposed sighting of Cassandra Greyson and he was eager to discover if the information was correct.

He smiled when he arrived at his destination. Only one person was ahead of him in line at the car rental desk so he'd be able to get on his way quickly. He stood patiently waiting his turn. The female attendant glanced up casually from her computer, then gave him a second look over the shoulder of her current customer. Her eyes brightened with obvious interest as she took in his appearance. He smiled to himself. While not conceited, he knew the effect he had on women and at times used it to his advantage. This might be one of those occasions.

Minutes later he was casually leaning against the counter, chatting to the girl as she processed his request. As usual, he'd managed to charm his way into a nicer vehicle and a better deal than most customers could manage.

"So, Bryan, how long will you be in Vegas?" The redheaded woman looked up at him through her lashes as she filled out the required forms.

"A week, maybe longer." He smiled at her, slowly letting his eyes move over her body. She blushed, but smiled back at him.

"If you're bored or have some free time—"

"I'll think of you." He grinned, finishing the phrase for her. As he reached out to take the keys, her fingers entangled with his and a bit of paper poked at his palm. He withdrew his hand and noted that a sticky note accompanied the keys. Carefully, he read the paper, the corners of his mouth curving slightly. As he suspected, it was her name and number. He folded it and tucked it into his pocket, giving her a knowing wink before walking away. She was easy on the eyes, so maybe...

He stepped out of the terminal and was immediately hit by a wave of heat. God, how did people manage to live in a place like this all year round? The pilot had warned them before landing that Vegas was in the middle of an unseasonal hot spell. The man hadn't been lying.

Longingly, he thought of the cooler air and shadowy depths of the forest back in Canada. Hopefully, he'd find the Greyson girl quickly and be able to head back home before he died from heat stroke. Sweat was already forming on his brow just standing there, so he hurried down the sidewalk, eager to find his car and crank up the AC.

It wasn't long before he was settled in a motel room; not one of the large casinos, but a smaller establishment closer to the suburbs. If Cassandra Greyson was working in a grocery store, she probably lived near the place so it made sense for him to be close to his quarry.

Kicking off his shoes and removing his shirt, he dropped onto the bed, resting against the pillows. His body relaxed into the soft surface and he sighed, taking a moment to enjoy the feel of the cool sheets and the quiet of the room before pulling his cell phone from his pocket. He'd better check in with Ryne first. Folding one arm behind his head, he propped the phone between his shoulder and ear, absentmindedly scratching his chest while waiting for someone to pick up.

"Hello?" A breathless Mel answered.

"Hey, Mel! It's Bryan. How are you doing?" He shifted his arms and grabbed the phone securely.

"Uh...fine. I guess."

"You guess?" He frowned. Something must be wrong.

"Yeah." Her voice lowered to a whisper and he mentally pictured her turning her back to the room and cupping her hand over her mouth so her voice didn't project anywhere but into the receiver. "Can I tell you something? Something you have to promise not to share with Ryne?"

"That depends what it is. He *is* our Alpha." He hedged his answer and sat up straighter. What information did she feel she could share with him, but not her mate?

"Right." He could hear her breathing heavily, maybe even sniffing as if she'd been crying. He waited patiently for her to continue. After a moment, she must have made up her mind, for she started to talk again. "Okay. Here's the thing. I had a message from the Lycan Link. You know how they've been looking into my background, trying to figure out who my father might be?"

"Uh-huh. Do they have a lead?" He leaned forward, resting his elbows on his knees as he tried to guess what she might have found out.

"Maybe."

"Then why not tell Ryne? He'd be happy for you."

"It's just that... Oh damn! Here he comes. Please, Bryan! Promise not to say anything to him, please?"

He exhaled gustily, feeling torn, but deciding once again to placate her. He didn't like this business of keeping secrets from his Alpha, but Mel's parentage wasn't life and death news; he supposed her could cut her more slack. "Okay. But I want an explanation next time we talk, all right?" His voice held an added sternness as he uttered the last phrase.

He could hear her breathing a sigh of relief. "Thanks, Bryan. You'll understand when I tell you." Muffled sounds followed, then Ryne came on the line.

"Bryan? Are you making Melody cry?" The Alpha's voice was suspicious.

"Me? No! I just started talking to her a minute ago." He didn't have to feign his nervousness. He didn't want Ryne angry at him; the guy was pretty laid back unless someone pissed him off or upset his mate.

"Huh." Ryne sounded puzzled and more than a bit frustrated. "It must be those damned pregnancy hormones. Melody's moods are all over the place lately. I can't keep up."

Bryan laughed softly, imagining the man running agitated hands through his hair. Ryne didn't do female emotions very well which was why it was a good thing Mel wasn't like this all the time. "Maybe you should talk to Kane? He's been through it twice so he might be able to give you a few pointers."

"Yeah, maybe I'll do that." Ryne sighed heavily before changing the topic. "So you made it to Vegas all right?"

"Yep. Just checked in. I'll grab a bite to eat and then see if I can find the grocery store where the girl in the picture works. With any luck she'll be there. If not, I'll ask one of the other employees when she'll be in."

"Be careful you don't sound too interested or they'll think you're some type of stalker."

"Hey, remember who you're talking to. I'm great at subtle."

Ryne grunted in acknowledgement. "Right. Give me a call tomorrow and let me know how you made out. If it's her, I'll start to work on getting her into Canada. And remember to be careful; rogues can be unpredictable."

The Finding

Bryan rolled his eyes. Ryne was really stuck on this rogue business for some reason. Cassandra Greyson was a kid. Handling her would be easy. He kept his thoughts to himself however; he'd prove Ryne wrong once Cassandra was part of the pack.

They continued to talk for a few more minutes, going over the technicalities of transporting a Lycan across the border then ended the conversation.

As he hung up, he felt guilty for not telling Ryne why Mel was upset, but reasoned that he didn't really know for sure. Finding her father was no big deal. Ryne was probably right; pregnancy hormones were throwing her off kilter. Besides, she'd likely break down and explain it to Ryne herself, long before he next spoke to her.

Putting the matter aside as just another of the weird interludes that Ryne and Mel shared, he headed to the bathroom for a quick shower. Travelling always made him feel grubby. Adjusting the water temperature, he stripped and stepped under the pounding stream.

At first he closed his eyes, revelling in the sensation of the hot water cascading down his body. Steam rose around him and he rolled his shoulders to ease the tension in them before grabbing the soap and lathering up. Washing automatically, he pondered how to proceed in his search. They didn't have a clear picture of Greyson, just Ryne's description of her and, if the girl had any measure of sense, she wasn't using her real name. So how to establish her identity?

A good sniff would determine if she was a Lycan, but other than that, all he had was a vague memory of her scent, which he'd detected in the motel room in Kansas. Would it be enough? His inner wolf rumbled in the affirmative. It hadn't forgotten the girl's unique essence.

He shifted uncomfortably as his body stirred to life. The beast inside had developed an exceptionally keen interest in the girl. It was more than the thrill of the hunt; for some reason the animal was eager to mate her, sight unseen. Down boy, he scolded. A sexual encounter was a possibility if the girl was willing, but don't start planning anything permanent, okay?

An inner silence greeted his warning. He frowned; the wolf hadn't automatically agreed, which was odd. Usually they were of one accord. He hoped it wasn't going to prove difficult. He'd have enough to deal with once he found Cassandra Greyson. A contrary inner-wolf would further complicate matters.

Shutting off the water, he grabbed a towel and quickly dried off before donning clean clothes. He'd grab a bite to eat, then search out the grocery store. If luck was on his side, the girl would be working and he could check her out. Should she prove to be Cassandra Greyson, he'd make contact and...

His thinking screeched to a halt as he pondered what to say to the girl.

'Hi! I'm Bryan, a fellow Lycan. The Finding clause means you're part of my pack, so come along quietly.' Shaking his head, he chuckled imagining how well that would go over. After a few more minutes of considering the situation, he shrugged and decided to play it by ear. Talking to women had never been a problem for him. The Greyson girl probably wouldn't prove any different.

Chicago, Illinois, USA...

Marla stepped into Aldrich's office and sat down in a seat near his desk. The man was still with his nurse, Sylvia Robinson, whom he employed to help deal with his trach tube. It required some daily maintenance and the man preferred to have a professional deal with it, even though most individuals managed fine on their own.

As she sank back in the leather chair, Marla looked around, pleased with the decor she'd chosen. Aldrich had given her free rein with decorating the penthouse and she'd gone with a modern look; chrome, leather, stark white walls with vivid splashes of colour. Some might think it was cold, but to her it fairly screamed exclusive, elegant, expensive. A faint smile curled her mouth at the memory of the purchasing spree she'd had.

The Finding

A contented sigh escaped her and she began to examine her nails for chips as she waited, not really caring how long Aldrich spent with the nurse as long he didn't expect her to help care for the tube. Thank heaven he kept a silk scarf over the opening. While it wasn't really ghastly to look at, she preferred to ignore the more unpleasant aspects of life. The nurse was welcome to the job.

Mrs. Robinson had started a month ago and was the eighth nurse he'd employed since the accident, the others having lasted only a matter of months each. Either they hadn't been able to put up with his moods or they'd shown signs of excessive interest in the man. In the former case, they quit of their own accord; in the latter, Marla herself made sure they left. She wasn't having anyone poaching in her territory and she'd already staked her claim on Aldrich, even if he didn't know it yet.

A quick glance at her watch told her he'd still be another ten minutes. Aldrich's life was rigidly ordered and he demanded punctuality, which was why she'd arrived early for their meeting. It also provided a good opportunity for gathering information.

Getting up, she wandered casually around the room, appearing as if she were staring at the pictures on the wall. The man was obsessed with security and he was always moving the surveillance cameras. As she moved about, she surreptitiously scanned the room, trying to determine their latest locations.

There was one over the door, pointing at the filing cabinet and the other one... She bit her lip and continued to search...there! Near the bookshelf. It was aimed at his desktop. Judging the angle carefully, she determined the computer wasn't within the viewing area, though it had been last time.

Smirking, she worked her way to the window and made a show of peering through the blinds at the view. Idly she noted how sparse the trees were and the lack of green space.

Not a suitable place for us to live.

She frowned and pushed her inner wolf's foolish idea away.

Letting the curtains fall back into place, she ensured she was out of camera range, then carefully reached forward to jiggle the computer mouse. The screen came to life and she began to read the information displayed. It never hurt to know what Aldrich was up to when she wasn't around. He liked to spring surprises on her and she'd found that some judicious snooping helped her keep one step ahead of him on most things.

The computer file that appeared had to do with Cassandra Greyson, an image of the heiress at the top of the screen. It showed a young girl with long, dark brown hair, green eyes, and golden skin. A mischievous smile lurked behind her full lips as if she were secretly mocking the photographer. It was a candid shot, one of the few that had apparently ever been taken of the child.

She didn't know much about the girl. Aldrich kept the whole thing close to his chest, but she had gleaned some information over the years.

The missing heiress had disappeared the night Anthony Greyson was 'accidentally' shot by Aldrich who purportedly had been trying to scare off an attacking dog. If it hadn't been for the severity of his own wounds, Marla might have thought Aldrich had arranged the whole thing; it would have been such a convenient way of eliminating Greyson. However, Aldrich had been near death, so it really must have been just a freak occurrence.

A wild dog attack was so unlikely in Chicago. At times she mused if a Lycan could have been involved, but decided it was simply her own paranoia. Lycans kept a low profile and as far as she could determine, neither Greyson nor Aldrich had been dabbling in anything that might have provoked an attack.

Returning her attention to the screen, she skimmed over Cassandra's file. Name, date of birth, mother's name. No father was listed. After her disappearance, she'd been traced as far as Kansas and then the trail went cold. Nothing Marla didn't already know.

About to turn away, she saw a footnote. This file was linked to the Greene file. She growled in frustration. There were certain files Aldrich kept encrypted and this was one of them. He'd never shared the password with her and so far she hadn't been able to crack it. The only other person who might know how to get in was his former assistant, Mrs. Sandercock.

Mrs. Sandercock, however, was unlikely to provide any help, should anyone contact her over the matter of secret passwords. The woman was rather bitter; something about an unexpected letter of dismissal from Mr. Aldrich. Marla smirked, thinking of how she'd bamboozled both Sandercock and Aldrich; each believing the other had terminated their association. Aldrich had barely been out of the hospital and in no condition to begin interviewing for the job, so naturally Marla had just slid into the permanent position. As for Mrs. Sandercock… Marla shrugged. Someone had probably hired the woman eventually; not everyone demanded letters of reference.

Checking the time, Marla realized Aldrich would be finished with his nurse soon. Casually, she strolled back towards her seat. On the surveillance camera it would appear she'd been studying the view and the paintings on the wall, while awaiting Aldrich's appearance. The computer screen would fade to black in a minute, erasing all evidence that anyone had been looking at it recently. Everything would appear untouched.

Gracefully settling into her seat, she pasted a placid smile on her face, crossed her ankles, and arranged her skirt so that a sufficient amount of skin was showing. Now all she had to do was wait for her employer. Inside, her wolf whimpered, saying it was tired of the game she was playing, but she shushed it sternly. This was not the time. Everything would work out perfectly fine.

Chapter 6

"Thank you, Sylvia." Aldrich slowly got up from his chair and nodded at the nurse who was putting away her equipment.

His doctor had assured him there was no need for a private nurse, but Aldrich wasn't taking any chances. Sylvia suctioned the tube each morning and night as well as before meals and whenever else the need arose. She was also in charge of checking the condition of his stoma twice a day, ensuring proper humidification of the air, ordering supplies, cleaning, and maintaining his suctioning machine. The woman was well worth the price of her paycheck. Besides, he had his hands on the Greyson estate; money wasn't a problem.

"You're welcome, Leon." She smiled at him briefly, as she continued with her task.

Aldrich spared a moment to watch his nurse, not minding the familiarity with which she addressed him; her faint British accent was pleasing to the ear. Sylvia was fiftyish, slightly plump and had strands of grey hair appearing, but was still an attractive woman. Plus, she didn't grate on his nerves and showed absolutely no interest in him whatsoever. Not since Mrs. Sandercock—damn her for leaving with no warning—had he appreciated the calm, soothing presence of the fairer sex.

His cheek twitched as he thought of the other female in his employ; Miss Matthews, or Marla, as she kept asking him to call her. The woman was beautiful and efficient, but as cold and calculating as himself. She thought she had him wrapped around her finger with her pouting lips and oft-displayed cleavage, but he knew her game.

Miss Matthews was out for whatever she could get and she'd set her sights on him, or more precisely, the Greyson estate. If it wasn't for the fact she was damned good at her job, he'd have sent her on her way ages ago. As it was, he could put up with her as long as she didn't step too far out of line.

"Leon? Is something wrong?"

Aldrich realized he was scowling at the nurse and hastened to reassure her. "No. Just some business I was thinking of." He paused, then spoke hesitantly. "I...I believe the British are known for taking afternoon tea. Is it a practice you follow?"

Sylvia smiled. "I do like to have a cup mid-afternoon. Are you fond of tea?"

He studied her for a moment, then nodded.

"If you'd like, you could join me one day." As she made the offer, a pinkness appeared on her cheeks. Aldrich found it fascinating.

Suddenly aware he was staring, he rubbed the back of his neck, feeling inexplicably embarrassed—he was never embarrassed—and left the room, only realizing after the fact, that he'd never answered her.

He left the area designated as the nurse's room utterly bemused by the exchange, arriving at his office door without even being aware of the fact. The door was open a crack and he could see long, silky legs carefully arranged for his viewing pleasure. He couldn't help giving the displayed limbs an appreciative look. The woman was as sexy as hell and a certain portion of his anatomy couldn't help but respond to the fact.

Wondering what was wrong with him—first Sylvia and now Miss Matthews—he gave his head a shake and corralled his wandering thoughts. Putting on his usual bland expression, he entered the room.

"Miss. Matthews, I'm sorry to have kept you waiting." He uttered the socially polite words, not really caring if she had been waiting or not. After all that's what he paid her for, wasn't it? Still, he prided himself on maintaining a cloak of civilized respectability.

"No, you're right on time as always, Leon."

He paused in the act of sitting down behind his desk and looked at her with one raised brow. She caught his gaze, lowered her eyes demurely and with a blush—fake no doubt—corrected herself.

"I mean, Mr. Aldrich, sir."

He gave a nod of approval and finished seating himself. Leisurely, he surveyed the surface of his desk, noting all his papers were exactly where he'd left them. Good. She hadn't touched anything. The surveillance cameras would have caught her if she had. He picked up the file she'd prepared the previous day and flicked it open. After a brief perusal he commented on her report.

"The Greyson Estate continues to function well and is in good repair, I see."

"Yes." Miss Matthews leaned forward, as if she were eager to talk to him.

Was it a coincidence her blouse gaped open? He thought not.

"The monthly expense report for maintenance supplies, utilities, and employee wages is included." She gestured towards the file.

He glanced at the next page and nodded. "Anything else?"

"Just the matter we discussed earlier; Franklin's advancing years." She shook her head and made a little moue. "I fear he's getting quite forgetful. The errors in the content inventory, claiming we've had conversations which we haven't..." Her face was a picture of regret as her voice trailed off, but he studied her eyes instead; they were flat and cold. The woman was up to something.

"Be that as it may, he and Mrs. Teasdale were appointed by the courts as interim caretakers and Franklin's last medical report deemed him capable of the job. We'll have to rely on your continued diligence to ensure things don't get out of hand."

The woman preened at his supposed praise while Aldrich kept his face neutral. He recalled Swanson's report about her stop at Albert Winter's, the antique dealer, last time she visited the Estate. There was little doubt in his mind Miss Matthews was pocketing small items and selling them, thus acquiring a tidy nest egg. He admired her ingenuity; it was something he might have done himself in the early days.

As long as she confined herself to the occasional bout of petty theft, he'd let it go. Her activities were actually providing him with ammunition should he need to use some leverage against her in the future. Knowing deep, dark secrets about an employee could be so useful.

"As always, I'll do my best." She smiled at him and, not for the first time, he noted her white, longer than normal, canine teeth. They had an unsettling effect on him when she smiled widely. He briefly mused why she'd never had them fixed.

He gave his head a minute shake and continued on with the business at hand. "Swanson will be reviewing the Estate's security system next week. I'd like you to accompany him and make note of anything that needs upgrading."

"Yes, sir." She began making notes, then queried in a deceptively casual voice. "If you don't mind my asking, sir, how are you progressing on the matter of the missing heiress?"

"Cassandra?" He flicked a glance at his computer and then at Marla. How did she know that was the file he'd been reading? Coincidence or...? Eyeing the surveillance camera mounted on top of the bookshelf, he narrowed his eyes. Did Swanson get the angle wrong or did it actually encompass his computer? Damn! He'd have to check the footage tonight.

Marla continued. "Yes. I was wondering if the latest batch of missing person posters had yielded any results."

"No, not yet, but we'll keep trying. She has to be somewhere. All it takes is for the right person to see the poster and for her picture to jiggle a memory."

"And when you find her?"

"I believe that falls under lawyer-client confidentiality at this point. If you ever need to be appraised of the situation, I'll let you know."

"Of course." She nodded and he wondered what was going on behind her demure expression. Was she laying plans for when or if Cassandra re-appeared? Perhaps planning on befriending the girl, becoming her companion? Or possibly arranging an accident, should the girl ever be located. The latter was more likely. Marla was probably hoping he'd remain in control of the Greyson estate for some time so the financial perks would continue to filter down to her. And once the estate was settled, a substantial sum would come his way. She'd love to get her hands on that.

Well, no matter what Miss Matthews was concocting in her head, he had his own agenda where Cassandra Greyson was concerned.

Swiftly dealing with the remaining items on his desk, he sent Miss Matthews on her way, much to her obvious annoyance. The woman always wanted to linger and fawn over him, making annoying small talk, finding reasons to touch him. On occasion, he put up with her wandering hands, but today he wasn't in the mood. Once free of her presence, he turned to his computer and thoughtfully studied the information before him.

Cassandra Greyson's background puzzled him. From what little information he'd garnered, the girl was the daughter of some woman named Luisa, with whom Greyson had hooked up with briefly, though Greyson wasn't the father; that person was listed as an unknown. Upon Luisa's death, he'd raised Cassandra as his niece and made her his heir.

Aldrich pulled at his lip, still impressed Greyson had managed to keep the child hidden all those years. It had come as a shock when Greyson suddenly announced the existence of a ward. In fact, the announcement had been so startling it had aided the werewolf's attack. Staring at Greyson in amazement, he had been unaware of the wolf until a streak of movement caught his eye. He'd swung towards the wolf; in his surprise tightening his grip on the gun and unintentionally shooting his boss, Anthony Greyson.

The incident had been deemed an accident caused by the 'wild dog' attack; that's how the doctor at the hospital had listed the cause of the injuries to his throat. He'd done nothing to disabuse them of the fact.

With Greyson dead, Cassandra had become heir to a multi-million-dollar estate. Unfortunately, she'd gone missing the night of the accident and no one seemed capable of finding her.

Originally he was of two minds as to how to deal with the situation. Both options had merit. In one, the girl was simply eliminated. If she never returned as heir, he'd be in charge of dispersing the estate's funds. He already knew of several ways to ensure a goodly portion ended up in his hands. Even now, as executor, he was able to use his own discretion to access a percentage of the money. The main drawback was the seven year waiting period for missing heirs. It would be another four years before he had complete control.

The other possibility was finding the girl and bringing her back. He'd have her declared incompetent, which wouldn't be hard, given her background. She'd been raised in a figurative glass cage and had no family or friends to vouch for her. There was even a nurse who had worked with the girl mere hours before Greyson's death. According to the woman, the girl was unstable, incorrigible and needed heavy sedation for some mysterious condition. Pampered, alone in the world, ill and a runaway. Having himself appointed guardian should be easy.

Her 'condition' was of special interest to him. Based on her uncle's declaration just minutes before his death, Aldrich had his own suspicions as to what ailed her. If he was correct, the girl would serve more than one purpose if he kept her alive. He chuckled darkly. Yet another pawn for him to use in the chess game of life.

Las Vegas, Nevada, USA...

Cassie shifted on her feet and rubbed her lower back. Standing at a cash register for hours was tiring and she couldn't wait for her break. She flicked a casual glance at the customers still waiting to check out, while her present customer—an elderly woman named Mrs. Mitchell—found the money to pay for her groceries.

The Finding

Most of the people in line were regulars, except for the third man back. He could be a tourist, though she didn't see many of those in the store; they usually stuck to the casinos and other attractions. She smiled vaguely at the customers and turned her attention back to Mrs. Mitchell.

"Three dimes—that's thirty. A nickel—that's thirty-five." Three more pennies appeared. "Thirty-six, thirty-seven, thirty-eight! There you go. Twenty-nine dollars and thirty-eight cents exactly." The older woman looked triumphant at having completed the task.

"The exact change as always." Cassie smiled back as she picked up the coins from the counter and placed them in the till.

She didn't mind waiting as the customers dug around for exact change. Many of them were seniors and lonely. Their time at the grocery store was a social outing rather than just a necessity.

She understood loneliness. Her family—Uncle, Franklin and Cook—were all gone now. She only had Kellen. Some, like Mrs. Mitchell, were almost family; the grandmother or great-aunt she'd never had, but it wasn't a real relationship, more wishful thinking.

"Do you need help carrying those bags to the car, Mrs. Mitchell?"

The older woman reached across and patted her arm. "No, but thank you for asking. The doctor said it was good for my old bones to carry a few heavy items; resistance I think he called it."

"All right. But don't do too much at once." She turned her attention to the next person waiting to check out while Mrs. Mitchell moved to the end of the counter and dug through her purse, most likely searching for her car keys. The poor dear was always misplacing them.

As she dealt with her new customer—a young mother with a toddler in her arms—Cassie experienced a prickling feeling, as if someone were watching her. It wasn't the first time this had happened. Several times this past week, she'd found herself staring around the grocery store looking for the source, only to find nothing.

At the time, she'd attached no importance to the phenomenon. But now that Mr. Bartlett had mentioned someone asking about her she wondered if it was more significant than she had initially thought. Could the beast inside her be aware of danger on some level? Inwardly she rolled her eyes, thinking the creature might have one redeeming quality after all; though sensing someone was watching, and knowing exactly who it was and why, were two completely different things.

Shrugging her shoulders, she tried to rid herself of the uneasy feeling, but it didn't work. Flicking a glance up from the bar code scanner, she locked eyes with the man—the one she'd dubbed a tourist—and found he was studying her, his eyes narrowed in concentration.

Quickly, she looked away. Her mouth suddenly seemed dry and the air around her was much warmer than a few minutes ago. Inside her, the beast stirred with excitement. Another quick peek revealed the man was frowning now.

Was he upset the line was moving so slowly? She tightened her lips. There were only two checkouts open, so he'd just have to wait his turn! She continued to scan the groceries while trying unsuccessfully to ignore his presence. He had an arrogant look about him, as if he expected everyone to notice him. Too bad, she wasn't going to speed things up to make him happy!

Seconds ticked by. An uncomfortable feeling began to grow in her stomach. Her heart rate sped up and her senses heightened; the brightness of the overhead lights hurt her eyes and the beeping of the scanner was like a hammer inside her head. Scents she wasn't normally aware of assaulted her nose and she mentally identified them while trying to concentrate on her job; baby powder, raw meat, cleaning products, sweat. Something new was in the mix though. She sniffed and wondered what it might be. An animal of some sort? Weighing a bag of grapes, she looked at the man through her lashes.

Damn! He was still staring at her. Her gaze locked with his. She couldn't look away. His eyes were hazel, his stare intent as if he were trying to see inside her. A shiver swept over her, followed by a heated feeling. Darting out the tip of her tongue, she wet her lips and he followed the movement with his eyes before looking back up at her. One corner of his mouth curled up and her discomfort increased. A desperate need to escape was coming over her; the wolf inside her was prancing; excited by the man's presence yet at the same time wanting to run so he would give chase.

She swallowed hard and wrenched her attention back to the task at hand. Her voice wavered as she announced the total.

"That will be forty-five, eighty-seven."

The woman handed over sixty dollars and Cassie took it. Her hand shook as she made change, dropping the coins and cursing softly under her breath. A chuckle came from the direction of the tourist and she wondered sourly what he found so funny.

Working on autopilot, she commented to the mother about the baby, all the while thinking that the man was next in line. She didn't want to deal with him; in fact she was almost light-headed at the very idea. Frissons of awareness darted up and down her spine at the thought of him being inches away, hearing his voice, breathing in his scent, their fingers possibly touching as he handed her some bills.

"Hey, Sandy! Break time." A cheerful voice sounded behind her and she almost slumped in relief. Debra, her replacement cashier, was there. With more haste than dignity, Cassie traded places with the other girl and moved to leave.

"Sandy, dear?"

Oh God, Mrs. Mitchell was still here! All Cassie wanted to do was get away before that man came any closer. Forcing herself to pause, she looked at the older woman. "Yes, Mrs. Mitchell?"

"I meant to ask you how your anniversary dinner went. Was Kellen pleased?"

"Er..." She looked over her shoulder. The man was still watching her, a scowl on his face. What was his problem? Obviously he was upset, but why? She'd never met him before, so perhaps she was being paranoid. Dragging her attention back to the older woman, she stumbled over her response.

"I'll...uh...I'll tell you about it next time you're at the store. I...er...need to use the washroom."

"Oh, then don't let me keep you. I know what that's like." Mrs. Mitchell waved her off, and Cassie walked away as quickly as she could, ducking down the cereal aisle. As soon as she was free of the man's gaze, she started to feel better.

"Now that was weird," she muttered to herself. Her heart rate was calming, the sights and sounds around her were fading to a normal level of awareness. Biting her lip, she cautiously peeked around the corner of an instant oatmeal display. The man was still there, only he'd moved closer to the door and was now chatting to Mrs. Mitchell.

She clenched her hands, wishing she knew how to read lips. Even by straining her ultra acute hearing, she couldn't make out the words over the background noises. What were they talking about? Mrs. Mitchell laughed and the man smiled at her, then looked in Cassie's direction. She ducked back. Had he noticed her spying? Not willing to take the chance he'd seek her out, she scurried to the back of the store and ducked into the employees' rest area.

Once there, she sat at the table and held her head in her hands, grateful no one else was around. Didn't she have enough to worry about right now without this? Who was that man and why did he make her so uncomfortable? Was he the same person Mr. Bartlett had been referring to? And if he was, what was the reason behind his interest? And why was he talking to Mrs. Mitchell?

While it could be the man wanted to ask her out on a date, she doubted it. There was a certain aura that had come off him. Earlier, she'd dubbed it arrogance, but on reflection perhaps it was danger. Whatever the case, he made her nervous and stirred the beast inside her.

Could he be another werewolf? It had been three years since the incident and there was no indication the wolves knew where she was, or that they were even looking for her. No. She was simply being paranoid where they were concerned. The only werewolf around was the hated creature inside her.

The Finding

Rubbing her hands over her arms, she considered the other possibility; that the mystery man had something to do with Kellen's gambling. She hadn't had a chance to talk to Kellen about it yet; the first night when he'd made her dinner, it hadn't seemed appropriate and since then they kept missing each other. A nasty voice inside her head insisted Kellen was purposely avoiding her.

She sighed heavily. Quite likely the voice was right. All the signs pointed to the fact that Kellen was in debt again, likely for a significant amount this time, and the people he owed were getting impatient. Maybe they thought she'd bail him out, or by harassing her it would force Kellen to pay up. An inelegant snort escaped her. Kellen had little in savings; it would likely be a long wait before he made any sort of dent in the total, whatever it might be.

The man in the check-out line certainly matched her image of a thug sent to collect a debt. Tall and muscular, too intelligent looking for a run of the mill goon. And too good looking, she added as an afterthought. His nose wasn't broken, there were no visible scars, and he had all his teeth—she'd seen them when he smiled at Mrs. Mitchell. Cassie frowned. Okay, maybe he didn't look like a thug. But he did have an air of danger about him. Not in a violent way though; it was actually sort of sexy. Like he could be dangerous if he lost control.

Just thinking about the man caused the wolf inside to stir again. Reluctantly, she acknowledged that the man affected her as well. His hazel eyes had been fringed by long lashes and his dark blond hair was thick with a slight wave. Her palms tingled as she wondered if it would feel as soft as it looked. She bit back a smile as she recalled that a dimple had appeared on his cheek when he'd been laughing with Mrs. Mitchell. A thug with a dimple? She shook her head, chastising herself. Mooning over a man with probable criminal connections was not a good idea.

Taking a deep breath, she brought her mind back to the business at hand. She had two possibilities; werewolves or thug. Neither one was overly palatable, though she felt the thugs might be less of a threat. At least she could go to the authorities about them.

Checking her watch, she decided to ask Mr. Bartlett to let her leave early. If she went home now, she'd be able to talk to Kellen before he left. She'd put off discovering what sort of a mess he was in long enough. It was time to get to the bottom of things.

She grabbed her purse from the small locker assigned to her. The bus would be leaving soon, so if she hurried...

Bryan had rolled his eyes when the young woman ducked back behind a cereal display. How she'd thought that could possibly hide her presence, he had no idea. Her scent gave her away just as easily as her physical presence. She was definitely a Lycan—that had been easy to determine—but there was a subtle essence that was uniquely her. He closed his eyes and inhaled; exotic and spicy, with floral undertones.

That particular scent was one he couldn't forget. It had plagued him for the past three years, ever since he'd caught the faintest whiff of it in the motel room in Kansas. The girl was definitely Cassandra Greyson.

She'd peered at him for a moment before moving deeper into the store, her scent fading as it blended with those of the various foods for sale. He'd snorted. Did she really think she was hiding her trail? If she did, she was sadly mistaken. An experienced hunter such as himself wouldn't be easily led astray by the tempting aromas of meats and baked goods.

He shifted his gaze to the magazine racks and the large man lurking there. Now *that* was an inexperienced hunter. The man had been staring at Cassandra Greyson for the last half hour while trying to look inconspicuous by supposedly reading a magazine. The problem was the fellow hadn't turned a page the whole time, nor had he taken his eyes off the young woman. Who was he and why was he watching her?

The man had made no move to follow Cassandra when she left her work station. If he had, Bryan would have followed. Instead, the fellow had made a brief phone call and then picked up his magazine again, apparently planning on waiting until she reappeared.

Deciding the man wasn't planning on making any moves towards Cassandra in the near future, Bryan nodded as the older woman beside him continued to chatter away. He'd approached the senior citizen after paying for the groceries he didn't need, but that were part of his cover. As he'd bagged the items, he'd struck up a conversation with Cassandra's elderly customer offering to carry her parcels to her car. While she declined, it proved to be the perfect way to make her acquaintance.

"You're just like Sandy. That's the girl who was working the checkout a minute ago. She wanted someone to help me as well, but I said no to her too. Such a sweetheart. She lives a few blocks from me in the cutest little house. Her boyfriend, Kellen, shares it."

He'd been checking on the magazine-man again when her statement caught his full attention. The news that Cassandra—or Sandy as the woman called her—was involved with someone didn't sit well with him or his inner wolf. It was unreasonable to think the girl would have remained unattached all these years, but that didn't mean he had to like it. Such a living arrangement was inconvenient to his present purpose.

He tried to put a logical spin on his feelings; he had a right to be annoyed. If she was living with someone, it would make it all the more difficult to bring her into the pack. She'd be reluctant to leave the man behind and bringing a new wolf plus her human companion into Canada would increase the complexity of their original plan.

They were at the store's exit now and he let the older woman leave first. She was still talking about this Kellen person.

"—works here too, though it's a night shift, so I've only seen him a few times. He's a good looking fellow, but," she shook her head, then leaned closer whispering in a conspiratorial manner. "I'd never say it to Sandy—I don't believe in poking my nose into other people's business—but sometimes I wonder about her relationship with him. I'm sure he's a fine young man, just not the one for her. They don't see much of each other, what with working opposite shifts, and she has this look. Not exactly unhappy; more as if she's restless inside, like something important is missing in her life."

He made suitable noises and continued to walk beside the woman as she made her way across the parking lot. So Cassandra—Sandy—was restless. He felt the corners of his mouth curve upward at the news. If her wolf was restless, it probably was feeling the strain of not being part of a pack. Well, he was here to offer a solution.

Mrs. Mitchell bid him farewell and climbed into her vehicle. He continued on his way as if searching for his own car, but once the woman drove out of sight, he circled back. The man by the magazines was still in the grocery store, and he had no plans of leaving Cassandra unguarded until he knew the man's intentions.

His hand was reaching for the door when the wind shifted and her scent drifted by. What...? He turned in a circle, scanning his surroundings. Cars, shoppers, grocery carts. There! A slim dark haired woman getting on a bus. Instinct told him it was definitely Cassandra Greyson.

As the bus pulled away, he started to run across the parking lot, intent on following her, but then drew himself to a stop. No. He'd have to shift into wolf form in order to keep up and the citizens of Las Vegas wouldn't be used to seeing a wolf running down the street chasing a bus.

He shifted the bag of useless groceries in his arms and glared in the direction of the departing vehicle, cursing himself for making such a rookie mistake. Dammit, he never should have taken his eyes off the girl! Now he'd have to start searching for her all over again. Growling, he wished he at least had her last name. Then he could have done a search to find out where she lived. All he knew at this point was that she was known as Sandy.

All right, he'd have to do things the hard way. First he'd find a map that outlined the city bus routes and then he'd follow it along until he caught her scent again. She had to get off the damned bus at some point and then he'd have her.

As he headed back towards the small strip mall that contained the grocery store, he saw the large man from the magazine rack was leaning against a white van, once again making a phone call. Too bad he wasn't close enough to hear what was being said. At least he could see the license plate. He committed it to memory so Daniel could trace it for him once he got back to the motel. First, however, he had to track down Cassandra.

Compressing his lips, he grumbled thinking of how long it might take to pick up her scent again. Waves of heat rose from the sidewalk and he felt sweat trickling down the indent of his spine. Damn, they would have to be having an unseasonal heat wave just when he arrived in the city. He'd have heatstroke before he found her. The cool forests of northern Canada had never been so appealing.

Chapter 7

Chicago, Illinois, USA…

Aldrich looked over the information that Nate Graham had sent him. The Nevada situation was salvageable, but only if they were able to get their edge back. Things had been allowed to slide under the less than competent leadership of Eddie Perini.

Flicking through the pages, he shook his head in disbelief. He'd made a serious error in judgement when he'd put the man in charge. Perini wasn't ruthless enough; his clients didn't respect him. The point returns weren't nearly as high as they should be. Eddie needed to apply pressure, instil some fear. Fear kept people in line, not idle threats.

He threw the report down, disgusted. There was no excuse for this except poor management on Eddie's part. Narrowing his eyes, he considered the possibilities.

At first, he'd considered folding the company and taking his losses, but that smacked too much of giving in; it gave people the wrong impression. Even if he dispatched Eddie, the failure of the business would still be a fact. Should word ever get out, it could negatively impact on his effectiveness in other areas of business. Failure clung to one's name and reputation like gum to a shoe.

No, he had to pull Dollar Niche out of the fire first. Once it was suitably profitable again, then he could rid himself of it. In the grand scheme of things the company was a minor concern, a leftover from the days when his goals hadn't been quite so lofty. But he needed to exit the scene with his head held high.

He gave a decisive nod. Having chosen a course of action, there was no point in waiting. He picked up the phone and dialled.

As it rang, he drummed his fingers impatiently on the desk, waiting for an answer. Some might view his plan as a severe step, but it was necessary in order to re-establish the fact that Dollar Niche was not a company to be toyed with.

If memory served him correctly, Eddie was a squeamish sort. The man's reaction to this new business plan might even prove to be mildly amusing. Idly, he thought Eddie's career choice was definitely at odds with his personality; the man would have done better if he'd followed the elder Perini's career path and become a part time preacher. Bilking people out of their hard-earned money with promises of salvation didn't involve any rough stuff.

Finally, the phone was answered, but a clattering noise met his ear as if whoever was picking it up wasn't really paying attention and had fumbled the receiver. The sounds of a sports announcer drifted over the line and then, after some delay, an actual voice spoke.

"Eddie Perini. What can I do for you?" The man's casual answer let him know Eddie hadn't checked who was calling before answering. He sighed; still the same old Eddie, he thought to himself, always thinking life was a lark. They'd grown up in the same neighbourhood; giving Eddie the job of managing the company had been an uncharacteristic spur of the moment decision based on that long ago friendship. Well, he'd known it before and this reinforced the fact that sentimentality had no place in business.

"Edward, this is Leon Aldrich speaking." He chuckled to himself, knowing the use of the man's formal name would rattle the fellow; memories of Mama Perini bellowing down the street drifted by while Eddie tried to gather his composure.

"Uh... Leon...er...Mr. Aldrich, sir. How are you? Nice of you to call."

He could hear the nervousness in the man's voice and mentally formed the image of Eddie sitting up straighter and shuffling the papers on his desk into some semblance of order as if the disorganized office could actually be viewed through the phone. Good. The man had been lazy in carrying out his duties and deserved to sweat a little.

"I've been going over the accounts and see no improvement since the last time we talked."

"That's not precisely true, Leon."

Aldrich raised his brows at the man's denial and leaned back in his chair. "I beg to differ. My representative is in Vegas at this very moment, checking out the situation. Word on the street is that Dollar Niche is an easy mark."

Eddie didn't answer immediately, no doubt realizing a noose was closing in around him. "I wouldn't say that exactly. I...I've gathered a number of new clients—"

"Profitable clients? Or men who use Dollar Niche because it's seen as a pushover?"

"No. Of course not. They've made their payments!"

"Paltry sums, Edward. These individuals have borrowed substantial amounts from the company and have reaped the benefits of our generosity. Repayment—swift repayment—is needed if the company is to make a profit." He kept his voice slow and calm, knowing the raspy sound was more effective that way. At least the damned tracheotomy was good for something, he mused.

"Some of these people don't have that much lying around, you know. They pay off what they can."

"Edward, we are not running a charity. People always claim to be hard up. If sufficient incentive is applied, they find the needed resources."

"We pressure them, Leon...er...sir."

"Perhaps your concept of pressure is different from mine, because what I envision as pressure would have yielded much greater results than those I see on the page before me."

"Exactly what are you getting at?"

"I need you to set an example. To show your clients you mean business. Choose someone and make sure everyone knows what happens when a person falls behind in their payments."

"You mean—" The man's gulp was audible over the phone line.

"I mean you do what is necessary, Edward, to make a *lasting* impression. This company has been falling apart over the past few years. I admit it's partially my own fault. You obviously weren't up to the job." He heard Eddie sputtering protests, but ignored the attempted interruption. "And I didn't take sufficient notice of the quarterly reports. However, that is all water under the bridge. The situation will be reversed or someone will be held accountable. I don't think I need to spell out who, do I, Edward?"

"No, sir." The answer was given as part of a heavy sigh.

He smiled coldly. "As long as we understand each other. Goodbye, Edward. I'll be in touch." He hung up the phone and leaned back in the chair. All that talking had been exhausting. Rotating his shoulders to ease the tension, he contemplated his next move. Perhaps, he'd go find Sylvia; she still kept the quaint British custom of afternoon tea.

Hanging up the phone, Eddie Perini rubbed his hands over his face. God, he wasn't cut out for this. He could do the lending, fake a tough guy voice and issue threats to a mark, but carrying them out had never been his strong point. Having a guy roughed up was one thing, but doing serious bodily damage or going after a guy's family wasn't something he wanted to do.

He looked around the room for inspiration, but found none. The place looked like it came from some Hollywood B-movie; worn furniture, dull paint, the air stale with smoke. Beyond this office, the 'waiting room' wasn't much better, consisting of a few chairs lining the hallway. Yeah, it was pretty shoddy, but a high-class place wouldn't draw in the type of customers they serviced.

Sure, Dollar Niche wasn't making the profits it did a few years back, but there was a bloody recession going on! Even a shady business like this one was feeling the pinch. He cursed Leon for sticking his nose in where it didn't belong. The guy sat in some ivory tower surrounded by money and had no idea what happened in the real world. If they started beating up all the clients, new marks would shy away.

Eddie sighed. It was no use complaining. Aldrich was a bastard and if he didn't follow through, he'd be in big trouble; at best losing his job, at worst... Well, he didn't want to think about that.

Rumours concerning Leon had grown over the years. The man had clawed his way up from the streets they'd both lived on to the position of a big time lawyer who worked almost exclusively for a multi-millionaire. When said millionaire had been killed in an accidental shooting, it came as no surprise to Eddie that the gun had been in Aldrich's hand, though no blame had ever been laid. That, combined with whisperings of how Aldrich had helped make certain individuals 'disappear' made people exercise extreme caution when dealing with the man. No one knew for certain exactly what he was capable of doing and no one was anxious to find out, either.

Pulling a thick file forward, Eddie flipped through the pages, scanning the lists of names. He had to make an example of someone, but who? And how? Aldrich had insinuated serious injury or maybe even death. Eddie's stomach lurched at the idea. He wasn't into blood and had no desire to spend time in jail for murder. Maybe he should have become a part-time preacher like his father. Nah, he liked having his weekends free.

Muttering under his breath, he decided to let fate make the choice. Closing his eyes, he stabbed the page randomly with his finger. Okay, this was the guy. Eddie stared at the name and screwed up his face, trying to picture who the man was, but nothing came to mind.

Shrugging philosophically, he picked up the phone to call Hugh, his recently acquired 'muscle'. The man had appeared at the office one day and before Eddie was even sure how it had happened, Hugh was working for him. Not that he minded. Hugh liked doing the leg work, checking up on clients, giving them a squeeze; Eddie preferred to hang around the office in the air conditioning.

Hugh hadn't had much to do yet beyond shaking someone by the scruff of the neck, a fact he often bemoaned. Apparently, Hugh appreciated opportunities to flex his muscles. Well, this would be his chance.

"Hugh? Eddie here. I've got a job for you."

The man on the other end of the line grunted and Eddie took that to mean Hugh was listening. Either that or he'd just woken up.

"Yeah, the big boss wants us to make an example of somebody. He thinks we're being too easy on the clients."

Hugh's grunt was more enthusiastic than last time. Hugh liked action.

"So I need you to track down this guy for me, and bring him in. We're going to give him an ultimatum and if he can't keep it then people will know that if you don't pay up, Dollar Niche means business."

He listened as Hugh gave his approval of the plan.

"What's that? Oh yeah, the poor sucker's name. It's...uh..." Eddie checked the name he'd randomly picked. "It's Anderson. Kellen Anderson."

Cassie got off the bus and hurried home, anxious to speak to Kellen. It was obvious to her now that he'd been purposely avoiding her, rather than just a serendipitous series of events keeping them apart. What kind of a mess was he in and how much did he owe? In the past, she'd relented and paid off his debts, all the while scolding him for borrowing money he couldn't repay. Afterwards he was always repentant, staying on the straight and narrow for a period of time but then falling into the same trap again. He'd meet new friends, start spending evenings 'out with the guys'.

She sighed heavily. Those nights out always led to trouble. Because of them, they'd moved to a smaller house where they had to pay less rent, given up having a car and now relied on public transportation. And despite the changes, money still was tight. Her patience was growing thin. Kellen needed to be responsible and he needed to control himself.

The Finding

The few people that knew about Kellen's gambling in the past had hinted that she'd be better off without him. Mr. Bartlett had said as much today when she asked to leave early. There'd been a pitying look in his eyes.

"When you bail him out, you're just enabling him." The older man had said. "You need to let him hit rock bottom. That's the only way to make him realize how big his problem is and that he needs to get professional help."

She'd thanked him for his concern, but didn't know if she could really turn her back on Kellen. Sure, she threatened to let him figure it out for himself, but he'd done so much for her in the past. Wasn't supporting him a way to pay back his kindness?

Rounding the corner, she saw that Kellen's bike was gone. She frowned. Had she missed him? Perhaps he'd parked it out back to tinker on it. The machine was old and always in need of some type of repair.

She let herself into the house and looked around but there was no sign of him. A glance in the kitchen revealed that he hadn't left a note on the message board either, not that she'd really expected one. He'd been disappearing on his own a lot lately, only speaking in general terms of being out with friends. Experience told her that meant gambling. And for the past few days... Well, she had no idea where he was. His bed was slept in and dirty dishes were in the sink, but other than that, there was no sign of him. So much for his great show of repentance the other night.

She wandered into the living room, hands in her back pockets. He had to come home sooner or later and she'd be waiting for him. In the meantime, she might as well keep herself busy. The living room was still relatively tidy, so perhaps she'd do the laundry.

As she gathered clothes from the bedrooms, she thought about the man she'd seen at the grocery store. Why did he bother her so much? It went beyond the fact that he might be a thug. His very presence had set her whole body on edge and had the creature inside her pacing restlessly, whining and eager to be set loose.

A frisson of fear swept over her at the thought of the beast escaping the tight reins she kept on it. Her body was already in a constant state of tension, always on guard after the slip-up in the back yard the other day. She was careful of her thoughts and tried to avoid letting her mind drift for fear the creature might surface and gain the upper hand. At night she forced herself to sleep lightly, in case deep slumber allowed the wolf to sneak past her defences. And now this man appeared, stirring the animal up, exciting it.

Yes, he's the one. He's the answer...

The words whispered in her mind and she was almost tempted to question the creature. What 'one'? The answer to what?

It was utter nonsense, of course. Why would she waste her time talking to an animal? Clamping her mouth tightly shut, she headed to the laundry room, her arms full of dirty clothing. Absentmindedly, she sorted the items by colour and checked pockets, frowning as she pulled loose change, matches, and a crumpled note from Kellen's jeans. Why couldn't he remember to empty his pockets before dumping his clothes in the laundry? He was supposedly the expert. She'd only learned how to do laundry a few years ago, yet here she was... Her train of thought screeched to a halt as she glanced at the note in her hand. She felt her eyes widen. He owed how much...?

She actually stumbled backward in shock. Fifty thousand dollars! What was he thinking to borrow that amount? She looked around the room and then at the note again, hoping she'd been wrong. No. It was still the same number of zeroes.

Her legs felt wobbly and she sat down on the small stool that was in the room. Oh God. This was way more than the usual amount. It wasn't a few thousand that he'd racked up playing small time poker with his friends.

She stared at the note for a few minutes, noting the name 'Dollar Niche' at the top before crumpling it in her hand and swearing under her breath. Kellen had promised her he'd never get deeply into debt again, like he'd been when they'd first met. By maxing out her credit cards and emptying all her accounts, she'd been able to pay off what he'd owed three years ago and still have a tidy nest egg left over, but this... This would take almost everything she had saved!

Anger surged inside her. That was her money in the bank; her safety net in case she ever needed to run. Why should she use it to bail Kellen out again? No. She wouldn't do it. Kellen had gone too far this time. Mr. Bartlett was right. If she kept rescuing him, he'd never learn; the cycle would never be broken.

Shaking with a combination of hurt, anger, and shock, she stumbled into the living room and sat down on the sofa, facing the door. She'd wait right here and confront him as soon as he stepped in the door.

Damn the man! How dare he mess up her life this way? Wasn't it enough that she had to deal with being a werewolf? Well, this certainly explained the man at the grocery store. If Kellen owed this much money, the loan shark would be wanting weekly payments and wouldn't be adverse to applying any kind of pressure needed to ensure Kellen coughed up the amount. No wonder the creature inside her was fighting to get out. The man at the store obviously represented danger!

A niggle of doubt worked its way into her resolve to let Kellen take the fall for his own actions. Could she stand by and let Kellen get hurt? She nibbled on her lip. Not really. But that didn't mean she'd pay off the loan shark for him. No, once she knew the facts and if there really were threats being made against Kellen or herself, she'd contact the authorities.

The beast inside her whimpered and she acknowledged that it had good cause. She'd been living her life under the radar for three years now. Her fake identity as Sandy Grant had served her well, but it hadn't come under close scrutiny either. And her use of drugs—not quite street drugs, but illegally purchased none the less—wasn't something she wanted brought to light.

An angry snarl erupted from her mouth, surprising her. Even though it was just days until the full moon, the creature had never done that before. Nervously, she clenched her fists on the arm of the chair exerting more inner control. It was getting stronger, fighting against the restrictions she placed on it. Would she have to take medication daily to keep it under control?

Another discontented growl rose within her. The animal hated the drugs. They were a chemically induced jail that kept it from roaming as it wished. But necessary, she argued with herself, thinking of the panic that had overwhelmed her just days ago. Las Vegas was highly populated and werewolves were dangerous. It—she—they—could kill someone. Hadn't she seen the power and destruction a creature such as herself was capable of with her own eyes?

She frowned as a new problem occurred to her. If Kellen wasn't here, how would she get her pills? There were only enough for another few months. Thoughts whirled in her mind as she contemplated all the implications of Kellen's gambling debt. Any course of action she took would have far reaching consequences. Leaning her head back against the cushions, she closed her eyes and massaged her temples with her finger tips as she tried to reason her way through the situation.

Bryan padded down the street, pausing to sniff at each bus stop. So far no one had given him a second glance, probably thinking he was someone's pet husky that had escaped from a backyard. He paused at a corner and sat down in the shade cast by a mailbox, panting from the excessive late afternoon heat. Las Vegas was no place for a wolf. His fur coat served him well in the cooler Canadian climate or even in the north western United States where he'd grown up, but this was ridiculous. Once he found Cassandra, he promised himself a large, cold drink.

At least it was cooler now than it had been in the middle of the afternoon. From all he'd heard, the temperatures would continue to drop as night approached. He squinted up at the sky, judging it to be around supper time. His stomach growled in concurrence and he thought longingly of the fast food restaurant that was directly across from his motel.

Realizing he wouldn't be eating in the near future unless he managed to track the girl down, he rose to his feet. Giving his body a shake, he continued on his way, sniffing the ground as he went. A bus drove past him and paused at the stop up ahead. He slowed his pace and watched the people disembark and hurry on their way. Then the vehicle roared to life again, spewing exhaust his way. His coughed and sneezed as the smelly fumes irritated his sensitive nose.

Snorting to clear his airways of the obnoxious odours, he approached the bus stop. Carefully, he sniffed the surrounding ground, then froze when a familiar scent tickled his nostrils. Exotic and spicy with floral undertones. That was it! He looked up sharply and gazed around. No one was watching him yet. He pulled his lips back in a wolfish grin. Gotta love the way everyone minds their own business around here, he thought to himself.

Nose to the ground, he set off at a brisk pace, eager to find the Greyson girl and make contact. She was a lone wolf but still young enough to be handled with ease; wolves who had been on their own for years were the ones who could prove dangerous. A wolf's psyche wasn't programmed to live a solitary lifestyle. After a while, they became unstable and then the options became more limited and less pleasant.

But Cassandra wasn't that far gone; he was sure of it. She might be experiencing some mental conflict but that would be the extent of it. And once he talked to her and she saw reason, he could head back to his motel. He'd grab some food and get cleaned up. The thought of a shower made him grin; the grit of the city had invaded his fur and he couldn't wait to be rid of it.

His nails clicked on the sidewalk, the heat from the sun-baked cement penetrating the pads of his paws. He didn't care; the joy of tracking filled him, pushing all other cares aside.

He sniffed the corner of a mailbox and could almost envision her brushing against it as she walked past. A little further down the road and he found a spot where she'd paused to cross the street, perhaps waiting for traffic. Her hand had been pressed against a lamp post, the sweat and oil from her palm was as distinctive as a neon sign to him.

He began to scan ahead, wondering if he'd catch sight of her even though he knew it was unlikely. His wolf wanted the thrill of sighting its prey followed by a chase. Not this time boy, he told the beast. Chasing her down won't endear us to her. Besides we're in a city, not the woods back home. We have to try to blend in.

The beast whined but conceded.

Padding around a corner, he paused then picked up speed. Close, so close. There! She'd gone up this sidewalk. He trotted up to the house sniffing carefully. Yes, this had to be her home; her scent permeated the surrounding area. His wolf rumbled happily, tail wagging at the knowledge that she was nearby. Circling around to the back of the building, he continued to sniff, analyzing the location. No pets, a motorcycle partially dismantled, fresh laundry, a male human. The hair on his neck rose as he considered this last bit of information.

Mrs. Mitchell, the elderly lady at the grocery store, had mentioned that a man by the name of Kellen lived here and this confirmed it. The knowledge didn't sit well with him or his wolf. Anger wafted from the beast within him and he struggled to stay in control and keep the animal in check. He had no claim on the girl and couldn't attack the man she lived with even if his presence was an unwanted complication.

Was the man inside at this moment? Bryan cocked his ears and listened. The house was silent so it was hard to know. He'd have to shift back into human form and knock on the door. Stepping into a shadowed area behind the house, he transformed into a man again. Straightening his shirt, he was thankful once again that he didn't need to worry about the inconvenience of carrying clothing with him, like some half-blooded Lycans did. Appearing naked at the girl's door would definitely not make a good first impression. And should her boyfriend answer... He shook his head at the thought of the fireworks that could cause.

Walking along the side of the house, he scrutinized in the windows. Curious. The first window revealed a very feminine bedroom with lace ruffled curtains while the next was a plain dark blue. He paused and tested the air outside this last window. Even more curious. Unless his nose was deceiving him—which he seriously doubted—they didn't share a bedroom; her scent was too weak. That tidbit of knowledge pleased him no end.

Rounding the corner, he went to the door, glancing in the front window, which was located to the right. Even with a set of blinds, it offered a perfect glimpse inside the living room. Through the partially closed slats, he noted the worn furniture, the older style TV and Cassandra. She was curled up on the sofa, sound asleep. Her hand cradled her cheek and her plump lips were softly parted. He stared at them for a moment and imagined how they'd feel against his own; soft and warm, moistly sliding. His tongue slipped out of its own volition and wet his lips. It was as if he could already taste her.

Curling his hands into fists, he forced his gaze to move on, noting her lashes were as dark as her hair and fanned out over her cheeks in a perfect arc. They scarcely hid the dark mauve shadows marring the skin below her eyes. She was exhausted. Protective instincts rose within him. Why wasn't she getting the sleep she needed? His wolf pushed against its restraints, wanting to immediately enter the house and curl up around her, offering protection and warmth as she rested.

We'll keep her safe. Once she knows she is ours, her rest will be peaceful.

He laughed softly. If only it were as simple as his wolf would like to believe. Something told him Cassandra wasn't going to welcome him with open arms. And the fact that she belonged to him...er...the pack, that is, would be a shock let alone the news about moving to Canada.

He stood quietly watching her for a few more minutes, appreciating her beauty. His wolf rumbled its approval as well. At the store she'd appeared to be of average height and build, though the cashier's apron she'd worn had hidden her body from view. Now, her tight yoga pants showed shapely thighs and delightfully curved hips.

Her top had ridden up and was twisted under her, baring part of her belly and pulling taut over luscious breasts. Cassandra Greyson was an enticing bundle and his palms tingled with a longing to stroke her. Somehow he knew her golden skin would be warm and supple to the touch. His lids grew heavy as he thought about how it would feel to have her naked body pressed against his, her softness complementing his hardness, her limbs entangled with his. The stirring of his body had him shifting uncomfortably. Damn, his wolf's lusty thoughts were invading his own. He cleared his throat and once again schooled his mind to the task before him.

He raised his hand intent on knocking, then hesitated just inches from the door. A glance upwards revealed the sky was starting to darken. She'd be surprised to find him at her door at this late hour. And he still had no idea how he'd break the Finding to her either. Besides, she was sleeping so soundly; it was a shame to wake her when nothing could happen until tomorrow. Perhaps he should return in the morning. She might be more receptive after a good night's sleep.

For a moment he weighed the pros and cons, before letting his hand fall to his side. He knew he was coming up with excuses and couldn't understand why his human half was reluctant to actually make contact with her. Was it because his wolf was so keen on her, he felt the need to act contrary and assert his dominance over the beast?

Or because you are denying the truth that I already know?

He frowned, displeased with the creature. His wolf was getting way too pushy of late. They might be as one in most things, but when it came right down to it, his human half was ultimately in charge. Lifting his chin, he stepped off the porch and away from the house, ignoring the animal's protests. Tomorrow morning would be soon enough to talk to Cassandra. He'd head back to his room, get cleaned up and...

But what about the other one?

Kellen? Her live-in?

The one in the store.

Damn! He'd almost forgotten the guy who'd been watching Cassandra. He paused mid-stride, looked around and lifting his head, tested the air. No one was around, but just in case, he altered his plan. He'd grab a bite then come back and spend the night under a nearby shrub. If anyone approached, he'd be there to defend her. And if nothing happened, well, first thing in the morning, he'd approach her as planned.

His wolf rumbled happily and he sourly realized the beast had gotten its own way. We need to have a long talk about who's in charge, he warned the animal.

Chapter 8

Hugh pulled the van into a parking space down the road from Anderson's home. Eddie wanted him to find the man and bring him in so this was the logical place to start. It also provided another opportunity to check out the girl. He'd watched her at work earlier in the day; a pretty little thing, probably with a Latino background. She seemed ordinary enough, working an early shift at a grocery store, taking a bus to and from work. From what he'd observed she was good at her job; quick, friendly with the customers. The only strange thing was how she'd suddenly looked spooked and left work early.

There'd been nothing unusual that he could see. Just a line of customers anxious to pay for their groceries. Still, something must have happened since she hadn't appeared ill. Hugh knew he wasn't the brightest man on the planet, but he was good at his job and when something was off, he noticed. Something was off about Anderson's woman; exactly what, remained to be discovered.

He glanced up and down the street. Typical suburbia, no one home during the day and when they did come home at night they all hid inside, watching TV or surfing the internet. It worked to his advantage; the fewer witnesses the better.

A hat on his head and a pair of sunglasses served as an easy disguise. Reaching into the glove compartment, he pulled out a picture of a dog. Claiming he was looking for a lost pooch would explain his presence should anyone ask.

Sliding out of the vehicle, he crossed the street while surreptitiously checking for observers again. He strolled down the street with purpose; peering into yards as if conducting a search.   When he reached Anderson's, he tried to act like something had caught his eye and walked up the driveway.

Hugh approached the front door. He'd knock and ask if he could search the backyard. It would give him a chance to see if Anderson was home. Intent on knocking, a casual glance in the front window revealed Anderson's woman dozing on the sofa. Searching the interior, he saw no sign of movement. The house seemed quiet. Instinct told him Anderson wasn't home. He sighed. Now he'd have to go searching out the man's other haunts.

He eased backwards off the step, keeping one eye on the woman inside. She didn't stir and he quietly breathed a sigh of relief. Good. No awkward explanations needed as to why he was looking in her front window. Should he circle around the house, go in the back way and 'persuade' her to reveal Anderson's whereabouts?

A glance over his shoulder showed someone coming down the street. It was an elderly woman walking a dog. Damn. He'd better not chance it. Besides, Eddie hadn't sanctioned any action against the girl...yet.

Maintaining his cover, he continued down the block, moving away from the dog-walking woman and then back up the other side as if searching for his own pet. When he reached his van, he got back in and removed his hat. Okay, no Anderson, so now what? He checked the brief file he'd compiled on the man to see where he should next look.

Since Hugh had started at Dollar Niche, he'd made a point of checking out quite a few of the clients who owed larger amounts. Eddie never bothered, but Hugh firmly believed in knowing who he was up against. In Anderson's case, his research revealed a simple gambler in over his head, nothing else.

Hugh drummed his fingers on the steering wheel for a moment, then gave a nod. Anderson had been referred to Dollar Niche by a fellow named Scott. Scott's address was on file; he'd go there next. He started the engine and then eased away from the curb. Anderson had a meeting to attend and Hugh intended to make sure that he kept the appointment.

The Finding

Kellen stood in the depressing hallway, his fists shoved into his coat pockets, and his shoulders hunched. It had to be at least two in the morning and the chill of the desert air had crept into the building making him shiver. He hadn't planned on being here, but Hugh—he shot a glance at the muscle bound man who stood a few feet away—had been insistent that he meet with 'the boss.' When Hugh insisted, Kellen suspected few declined. He rolled his shoulder, still able to feel the impression of Hugh's fingers there.

He'd been at a poker game, just as he had been every day for the past three days, trying to win enough to pay off the huge debt he'd accumulated, when Hugh appeared. How the man had found him, he didn't know, but Hugh claimed to be a representative of Dollar Niche and that Kellen Anderson's presence was requested immediately at the office.

So here he was, waiting to talk to Eddie Perini about the considerable debt he'd run up. Dollar Niche was basically a loan sharking business that asked no questions and charged exorbitant interest rates. He hadn't set out to borrow money from them, but when a winning streak suddenly cooled, he'd been desperate for funds so he could stay in the game. His new friend, Scott, had made a phone call to Dollar Niche and gotten him a small loan and that's when the trouble had started. The game had continued to sour. He'd borrowed more, hoping to recoup his losses, but the downward slide wouldn't stop.

Now his first week's payment was due and the people who ran the business must have discovered he didn't have enough to cover the amount. Well, it was his first instalment, he thought hopefully. They wouldn't be too rough on him and from what he'd heard, Dollar Niche was one of the easier establishments to deal with. He thanked his lucky stars over that one.

Kellen eased his weight onto his other leg. How long would he have to wait? It was getting late and he'd already missed his shift at work—again. That wouldn't go over well with Sandy or Mr. Bartlett. He hoped he could talk the man into giving him another chance. Sandy would kill him if he lost that job.

Trying to distract himself, he began reading the various flyers posted on the wall across from him. Free kittens, religious revivals, used furniture for sale; it was an eclectic mix. One in particular caught his attention. It was half hidden under another page that was advertising cleaning services, but something about the partially covered colour photograph niggled at him. He stepped away from the wall, intent on getting a closer look.

"Where are you going?" Hugh stood up straight and grumbled at him, thick arms crossed over his chest.

Kellen gave a lopsided grin and nodded his head towards the wall. "Just looking at the flyers posted over there. You never know when you might find something you need. My carpets need cleaning and this seems like a good deal."

Hugh grunted and returned to leaning against the wall in a half dozing state.

Doing his best to ignore the man, Kellen lifted the cleaning ad out of the way and then inhaled sharply. He was staring at a picture of Sandy! Blinking, he studied it carefully, thinking he must be mistaken, but he wasn't. It was her—a few years younger possibly—but definitely her.

Careful to not attract Hugh's attention, he scanned the page. Cassandra Greyson. Missing heiress. Apparently she'd disappeared three years ago and there was a hundred thousand dollar reward for information leading to her whereabouts. There was a number to contact, too.

He gulped. Sandy was an heiress? And whoever was looking for her was willing to pay one hundred grand for information concerning her. Wow! She must be worth a fortune if they were offering that kind of money. But if she was rich, why was she hiding in the Las Vegas suburbs and working in a grocery store?

Kellen recalled the first night she'd spent in his apartment. She'd awoken screaming and once he'd calmed her down, she'd slowly told him some of her story. How she'd seen her uncle killed and another man murdered. How one of the killers might still be looking for her. He'd suggested going to the police and she'd been adamant that she couldn't. Supposing she'd witnessed some illegal deal—maybe drugs or weapons—and just wanted to start a new life away from a seedy past, he hadn't pressed the issue.

Furrowing his brow, he realized that if she was indeed an heiress, it would explain why she hadn't known how to complete even the simplest of daily tasks. That part had always puzzled him. She hadn't been able to cook or clean, had no idea how to do laundry or use public transit. Now it all made sense. Sandy—Cassandra, he corrected himself—had likely been raised like a princess in an ivory tower. He chuckled to himself thinking of how the 'princess' had cleaned his toilet and washed his socks.

Raised voices broke into his thoughts and he turned towards the source, letting the cleaning ad fall down over Sandy's picture. The noise was coming from the office at the end of the hallway. The door swung open banging loudly against the wall and a middle-aged man stumbled out, his face ashen.

"And you better have the money next week if you know what's good for you. Dollar Niche is tired of carrying you along. Pay up or else." An angry voice blared out of the office and the man nodded as he backed away. Turning, he cast a nervous glance at Hugh then gave Kellen a sympathetic nod before hurrying around the corner out of sight.

Kellen inhaled deeply and straightened his shoulders. Okay. Yelling and verbal threats. He could handle that.

Hugh grunted. "Your turn."

"Thanks." Kellen nodded as he walked past, but Hugh didn't respond. Stepping into the office, he looked around briefly before settling his gaze on the man who was walking around the desk. The fellow was breathing deeply, as if trying to calm himself down, which Kellen supposed he was. Yelling that loudly would tend to work a body up.

Running his hands through his hair, the man eased down into his chair and negligently waved a hand at him.

"Mr. Anderson, I'm Eddie Perini. Please, take a seat."

Slowly, Kellen walked towards the chair indicated and sat down, not sure what to expect. The man before him didn't look like a mobster. He was average size, had dull brown hair, wore a rumpled shirt, and needed a shave. In fact it was hard to believe this mild mannered man was the person who'd been yelling a minute ago.

"Forgive the unpleasantness you overheard just now. Frank—the man who was here before you—needed a pep talk to keep him motivated." Eddie chuckled and looked pleased with himself.

Kellen nodded and eyed Eddie warily.

"I'm sure you're wondering why I've brought you here."

"The thought did cross my mind." Kellen shifted in his seat, not at all sure what the protocol for this situation might be and not trusting the calm facade the man was presenting.

Eddie Perini smiled. "I'm sure it did. You owe us quite a large sum, Mr. Anderson."

Kellen winced and licked his lips nervously before replying. "I know. The first payment is due tomorrow." There was no point in denying the truth. It might make the fellow angry and he'd prefer to remain on the man's good side. After all, Eddie did control the blond gorilla in the hallway known as Hugh.

"And will you be able to make the required payment?"

"Well..." Kellen hesitated.

The man raised his brows. "As I suspected." He steepled his fingers and peered at Kellen for a moment before speaking. "Mr. Anderson, I'm not a violent man. I'm a business man. I lend money for a fee and then await payment. When payment is made on time, I'm happy and my boss is happy. When payments are late, it causes distress. I don't like being distressed."

Not sure what to say, Kellen gave a nod. Eddie continued.

"Normally, I believe in giving my clients the benefit of the doubt. Most people are honest and try to pay me back as soon as possible, but not everyone has the same philosophy as me. My boss for example. He is *displeased* with the rate of return we are getting on our investments. As you just heard with Frank, I've upped my usual level of incentives. However, Leon—my boss—doesn't feel that is sufficient. He wants me to make an example of someone."

"An example?" Kellen didn't like the turn the conversation was taking. He'd watched enough movies to know that 'examples' could have their legs broken, fingers removed, or even be killed. A cold sweat broke out on his body. Bravery was never one of the qualities he'd claimed to have. Whenever possible, he avoided unpleasantness. This couldn't be happening to him!

"Correct. It upsets me to tell you this, but you've been chosen as the example."

"Me?" Kellen gripped the arms of the chair, his stomach feeling as if it had dropped to the floor.

"Yes, unfortunately yours is the name that was picked."

"But...but...the first payment isn't even due until tomorrow!" Kellen leaned forward, pleading his case. Even as he spoke, there was a buzzing sound in his ears and the room seemed to grow darker. There wasn't enough air.

"Technically, it's already tomorrow, but let's not split hairs. I have a proposal for you. If you can make your payment on time, I'd have no reason to use you as my example. Instead, I could report to my boss that the mere threat was enough to bring you to heel."

"All right. I can do that." Kellen swallowed hard and nodded, not sure how he'd make the payment, but willing to promise anything. The darkness that had been encroaching on his vision started to fade and the tightness in his chest eased.

"I was hoping you'd say that. As you might have guessed, I'm a civilized man. Carrying out my boss's instructions with respect to this matter has little appeal to me, but I will if necessary. Might I ask how you plan to get the needed funds?"

"Um..." He wracked his brain. "A friend of mine. She has a lot of money."

"And this friend is willing to lend you money now, but she wouldn't earlier on?"

Kellen nodded, vaguely thinking that his head must be going up and down like one of those bobble-headed ornaments on the dash board of a car. "I didn't want to bother her."

He prayed Sandy would come through for him one last time even though she'd said she wouldn't bail him out again. She'd threatened that before, but always caved in if he begged hard enough. Hopefully she had sufficient savings in her bank account.

Wait. She was an heiress. Of course she'd have enough money!

A wave of relief washed over him. Why was he worrying? He relaxed his tense muscles, a smile forming on his lips. Standing up, he cocked his head to the side and raised a brow, feeling more confident than he had a moment ago. "Can I go now?"

"Of course." Eddie eyed him with a curious expression. "And Mr. Anderson? I'll be sending Hugh to your house around noon."

Kellen started to nod, but then stopped himself. Reaching back, he grasped the door knob. "Sure. That won't be a problem."

"Good. Could you ask Hugh to come in as you leave?"

Kellen gave Eddie Perini a quick salute and exited the room. As he walked down the hallway, he paused near the poster that claimed Sandy was an heiress. Checking over his shoulder to ensure that Hugh was in the office, he ripped the paper from the wall and shoved it in his pocket. He suppressed the desire to whistle as he ambled down the narrow stairway. Lady luck was on his side again!

Hugh leaned against the doorway and observed his 'boss'. The man was grinning like a Cheshire cat.

"That was a good performance, wasn't it, Hugh?" Eddie leaned back in his chair and propped his feet on the desk. "Anderson really believed I was some big crime lord. The way I yelled at poor Frank and then was so overly polite with him. And I loved the way I said 'late payments cause distress' in that cool, detached way. Anderson will be running home and finding some cash, I'm sure of it."

The Finding

Grunting, Hugh sat down not nearly as gleeful as Eddie. He'd overheard the whole conversation and Anderson had seemed too certain he could find the needed money in time. Something was off and further investigating was definitely in order. "Perhaps. But what if he doesn't?"

Eddie dropped his feet to the floor, his expression sobering. "For his sake I hope he manages. Aldrich really wants results; greedy, old bastard."

Ignoring the latter comment, Hugh gave an update on Anderson, unsolicited though it was. "I've checked out Anderson. He lives with a girl and they both work at a grocery store; both low income jobs. They rent a small house, but Anderson does own a motorcycle. It's old, but some might call it a classic, though you'd need to find the right buyer." He shrugged. "If you want money from him, the best bet is to go after the girl. She leaves for work pretty early in the morning; usually no one's around. I can grab her easily. Anderson will find a way to cough up some money for her sake."

Eddie rubbed his chin. "No. Hold off on that. He said his friend has some money. Let's give the guy a chance. If Anderson doesn't come through with a substantial payment tomorrow, we can still try Aldrich's way. No harm done in waiting. Aldrich isn't here. He has no idea what's really going on."

Hugh stared at Eddie thoughtfully. "Sure. You're the boss." He managed to keep his voice neutral.

Eddie burped loudly and grimaced. "This sort of stuff is bad for my digestion. I'm heading home. Can you lock up?" Hugh nodded and Eddie grabbed his jacket, swinging it over his shoulder as if he hadn't a care in the world. He didn't even bother to lock the filing cabinets.

Such negligence could prove deadly in this business, Hugh thought as he stared around the tired room. The decor reflected Eddie's careless attitude. Worn furniture, papers strewn all over, file drawers left partially open. Giving a derisive smile, he went to the small window and eased the blind aside so he could see the dimly lit alley below. After a few minutes a door opened and a

131

shadowy figure stepped out. A security light briefly illuminated the individual and revealed that Eddie was heading for his car.

Satisfied that he was alone, Hugh let the blind fall back into place and wandered over to the filing cabinet. He pulled a drawer open and began rifling through, pausing every now and then to read a bit here and there.

Nate Graham had hired him to get inside Dollar Niche and find out how the business operated. Hugh wasn't too sure why Graham wanted the information, but he was getting paid and that was what mattered. Well, that and the fact that he might get to beat somebody up. That was an added bonus.

Hugh knew some might question his ethics; working for two different employers, being paid to spy on one of them. He shrugged. Such minor details didn't bother him. It was a cut throat world and he was available to the highest bidder, plain and simple. Sure he was clever enough to 'make something of himself' as his granny used to say, but using his brain had never appealed that much. It was the darker side of life that drew him.

He copied a few pages to give to Nate and shoved them in his pocket. He'd drop them off then cruise by Anderson's place again. There was something strange about that setup and he wanted to know what it was.

Bryan shivered and bit back a sneeze. It had been drizzling for almost an hour now. Vegas wasn't known for its rainfall, but given his luck, he wasn't surprised that it was happening tonight when he was sleeping outside. Between the dampness and the cool night temperatures, he was miserable.

The local vegetation provided minimal shelter. Cassandra's yard was a typical desert garden with cacti and... He frowned up at the plant he was huddled near wondering what it was called. An agave? Or maybe a yucca? Whatever it was, he'd give almost anything for a good old broad leaf maple that would keep the water from dripping on his head.

Feeling sorry for himself, he rested his chin on his paws and kept one eye on the house, the other on the road. It had been a quiet night; only a few vehicles passing by. No one had approached the house, not even this Kellen character she lived with.

His wolf snorted. *What type of male leaves his female alone all night? It's obvious he doesn't care. Once she is ours, such a situation will never occur.*

She isn't ours, buddy. He felt it necessary to remind the animal within of that important point. Sure, Cassandra is a lovely little bundle, but that doesn't mean anything. There are lots of women in Las Vegas. Remember the one at the car rental? He paused expectantly, but his wolf wasn't impressed and retreated to mope.

Grimacing, he conceded the animal had a point. Cassandra was much more alluring than the redhead. An image of her pressed flush to his body popped into his head and he was sure he could smell her heady scent, feel her warmth, taste her. His body stirred in response to his mental imagery and he had the distinct impression that his wolf was smirking.

Sighing at the contrary creature, he lifted an eyebrow and watched with casual interest as a white van came down the street. It slowed as it approached and he raised his head to watch more closely. This van, or a similar one, had been by before. He squinted trying to see the driver, but could only make out a silhouetted figure. Sitting up completely, he tested the air for a scent. It was vaguely familiar. Hadn't he detected it around the house when he returned after eating? He'd assumed a friend or neighbour had stopped by, but this wasn't the usual time for social calls.

When the van came to a complete stop, he got to his feet, ready for action if need be. He sensed the driver was hesitating, wondering if he should stay in the vehicle or get out and take a closer look at the house.

Just as the van's door began to creak open, a figure appeared strolling down the sidewalk. Someone was out walking their dog in the rain! He scowled, but stepped back and shifted into his human self. While his wolf form was better for sneaking up on the individual in the van, it would attract the dog's attention more. He pressed himself back into the shadows and watched.

Whoever was in the van noticed the dog-walker as well, for the door slammed shut and the van started. It pulled away sedately, and he narrowed his eyes. Whoever was driving knew how not to attract attention.

Stepping out of his hiding place, he quickly walked to the road, trying to catch a glimpse of the license plate, but the van was already turning the corner. Wasn't it the same van he'd seen in the grocery store parking lot the previous day? If so, he already had the plates committed to memory. Now he just needed time to send them to Daniel to be traced. He cursed himself for not taking care of that little job earlier.

Questions bounced about in his brain. Why was this guy watching Cassandra Greyson? He'd been observing her at work and then snooping around the house earlier this evening. Was the man a stalker or a rejected boyfriend? Or was there some other reason for his interest? A frustrated growl sounded low in his throat. No one had the right to be watching Cassandra except himself! He turned abruptly, intending to return to his hiding place and resume his guard duties.

"Hello!" A voice—elderly and female—called out and he swivelled his head towards it. Mrs. Mitchell, the elderly lady from the grocery store was approaching, with an overweight dachshund trotting beside her.

"Mrs. Mitchell, nice to see you again." He nodded and tried to look casual, as if he belonged in the neighbourhood.

She beamed up at him. "You like walks in the rain, too, I see."

He opened his mouth to answer, but she continued on without waiting for a reply.

"We don't get much rain so when we have the chance, Netty and I head out, no matter what time it might be."

He glanced at the fat dog he assumed was Netty. It didn't appear to be enjoying the rain at all. Instead it was staring woefully at him, its eyes begging for an appeal from the damp, early morning outing.

The Finding

"I know how you feel." He muttered under his breath as he wiped a raindrop from his eye, then pulled at the damp shirt that stuck to his chest.

Mrs. Mitchell didn't seem to notice. "You must have just moved here. I know all the neighbours. You're in the Thompson's old house, I bet!" She patted his arm and nodded towards Cassandra's house. "That's where Sandy lives. You remember her, the girl from the grocery store? You're almost next door neighbours now. If I were you, I'd take lots of walks down this street. You might bump into her and I think you might be exactly what she needs."

The older woman glanced towards the horizon. "The sun will be rising soon. It's going to be a beautiful day, you know. The desert always blooms after a rain. Well, we'd better be on our way. Come along, Netty. I'm sure I'll see you around, Mr... Er... What was your name again?"

"Bryan."

"Mr. Bryan. Of course. I'll have to try to remember that." She smiled at him then jiggled Netty's leash and headed on her way.

He shook his head as he watched her disappear around the corner. Strange woman. Cocking his head to the side, he considered their exchange. She hadn't told any lies, he was sure of it—humans gave off a number of signals when they were being deceptive—but she hadn't been completely honest either. Pursing his lips, he considered the situation, then decided to forget about it. Mrs. Mitchell was an interesting old lady, but in the grand scheme of things, had little impact on him and his dealings with Cassandra.

Using his sleeve to wipe the rain from his face, he glanced down and frowned at the damp material that clung to his body. Going back to the motel and changing sounded eminently appealing, but even as the idea came to him, a light flicked on inside the house. Cassandra was awake. Hmm... He couldn't stand around on the sidewalk, staring at the house. One of the neighbours might notice. Perhaps, he'd wait beside her house.

When she came out, he'd walk up to her casually and introduce himself.

Cassie awoke to a feeling of discomfort in her neck and back. Gingerly, she stretched and tried to roll over, moaning as pain shot through her body. She grimaced, and opened her eyes, slowly coming to realize that she was in the living room. No wonder she was stiff, she'd spent the night sleeping on the couch.

She yawned and stood up, more aches and pains making themselves known. Squinting at her watch, she saw that it was still early, barely five-thirty. A glimmer of brightness was beginning to appear in the sky outside her window. Stumbling into the kitchen, she prepared the coffee maker, then made her way to the bathroom, functioning on autopilot.

It wasn't until she'd stood under the hot shower spray for a few minutes that her brain registered the fact that she'd been waiting up for Kellen. Had he come home last night? Scrunching up her brow, she tried to recall if she'd heard him or not, but her mind was a blank. She'd slept soundly last night, which was strange given her uncomfortable location. For some reason a feeling of security had wrapped itself around her, as if all was right with the world and a guardian angel was watching over her. A foolish idea. No doubt, sheer exhaustion had been the cause. Thankfully, it appeared the animal inside her had slept too.

Quickly, she finished her morning ablutions, wrapped herself in her bathrobe, and hurried down the hall in search of Kellen. They really needed to talk. She stood outside his bedroom, listening intently for a moment, but heard nothing. Giving the door a soft knock, she called his name and turned the handle. A peek inside showed her that his bed hadn't been slept in and his work uniform was still lying on the chair beside his bed.

Exhaling loudly, she ran her hands through her damp hair in exasperation. He hadn't gone to work and he hadn't come home. That could mean only one thing; he'd spent his night gambling again. Damn him! Wasn't he deeply enough in debt? He owed fifty thousand dollars! Was he trying to make it up to a hundred? She felt tears welling in her eyes.

Slamming the door, she stomped into her own room and began to get dressed, pulling on her clothing while muttering dire threats under her breath. He'd definitely lost his job if he missed work again last night. Mr. Bartlett had already been more than understanding when it came to Kellen.

She yanked a comb through her hair and pulled it back in a ponytail. This was just great. She'd be their sole breadwinner again. With only half the income, how the hell were they supposed to pay rent and buy groceries, let alone try to pay off the money he owed?

Shoving her feet into her shoes, she headed to the kitchen, the smell of fresh coffee doing little to sooth her spirit. Leaning her hip against the counter, she sipped the bitter brew and scowled, contemplating all the things she'd say to Kellen once she finally tracked him down.

It was early to leave for work, but she decided to go anyway. Staying at home would only make her angrier. Maybe she'd even walk to the store, it might help burn off some of the anger inside her.

Turning off the coffee maker, she grabbed her purse and headed out the front door, only to freeze on the front step. Something was different. Narrowing her eyes, she looked around. It had rained last night; an unusual event to be sure, but that wasn't what had caught her attention. A strange scent was assaulting her nose. The animal inside her was instantly alert and pressing against its boundaries. She could sense the change within her. Normal sounds were louder, her skin seemed sensitive to the air around her. Even though the light of dawn was barely breaking, her eyesight was more acute than ever, catching the minute movements of insects. Slowly, she turned her head, searching the shadows for anomalies.

Something was here, something vaguely recognizable that called to the animal within her. Slowly, she bent and set down her purse, keeping a watchful eye on her surroundings. Instinct was telling her to be cautious. There was danger nearby, but...

She sniffed the air; it was alluring too. Her heart was beating faster, her skin tingled and warmth was pooling in her belly, stirring a memory.

She'd had the dream last night. The wolf had chased her, caught her, and forced her to the ground. It had been more realistic than ever; the feel of his hot breath, the weight and power of his body pressed to hers, his scent surrounding her.

Her eyes widened when she realized it was the same scent. The one from her dream was here, floating on the air around her house. Frightened, yet inexplicably drawn to it, she stepped off the porch and began to walk down the path that led to the driveway.

The scent was getting stronger. Her breathing quickened as excitement raced through her. The beast inside strained to reach the source. Pulled by some instinct she didn't understand, her feet unerringly led her to the edge of the house. She turned the corner and...

A screamed ripped from her throat!

The shadowy figure of a man stood at the edge of the building. Before she could even think, he grabbed her, spinning her around and clamping a hand over her mouth, effectively stifling her cry. Instinctively, she struggled, but he easily stilled her movements wrapping his arm around her waist and pressing her back tightly to his chest.

"Shh! You'll wake the neighbours," he scolded into her ear. His hot breath tickled against her skin, sending shivers down her spine and she froze, surprised by her own reaction. He used her momentary stillness to his advantage, turning her face so that she was looking over her shoulder and staring up into his eyes. Hazel eyes. A thrill shot through her as their gazes locked and she found herself unable to look away. They were so close, she could feel his breath against her face, fill her lungs with his scent. There was a compelling power about him that held her transfixed, unable to think or move.

His mouth quirked in a smile and amusement danced in his eyes. "That's better. Now, if I let you go, will you behave?"

The Finding

She found herself nodding and wondered why. This man had no control over her yet her free will seemed to be disappearing. Some part of herself that she wasn't even aware of was taking over, willingly bowing down before him.

He released her and stepped back, holding out his hand. "Hi! I'm Bryan."

She stared down at his hand, feeling dazed. The man had appeared out of nowhere, lurking around her house at an hour when most people were getting out of bed. The shock of him *being there,* when she hadn't really expected to see anyone, had made her scream and now he was holding out his hand making polite introductions? And she was just standing here? Okay, something was wrong with this picture.

He's not a threat to us, the voice inside assured her.

Why she believed the voice, she didn't know. It wasn't like she and the creature were on speaking terms. It crossed her mind that she should be running and calling for help. Men with honourable intentions didn't lurk outside your home in the early morning hours. Her brain acknowledged the facts, but seemed to stand back and blithely watch as she responded to the man's greeting.

"Um... Hi." She brushed a few strands of stray hair from her face and then slowly took his hand. Heat rushed up her arm at the contact and she broke free quickly, flexing her fingers and frowning at the unusual reaction.

"You're Sandy, right?"

She looked up at him warily, wondering how he knew her name. Then the sun's rays broke over the roof tops and his face was suddenly illuminated clearly. A gasp escaped her lips as she realized she had seen him before. He was the man from the store!

Fear rushed through her, breaking through the strange calm that had washed over her. Her mind raced as she stared at him with increasing trepidation. Oh, this was not good. It couldn't be a coincidence that he'd ended up outside her house after watching her so intently in the grocery store. And how had he found out where she lived anyway? Her human logic told her he was probably some kind of stalker. The animal inside whined in protest at the idea, but she managed to ignore it.

"Nice to meet you, but I have to go now." She started to back up and the man—he'd called himself Bryan—frowned at her, possibly realizing she'd recognized him.

He took a step closer to her. "There's no need to be afraid."

Right. Those were the words every psycho used just before attacking. Giving no warning, she pivoted and ran back towards the front door.

"Hey!" He shouted and followed her.

She could hear his steps close behind her, sensed him reaching, trying to catch her. Panic began to rise inside of her and she urged her legs to move even faster. His fingers fumbled, then clamped around her upper arm. Her body spun around as her forward momentum reacted to the sudden tug on her arm. A feral sound, half scream, half growl, ripped from her throat. His hands grabbed at her. She started to struggle, her vision blurred. Her whole body vibrated with a strange energy as survival instincts kicked in.

"Oh no you don't." Bryan's voice growled in her ear, but she had difficulty focusing. Everything felt so strange, as if her body wasn't quite her own. "Changing into a wolf won't help you escape me. Not that I wouldn't enjoy a good hunt—I could easily outrun you and take you down—but that might not go over so well here in the suburbs. So let's make things simple. I'm your Beta and I'm *ordering* you to not change."

As if someone had pulled a plug, the strange feeling began to subside, but she paid little attention to the fact. His words rang ominously in her head.

"Beta? Wolf? What are you talking about?" She stared at him, frozen in horror. He knew! Somehow he knew! How had she been discovered? Her heart was pounding so hard she was sure he must be able to hear it. This was her worst nightmare. He couldn't know. No one knew. Not even Kellen was privy to her secret; she'd taken great pains to ensure that fact. Besides, she'd never actually transformed completely so no one could have seen her; she stayed locked in her room, drugged almost out of her mind during the dangerous phases of the moon.

It couldn't be true. The only way he could know she was a werewolf was if he were connected to the incident in Chicago. She shook her head in denial. No! It couldn't be happening. Not now after all these years. Suddenly the frozen state she was in disappeared and she began to kick and squirm. She had to get away. Her very survival depended on it.

His fingers bit into her arms even more tightly as she struggled and she winced at the controlled strength she felt emanating from him. She looked around frantically. Where were the neighbours? Why wasn't someone outside and coming to her rescue? Perhaps, it was all a bad dream. Surely, she'd wake up any minute and find out it was a strange new twist on the dream she frequently had.

"Cassandra, behave!" He growled the words at her as he thwarted all her attempts to free herself. "You know exactly what I'm talking about. I'm the Beta of our Lycan pack and you're coming with me."

"Lycan pack? What the hell is that?" She struggled harder.

"Lycan is the proper term for a werewolf. Now stop this nonsense. You're coming with me."

"With you?" Her voice rose as terror gripped her. He was one of them! Oh God, no! She couldn't go with him. Werewolves were monsters. They murdered people. She'd seen it with her own eyes. She wasn't like that! She'd never be one of them. Never!

"No!" A rush of energy such as she'd never felt before burst from her and she ripped herself from his arms, stumbling backwards. As if in slow motion she felt herself falling, the impact of the cement rippling up her spine as her rear end struck the ground. Then the rest of her body tipped back and she caught a glimpse of Bryan's shocked face, followed by a view of the sky as she continued to be propelled backwards. Finally, pain exploded in her head as her skull struck the edge of the step and then...darkness.

Chapter 9

Kellen sat nursing a cup of coffee in his favourite restaurant. It wasn't an expensive place, more of a diner than an actual restaurant, but the food was good, and the prices weren't inflated.

A smile played over his lips. Expense might not be a problem in the near future. Reaching into his pocket, he pulled out a piece of paper and stared at it; one hundred thousand dollars for information leading to the whereabouts of Cassandra Greyson. It was a staggering sum of money, and who knows... He might even get more since he not only had information, he had the actual girl!

This was a turn of fortune that he'd never foreseen. As a matter of habit, he never looked at the bits of paper posted on bulletin boards. Sandy's picture might have been posted for ages and he would never have seen it. Apparently Lady Luck was back on his side. Why else would she have put him in a hallway directly across from Sandy's picture? To think he'd been shaking in his boots, when the answer to all his problems was already with him. He laughed softly and leaned back in his seat to stare out the window, dreaming of the future.

What would he do with the left over money, once he'd paid off Dollar Niche? Move to a bigger house? Take a vacation? Fix his motorcycle? Sandy would tell him to save it for a rainy day; she was always so practical, scrimping and saving. Sandy. Hmm...

Raising his cup to his mouth, he fixed his gaze on an alley a short distance away. That's where he'd met her. And the table he was at was the one they'd shared during their first meal together. An image of her frightened face flashed in his mind. She'd been wary of him, but eventually had learned she could trust him, that he wasn't going to attack her or murder her in her sleep.

Not that he hadn't been tempted—well, not to attack or murder—but to make some form of advances towards her. He'd immediately noticed her physical appearance though she'd seemed unaware of it; the fact that she hadn't been flirty or obvious had been rather sexy to his way of thinking. Then, as he'd gotten to know her, he'd discovered she had a mischievous streak and a quirky sense of humour; that she was eager to learn about the world and willing to tackle any task be it learning to cook or mastering public transit. She'd been an intriguing mix of child and unawakened woman.

Often he'd find himself staring at her, looking for some hint that she was aware of him as a man; that she returned his interest, but it never happened. Well, there'd been that one inexplicable yet amazing time when she'd crawled into his bed, but beyond that...nothing.

Instead, he'd had to content himself with her friendship and the vague hope that maybe someday she'd change her mind. It was foolish, of course. Obviously, the spark wasn't there for her and now, perhaps he knew why.

Given the size of the reward, it was obvious she came from a wealthy background and probably was used to rubbing elbows with the rich and famous. Why would she be interested in him? Kellen Anderson was a nobody; kicked out of home and forsaken by his family because of his gambling. He hadn't talked to his parents in years, not since they'd had to re-mortgage their house to get him out of debt. And all the friends he'd grown up with... Well, he owed them tons of money too, and they'd likely string him up if their paths ever crossed.

A wry chuckle escaped his lips. Here he was, right back where he started; in debt up to his ears with threats being made against his personal safety. At least this time, he'd be able to get out of the mess on his own. The ticket was right here in his hand or, more exactly, in his house.

He stroked a finger over Sandy's image. She was laughing in the photo and he smiled in response. It would be good for her to be back where she belonged; life here wasn't caviar and silver spoons. He shook his head. How had she ever put up with their pokey house and the monotony of working at a grocery store when she could be living in the lap of luxury? If he were in her shoes, nothing could have convinced him to leave all that wealth behind.

Why *had* she left? Her story about her uncle being murdered didn't quite ring true now. He'd always assumed there was some illegal activity involved, but if she were wealthy, why hadn't she simply called the authorities? And why had she stayed away all these years? She must have known there was money awaiting her, even after she'd emptied her bank accounts. Who in their right mind would turn their back on all that? He tightened his lips; there was something about this whole situation that bothered him.

His watch beeped and he checked the time. The crystal was cracked—Hugh's fault probably—but he could still make out the time. He added getting a new watch to his list of things to buy with the extra reward money while swearing under his breath at the passage of time. Damn! He'd been sitting here longer than he'd planned. Hugh would be at the house in a few hours, looking for the money. He stared at the paper in his hand one more time and then folded it carefully before tucking it back into his pocket with a sigh. After tossing a tip on the table, he walked out, frowning, deep in thought.

Bryan balanced a tray of coffee and a bag of donuts in one hand as he pulled open the door to the motel and quickly crossed the lobby, hoping Cassandra hadn't come around during his brief absence. She hadn't stirred once when he'd scooped her up off her sidewalk and driven her to his motel. Nor had she shown any sign of gaining consciousness when he'd dried off and changed out of his damp clothes, so he'd figured there was enough time to head across the street for food.

The bump on her head hadn't appeared serious and given the fact that she was a Lycan, he knew she'd quickly heal. Most likely it was shock more than the injury that was causing her unconscious state.

He chuckled softly. When she'd knocked herself out, he'd had flashbacks to his first meeting with Mel back in Stump River. Mel had been running from him and had smacked right into a tree, knocking herself out. He'd ended up carrying her back to the house, thinking he'd found a pretty bit of fluff to play with for a while. Of course, Ryne had taken one look at the woman and subconsciously claimed her, giving 'back off' signals that were hard to miss.

This time, he was the only male around so that wouldn't be a problem. Not that he had anything but a professional interest in Cassandra. He was here to do a job and that was as far as his involvement should go. It didn't matter that she'd been soft and warm in his arms, or that her scent had wrapped itself around him causing his blood to thunder in his ears. No, it was just the adrenaline rush of finally finding her.

He frowned and shushed his wolf's protests before it could even speak. Her plump red lips and smooth golden skin had only a minimal effect on him. And the fact that he could see her cleavage and feel the swell of her breasts brushing against him as he carried her from his car was irrelevant. He stepped into the elevator and surreptitiously adjusted the crotch of his pants; okay, so she did have *some* effect on him.

He clamped his mouth shut and applied cool logic to the situation. Cassandra *was* attractive and it was only natural that he responded to her, especially considering how his wolf was acting lately. It even explained his appalling lack of judgement with regards to how he'd introduced himself. Duh! He gave himself a mental forehead slap. 'Hi! I'm Bryan.' Yeah, that hadn't been the cleverest introduction.

She could be bordering on going rogue and he should have been more careful until he'd fully assessed her stability. It was little wonder she'd freaked out. To her way of thinking, he'd been lurking in her backyard, like some crazy stalker and her wolf might even consider him an invader of her territory. He should have had some excuse prepared or better yet, have avoided the yard altogether. Casually walking down the street and bumping into her would have provided a perfect opportunity to strike up a conversation in a non-threatening manner. He was glad Ryne wasn't around; he'd never hear the end of it after his boasting that he knew how to handle women.

He considered another point of view; she might still have reacted badly to him, no matter how he introduced himself. She'd become even more agitated when he mentioned wolves and the pack; the idea of another Lycan seemed to scare her to death for some reason. He knew she'd been raised by humans, but Greyson had been seeking out a Lycan pack for her to join, so why had she been on the verge of hysterics?

The elevator gave a pinging noise announcing he'd arrived at his floor. He took a deep breath wondering what he'd find when he got to his room. There was some major damage control to do and it was all his fault. Hopefully, she'd just be waking up and they could start off on a fresh note. He had coffee and donuts as a peace offering. And maybe he'd even try a bit of humour. That usually helped break the ice.

The pillow beneath her head was softly scented with the most delicious smell. Cassie buried her face into it and inhaled deeply, a smile forming on her face as a sense of warmth and security filled her. Reaching out, she searched for the covers, anxious to pull them up around her shoulders and drift back to sleep.

Her grasping fingers didn't find a blanket and she muttered in annoyance, wondering if it had been kicked onto the floor. Usually, she wasn't a restless sleeper except during a full moon. Frowning, she tried to recall what day it was.

Could it be the full moon already? Her brain responded sluggishly as images and memories drifted past. For some reason her thoughts were hazy and focusing was difficult. She was often confused or disoriented during a full moon, so possibly that was the case. Rolling over, she groaned, the back of her head throbbing lightly as it pressed into the pillow.

"Must have been thrashing around and hit it on something." She mumbled to herself as she manoeuvred her head to the side. Ah! That was better. Still half asleep, she brought her hand up to touch the tender area. Her fingers encountered a small lump, but there was no stickiness to indicate blood. That was a good thing. During a full-moon, it wasn't uncommon for her to awaken bruised and battered, having only the vaguest recollections of what happened while she was locked in her room. On a few occasions, she'd even managed to escape the house, waking up in some of the strangest places.

The first time it happened, she'd ended up in the alley where Kellen had found her. On another occasion it had been a neighbourhood park and once she'd even found herself in the employees' room at the grocery store. Luckily, she'd always been able to make her own way home or find a means of contacting Kellen.

A smile drifted over her face as she thought of Kellen. He always came to get her; scooping her up, lecturing her about her drug habit. Recalling all the lies she'd told him over the years had the smile fading. She wished she could share the truth with him, but it was too dangerous. No one could ever know what she really was.

It was amazing that no one had ever discovered her wandering the streets in a semi-conscious state; at least to the best of her knowledge, no one had. She always scoured the news after the fact, praying that there would be no reports of strange inexplicable attacks by wild dogs. There never were, but she always worried. The animal inside her wasn't to be trusted.

She shifted back onto her side, keeping her eyes closed as she hovered on the edge of sleep. It was puzzling how she ended up in those places. They were usually locations she was thinking about just before the pills took effect, but she never had any recollection of how she got there. And when she returned home, the door to her room was still locked, so how had she managed to escape?

Over the past three years, she'd done her share of research on werewolves, trying to understand this mysterious other half of

The Finding

herself. There were so many sites and so much information, but no real way to authenticate what she read. Most of it was the stuff Hollywood movies were made of; images of grotesque and painful transformations, creatures howling at the moon. At least she hoped it was all fanciful cinematography. Still, her own experience allowed her to glean a few nuggets of truth such as the monthly effect of the moon.

One site had mentioned supposedly 'royal' or 'blue-blooded wolves' being able to teleport, or move from place to place, simply by thinking of a location; apparently it was a skill that was hard to master. She wasn't sure if that was what she did or not, though it was a possible explanation.

The main flaw in the theory was the whole idea of being werewolf 'royalty'. It was farcical to her to suppose that savage beasts could ever organize themselves into an aristocracy! Yet again, she shook her head in disbelief of the very idea, wincing as the movement reminded her that her head hurt. She sighed, supposing she should get up and put some ice on the lump.

Slowly stretching, she reluctantly opened her eyes and then froze, her arms still extended at her sides. A gasp escaped her lips as she took in the unfamiliar curtains and furniture. This wasn't her bedroom! She bolted upright and everything seemed to spin wildly for a moment before slowly righting itself. Her heart pounding, she looked around finding herself in a totally unfamiliar room.

The decor led her to believe she was in a motel, but where? She half fell off the bed and rushed to the window to peer outside. A parking lot and the back of a building met her inquiring gaze. There was no visible sign to indicate the name of the place, but at least it appeared she was still in Las Vegas; the palm trees and cacti that bordered the parking lot were reassuringly familiar.

Letting the curtain fall back into place, she scanned the room, her gaze lighting upon a pile of clothing on the floor and an open suitcase sitting on a chair in the corner. She approached it hesitantly, fearful of what she'd find. The clothing was damp to the touch and a towel was folded across the arm of the chair.

Nervously, she began to search the contents of the suitcase. Men's shirts, pants, underwear. She quickly dropped them, wiping her hands on her pants. Dear heaven, they weren't even Kellen's; he wore boxers not briefs!

A horrid thought suddenly popped into her head, and she looked down, running her hands over her body, relieved to find she was fully dressed except for her shoes. For a moment, she'd feared she'd gone into an early heat and ended up with some strange man! Relieved that at least she hadn't done something totally inappropriate, she rubbed her forehead trying to recall who owned the suitcase and how she'd come to be here.

Before any answers came to mind, a sound behind her alerted her someone was coming. Swinging around, she faced the door and watched with trepidation as it swung open. A tall, well-built man walked in, and that's when it all came rushing back to her.

Oh God, it was Bryan, the stalker guy from the grocery store! Somehow, he'd followed her to her house and had been waiting for her when she left for work this morning. And, worse still, he claimed to not only know about werewolves; he said he was one, the pack Beta no less! Warily, she backed away from him, her legs hitting the bed and causing her to sit down on the mattress with an undignified bounce.

He chuckled as if her retreat was funny. "Just the sight of me already has you falling into bed, eh?"

"Stay back! Don't come any closer." She issued the warning while managing to right herself and then skitter across the bed, pressing herself to the headboard. The beast inside her was bouncing up and down like a puppy presented with a juicy bone. Its obvious pleasure in seeing the man was in stark contrast to her own horror. Did the creature have no sense at all? So what if the man was drop dead gorgeous, had intriguing hazel eyes and lips curved in a smile that begged to be tasted?

The man stepped even closer and her breath caught in her throat. Was that a leering expression on his face? Her skin tingled with expectant awareness, waiting for the touch of his fingers, the brush of his lips. A mental image of his mouth on her flesh, his body pressing hers to the bed popped into her head and—how embarrassing—an ache began low in her belly at the idea of being ravished. No! These couldn't be her thoughts; the creature was taking over, that had to be it!

Her eyes fixated on his gleaming white teeth, the longer than normal canines. She took in his broad shoulders and muscular forearms, part of her longing to run her hands over their surface while another piece of her acknowledged she'd never stand a chance against him in a real fight. A distressed whimper escaped her lips and she snatched up a pillow, clutching it to her chest even though it would provide no protection. The man had claimed to be a werewolf and she knew what werewolves could do.

Las Vegas, Nevada, USA...

Marla finished the electronic transfer that deposited money into Nick Grant's bank account as per Aldrich's instructions, then sighed heavily and finger combed her hair away from her face. Wrinkling her nose, she mentally went over the tasks she still had to complete; double checking the other employees had been paid, dealing with the utilities, setting up an appointment with Swanson for a security check of the Estate. She hated this part of her job. Travelling in the limo was one thing; sitting at a desk was sheer drudgery.

Trapped inside, always trapped inside. When will it end? Where is the freedom to roam, to run? Her inner wolf paced back and forth in the cage she had imposed upon it. *A real mate, a real pack, our own kind.*

Rubbing her forehead, Marla tried to ignore the relentless questions, the inner agitation. Whining and complaining will do you no good, she scolded. This is the best course for us. We never did fit into a pack, nor enjoyed our packmates, remember?

You didn't, the wolf scolded back, *but then again you never tried. Always out for yourself. Pack is everything, our family, our reason for being.*

Family, she scoffed. I have no family. My father is dead, my mother left me behind.

You chose to stay, the wolf reminded her.

Only because she didn't really want me. No one ever really wanted me. Pack is nothing! This, she swept her arm out encompassing the room, is real. Clawing and scraping your way ahead, finding a secure source of money. Then we'll be independent and need no one.

No one? The wolf answered sadly. *How lonely.*

Shaking her head, Marla stood up and paced the room, trying to calm down from the argument she'd had with herself. Thankfully, no one had come in. She ran her fingers through her hair again and straightened her dress. Then, chin lifted, she sat down, tucking her chair in near the desk, once more the image of an efficient employee.

Her job had evolved over the past few years, moving from simply being a temporary secretary to that of personal assistant. Aldrich seldom visited his offices anymore, conducting most of his business over the phone or the internet, so she spent a great deal of time stuck in his penthouse. At least if she was in an office building, she'd be able to ogle the men that worked there. Instead, here she was surrounded by the same boring people day after day, dealing with Aldrich's personal bills, consulting with his housekeeper over menus and generally overseeing almost every aspect of his life.

At first, she'd been pleased, seeing her work here as a stepping stone to gaining his confidence and becoming more intimately involved. She'd envisioned accompanying him on business trips and to social functions where she'd be required to wear designer gowns and drink champagne. Instead, Aldrich had become increasingly reclusive and, while the man allowed her to balance his household accounts, he was proving to be annoyingly immune to her charms.

Oh, he appreciated her physical attributes, but she never got a sense that he truly trusted her. It was frustrating, considering all the time and effort she'd put into this project.

See? It isn't worth it. We need to leave, find one who suits us better.

Marla chuckled dryly, for once agreeing with her inner wolf. She really didn't want to marry the old man, but he was in line to receive a considerable sum of money and some sacrifices were to be expected if she was to get her hands on the main prize. However, she hadn't expected the sacrifices to be quite so mundane.

When she'd first begun working for Aldrich, he'd been in the hospital and dependent on her to carry out his wishes. It had seemed a perfect opportunity to worm herself into his life, and she'd succeeded to some extent. In the beginning, he'd relied heavily on her, but lately the plan was losing its momentum.

She frowned, wondering what she was doing wrong, then smoothed her forehead not wanting to cause wrinkles. A wrinkled brow wouldn't help her win over Aldrich, or any other man for that matter.

A knock on the door had her looking up and a middle-aged woman popped her head in, smiling cheerfully. "Marla, I'm making a pot of tea, if you'd care to have some."

"Thank you, Sylvia, but you can start without me. I need to clear my desk first." Marla returned the smile, and Aldrich's nurse left with a nod and a wave. As soon as the woman was out of sight, the pleasant expression fell from her face.

Annoying old cow. The nurse was unfailingly friendly and appeared happy to go about her job of caring for Aldrich's tracheotomy, claiming how lucky she was to have landed such an easy, yet satisfying job. Marla shuddered, wondering how suctioning mucus could be viewed as satisfying. The woman's affable presence was grating on the nerves, though Aldrich actually seemed to like the old biddy. They even called each other by their first names.

She tightened her lips as she recalled that not once in the three years she'd worked for him, had Aldrich ever called her Marla. She was still 'Miss Matthews' to his 'Mr. Aldrich'. In fact, the few times she'd tried to use his name and called him 'Leon' he'd stared at her as if she'd taken leave of her senses.

Could Sylvia be a rival for the man's affections? The idea was too preposterous to even consider. The woman was actually dowdy whereas she, with her Lycan metabolism, had the luxury of always looking sleek and fit. Plus, she aged more slowly, so sags and wrinkles were still years in her future. Sylvia had crow's feet by her eyes, an overly round figure, and grey at her temples. Marla grinned; the other woman's shortcomings made her feel quite happy.

She bent over her desk intent on getting the menial tasks done as quickly as possible, only to look up sharply when the sound of raspy laughter drifted down the hallway. Tuning in her acute hearing, she heard her employer joking with the nurse. Marla's fingers tightened on her pen until the plastic casing cracked. Laughter was not a good sign; not good at all. Leon Aldrich never laughed. The man didn't even know the meaning of the word humour.

He is interested in the woman. She is for him in a way we never will be.

Compressing her mouth into a straight line, Marla fumed in her small, stale office. Despite all logical arguments to the contrary, Nurse Robinson was getting under Aldrich's guard. And if Aldrich let the woman in, she could very well ruin all of Marla's plans to get her hands on the money from the Greyson estate.

Tapping the desk with the broken pen, she narrowed her eyes, annoyed that this new obstacle had popped up. It would seem there was only one way to deal with a situation such as this.

Leave? Give up this ridiculous plan? The wolf perked up, its spirit soaring at the possibility.

No. Sylvia Robinson would have to go. Hopefully, she'd be as easy to get rid of as the other nurses had been. If not... Marla curled her lips. There were ways to make even the most unwilling person leave.

Stump River, Ontario, Canada…

Mel paced the room, her arms wrapped around her waist as if she could ward off the trouble headed her way. Nervously, she nibbled her lower lip, not sure what to do or who to turn to. The email she'd printed was clutched in her hand, the only remaining evidence of the message she'd received. She'd double checked the computer to ensure it was truly deleted from memory, even dumping the recycle bin and checking the temp files.

In other circumstances, she might have found her actions a humorous re-enactment of Ryne's some three years ago. At the time, they'd just met and he'd been suspicious of her motives. When she accidentally downloaded pictures from his camera onto her computer, he'd been furious at her invasion of his privacy. He'd deleted the file, but neglected to dump the recycle bin, a fact that she'd hesitated to use until circumstances forced her hand. She'd ended up using the supposedly erased photos to create a report on him for her employer, Anthony Greyson. That report unwittingly precipitating a series of life-changing events.

In the end, her snooping in the recycle bin had led to a greater good, or at least that's what she liked to think. If she hadn't found the pictures Ryne had deleted, he might not have felt compelled to track her down and he wouldn't have been there to rescue her from the evil clutches of Leon Aldrich. Ryne argued otherwise, but that was her version of the story and she was sticking to it.

A faint smile crossed her mouth at the memory of how the whole episode had ended; her real heritage being revealed, she and Ryne becoming mates. The smile faded quickly from her face. If only she'd known then what she knew now. This past week, she'd felt as if her happy world was being ripped apart. Her fingers clenched into fists causing the note in her hand to crinkle. She read the message again and a wave of nausea washed over her. Rushing down the hall, she made it to the bathroom just in time.

Once the ghastly experience was over, she splashed cold water on her face then leaned against the cool tiled wall and sniffled sadly. Her life had been going so well. The pack was her new extended family, Ryne her loving mate and now a baby. Why did this have to happen? She poked the note that had fallen on the floor with her toe.

A knock on the door had her lifting her head.

"Mel? Are you all right?" It was Olivia, Marco's mate.

"Just a minute." She picked the note up and shoved it in her pocket before opening the door.

The other woman was looking at her with concern. "Still having some morning sickness?"

Mel gave her a watery smile before answering evasively. "Maybe, or it could be something I ate."

"Do you want some tea? Or crackers? They always helped soothe my stomach when I was pregnant with Maria."

Olivia was one of those calm, competent women who never looked fazed by anything. She had two children—Angelo who was four and Maria who had just had her first birthday—yet Olivia never seemed tired by their antics. Mel hoped to be even half as good a mother as the woman who stood before her.

Refocusing her attention on Olivia's question, Mel nodded slowly. "The tea might help." She brushed her hair from her face and noted that her hand was shaking.

Olivia gave her shoulder a sympathetic squeeze. "Being sick to your stomach is the worst part of being pregnant. Why don't you go lie down and I'll bring a tray to your room."

"Thanks, but I think I'll sit in the kitch—"

"Melody!" Ryne's voice boomed down the hallway and Mel cringed. She didn't want to see him right now, so she stepped back into the bathroom, foolishly intent on hiding in there until she was more composed, but it was too late. Before she had time to even grab the door, Ryne was there.

His piercing blue eyes searched hers, concern evident on his face. She looked down at the floor, too unnerved by the secret she possessed to meet his gaze. Her hand reached for the door knob and gripped it tightly, her fingers tuning white.

"Melody, what's this about you being sick?"

Mel tightened her lips. Damn his Lycan hearing! He'd picked up on the conversation with Olivia, maybe even heard her retching. In vain, she tried to shrug it off. "It was nothing."

"Like hell it was nothing. I overheard Olivia saying you were sick. The pregnancy book I've been reading said you should be over the nausea by now."

The Finding

"Ryne, you know I never follow the rules." Mel gave a brief laugh and moved to walk past him. He shot his hand out and caught her gently by the arm. A familiar tingle washed over her at the point of contact. It was always that way when they were together; the attraction between them was like an electric current. Normally, she revelled in their connection, but today it made her cringe away.

Of course, he noticed her withdrawal and gave her a puzzled look. She strengthened the mental block she'd created, not allowing him access to her thoughts. Being blood-bonded had its drawbacks when you were trying to keep a secret, and this wasn't something she could spring on him. Besides, her own feelings on the matter were still in a muddle.

A hurt look passed over his face as he realized she was keeping him out. Olivia must have sensed something was wrong, too. She quietly left, murmuring that the tea would be ready whenever Mel wanted it.

"Melody?" Ryne cupped her face and forced her to meet his gaze. He seemed to be searching her eyes for an answer, but she had none to give him yet. Tears welled and she blinked trying to keep them at bay. "Ah, Melody, don't cry!" Gathering her close, despite her resistance, he rocked her in his arms. His tender gesture made her cry all the harder. Ryne wasn't one to display his feelings; he was more of a rough-around-the-edges kind of guy. When he showed his softer side, it always made her emotional. It was only for her that he was willing to be vulnerable and expose his true self.

She clutched at his shirt with her fingers and sniffled, her tears slowly fading. The warmth of his body seeped into her and she began to relax, knowing it was wrong, but unable to resist.

For a moment, she'd pretend everything was fine.

Chapter 10

Chicago, Illinois, USA…

The tea kettle whistled softly on the stove in the kitchen of the Greyson Estate. Through the large windows, Franklin could see the grey clouds hanging low in the sky. With the temperature hovering at the freezing mark, they could herald a spring snow or a cold rain. Dampness permeated the air and he pulled his chair closer to the old, stone fireplace, enjoying the warmth emanating from it.

He murmured his thanks as Mrs. Teasdale placed a cup of tea in front of him before sitting down opposite him.

"How do you think our young miss is doing?" She curled her hands around the cup. No doubt the dampness was making her arthritic fingers ache.

"I'm sure she's fine." He stared at the steaming liquid, holding back a smile at the good news he had to impart. It would take her mind off her aching joints.

"That's what you always say." Mrs. Teasdale scolded him gently, then sighed, wrinkling her brow. "I wish she was here, where we could take care of her."

Franklin took a sip of tea before responding. "She has her reasons for staying away, I'm sure."

"It's been three years. Surely by now...?" She let her voice trail off and looked at him pleadingly.

"She's special, we both know that. When the time is right, things will happen."

"But what if we wait too long?" The elderly cook leaned forward setting her cup down. There was an urgent expression on her face.

He shrugged. "Greyson tried his way and it blew up in his face. We obviously can't force contact. Letting a pack find her on their own is a risk, but what other option do we have?"

Mrs. Teasdale smacked the table with her open hand. "Bring her home! We'll take care of her."

"And when we're gone? She'll be alone again and all the money in the world will be of no use to her." It was an old argument; one they had every few months. He reached across the table and patted her hand. "We agreed to let fate take its course. If she stays away and ends up losing the estate, then so be it. At least she'll be with her own kind."

"But will she find her own kind?"

"Perhaps." He smiled. "Though I think they might be finding her."

Mrs. Teasdale sat back, looking surprised that their habitual conversation was taking an unexpected turn. "Are you hiding something from me?"

He tried to look mysterious, glancing side to side before leaning forward to whisper. "I've had a positive report."

"Really?" She clasped her hands to her ample bosom. "What did Meredith have to say?"

"Just that a man has been around." He leaned back and tried to act casual, but couldn't keep the smile from his lips. "And not that young fellow she's presently with."

Mrs. Teasdale snorted. "Kellen Anderson. I've never liked him."

"Cassie's an adult now. We have to accept her choices." He chided her gently.

"But we don't have to like them."

"True." He conceded the point. "Anyway, Meredith called this morning to give a report. It's not definite, but she claims the man had a certain air about him; the way he moved, the way he held his head and watched Cassie. According to Meredith, he matched most of the signs Mr. Greyson used to identify that young reporter, Melody Greene, a few years back. Even Netty concurred."

Mrs. Teasdale chuckled. "Netty wouldn't know a werewolf from a hole in the ground. Meredith was pulling your leg on that one."

Franklin laughed softly. "I know, but she does a good job, so we can let her have her little delusions about her pet. What's important is that this is the first real sign of interest that we've ever noticed."

Nodding in excitement, Mrs. Teasdale started to push her chair back from the table. "If it's true, I'd better start to get ready. I'll get out my recipes for our Miss Cassie's favourites."

"She might not come back," he cautioned. "If she takes up with a pack, they might not allow it."

She stilled her movements. "I know she'd not be here forever, but surely a visit...?"

"We can only hope, but their ways might not be ours."

"Hope's all we've had these past three years. What with Miss Matthews always coming around and helping herself to Miss Cassie's things and that Mr. Aldrich meddling with the accounts. It's a good thing you kept your connections when you retired from the Service."

"They have proven useful, haven't they?" He gave a pleased smile. "The two doddering old retainers know more about Cassandra Greyson than all the supposed professionals who are looking for her."

Mrs. Teasdale nodded. "It's been a blessing knowing where she is and that she's safely tucked away from Aldrich's machinations."

"Indeed." He sipped his tea again, enjoying the warm sweetness. "Meredith and Netty were a tad worried earlier this week. Someone else was snooping around, but they're placing their money on this young fellow being the right one. And if he is, then Miss Cassie will be fine. He'll take good care of her."

Las Vegas, Nevada, USA...

Bryan stood inside his motel room staring at the young woman cowering near the head of his bed. She was clutching a pillow defensively to her chest and seemed scared out of her wits. He'd hoped she'd be calmer by now, but apparently that wasn't the case. Why didn't her wolf sense that he meant her no harm? Was she already going rogue? Losing her grip on sanity? No. She was too young for that, wasn't she?

Still, her reaction made no sense to him; it wasn't as if he'd attacked her. The fact that she'd fallen and hit her head was her own fault. In fact, he'd gone out of his way to assist her; bringing her here until she recovered, getting her food. He glanced down at the coffee and donuts in his hand and set them down along with his keys and cell phone, while searching his mind for a way to make her feel at ease. Perhaps some humour would help. Tilting his head, he looked at her quizzically before speaking. "Now this is a new one."

"Wh... What do you mean?" She eyed him warily, her body tensed as if to ward off his advances should he decide to pounce. His wolf rumbled its approval of pouncing, but he mentally shook his head. Explaining his real purpose for seeking her out had to come first. Remember what Ryne said? Business before pleasure. The wolf inside slunk to the ground as it recalled the Alpha's command.

"Women don't usually cringe at the sight of me. More often than not I have to beat them away with a stick." He shoved his hands in his back pockets and grinned at her, letting his amusement reflect in his eyes.

She didn't return the smile. If anything, she looked even more nervous than before. He felt the grin slip from his face as she pressed herself even tighter against the headboard. Okay, perhaps his choice of humour might not have been in the best of taste, given the circumstances.

Damn, but he was messing this up. He ran his hand through his hair in frustration looking around the room for inspiration and wondering where all his purported common sense had gone. Something about this situation was throwing him off his stride and instead of swaggering through his encounters with Cassandra, he felt like he was stumbling.

The Finding

Dropping his hand to his side, he took a deep breath. Okay, on to plan B, which he was devising at that very moment. Hmm, soft words and some hand holding to soothe her nerves might be the key.

"I won't hurt you, you know." He spoke in low, gentle tones as he stepped closer, then sat down on the edge of the bed. "I want us to get to know each other better."

Cassandra gave a squeak and pulled her feet even closer to her body. The scent of fear rippled off her. Fear and—he sniffed carefully—a faint undercurrent of arousal? He blinked rapidly trying to process that fact. They'd just met, and while he wasn't unaware of his own sex appeal, for her to be turned on by him was extremely curious. Searching for an explanation, the lunar cycle came to mind. Perhaps the nearness of the full moon was affecting her wolf and bringing it into heat. It was spring after all. He mentally rolled his eyes; just what he needed, a sex-starved young she-wolf to keep in line.

He rubbed the back of his neck and eyed her speculatively. Her fear, inexplicable as it was, was bringing out the Beta in him; not the enforcer, but the need to protect and reassure the weaker members of the pack. He reached out his hand in a gesture of comfort, only to be rewarded by her swatting at him.

"Hey!" Jerking his hand back in surprise, he glanced at it. The tip of her nails had caught the skin and the thinnest line of blood was appearing. An instinctive growl rose from his throat, chastising her for her actions. Another Beta characteristic was coming to the fore; demanding respect from the pack members and enforcing the rules, one of which was not striking out at superiors unless you were trying for a coup.

Much to his surprise, given her meek cowering moments before, instead of showing submission in the face of his reprimand, she shouted at him.

"Don't you dare growl at me! Take that, you filthy beast!" He caught a glimpse of her face, furiously contorted just before she swung the pillow at him.

"What the—!" He blinked in shock as the pillow slammed into his face. As blows went, it wasn't much. He'd endured far worse in a bar fight. It did, however, catch him by surprise.

Reflexively, he raised his arm to deflect a second blow and saw her dive across the bed. He shot his arm out, managing to grab her ankle and pulled her back towards him. Her nails made a faint scratching sound as she clawed at the bedspread, trying to pull herself across the surface while her free leg kicked back at him. It caught him in the stomach and his grip loosened as the air whooshed from his lungs. The hellcat!

In that brief moment, Cassandra reached the end of the bed. Pivoting around, her feet hit the floor and she was almost completely upright by the time he lunged across the mattress. Wrapping his arms around her waist, he yanked her against his chest, intent in holding her in a bear hug. With impressive speed she reacted to his move, jerking her head backwards. If he hadn't anticipated her actions and swung his head to the side, she'd likely have broken his nose with her move. Some part of his mind registered the fact that whoever had taught her to fight, had done a damned fine job. Unfortunately, that meant he had his work cut out, trying to subdue her without causing any actual injury.

"Oh!" An infuriated scream came from her throat as he tightened his grip and she realized her head butting had been unsuccessful.

Arms and legs flailing, she repeatedly tried to strike out at him. He was glad that his early command to not shift form was still stuck in her wolf's mind. If they were struggling as wolves right now, their growls and snarls would have caused suspicion in the mind of anyone passing by the room. As it was, the thumping of the bed against the wall combined with the grunts and heavy breathing would lead a passerby to suspect rambunctious sex was taking place, rather than a fight.

In the end, despite her efforts, his superior strength and weight won out. He lay on top of her, his arms and legs wrapped around hers, their bodies pressed together from chest to thigh. They were both breathing heavily and he could feel her breath against his face, smell the sweat that had gathered on her skin. As close as they were, he was staring right into her eyes; incredibly deep green pools with thick dark lashes.

If the circumstances had been different it might have been rather sexy to have her pinned beneath him after subduing her. Crap! No point in lying to himself. It *was* incredibly sexy and it was turning him on, even if he was mad at her.

And she was interested as well; the faint musky scent of her arousal hung in the air around them, stirring his instincts even further. She probably wasn't aware of the fact, but she'd pushed her hips up towards him. Her wolf was instinctively offering itself to him and for a moment his own self-control slipped too. Grinding his hips against her shot a thrill of heated lust up and down his spine and a rumble rose in his chest.

Gritting his teeth, he fought against his desire, trying to channel the emotional energy elsewhere. He inhaled deeply and let his temper rise to the surface instead. This young wolf was insubordinate and disrespectful, challenging his authority, attacking her superior. Some of the blows she'd landed with her elbows and knees had really hurt! A spot on his inner thigh throbbed from her unsuccessful attempt at kneeing him in the groin.

Deciding it was time to lay down the law, he glared at her, rumbling a warning. "That's enough, pup. Stand down or face the consequences." The tone he used, and the words themselves, should have had her cowering. For a moment their eyes locked and he waited for her to drop her gaze in acknowledgement of his position.

The faintest flicker of indecision could be seen in her eyes, then she squared her jaw and spat in his face!

His wolf surged to the surface and he bared his teeth, his fingers tightening on her arms as an angry growl rose in his throat. She was treading on thin ice now, and her next move would determine her fate. If she didn't change her attitude, he'd tie her up and ship her to Canada so fast her head would spin!

Cassandra froze and he knew she was seeing the animal in him lurking behind his eyes. A frightened whimper escaped her and she paled, her straining muscles relaxing as if admitting defeat. Good. She needed to learn who was boss. While he was willing to cut her some slack, there were limits.

He waited a moment, keeping his gaze steady, letting her know he wasn't pleased and he wasn't backing down. She flicked a glance at him, but quickly looked away, remaining limp and passive beneath him. Gradually, he eased his grip while continually monitoring her response. There was no indication that she planned another aggressive move, so he slowly sat up all the while watchful in case she made a sudden move. Her sudden acquiescence was suspicious, but when there was not so much as a twitch, he finally relented and leaned back on his heels, though he still straddled her hips.

Using the sleeve of his shirt, he wiped the spit from his face and grimaced. "That was really rude, you know. Didn't anyone ever teach you not to spit at people?"

She didn't answer, but he was sure he saw a flash of regret in her eyes before she hid it with a defiant thrust of her chin. Oh, she was a feisty one, he thought to himself, holding back a smile of appreciation. However, while he liked some spirit in his women, she'd have to learn respect if she was going to survive in the pack. Ryne wouldn't put up with that sort of crap. Deciding to capitalize on the situation, he pressed his point, keeping his voice deep and implacable.

"Your attitude had better change once we get back to Canada. Our Alpha will be taking you to task himself if you even try a stunt like that on him."

"Canada!" Her voice squeaked as she spoke the word.

He nodded, pleased she was at least talking now, rather than cowering in fear. "Uh-huh. That's where the pack is located. Under the Finding clause, you're now a member. We'll be heading back as soon as I can finalize the arrangements."

"Finding clause? Arrangements?" The words came out as a bewildered whisper.

"Yep. Rogue or lone Lycans such as yourself can cause a lot of trouble, so when one is found we usually hunt them down." His cell phone rang at that moment interrupting his explanation.

The Finding

He patted his pocket, before realizing it was on the dresser. Leaning forward, he found he couldn't quite reach and grunted in frustration.

For a moment he hesitated, eyeing the woman beneath him. The phone rang again and he sighed heavily, then issued a warning in his sternest voice before climbing off her. "Don't do anything stupid like trying to leave because if you do, I'll track you down again and the consequences won't be pleasant. Stay right here while I get my phone." She didn't move when he stood up, only her eyes followed his progress as he backed towards the phone, reluctant to let her out of his sight. He still didn't trust her sudden acquiescence.

He picked up the phone without even looking to see who was calling. "Hello?"

Mel's voice sounded in his ear. "Bryan?"

"What's the matter? I'm sort of busy right now." He answered her absentmindedly, his thoughts more on the girl before him than his Alpha's mate. Cassandra Greyson was a puzzle; scared yet defiant. How had she survived for three years on her own? Keeping her wolf in check with no one around to guide her couldn't have been easy.

"Oh, I'm sorry. I...I'll call back later." Mel's voice sounded wobbly, as if she were on the verge of tears. That grabbed his attention.

"No! Don't hang up! What can I do for you, Mel?"

"Oh Bryan, I..." She paused and sniffled.

A sound from the bed caught his attention and he looked up to see Cassandra was now sitting on the edge of the bed. She had her arms wrapped around herself and was staring at the floor. Her whole demeanour projected defeat. He grimaced, thinking he'd been too harsh with her. The girl had had a rough go of it, no doubt. Being a lone wolf was no fun.

"Bryan? Are you still there?"

"I'm here, Mel. I was distracted for a minute. What's upsetting you?" He turned his body away from the bed, in an attempt to help himself concentrate on Mel.

"You know how you saw me at the computer the other day, and I was acting sort of strange?'

"I remember." A quick glance over his shoulder revealed that the Greyson girl hadn't moved. He relaxed and listened intently to Mel, trying to think of what the problem could possibly be. Mel wasn't the sort to fall apart over nothing, however, since she'd gotten pregnant her moods were unpredictable.

"I've been getting some correspondence from—"

A sound behind him had him starting to turn towards the spot he'd left Cassandra when pain exploded in his head. He gave a brief cry, felt his knees buckle and then the carpeted floor seemed to rush up to meet him.

Cassie stood frozen, staring at the results of her actions. Bryan was lying on the floor, a thin trickle of blood seeping from a cut on his cheek. She couldn't believe she'd actually knocked the man out! Sure it always worked in the movies, but this was real life. Using the lamp had been an act of desperation and now that she'd been successful, a queasy feeling was filling her stomach.

She swallowed hard, forcing herself to look around for her shoes. Her purse was by the door and she breathed a sigh of relief, thankful that Bryan had brought it along. All her ID was in there and while it was technically all fake, they were the only documents she had at the moment. The irony of her thanking her kidnapper for not losing her purse struck her and she gave a derisive snort before resuming the search for her shoes. Even though he was unconscious now, she didn't hold out much hope that he'd stay that way for long. After all, he'd admitted he was a werewolf and they were purported to be quick healers. Heck, who was she kidding? She'd seen the phenomenon herself; her own minor cuts and bruises always faded much faster than would be considered normal.

The memory of watching her skin knit itself back together before her very eyes made her uneasy. She didn't want to be a werewolf and anything that reminded her of the fact was upsetting.

"Bryan? Bryan!"

A voice—a female voice—could be heard over the phone and she paused in her search for her shoes. Bryan had indicated he was popular with women; was this one of his girlfriends? He'd called her Mel. Was that short for Melissa or Melanie? Not that it mattered.

She wondered if Mel was a human or another werewolf. If the other woman was human, maybe she should warn her about her boyfriend. She quickly dismissed the idea. Escaping was her priority at the moment. Besides, the person on the other end likely wouldn't even believe her.

"Hello? Hello? Is anyone there?"

Ignoring the frantic sounding voice, she peered under the bed, grunting happily when her shoes came into view. Pulling them on, she stood and stared at Bryan again. He was breathing steadily, so no real damage had been done. Perhaps she should tie him up? Eyeing the bed sheets, she decided against it. It would take too long and probably wouldn't slow him down significantly. The power of his body had been more than revealed to her when he'd had her pinned to the bed. Muscles covered every inch of the man. Muscles and... Her gaze drifted to his crotch.

Their struggle had aroused him. She'd felt the evidence pressing against her and the beast inside her had responded, her panties growing moist. The smell of his body, heated from their exertions, had filled her nostrils and she'd had an overwhelming desire to nuzzle against him and lick the strong column of his throat. Thankfully he hadn't noticed and she'd been able to project a defiant facade.

But a facade was exactly what it was. The creature inside her was fighting to get out like never before. Hot, wild thoughts kept racing through her mind; images of naked, sweaty bodies twisting and writhing together. Even now she could almost imagine what it would be like to have her legs wrapped around his hips; to feel his hands gripping hers.

The man on the floor gave a light moan and she jerked back to reality. Her breathing was rapid and there was an ache between her thighs. Oh God, this was crazy. Here she was contemplating sex with a werewolf! With a cry of self-disgust, she turned and fled the room, anxious to put as much distance between them as possible.

Once she was outside the motel, she looked around getting her bearings, trying to calm herself enough to think logically. Luckily, the place he'd taken her wasn't that far from her house and it was on a public transit route. And a bus was coming! She sprinted across the parking lot, arriving just in time to climb on.

Settling in her seat, she breathed a sigh of relief. She could have walked home, but this was faster and she wanted to put as much distance as possible between herself and that werewolf.

His motives for searching her out were puzzling. While she'd been more intent on escaping than listening to what he was saying, a few of his words had sunk in.

He'd said something about finding her and that she was now a member of his pack. And he was going to take her to Canada! She shivered, thinking how a few days ago she'd been contemplating the fact that she'd need to move away from civilization before the animal inside her caused any harm, but Canada! It seemed a bit extreme.

How had he found her if he was from such a faraway place and, for that matter, why was he even looking for her? It made no sense. She recalled his arousal. Was he looking for a mate? Some of the websites she'd visited had said werewolves hunted for mates, but was that true or a myth? The idea frightened her human side, while the animal within squirmed in delight.

Yes, our mate! And a pack in the wilderness!

She grimaced at the creature's excited response and squashed the beast down. She needed a clear head right now, not crazy thoughts about mates. A shudder of distaste ran through her at the very idea.

Nibbling her lip, she considered the situation. Possibly, Bryan was connected with the werewolf in Chicago. Most definitely, he wasn't the same wolf she'd seen on the estate. That beast had been a dark haired man before it had shifted, but perhaps Bryan knew this other werewolf? There'd been mention of a pack, but Canada and Chicago weren't that close together. Her head began to pound as the situation became more and more muddled.

She gave up trying to figure out the how and why of Bryan finding her. It was more important to plot her course of action. Having escaped him once, she wasn't sure she could do it again, so running was essential. All the money she'd saved for an emergency was going to be put to use now.

As soon as she got home, she'd pack a few things and head to the bank. She'd close the account, go to the airport, and get a seat on the first flight out. It didn't matter where it was headed. Any place would do.

But what about Kellen? She clenched her hands in her lap. She couldn't leave him behind, despite her earlier anger over his gambling. It was too dangerous and Kellen was her family. The werewolf knew where she lived. He'd find Kellen and most likely kill him, assuming she'd shared the secret of werewolf existence.

She'd have to take Kellen with her. Hopefully he'd be willing. Given the debt he'd run up locally, she didn't believe he'd protest too much. A fresh start would be good for him.

Crossing her fingers, she hoped Kellen wouldn't question her impulsive desire to relocate. He liked adventure, so maybe it would appeal to him.

The bus was approaching her stop, so she gathered her purse and made her way to the door. It only took a few minutes to reach her house. Vaguely, she noted the day was clear and hot, much warmer than was typical for Las Vegas at this time of year. The sun was high in the sky, so it must be almost noon. Kellen should be home from wherever he'd spent the night. If he wasn't, she didn't know what she'd do. She couldn't leave him behind to face Bryan's wrath, yet how would she find him?

As quickly as she could, she walked down the street not wanting to draw attention to herself by running, but eager to get home so her escape plan could be set in motion. Over the years, she'd played out a scenario similar to this so she'd be prepared if the time ever came. Of course, she hadn't expected to be kidnapped by a sexy werewolf, nor had she factored in the possibility of Kellen not being home.

Her house was before her. She trotted up the walk, grabbed the front door, and breathed a sigh of relief as the door knob turned under her hand. Kellen was home. There'd be no need to try to track him down. The door swung open and she stepped inside.

"Kellen? Kellen, where are you? I've got something to tell you."

Cassie dropped her purse on the coffee table, peeked into the kitchen, then hurried down the hall towards the bedrooms. Kellen's door was ajar and she could see him standing by the dresser, staring at a piece of paper. She ignored it and looked at him instead.

"Kellen, I have a surprise for you." She'd decided to tell him they were going on a vacation, that one of the women at work had to back out of a trip and she'd taken over the tickets. It wasn't a very strong story, but she hoped he'd be too excited to question her. Once they got to wherever they ended up, she'd probably have a better story concocted. Right now, getting away was the most important thing.

"Hmm?" He looked up at her distractedly. "Oh. Sandy. Good. I was hoping you'd be home early from work. I need to ask you something."

Damn! She'd forgotten work. Mr. Bartlett wouldn't be happy that she'd missed her shift and not called in. Of course, if she was leaving town, it didn't really matter.

"You can ask me later, Kellen. I've got great news. We're going on a vacation, today! I got tickets really cheap, but we need to get to the airport right away. Grab the bare essentials and we'll head out." She infused her voice with an excitement she didn't feel, talking quickly, and giving him no chance to ask questions. She saw a duffle bag on the floor and tossed it at him. "You start packing and I'll gather up a few of my things. Won't this be exciting?"

The Finding

She left the room and hurried to her own, a sense of urgency coming over her. There was danger coming, she just knew it and they needed to leave quickly. All but running into her room, she pulled a small carryall from her closet and moved to the dresser. A movement near the door caught her attention. Kellen was standing there.

She smiled at him brightly, trying to hide her exasperation. Why wasn't he cooperating? "Are you packed already?"

"Um...Sandy."

A corner of her mind noted that Kellen seemed to find saying her name awkward. That was strange.

"I need to talk to you." Kellen looked sober, like there was bad news in the offing. A sinking feeling formed in her stomach. She tried to push it away and began shoving underwear into her bag.

"We can talk on the plane, now go pack."

Kellen stepped into the room and grabbed her wrist, pulling her around to face him. She froze, a handful of lacy bras dangling between them.

"Kellen?" His face was unreadable, but she sensed something was seriously wrong. Damn and double damn. They didn't have time for this right now.

"Sandy, you need to stop and listen to me. I..." He paused and flattened his lips, his eyes appearing tormented with some inner struggle. "What was your life like before we met?"

The question shocked her and she blinked at him, not sure what to say. In all their time together, he'd never asked. It was like an unwritten rule between them. They didn't delve into each other's past. Here and now was what mattered.

"Why do you want to know that now?" She kept her voice light and tried to pull away from him, but he tightened his grip on her wrist.

"I was curious. I know that you said things ended badly, but before that, were you happy? Was it a good life?"

His question unsettled her. She didn't think about her life with her uncle anymore. It was too painful. Twisting her arm, she managed to break free and dropped the bras in her bag.

"Maybe. I don't think about it a lot. Does it really matter?" She turned her back and picked up some items off the top of her dresser.

Behind her she could hear a paper rattling. "Yeah, it matters. I wouldn't want you to be unhappy."

"That's silly. How could I be unhappy? We're leaving on a vacation any minute. That is, if you get your act together and start packing." She turned, a teasing smile pasted firmly on her face.

Kellen wasn't looking at her. He was staring at a piece of paper again. Curiosity won out and she stepped closer to see what he was looking it.

Her breath caught in her throat as she saw a picture of herself. It had been taken four years ago when she'd gotten her driver's license. She recalled the moment clearly. Her uncle had presented her with a sensible little car. It was bright red and he'd had a large white bow tied around it. Franklin had led her outside, her eyes blindfolded and then her uncle had given the order for her to finally look. Excitement had welled inside her and she'd been grinning happily. Cook—Mrs. Teasdale—had been there and had snapped a picture of the event. Her uncle had seldom allowed pictures of her to be taken. A wave of sadness washed over her as she wondered what had become of Franklin and Cook. They'd always seemed old to her. Were they even still alive? Or had the werewolf attacked them as well?

Not for the first time was she filled with guilt. Why had she only thought of herself? Why hadn't she taken Franklin and Cook with her? If the werewolf had killed them, it was her fault. Instead of warning them of the danger that was lurking in the woods, she'd simply fled. There'd been no mention of their fate in the papers. She'd checked the obituaries, but would anyone have even bothered to write one for them? Their fate was a mystery to her, yet she'd never dared make inquiries for fear of her own location being discovered.

The memories brought a wave of pain as she recalled all she'd lost; her uncle, the two servants who'd been more like family to her. "Where did you get this?" Her voice sounded harsher than she intended, but she didn't apologize.

"I found it posted on a wall along with a lot of other advertisements. Sandy...er...Cassandra—I guess that's your real name—you're an heiress. You're probably worth millions of dollars!"

She blinked. On some level she supposed she'd always known her uncle was rich, but she'd never really thought of what had happened to the money once he died. Her eyes drifted to the flyer in Kellen's hand. It called her an heiress. Apparently her uncle left at least some of his money to her.

A short, dark laugh escaped her. All these years of struggling to make ends meet and she was rich. Not that she cared. The money meant nothing. She'd much rather have her uncle back and be free of the threat of werewolves.

Werewolves. That brought her up short. Bryan had to be conscious by now and was probably on his way here at this very moment. She returned to packing, talking to Kellen over her shoulder.

"I'd never thought about it, but yeah, I guess I am worth a bit of money. Not that it matters. I don't want to go back to that life." She compressed her lips and blinked back tears thinking of how empty all the fine homes around the world would be without her uncle, Franklin and Cook. "Look, we'll talk later. Right now, we need to get packed and get out of here before it's too late."

"But—"

His protest was cut off by a knock on the door. A feeling of horror washed over her. They were too late. Bryan was already here. She turned towards Kellen who was looking at her with an equally stricken look.

"Don't answer the door!" They both said simultaneously.

Chapter 11

Kellen gulped as a knock sounded on the front door again. For some reason Sandy looked frightened as well. He wondered why, but didn't have time to ponder the fact as the sound of cracking wood came from the general area of the front door.

"Damn!" The goon from Dollar Niche was early and obviously not feeling patient; the strength of his knocking was splintering their old front door. He turned to go head the fellow off, not wanting Hugh to get a glimpse of Sandy; the guy had slimeball written all over him. Kellen didn't trust the man to behave himself.

"Sandy, you stay here. I'll see what's going on." He didn't even manage to take one step, when she grabbed his arm and tried to thrust herself in front of him.

"No. It's too dangerous. You don't know what you're dealing with!"

Her fingers clutched his arm tightly and her obvious concern warmed him. It was good to know she still cared.

"Anderson! Get your ass out here." A deep voice called from the living room; obviously the door hadn't been latched or perhaps it had given way. Kellen winced. Hugh appeared to be in a bad mood.

"I'll be fine." He pried her fingers from his arm. They weren't as tight as they had been and she looked rather surprised as if she'd expected to hear someone else. He didn't have time to consider the point though. "Stay here. I'll deal with the guy in the other room."

He took a deep breath and walked to meet the beefy blond giant he knew was waiting for him.

"Anderson." Hugh nodded at him as he stepped into the room. "Eddie sent me to make sure the money is delivered on time."

"You're early. It's not due for a few more hours."

Hugh grinned and cracked his knuckles. "I'm here to help you get it and to make sure you don't skip town."

Kellen laughed, all the while thinking that Cassie was busy packing her bags in the next room. He hoped Hugh didn't take it into his head to go snooping through the house. "Me? Leave town? I wouldn't think of it." He leaned casually against the wall and crossed his legs.

"You wouldn't be the first guy to try and get out of paying up. Not that I'd mind exactly. Tracking you down and reminding you of your obligations would be kind of fun. I haven't broken any kneecaps in ages."

Taking in the guy's thick arms, broken nose and scarred knuckles, Kellen could only imagine the kind of fun he was referring to, and gulped. The paper in his hand crinkled as his fingers twitched. He'd forgotten he was still holding it.

Damn! What should he do? The reward money for revealing where Sandy was would pay off his debt to Dollar Niche and there'd be a tidy sum left over. But Sandy hadn't seemed overly happy when talking about her former life. He wished he'd had more time to discuss this with her, to see if she wanted to go back. This had been such a good idea at two in the morning, but not now. Maybe he shouldn't.

Hugh settled his large body in a chair and folded his hands behind his head. His legs stuck out halfway across the small room. Shifting into a more comfortable position, the furniture creaked under the man's weight. "So where's all this money suddenly coming from?"

Kellen frowned. Suddenly Hugh was acting a lot more intelligent than he had a few minutes ago. There was a calculating gleam in his eye. Was the 'tough guy act' just that? An act to throw him off? But if so, why?

"Er...about that." He wasn't sure what he was going to say, but a voice behind him made it a moot point anyway.

The Finding

"Money? What money?" Sandy's voice suddenly spoke from behind him and Kellen swore under his breath.

"I thought I told you to stay in the bedroom." He whispered harshly, glaring at her and trying to block her entrance into the room. Of course, it had no effect. Sandy could be headstrong when she had a bee in her bonnet.

"What money is he talking about, Kellen?" She stepped into the room, her face strained and her voice higher pitched than normal. A knot formed in Kellen's stomach knowing Sandy must be drawing some of her own conclusions. She wasn't slow. She'd have seen the reward printed on the flyer and connected it to Hugh's talk of sudden money.

Hugh took Sandy's appearance in the room in stride, answering her question before Kellen could think of what to say. "Your friend here claims to have some quick cash coming his way. Lucky thing too since Eddie wants to make an example of someone and Anderson here was his first pick."

Sandy looked at Hugh and then back at Kellen, anger sparking in her eyes. "Explain, Kellen."

"It's not what you think."

"Not what I think? How can it not be? You start asking me about my past for the first time in three years. Then you have this poster, saying there's a reward out for me." She pulled the paper from his hand and jabbed at it with her finger. "Then lunk-head over there says you're talking about coming into a large sum of money. How can it not be what I think?" Her voice rose in volume as she spoke and she waved her arm wildly. Kellen winced, knowing it looked bad.

Hugh had stood up as she was talking and wandered over to where they were. "Don't call me lunk-head, kid." He glowered at Sandy who merely looked at him in annoyance, most likely too perturbed to perceive the threat Hugh imposed.

Kellen watched in dread as Hugh plucked the paper from Sandy's hand. He tried to snatch it back, but Hugh held it out of reach, his gaze shifting from the picture to Sandy then back before understanding dawned. "Hey! You're the girl in this picture." A grin spread over the man's broad face and he reached

179

out and punched Kellen in the arm. "You did good, boy. She's worth a hundred grand at least. Maybe even more. I've got to tell Eddie about this."

Kellen made another grab for the paper, but Hugh was already moving away, pulling out his cell phone. When he would have followed, Sandy grabbed at him. "And where do you think you're going? We need to talk about this!"

"Sandy, I—" He cast an agonized look at her and then at Hugh who was already talking to someone, no doubt Eddie. His gaze swung back to Sandy who was looking hurt, angry, betrayed.

She jabbed him in the chest with her finger. "You were basically going to sell me out, weren't you? You were gambling again, ended up in debt, and decided I was your cash cow."

"No! I wasn't going to… I mean, at first maybe the idea crossed my mind, but then I decided—" He sputtered, trying to explain that he'd been having second thoughts, but she wasn't listening.

"God, and to think I was worried about saving you from the—" She suddenly stopped and clamped her lips tightly shut.

"Saving me from what?" What was Sandy talking about? Surely she hadn't known that Eddie Perini was threatening him with bodily harm?

"Nothing, I—"

"Hey, Anderson!" Hugh's booming voice cut into their conversation. "Eddie says to bring her over to Dollar Niche. We'll split the reward money and he'll cancel out your debt."

Shock washed over Sandy's face and he was sure it was mirrored in his own as he protested the plan. "No! That wasn't part of the deal."

Hugh laughed derisively. "You guys always think you have more options. Sorry. New deal. Eddie's in charge of this now. Behave before he cuts you out completely."

The giant of a man grabbed Sandy's arm and she yelped in protest before starting to struggle. Kellen stepped forward and gripped Hugh's other arm.

"Let her go!"

The Finding

With a simple shrug, Hugh shook him loose, and Kellen stumbled backwards, hitting the wall. "Come on. We're all going to visit Eddie."

Sandy reacted wildly, kicking and yelling as Hugh began to drag her towards the door.

Kellen regained his footing and rushed forward, launching himself at Hugh. "No!"

The thug fell backwards at the sudden addition of Kellen's weight hanging off his arm. He let go of Sandy and she landed on the coffee table.

There was a crashing sound and Kellen had a vague impression of Sandy sitting on the floor surrounded by bits of wood, but most of his attention was on Hugh. He gripped the man's wrist with both of his, but it made no impression. Hugh had him by the throat and merely laughed, wrapped his fingers more tightly and began to squeeze.

Kellen thrashed and struggled, but the man was no match for him. He fought to breathe, spots beginning to dance before his eyes. His fingers clawed at Hugh's hands, but to no avail. The world started to turn grey and a growling sound filled his ears. Strange. Wasn't it supposed to be a roaring sound?

Cassie looked up from where she lay in a crumpled heap on the floor. Her whole body ached from its impact with the coffee table and her vision blurred. Shaking her head, she tried to focus on what was going on around her. The sound of grunts and heavy breathing met her ears. She blinked and the blurred images before her became clearer. The huge blond thug had Kellen by the throat! Kellen was fighting back, but it seemed useless, his blows having no impact on the man's mammoth body.

She struggled to her feet, not sure what to do, but knowing she had to try to save Kellen. Staggering, she made her way over to where the two men were fighting and pounded on the thug's back, yelling for him to let go. Her blows were ineffectual. Kellen's face was changing colour; deep red, purple, blue.

Icy fear washed through her veins and there was a buzzing in her ears. Oh God, Kellen was going to die! Her mind flashed back to that night three years ago; the sight of her uncle falling to the ground, a bullet hole in his forehead. She saw Mr. Aldrich fighting against the werewolf, blood running from his throat. Now another person was going to die in front of her!

"No!" A scream ripped from her throat. The air around her shimmered. Her skin crawled. It was just like when Bryan had caught her this morning, only worse. She gripped her head with her hands, trying to fight the feeling, but it overwhelmed her. Her muscles contracted, an unbelievable tension filling her, squeezing her until she was gasping. Half pain, half pleasure she hovered on the edge of a precipice, fearful to take the final plunge yet knowing it was inevitable. Something called to her, urging her to move forward. She hesitated, fearful, but unable to resist the pull. A flash of light exploded behind her eyes, the bubble of tension finally bursting and she found herself plummeting back to earth.

She was on the ground, the world around her inexplicably strange. The images were sharper; the scents and sounds more acute. Sounds! Kellen was still struggling with the man, his arms were only moving feebly now. A horrible rasping noise came from him as he fought for air. The thug was laughing. She rushed to her feet and lunged forward, feeling clumsy as if her body wasn't her own, but intent on doing whatever she could to save Kellen.

A strange sound—a snarl—erupted from her throat and she found herself clinging to the man's back. Digging her fingers in so she wouldn't fall, she bit at the back of his neck, only vaguely wondering why such an action would seem natural to her. The man screamed and released Kellen.

Blood gushed into her mouth and she gagged, but bit down again intent on ensuring he didn't resume his attack on Kellen. Vaguely, she was aware that Kellen was free now, lying on the ground, gasping for air.

The man hit and kicked at her. She yelped in pain. Yelped? What...? Looking down she saw that she wasn't on her hands and knees as she supposed. Thin legs covered in brown fur were where her arms should be.

The Finding

Panic washed over her. It had happened! Despite her years of precaution, she'd turned into a wolf! A gurgling sound caught her attention and she realised she was looming over the thug, his blood dripping onto the floor.

Oh God! Oh God! She was just like the beast that killed her uncle's lawyer! Horrified by her actions, she backed away. Her claws made scratching sounds on the floor, reinforcing the fact that she was an animal, a ravaging beast and she'd attacked someone.

With a whimper she turned and tried to run, but stumbled, her legs uncoordinated. Uncaring that her movements were less than graceful, she pulled herself up and out of the house, staggering and weaving until she eventually found her stride.

How could she have done that? How could she ever face herself again? Horrified and ashamed she retreated from the reality of what she was while the beast inside surged to the foreground. It was taking over, exultant at finally being free. She briefly struggled to regain control, but then gave up; what did it matter now? She'd lost the battle; her life was over.

Bryan parked his rented car a block away from Cassandra Greyson's house and turned off the engine. He drummed his fingers on the steering wheel, pondering what approach he should take this time.

Walking up to her with a friendly 'hello' hadn't worked and the scene at his motel had proven to be a fiasco. He reached up and touched the spot on his head where she'd whacked him with the lamp. It was tender, but healing rapidly. Feisty, little rogue. If he wasn't so exasperated with the girl, he'd applaud her ingenuity. She'd played her cards perfectly, allowing him to think she was subdued by his authority and then attacking when he turned his back.

No, it wasn't the accepted way to treat your Beta, but then again, she didn't seem to recognize that he *was* her Beta. Her inner wolf was aware of the fact, but as for her human half... There was some sort of block there that he couldn't put his finger on. It was as if the two halves of her weren't communicating.

They were aware of each other, but functioning at cross-purposes. It made sense based on what he had gleaned of her early life. She'd been raised exclusively among humans. It shouldn't be surprising that she had a few quirks.

Rubbing his chin, he considered the situation. It could prove interesting, trying to integrate her into a pack. Mel would be of some help, having only discovered her own Lycan heritage a few years ago. She'd be able to relate to the girl and offer some tips on pack life. That is, provided she ever forgave Cassandra for scaring her half to death in the middle of that phone call.

When he'd come to on the floor of the motel room, Mel had been shouting into the phone, wondering what had happened to him. Upon learning that the Greyson girl had knocked him out when he turned his back, Mel had been both furious and remorseful; mad at the girl for hurting him and angry with herself for interrupting.

Finally, she'd calmed down and he'd discovered why she'd called. The news had come as a shock and he hadn't been able to offer as much help as he'd have liked to. Something was off with the situation and he'd told her as much which seemed to assuage the worst of her fears. Further investigation was definitely needed before she did anything drastic. He'd pointed out that Ryne was the one she should really be talking to, but she'd protested that until she knew more, she didn't feel able to broach the subject with her mate.

He could understand her point of view, even if he didn't totally agree. And after all, who knew what he'd do in a similar situation. Finally, he'd suggested talking to Daniel since he'd have more background knowledge about the subject. Reluctantly, Mel had agreed to involve another pack member and they'd ended the conversation with her promising to keep him abreast of the situation as more information became available. As he hung up, he wondered how Ryne would take the news and was half-glad, half-disappointed he probably wouldn't be there. His Alpha's reaction would be something to see.

Putting the matter aside, he concentrated on the Greyson situation. According to the Finding clause, she was the pack's responsibility. Should she ever reveal herself to a human or attack someone, the blame would be directly on their heads for not controlling her. Left alone, who knew how long she'd manage to control her wolf before a situation arose. If one did, all hell could break loose. An untrained Lycan could unknowingly do a lot of damage in a short period of time.

With a weary sigh, he got out of the car and began walking towards her house, idly noticing the changes wrought by last night's rain. The smell of the soil was different, richer and more pervasive, and splashes of colour were starting to appear as the desert plants that dotted the front yards sent out blooms. If he wasn't so busy thinking about Cassandra it would have been interesting to study the changes. However, he had more important things on his mind than desert flora.

This whole situation wasn't turning out at all the way he'd planned. The 'thrill of the hunt' was turning out to be more of a 'pain in the rear'. She was afraid of him, but he still had to make her listen. Maybe if he approached her at her own house, in broad daylight.

A blur of chocolate brown fur ran past him and he spun around, stunned at the sight. Was that a...? Dammit, it was!

A quick glance around revealed that there was no one on the street, but just in case, he ducked down behind a car to shift into his wolf form. Once he transformed, he took off after the little female Lycan. She was running as if the demons of Hell were chasing her. He sent up a quick prayer that no animal control officers were around and that she didn't run across the road and get hit by a car!

He raced after her, his longer legs quickly eating up the distance between them. They were coming to the end of the road, a playground was straight ahead. He scanned the area, thankful no children were there, then put on a burst of speed. He was almost upon her when she started to veer to the left. Quickly calculating her path, he cut across at an angle and leapt, slamming into her as she ran in front of him.

The impact sent them both rolling across the ground in a tangle of legs and tails. A cloud of dust billowed around them and he sensed rather than saw her turning around, preparing to bite her attacker. Agilely, he twisted away, the sound of teeth clicking together letting him know he'd had a near miss. Before she could make another attempt, he hip-checked her, knocking her off balance and then scrambled around to straddle her. Gripping the scruff of her neck firmly in his teeth, he issued a low, warning growl. She froze in response, only her heaving sides moving as she struggled to breathe after her headlong flight.

His wolf was excited to have her pinned beneath him and he flashed back to his recurring dream. This wasn't a forest, but in every other way, the circumstances were the same.

We've chased the female down and now she is ours!

Cautiously, he released the scruff of her neck and nuzzled her ear. She whined in response, tilting her head and exposing her throat. A rumble of pleasure sounded deep in his chest.

She is submitting to us! We should stake our claim and mark her!

He got up and circled around, sniffing her thoroughly. The scent of arousal was becoming stronger and the wolf in him fairly danced in excitement. Moving so they were nose to nose, he nipped and licked at her face, rubbing against her, marking her with his scent. She returned the favour, her breathing turning into excited pants.

Her scent was intoxicating and he couldn't wait to get closer. She seemed to feel the same way, standing and bumping her body into his. Licking her muzzle, his human side wondered what it would be like to kiss her full plump lips. No sooner had the thought crossed his mind, than he shimmered and changed forms, using the power of his own transformation to pull her along with him. Before he knew it, Cassandra Greyson was in his arms, kissing him passionately.

He sighed contentedly. It was just as he'd thought it would be. Her mouth was soft and responsive, her tongue grazing over his, teasing, then retreating while little sounds of pleasure emitted from her throat. He gathered her closer, gently pushing his hips against her. She responded in kind and his arousal throbbed heavily between his legs.

The Finding

Cassandra threaded her fingers through his hair, her nails grazing his scalp. A shiver of excitement raced down his spine. Inhaling deeply, her exotic spicy scent overwhelmed his senses, seeping into his every pore, filling him with her presence. He wanted her, desired her, needed her like he'd never needed anyone before.

He slid his hands up and down her back, marvelling at the feel of her warm, silky skin. His questing hands reached the flare of her hips and he paused, but she made no protest. In fact she moaned softly and nestled in closer. His wolf's elation at her nearness meshed with his own; his heart pounding, his blood racing.

He slid his fingers over the smooth curves of her butt, lightly tracing the cleft between her cheeks before cupping her bottom and pulling her more tightly to his aching erection. She felt so good in his arms; he couldn't wait until he too was naked and—

Whoa! Go back and repeat that thought. Naked? She was naked? He stilled his hands, shock running through his system. Damn, but she'd forgotten to think 'clothes' when she shifted. Either that or she was a half-breed. Whatever the case, they were in a public park and Cassandra being arrested for public nudity was the last thing he needed to deal with at the moment.

He hastily removed his hands from her oh-so-tempting rear and grasped her upper arms, pushing her away. She mewed in discontent, straining forward, trying to reconnect. He ignored her protests and looked around. Thank heaven there was still no one around.

"Cassandra! Hey, Cassandra!" He gave her shoulders a quick shake. She gave him a dazed look and he realized that her wolf side was still foremost in her mind. "Cassandra, snap out of it." He tapped her cheek lightly and watched as her eyes lost their unfocused appearance. Blinking, she gave her head a shake and he noted that the human half of her must be regaining the upper hand.

He made a mental note that he'd really have to work with her on integrating the two parts of herself. Right now it was as if she were two different beings. He'd never encountered a case like that; it reinforced his suspicions that she was probably completely uninformed about their species. Most Lycans conversed with their wolf as if it were a friend that was constantly with them. They shared thoughts and feelings, but the human half never completely submerged even when they shifted. The wolf within recognized and accepted that its human held the superior position in the relationship. Only a totally repressed wolf would seek to become dominant in order to be heard.

"Nice to have you back." He gave her a crooked grin and rubbed her arms soothingly, knowing it might be difficult for her to reorient herself.

Cassandra stared at him in surprise for a second before trying to escape his hands. "Oh no! It's you again!" She pressed her hands to his chest, perhaps intent on pushing him away, but something made her glance down at herself instead. Her face flushed red and an embarrassed squeak emitted from her lips as she realized she was naked. "Oh my gosh! What did you do with my clothes, you pervert?"

She shot him an accusing glare while quickly removing her hands from his chest and trying to cover herself with her hands in an age old gesture of modesty. He was tempted to protest that it wasn't his fault, but she was backing away from him and at the moment, hiding her from any prying eyes was more important than defending himself against her accusations.

He tightened his grip on her upper arms and pulled her closer despite her resistance. "It's better if you stay close to me." Casting a wary glance around the park again he explained his logic. "Less of you is exposed to prying eyes this way."

Upon hearing his words, she too flicked a glance around and then froze, a horrified expression on her face as she realized she was outside in full view of anyone who happened to be passing by. He could see the fear and confusion in her eyes as she tried to decide what was the biggest threat; being near him or running naked through a public park.

"Relax, there's no one around right now, though we don't want to push the situation. If you promise to not run, I'll let go of you and give you my shirt, okay?"

The Finding

Wide-eyed, she stared at him and then gave a quick, jerky nod.

Slowly, testing the fact that she wouldn't run, he released his hold on her. He left his hands hovering in the air on either side of her for a moment, thinking back to how she'd duped him earlier in the day. When she didn't move, he quickly unbuttoned his shirt and held it out to her. "I guess you forgot to think about clothing when you changed." He cocked his head. "Or are you a half?"

Cassandra snatched the shirt from his hand and turned her back. He watched with disappointment as the dip of her spine and her cute rear end disappeared from view. As she covered up, she talked over her shoulder.

"What do you mean, 'think about clothing'? And a half-what? You're not making any sense! And why are you following me around? And how did I get here?" She peppered questions at him like a rapid-fire machine gun, not waiting for him to answer. Now that she was somewhat covered, her fear seemed to be replaced by indignant anger.

As she swung around to face him again, her hair fell in front of her face and she lifted a hand to brush it away. The buttons on the shirt gaped open and he got an interesting flash of breast. He forced his eyes up; ogling her wouldn't put her at ease and calming her down was his main priority right now. Reminding himself to focus he tried to answer her questions.

"A few minutes ago, you came running past me like your tail was on fire. I shifted and followed to make sure you were okay, then things sort of got out of hand." He gave her a crooked smile and shrugged. "Our wolves like each other."

"My tail? Our wolves?" Her face turned ashen, her eyes wide. She stretched her arms out in front of her and looked at them, shaking her head in denial. "Oh God, you mean I was a...a...wolf?"

He nodded, puzzled by her reaction, but her next statement explained it all.

"No! It can't be! I've never done that before, never completely given in!" Cassandra clamped a hand to her mouth and stumbled backwards until she bumped into a tree. Her back pressed to the trunk, she put one hand on its rough surface, as if trying to brace herself. She looked as if she might be sick and he stepped closer, concerned at her extreme reaction. She held out a hand to stay him. Her eyes were shiny with unshed tears and she blinked rapidly, trying to hold them back.

"You mean you've never changed before?" He lifted his brows in surprise.

She shook her head. "No! I mean... Almost, but I've always stayed in control. Oh God I can't believe this." She looked around frantically as if searching for answers before locking eyes with him. "But how? It's still a few days until the full moon! I should have still been safe! It must have been because..." Her voice trailed off and then she gasped, a look of shock and dawning understanding sweeping over her face. "Oh no! Kellen! I left him with that goon!" She suddenly pushed off from the tree as if to run and he barely caught her by the arm, stopping her from another headlong flight.

"Slow down, you can't go running through the streets half-naked, not even in Vegas. You have no shoes on and my shirt barely makes you decent."

"But I have to get back home. Kellen's there. He might be injured!" She pulled against his grip, trying to free herself.

He compressed his lips, not at all pleased that she was so concerned about this other man. However, arguing with her would be a waste of time. "Okay, we'll go back to your house, but you'll have to go as a wolf until we can get you some proper clothes. Shift back."

"No!" Horror at the idea laced her voice. "I'm not some filthy animal. I don't want to be a werewolf!" Her struggles increased and definite panic was rising in her voice.

He pulled Cassandra closer in an effort to subdue her, forcing himself to ignore the way she squirmed against his body, the way the shirt rode up allowing his hand to brush against her bare thigh.

Firming his jaw, he concentrated on his duty. Bringing her under control was his main concern and he wrapped his arm around her, threading his fingers into her hair to hold her head still. He hoped no one came by. If they did, they'd likely think he was assaulting her. Frowning, he tried to figure the woman out. How could she call her own wolf a 'filthy animal'? And why wouldn't she want to be a werewolf? It made no sense to him. There were definitely some major underlying issues to be dealt with here, but first things first. He hardened his voice.

"Listen to me. Stop fighting. We'll check on your boyfriend, but we're doing it my way. My shirt isn't that long; it doesn't even completely cover your rear so there's no way you can parade down the street in it." He gripped her chin and stared into her face, letting the Beta in him come to the forefront. There was a stirring in the back of her eyes as the animal within awakened again, recognizing his dominance. "Shift!"

A shocked look flashed across her eyes, as the human part of her subsided and the wolf inside responded to his command. In less than a second, a chocolate brown wolf stood before him, looking up at him with a submissive gaze, its tail swishing from side to side.

He rocked back on his heels and gave a satisfied smile. He'd never had to do that before; forcing a Lycan to shift against its will. It was gratifying to know that it actually worked. And at least this way, he had Cassandra under control. He took a moment to examine the wolf before him. She was a beauty. Thick, chocolate brown fur, fine boned yet quick and strong. Her deep green eyes followed his every move as he circled around, looking her over.

This might work to his advantage. They'd head back to her house and she could listen without interrupting as he explained his plans for her. Anyone who saw them would assume he was taking a stroll with his pooch. He took off his belt and looped it around her neck. "I'm pretty sure there's an off-leash law in this city."

If looks could kill, hers would have had him buried six feet under. He chuckled at her feisty spirit and barked out the command "Heel." She gave him another disgusted look, but immediately got up and followed him as he walked out of the park. Yep, this might not be a bad arrangement at all.

Chapter 12

The sun beat down on his back as they strolled towards Cassandra's house, the warmth actually feeling good on his tense muscles. Bryan rolled his shoulders and took a few minutes to enjoy the moment. Everything was quiet except for the buzz of insects and the faint click of Cassandra's claws on the sidewalk. The neighbourhood appeared to be deserted, each house seemingly empty, the owners no doubt off at work. Still, he kept alert, scanning around looking for signs of danger. This wasn't his home territory and he felt somewhat ill at ease being so out in the open. After being used to the thick forests of Stump River, Las Vegas appeared almost barren.

He swatted at a fly that buzzed past and glanced down at Cassandra. She was trotting obediently at his side and he smiled at how right it felt to have her with him. Exactly why he wasn't sure and he spent a moment trying to analyze the feeling before giving up. Enough time for that later. Right now, he needed to bring her up to speed on the workings of Lycan law.

As succinctly as possible, he filled her in on the Finding clause; explaining that since his pack had found her, she was their responsibility and that was why he needed to get her to Canada. She wasn't pleased with the news; the occasional droop of her tail conveying that fact clearly enough. He suspected her wolf side was happier than her human half and he tried to work with that, painting a verbal picture of life in Stump River.

He talked about the pack members, relating funny anecdotes and then spoke of the vast woods which were perfect for running and hunting. He described the large home Ryne had for them and all the renovations they'd done, but nothing he said seemed to capture her imagination. Finally, he stopped, feeling affronted by her reaction. The pack was his family. What reason could she have to not want to be a part of it?

Watching her out of the corner of his eye, he puzzled over her reactions. She appeared more aware, as if her human half wasn't as overwhelmed by her wolf as it had been earlier. What was she thinking? Why had she panicked when he said she should shift? Was there a reason she was reluctant to join a pack or was she one of those oddities; a natural lone wolf?

Perhaps she was too concerned about her friend to really hear what he was saying. He gave a nod. It made sense. Okay, he'd reassure her this Kellen fellow was okay and then they'd have another talk. Once he understood her concerns, he could set her fears to rest and they'd be on their way back to Canada.

The house came into view and she whined by his side. He slowed his pace then came to an abrupt halt as he took in the scene before him.

A large blond haired man was dragging another man from the house. The first fellow had blood stains on his shirt and looked shaken, but angry. The second man appeared to have his hands tied behind his back and was considerably the worse for wear. Was that Kellen?

He glanced down at Cassandra. Her ears were flattened and her lips were drawn back, low growls emanating from her throat. He crouched at her side and put a restraining arm around her shoulders and neck. "Shh... You can't go rushing in there. Lycans take great pains to ensure their existence isn't discovered by humans."

She whimpered and pranced in place. He rubbed her fur soothingly. "Don't worry, we'll find out what's going on and see what we can do to help your friend. Looks like he really pissed that guy off though; drew some blood, too."

A sudden stiffness in her body, had him looking at Cassandra with dread. "Oh no. You didn't attack that big lug, did you?" He shook his head and looked at her with pleading eyes, already suspecting the answer. "Please tell me you didn't do that."

The Finding

The wolf hung her head and he swore under his breath, his shoulders slumping tiredly. "Great. Now the guy's going to go around telling everyone this big wolf-like dog attacked him. Rumours will start flying and lord only knows how long it will take until things settle down. I'll have to contact Damage Control and see what type of story they can concoct; maybe a rumour about an animal escaping one of the magic shows at the big casinos." He let his voice trail off and rubbed his forehead, feeling the beginning of a headache then winced when he touched the spot where she'd walloped him with the lamp. Cassandra Greyson was turning out to be a pain and he was starting to question his inner wolf's sanity in being attracted to her.

Cassandra wiggled in his arms and he tightened his grip, while looking up to see what the problem was. Ah! The big guy was shoving Kellen in the back of a white van.

He stiffened and narrowed his eyes; it was the same van he'd observed last night, he was sure of it. Testing the air, he caught a whiff of scent and confirmed his suspicions; it was the same man, too. Well, at least he knew why the fellow had been driving by; Anderson had been the draw, not Cassandra.

As the van drove away, he stood. "The coast is clear; we can head inside and find you some clothes so you can shift back." He moved towards the house, Cassandra tugging at her makeshift leash.

Once inside, Bryan took off her 'leash' and she shook her head, relieved to have the thing removed. It had chaffed at her neck and made her feel even more like an animal than she already did. While Bryan looped the belt back around his waist, she eyed him thoughtfully. Someday she'd have to return the favour if, heaven forbid, their association lasted that long!

Turning away from the annoying male werewolf, she looked around in dismay, noting the broken coffee table and the blood on the floor. Blood she'd drawn from another person! A sick feeling rose in her throat and she looked away. Someone—most likely the thug—had punched a hole in the wall. An overturned plant had spewed dirt across the carpet. The wooden frame of the front door was broken. The home she'd been so proud of looked a wreck. And what would the landlord say about the damage? The cost of repairs would ruin her budget. She closed her eyes to keep back the tears. Could the day possibly get any worse?

We're free! Our first transformation was successful and he has come for us. It is a day of celebration, not sadness.

The wolf's thoughts took control and against her will, she found herself leaning adoringly against Bryan's leg. His warmth seeped into her and she could feel the strength of muscle and bone. It filled her with a sense of safety, of homecoming. A contented sigh escaped her and she was aware of her tail thumping happily against the floor. Appalled, she struggled to bring her human half to the surface again and moved away from Bryan's leg. She hoped he hadn't noticed the wolf's behaviour; it had almost grovelled at his feet, for heaven's sake!

She didn't think he had. In fact, he was more intent on examining the room and gave a low whistle as he took in the damage.

"Looks like it was some fight that took place. Did you—" He started to ask a question, then paused and looked down at her. "Uh...I guess we'd better get you back into your human form before trying to have a conversation, right?"

He stared at her expectantly, one eyebrow lifted, but she didn't know what to do and shifted her weight from foot to foot while whining uncertainly. She had no recollection of how she'd managed to change in the park; vaguely she recalled the feeling of excitement and desire that had consumed her, the need to be with him, to press her body to his. Her face heated as images flashed through her mind and she was almost glad of the fur that hid her response.

"Okay, so I guess you don't know how to shift back either." Bryan rubbed his chin and then sat on the arm of the sofa, bending over so they were on eye level. "For centuries, shifting was considered magick and often it's still referred to that way, but actually it's a question of harnessing energy and directing it into a molecular restructuring of your form."

She whined and shook her head vigorously, her ears flapping against her skull. Oh great. Physics was always her worst subject. Now she'd be stuck in four-footed purgatory for the rest of her days!

Bryan must have read her body language or understood her whine for he paused and frowned. "I guess that's a bit deep at the moment. Umm... The way most of us do it is to think 'human'. We make a mental picture of ourselves; our hair colour, height, facial features and such. Of course, don't forget to include clothing in the picture or you end up naked. That's a mistake a lot of young Lycans make the first few times." He coughed and looked uncomfortable as he said the next part, "Unless you're only half-blooded; not that there's anything wrong with that of course. It just has certain disadvantages. Halves usually don't have enough control of the molecular energy around them to include clothing in the change process. If that's the case, you might want to try this in your bedroom or you could end up nude again."

She cocked her head to the side, having no idea if she was a full-blooded werewolf or half. All she knew was that she didn't want to chance accidentally flashing Bryan.

He wouldn't mind, the beast within said slyly.

Unfortunately, she was sure the animal was right. She could recall the feel of his body and the ridge of flesh that had pressed close. The memory caused a warm liquid feeling within her and she glanced up sharply at Bryan. He was eyeing her speculatively. Was it possible that he knew?

She got to her feet, feeling a strategic retreat was in order, and trotted down the hallway to her bedroom. Nudging the door open with her nose, she stepped inside and looked around. Lace curtains hung from the window, a colourful quilt was spread on the bed.

It was familiar yet different when viewed from this angle. She lowered her head and could clearly see a collection of shoes under her bed as well as a few dust bunnies and a forgotten novel. The half packed bag of clothing lay on the floor where she'd dropped it and dresser drawers were pulled open, their contents spilling over the edge. Lifting her...er...muzzle, she could see the clock on the bedside table. It had only been a half hour since she'd been rushing around, trying to get out of the house before Bryan appeared.

Bryan. She swung her head around and stared at the door. Not only was he in her home, but he was more in control of the beast inside her than she was herself. Said beast growled and she struggled to push it aside. The creature wanted to be heard and kept trying to take over. It had when the thug was attacking Kellen and later, as she'd raced down the road, the animal had rejoiced in the excitement of running and she'd totally lost control until coming to her senses in Bryan's arms. *Naked* in Bryan's arms, no less!

She recalled the deliciously wicked feel of his hands sliding over her body, cupping her buttocks to pull her closer to his arousal. Another wave of desire ran through her and she found herself panting in excitement. No! That wasn't a road her mind should be heading down. She was here to change back into a person, not lust after some half animal-like creature! Now, what had he said to do? Form a mental image of herself?

Closing her eyes, she considered the reflection she saw in the mirror each morning. Golden skin, deep green eyes, dark hair. For a moment she considered adding some highlights to the hair, but decided she'd better not chance it. Who knew what kind of a mess she could end up in? Abandoning the thought, she mentally dressed herself and concentrated on being human.

At first there was no response, then a quiver ran over her skin. She held her breath expectantly, waiting for something else to occur, but nothing happened. Harrumphing in exasperation, she hopped onto her bed and lay down, resting her chin on her paws.

I'm a human, I'm a human; she chanted the phrase to herself while concentrating intensely on transforming. Another quiver and a slight tingling about her nose. Her nostrils twitched and she sneezed which effectively chased the other sensation away.

The Finding

Disheartened, she let her head flop down and exhaled noisily, venting her frustration. A moment later, a soft knock on the door drew her attention. She lifted her head and perked up her ears.

Bryan peered into the room. "Any luck?"

She whimpered and lay her head down again. He pushed the door open further and stepped inside. "Want some help?" He shoved his hands in his back pockets and looked down at her. "I can force a transformation if you want. It's not something I do very often though so I can't guarantee the clothing." A soft laugh escaped him. "Not that I'd mind."

She growled and drew her ears back, ignoring how the animal within chastised her. Bryan took no offense. A crooked grin graced his face.

"Not keen on that part, are you? Don't worry, I was teasing." He sat down beside her and rubbed her shoulders. "Damn, your muscles are tight. Little wonder you aren't changing." His fingers began to dig into her fur, massaging the tense flesh underneath. At first she stiffened, annoyed at the invasion of her personal space, but the animal in her was ecstatic over the attention. Hmm... It did feel good. She gave a contented sigh and closed her eyes, relaxing with her chin on her paws.

"That's it." Bryan whispered in her ear. "Relax. Imagine you're lying on your bed, your arms and legs are stretched out, and the mattress is soft beneath your skin. Think of your fingers and toes, the way your hair is spilling over your shoulders." His voice was low and soothing, almost hypnotic. She could feel the tightness in her muscles slipping away. It was as if she were falling through space; slowly spinning, the breeze ruffling her hair and clothes as she floated downward.

Her whole body suddenly jerked and her eyes flew open. She was on the bed, lying on her stomach, her arms folded, and pillowing her head. Her arms! Pushing herself upright, she gave a happy cry. "I'm a person again!" A wide grin spread over her face and she looked triumphantly at Bryan.

His hands were still on her shoulders. He squeezed gently then stood up and nodded. "There. You did it. Your first unassisted change. And you're clothed, too, so you must be a pure-blood."

"Yeah. My first change." The elated feeling rapidly faded as the true meaning of what just happened sank in. Melancholy rushed in, filling the void left behind.

It was happening. For years she'd been fighting against it and now all her efforts had been in vain. Slowly, against her will, she was becoming that which she most hated and feared; a werewolf. And there didn't seem to be anything she could do to stop it. The drugs, her constant vigilance, the sleepless nights; it was all for naught. The animal inside her was winning; its presence constantly on the periphery of her mind, always looking for a chance to make itself known.

And now Bryan was here. He was able to command the beast inside her at will and she suspected that getting away from him wasn't going to be an easy task. It was like a prison door was slamming shut, trapping her in a world she never wanted to be a part of. All she could do was ineffectually rattle the bars and cry out against fate. She was doomed.

Reluctantly, she got up noting that she was wearing the same outfit she'd put on that morning. Her lip curled into a wry smile, her sense of humour surfacing for a moment as she wished she could have imagined herself back into nicer apparel. Being a werewolf sucked enough as it was; there weren't even any clothing perks. Sighing, she forced herself to look on the bright side; at least she wasn't naked.

"Are you okay?" Bryan was looking at her with concern.

"Yeah, just shaken up." She nodded and ran her hands through her hair. This wasn't the time to bemoan her fate; she had to try and rescue Kellen. He needed her help. There'd be time for grieving the loss of her humanity later on, for planning where she'd run to, how she'd keep the world safe from herself. Maybe a cave with a large boulder?

She took a deep breath and squared her shoulders. One problem at a time. "The guy who took Kellen, I think he's some thug who works for Dollar Niche. Kellen owes them fifty thousand dollars. From what I could figure out, the thug came here to make sure Kellen paid up and didn't skip town."

"Skip town, eh?"

Looking over at Bryan, she saw he was holding up her half packed bag. Her lacy underwear was hanging out of it and she wondered why that embarrassed her; he'd seen her naked already. What did a few bits of satin and lace matter? She snatched the small case from his hand anyway and tossed it in the corner, glaring at him out of the corner of her eye. For a moment she'd almost forgotten what he was. "Yeah. Apparently we both had people we needed to avoid."

"Trust me, Cassandra. You can't avoid me. I'll track you down, no matter where you run to." Bryan spoke calmly, but there was assurance in his deep voice. His eyes seemed to see right inside her and she found she was unable to hold his gaze.

Looking at the floor, she shrugged. "It's always worth a try." He muttered something under his breath, but she felt it was prudent to not inquire what. Instead she side-stepped him and headed towards the living room, talking over her shoulder.

"When the thug realized who I was, he called his boss, Eddie."

"What do you mean, he realized who you were?"

"That I was Cassandra Greyson, the missing heiress."

"And he figured this out, how? From what I've been able to determine, everyone here knows you as Sandy."

She nodded. "Sandy Grant. That's the name I came up with when I first met Kellen. He helped me establish a new identity and I've used it ever since."

"So how did the thug make the connection between Sandy Grant of Las Vegas and Cassandra Greyson of Chicago?"

"He saw a piece of paper in Kellen's hand. It was a flyer saying there was a reward for information leading to my whereabouts. I guess Kellen found it somewhere and was going to use the money to pay off his debt." She was rather proud of how she'd kept her voice steady as she spoke. Kellen's betrayal cut like a knife into her heart. Never would she have believed he'd do something like that to her. Staring up at the ceiling, she swallowed hard, forcing back the tears that pricked at the back of her eyes. God, she was a mess right now. Everything made her want to cry lately.

"I'm sorry." Bryan spoke from behind her, his breath softly caressing the side of her neck, the weight of his hands comforting on her shoulders. "It must have been hard to have a friend turn against you."

A part of her wanted to lean back against him and have his arms enfold her, but she couldn't give in to such weak thoughts. Despite what the creature inside her might feel, Bryan was a virtual stranger. She knew nothing about him except that he was a werewolf and wanted to lay claim to her because of some legal clause. Well, his laws had no bearing on her; she refused to acknowledge them, just as she refused to give in to the animal within.

Smiling tightly, she stepped away from his comforting hands. "From what I overheard, Kellen was being threatened with bodily harm. I guess he didn't know what else to do." Shoving her hands in her pockets, she wondered why she was defending Kellen. Apparently her loyalty ran deeper than his had.

"Friends don't sell each other out, no matter what. You'd never find a Lycan betraying a pack member like your friend is doing to you. Pack sticks together." He tilted his head towards the front door. "Come on. Let's go."

"Go where?"

"Back to my motel room. I need to grab my things and we can head to the airport. If we're lucky we'll be able to get some stand-by seats back to Canada."

"Canada? I'm not going to Canada with you."

"Oh yes, you are. Lycan law clearly states—"

"I don't give a damn about Lycan law!" She stared at him in amazement. "Kellen's been abducted by some goon and you think I'm going to fly off to Canada with you? You're crazy. Hell, I don't even know you and even if I did, I wouldn't abandon a friend." She paused, breathing heavily from the force of her emotion.

The Finding

"He's willing to trade you for money. Why waste your time on him?" Bryan stood before her, arms folded, looking and sounding annoyingly calm and logical. It irritated her to no end.

"Because he's my friend. F-r-i-e-n-d. Friend. Haven't you ever come across the word before?"

He narrowed his eyes, displeased. "I have, but I think we have different definitions."

She rolled her eyes, not wanting to debate the matter further. "Whatever. The thing is, I need to help him, no matter what he may or may not have been planning on doing and nothing you say is going to make me change my mind. Now as I see it, the thug told his boss about me and they probably decided to take Kellen, thinking I'll trade myself in for his safety."

Bryan cocked his head and looked at her quizzically. "And will you?"

"I..." She hesitated. Turning herself in meant going back to Chicago, to her old way of life. Everyone she had cared for was gone now, but then again, she had nothing here either. Her relationship with Kellen was severely damaged by this incident; staying with him as they were now didn't seem possible. And she'd bit the thug. Had he connected her sudden disappearance to the animal that attacked him? He might, and that made remaining too dangerous. She turned to stare blindly out the window. Where would she go? An empty, lonely pit opened up inside her as, once again, she realized she was all alone with no real home. There was just her, a big empty house in Chicago and the hated creature inside her.

"Cassandra?"

"Hmm?" She glanced behind her and saw Bryan watching her expectantly. What had the question been? Would she turn herself over to save Kellen? "If I have to, but if there's another way, I'll take it. Chicago has no appeal to me anymore."

"I was hoping you'd say that." Bryan looked pleased by her answer and she wondered why he cared. He rubbed his neck and looked around the room. "Um... Do you have any idea where they might have taken your friend?"

"No." She started to shake her head, then paused. "Oh, wait! The thug mentioned taking me to someplace called Dollar Niche. And I heard him use the name 'Eddie'. I think that's the boss."

"Dollar Niche? Okay. That's a start. And I have the license plate number from the van. Do you have internet?" She nodded. "Good, show me where it is. I have a friend, Daniel— he's a member of the pack—and he's a major computer geek. He'll be able to find out who owns the van and where Dollar Niche is located a lot faster than we'd be able to on our own."

"Why are you doing this? Helping me find Kellen, that is. You don't know him."

Bryan studied her for a moment before speaking. "I'm not helping Kellen; he's not my concern. I'm helping you and as for why... You're pack and like I said before, pack sticks together."

She bristled at what he was implying. "I'm not 'pack'."

His face was expressionless. "So you say." His eyes bored into her and she shifted uncomfortably, finally looking down at the ground.

"If you help me, do I have to promise to go with you once we have Kellen back?"

"That's not how I operate. When your friend is free, you and I will sit down and discuss your future."

He looked at her unwaveringly and a funny feeling rose inside her. As much as she wanted to continue arguing with him, she couldn't find the will to do so. Instead she changed topics.

"I'll show you the computer." She led him to the alcove off from the living room and then left him to contact his friend while she began to pick up the pieces of the coffee table.

It was broken beyond repair. She slowly ran her hand over the shattered wood recalling the day she'd bought it. It hadn't been expensive—a yard sale special—but she'd polished it so the scratches weren't as obvious. It had looked quite nice, she'd thought as she'd proudly shown it to Kellen. Of course, he'd only seen the imperfections and bemoaned the fact that it wasn't new. She tightened her lips and resolutely pushed Kellen's failings to the side; time enough for that once he was no longer in danger. For now, she'd clean up the mess and then see what Bryan had come up with in the way of a plan.

She snuck a peek at him; he was tapping away on the keyboard and staring intently at the computer monitor. She wasn't exactly sure why she was cooperating with him, especially since he was one of the creatures she'd been hiding from for the past three years. Perhaps it was because she didn't feel she had any other option. There was no one she could turn to. Not the girls at the grocery store or Mr. Bartlett. Certainly not Mrs. Mitchell or any of her other elderly customers. She didn't really even know her neighbours. And as for Kellen's so-called friends—she scoffed at the misnomer—they were the reason he was in debt to begin with!

So for the time being she'd have to rely on Bryan and accept his help, regardless of why he was giving it. That didn't mean she trusted him or believed she was part of his pack, though. She'd watch his every move and once Kellen was safe, she'd have to try to escape. Bryan planned to force her to go to Canada and join his pack, she just knew it. And that was something of which she wanted no part. While he looked and acted human enough right now, she could just imagine the way the beasts probably lived in the backwoods of Canada.

Uncivilized, dirty. She grimaced in distaste at the very idea. Sure, on their way back here, he'd told her about the werewolves Book of the Law and how it guided them, ensuring they lived peacefully and unobtrusively among humans. The very idea made her snort. She'd seen werewolves in action. The man in the woods had been covered in filth before shifting into a wolf and attacking.

According to Bryan's explanation, that same beast was the leader of his pack. And simply because it had seen her that fateful night, some clause called the Finding came into effect allowing the creature to basically lay claim to her.

No. That wasn't going to happen. A few minutes ago after shifting, she'd been feeling defeated, as if her fate was sealed, but she'd fight it. She'd fight being a werewolf until the very end if need be. Cassandra Greyson had been raised as a human being and that was what she was. The animal inside her couldn't be allowed to win.

Chicago, Illinois, USA...

Marla paced the length of her office, cradling a cup of coffee and considering her options. The more she thought about it, the more she knew Sylvia Robinson had to go. Aldrich had become more distant of late and she was sure it was due to the nurse, though why she had no idea. Sylvia was dumpy, dowdy, and dull. It made no sense for Aldrich to be interested in her, yet that was the only plausible explanation.

The man had actually had the faintest hint of a smile on his face when he stopped in the office a few moments ago. He'd had 'tea' with Sylvia, he'd announced. Unfortunately, his good mood hadn't lasted. One of the messages she'd handed him—some legal query concerning the Greyson estate and probate—had quickly had him scowling again and dumping more work on her desk, guaranteeing she'd have to work late.

Yes, Sylvia had to go. A falsified letter of dismissal had gotten rid of Aldrich's previous secretary, but Marla couldn't see that working with Sylvia. The nurse talked to Aldrich several times a day; the letter would definitely be questioned.

Possibly a car accident? That trick had worked when Marla killed the Alpha of her own pack. She knew how to sever a brake line and tamper with steering, but Sylvia only drove in town. The mountain roads had been key to the success of that scheme.

Wrong, so wrong. The wolf inside her growled in anger, still not forgiving or forgetting how she'd dispatched Zack. *He was our Alpha. He cared for us. Protected us.* Its ire rising, the creature pushed against the constraints she placed on it, trying to come to the fore.

No! You have no place here. Angrily she pushed the creature down and returned to her plotting. She nibbled on her lip as she thought, wincing when she accidentally nipped herself with her canine. Hmm... She could always dispatch Sylvia the old fashioned way. It had been years since she'd allowed her wolf out. The idea had merit, but there were certain drawbacks. For one thing, her wolf was decidedly contrary as of late. If she let it free, would it follow commands or try to take over?

The animal inside her stirred, excited at the prospect of being given some freedom. Marla rubbed her hands up and down her arms, feeling the energy coursing through her veins. It had been so long since she'd experienced a change and a full moon was approaching, too. Did she dare?

Cold logic told her to not chance it for several reasons. The creature inside her was growing unstable. It would be hard to explain away Sylvia's death without drawing attention and she might expose herself to other Lycans. True she had her perfume, but the formula might not be as effective if she was in her wolf form and being discovered by her own kind was dangerous.

She stared unseeingly across the room, recalling the events of three years ago. She'd been left for dead, her body battered and bleeding. Unwilling to give in to the darkness that had threatened, knowing it would've been the end of her if she had, she'd dragged herself through the woods by sheer force of will.

Once she'd reached her car, she'd used the last of her energy to pull herself into the vehicle. How she'd managed to drive the back roads without incident was a fact she still marvelled at to this day. When exhaustion and blood loss had finally made her stop, she'd pulled into a wood lot and slumped sideways in the seat. Her last clear thought had been that she'd have a better chance of surviving in her wolf form and had transformed just before blacking out.

Hours had passed as she'd laid there, hovering on the brink of death, drifting in and out of consciousness. When she'd finally come to, her mind clear for the first time in over a day, her wounds had been almost healed. Of course, changing while seriously wounded and lying there untreated had resulted in some permanent damage. The scar on her side and a slight limp constantly reminded her of what she had survived.

Pursing her lips, she pondered if ripping Sylvia to shreds was worth the risk and decided it probably wasn't. True, the presence of other Lycans in the area didn't mean they were actually looking for her; there could be other reasons. In fact, it was quite likely she'd been forgotten after all this time. Still, if ever she were discovered, word might get back to Kane and Ryne. Did she want to chance that? Not likely!

Years ago, sentimentality and a misplaced sense of guilt had attached Kane to her, but once he'd mated with Elise he'd switched allegiance. Marla sneered. The girl Kane fell in love with had been insufferably sweet and naive; it had almost been too easy to fool her. Too bad Elise had finally found some gumption that last day. If not for that fact, the plan to kill Elise, mate with Kane and then bleed the pack dry of funds might have worked.

As for Ryne, the man was arrogant and sexy as hell, but quick tempered too. She'd managed to string him along for a while before he'd finally grown wise to her game. Ryne was furious over how she'd duped him out of money and arranged that he take the blame for attempted murder and sabotaging the pack. No, he wasn't the type to let go of a grudge easily.

Moving to the doorway of her office, she watched Sylvia move about the penthouse, humming softly to herself as she tidied up from the afternoon 'tea.' Marla narrowed her eyes, recalling Aldrich's smile and the laughter she'd heard drifting down the hallway.

Stepping back into her office, she closed the door and leaned back against the wooden panel. Her fingers clenched, the nails digging into her palms. Yes. Sylvia Robinson must go. It was simply a question of how.

Chapter 13

Las Vegas, Nevada, USA…

Eddie Perini stared at the man that Hugh had dragged into the office, and his stomach did a flip-flop. Kellen Anderson had been much better looking last time he'd been at Dollar Niche. Right now, his eye was swollen shut, his cheek scuffed red and marks from Hugh's fingers stood out on his neck. His arms were tied behind his back and he sat awkwardly in the chair Hugh had pushed him into. Swallowing hard, Eddie wondered once again why he'd ever become involved in this line of work; serious re-evaluation of his career goals was needed. The idea of some sort of career in the theatre had always appealed to him. He gave a half smile at the idea.

He shifted his gaze to where Hugh was leaning against the wall, looking incredibly pleased with himself. Hugh fit this line of work like a glove; following clients, digging up dirt, dragging them in; no doubt feeling he was living out a fantasy from one of the gangster movies he claimed to love watching. Eddie hated to burst his bubble, but...

"Hugh, untie Mr. Anderson's arms. We can hardly have a decent conversation when the man can't even sit properly in a chair."

Scowling, Hugh did as he was told, but then stood with his muscles tensed as if expecting a sudden attack. Strange, Hugh wasn't the nervous sort. Come to think of it, Hugh didn't usually arrive back covered in blood. His neck sported blood encrusted scratches.

"What happened to your neck, Hugh?"

The blond giant kicked the chair Anderson sat in. "His damned dog attacked me; came out of nowhere and bit my neck, then ran off."

Anderson shook his head. "I told you before. I don't have a dog."

"The dog was in your house. Your house. Your dog." Hugh growled and kicked the chair again, causing it to tip precariously.

Quickly, Anderson shifted his weight and righted the chair preventing himself from landing on the floor. Anger flashed in his eyes and he stood as if to confront the other man. Hugh stepped forward, a pugnacious look on his face that caused Anderson to reconsider whatever he had planned. Slowly, he sank down in his seat and answered tightly. "It must have been a stray or maybe one of the neighbours just bought it."

It was quite apparent that Hugh didn't believe the statement. "That damned dog had better have had its shots. I don't want to get rabies." Gingerly, Hugh touched his neck, his jaw working with suppressed anger.

Eddie rolled his eyes. Hugh's injuries weren't his main concern at the moment and he wished he'd never broached the subject. "If you're concerned, Hugh, go to the doctor."

"No way." The man shuddered and stepped away to lean against the wall. "They give you needles in your gut if you've been bitten by a rabid dog. I saw it in a movie once. I hate needles." With that, the muscular man clamped his mouth shut and folded his arms across his chest.

"They don't do that anymore but believe what you want as long as you stay quiet." Eddie frowned at his supposed 'help'. Hugh puzzled him; a tough guy in some respects, the man was whimpering over a dog bite. When he had more time, he'd have to try to figure the man out. In the meantime... Giving his head a shake, Eddie cleared his throat and mentally got into his role. "Mr. Anderson...Kellen...I hear that you've made an interesting find."

Kellen shrugged, but said nothing, so Eddie continued on in a pleasant conversational tone. Hopefully the young man was going to be cooperative; this situation could prove to be extremely beneficial to both of them.

"Hugh tells me you've found the missing Greyson heiress. She's worth a tidy sum, more than you actually owe us in fact."

"I've changed my mind. She doesn't want to be found, so I'll pay you another way."

Eddie steepled his fingers and nodded slowly. "I see. She's a friend of yours?"

"Yeah, we know each other pretty well." Kellen stared at him, a look of wariness in his eyes. He was probably wondering where the question was leading.

"But as a friend, wouldn't you want her to have all the benefits of that money? I've done some quick research since learning of her presence in your life. She's worth millions and has houses all over the world. Surely, once she reconsiders, she'll see the benefits of claiming what's truly hers."

"Like I said, she doesn't want to be found." There was a determination in both the man's voice and the set of his jaw. Eddie frowned; apparently the man was going to be difficult.

"That *is* unfortunate, but we don't always get what we want in life." Eddie leaned back in his chair. "You see Kellen, I'm in a bind myself. My employer, Leon Aldrich, isn't pleased with Dollar Niche's profit margins. In fact, I strongly suspect that if things don't improve, my head could be on the chopping block; a situation I truly want to avoid."

Kellen shrugged. "So...?"

"So, by some amazing twist of fate the person who is looking for Cassandra Greyson is none other than Leon Aldrich." He smiled as the news had Anderson widening his eyes. "As I said, I've done a bit of research since Hugh called me with the news. Mr. Aldrich is the lawyer and executor of the Greyson estate. He's spent considerable time and money looking for this young lady. If we present her to him, I'm sure he'll be suitably grateful, forgiving the money you owe and looking on me in a much more favourable light than he has as of late."

There was a minute hesitation as if Anderson was tempted, but then he shook his head. "No."

"No?" Eddie raised his eyebrows in surprise. "It's a win-win situation for all of us, Mr. Anderson."

"Not for Sandy. She doesn't want to go. When I asked about her past, she looked sad. If she wanted to go back, she would have. Besides," He smirked, looking overly pleased with himself. "I've no idea where she is. Just before Bozo here broke into the house, she was packing to go on a trip. I'd imagine that he scared her enough that she's running away as fast as she possibly can."

"Oh dear." Eddie shook his head regretfully. "That does make your situation precarious."

"How so?" The smirk disappeared from Kellen's face.

Eddie noted a nervousness in the man before him. The fellow was putting on a fine show of bravado, but his breathing had quickened and sweat was appearing on his upper lip. Good. A few threats should be sufficient to change the man's mind.

"If you don't help us find Cassandra, I'll let Hugh play with you." Eddie chuckled inwardly at his own performance. If Anderson only knew how squeamish he really was. Keeping his face passive, Eddie reminded himself to stay in character.

Anderson glanced over his shoulder and Hugh stood straighter, a look of excited expectation about him.

Eddie felt a twinge of concern. Hugh really was too enthusiastic.

Chicago, Illinois, USA…

Aldrich set aside the file he was reading and pinched the bridge of his nose. His mind refused to focus on the documents before him, the legal phrases nothing but a sea of words floating on the pages. He was seldom restless, but for some reason, the confines of the office seemed stuffy.

Standing, he wandered over to the window and carefully pushed the curtains aside, allowing himself the barest glimpse of the cityscape. Some would say it was a million dollar view, but he seldom dared to appreciate it. A sniper could easily shoot him from the rooftops of the surrounding buildings. He wasn't sure if a werewolf would ever resort to high powered weaponry, but he wasn't taking any chances. He valued his skin too much for that.

Letting the curtain slide back into place, he folded his hands behind his back and paced the room. For three years now he'd lived in constant fear of an attack, basically a prisoner in his own home and now he was tiring of the fact. Unfortunately, there was no doubt in his mind that the wolves were still looking for him.

Three years ago, exposing the existence of werewolves had been a spur of the moment plan on his part. His excitement over the discovery had temporarily clouded his good judgement. If he'd been thinking clearly, he would have gathered a team of experts to help him control the she-wolf rather than trying to deal with her on his own. And then the appearance of the other one had completely thrown his plan off kilter.

Wistfully, he recalled his conversation with Sylvia. Over afternoon tea, she'd mentioned working in her small garden and taking walks in the park. She'd even suggested they go for a stroll together one day. The idea intrigued him. He'd never noticed the world around him, being too busy clawing his way to the top. But Sylvia had made the awakening of spring wondrous rather than mundane.

He sighed. He'd be too exposed walking in a park; werewolves could be lurking there. And he was sure they were like elephants, never forgetting, never forgiving. Not that he needed their forgiveness; there was nothing to forgive. Animals, that's all they were; freaks of nature. Real humans, such as himself, would one day prove to be their lords and masters, if only proof of the beasts' existence could be attained.

Should he ever find the Greyson girl he'd be able to finally proclaim the truth without being seen as a madman. The girl was a werewolf; Greyson had said as much before he died and it made sense. She'd been kept hidden away from the world; the nurse who'd tended her that last night, said the girl was under confinement once a month. Greyson's 'trips' had always been at the time of a full moon; no doubt trying to keep the young wolf under control.

Yes, if he ever got his hands on Cassandra Greyson, he'd expose her for what she was and then, once the truth was known, he'd finally be free. The werewolves would be hunted down and caged like the animals they are and he'd no longer need to hide from them or their Keeping law.

The clock on the wall chimed softly. Five o'clock. Quitting time for most of the world, but not him. He had nothing to live for except his work. An image of Sylvia flashed before his eyes. She was so calming, so ordinary. Pushing the idea aside, he moved to his desk. Work to do; always more work to do.

A note on his planner caught his attention. Eddie Perini. Ah, yes. He wanted to check on the man today. He suspected Eddie might need extra prodding to carry out his orders; perhaps tormenting the fellow would help lift his morose mood.

After dialling, he settled in his chair, quite surprised when Eddie answered the phone on only the second ring. He raised his eyebrows. Eddie wasn't known for doing anything quickly.

"Dollar Niche, Eddie Perini speaking. How can I help you?"

"Edward, how efficient you sound today."

"Leon...I mean, Mr. Aldrich. I was just going to call you."

"Really? With good news, I hope."

The man chuckled on the other end of the line. "Oh yeah. I think you're going to like this news. You know that girl you've been looking for? Cassandra Greyson?"

He frowned. Eddie had never spoken of her before. He tightened his grip on the phone and answered slowly. "Yes. What about her?"

"I've found her!" Eddie fairly crowed as he delivered the news. "Or at least the next best thing to finding her. She's been calling herself Sandy Grant and I've got a guy here who has actually been living with her for the past three years."

"And where is Miss Greyson now?" He struggled to keep the excitement from his voice. It was never a good idea to let others know you were too interested in what they were saying.

"Well...that's the problem." The exuberance in Eddie's voice faded. "We had her, but then she slipped away. Her boyfriend—Kellen Anderson—is here though."

He slumped in his chair. Damn! "Does he know where she is?"

"He says he doesn't, but Hugh—my muscle—will be roughing him up if he doesn't start talking soon."

Same old Eddie. All threats, but no action. Well, he'd take over from here. Anything that had to do with Cassandra Greyson was too important to leave to the likes of Eddie Perini and his 'muscle'. He rolled his eyes at the ridiculous term then began using his free hand to access the computer. Flights. He needed to arrange a flight. Distractedly, he talked to Eddie. "I want the man flown to Chicago as soon as possible."

"To Chicago? But why? The girl is here in Vegas."

"You say Miss Greyson has lived with the fellow for three years, correct? Then there will be a strong bond between them. If he's in Chicago, she'll follow."

"But..." Eddie sputtered on the line.

"We'll even provide an incentive. Allow Hugh to rough him up a bit, take a picture, and send it to Miss Greyson. I assume you have the address where she lives?"

"Yes, but..."

"Leave a note. Something to the effect that if she wants to spare her boyfriend further damage, she needs to head back to Chicago."

"But what if she goes to the police?" Eddie's voice reflected his discomfort with the plan. Really, the man was definitely in the wrong line of business. He made a mental note to remove Eddie from the organization once this was over, then focused on the possibility of Cassandra going to the authorities.

He considered the point carefully. Would she tell someone? No. Not likely. She was living under an assumed name and she was a werewolf. Attracting attention to herself would be the last thing she'd want. And even if she did tell someone, they wouldn't believe her because he already had papers drawn up declaring her mentally incompetent. There was even a doctor waiting in the wings to sign them. No one could imagine a sane person running away from millions of dollars.

"Don't worry, Edward. I have that taken care of. I'll arrange for a private plane to meet you at the Vegas airport. It will fly him directly to Chicago and I'm sure Cassandra will soon be hot on his heels. You just get the man on the plane."

"Yes, sir." Eddie sounded resigned to the plan, which was just as well since he really didn't have a choice. After a moment, Eddie spoke again. "Er...what about the reward? The hundred thousand dollars?'

"Edward, your...future...was rather precarious yesterday, wouldn't you say?"

He could hear the man gulp before answering. "Yes."

"It isn't now. Surely that's payment enough."

The man didn't argue but the disappointment in his voice was audible. "Yes, it's enough."

"I thought it would be." He paused, then continued. "And Eddie? You might want to start looking for another job before my benevolent mood wears off and I see the books for the next quarter. I think we should end our business association on this high note, don't you?" His comment was met with silence, then the sound of the receiver being hung up.

He chuckled to himself. Talking to Eddie had lifted his mood considerably. He rubbed his hands together. If the Greyson girl took the bait—and he'd bet his last dollar she would, given how foolish young lovers could be—he'd have control of her and her inheritance in the near future. Then after waiting a suitable length of time, and judiciously rearranging the estate funds in his own favour, he'd reveal her for what she was. When the news broke, it would make him famous and, more importantly, finally free him of the werewolf threat. The beasts would be too busy trying to run and hide to ever bother him again.

He chuckled, then began to cough as mucous gathered in his trach tube. Reaching for the buzzer that would summon Sylvia to his side he coughed again, managing to smile in anticipation of her gentle attention. It had certainly been his lucky day when she came to work for him.

The Finding

Bryan watched Cassandra as she moved about the living room, tidying up the evidence of the struggle that had occurred earlier. The scent washing off of her was a veritable smorgasbord of emotions; fear, anger, distrust, confusion...and reluctant arousal.

The arousal he could relate to; she was a pretty, curvaceous female and the male in him reacted to that naturally, but there was something else. It was more than basic lust. His wolf knew hers despite the fact they'd just met. Sure, he'd caught a faint whiff of her scent all those years ago, but it couldn't have been enough to bind the two animals together. Besides, Cassandra had never encountered him before this morning, yet the animal within her had shown no shyness of him.

An earlier conversation with Marco came to mind; how certain select wolves knew their mates in some dream world long before they actually met. The idea seemed far-fetched and yet there was his recurring dream of chasing a chocolate brown wolf. Coincidence or something more?

With half-closed eyes, he examined each detail of her appearance and compared it to the nebulous female in his dreams. Her breasts were full, her waist narrow. Rounded hips perfect for holding during mating. Long legs that would wrap around his waist, her heels locking in the small of his back as he—

A sound from the computer drew his attention and the erotic dream images he'd been recalling disintegrated into a million pieces. Damn, just when it had been getting interesting. Rather like his dreams, he thought morosely. They always faded at the good part, too.

He checked the computer screen. A message appeared from Daniel. He shook his head, as always amazed at what his friend could do when armed with a computer and internet access.

Leaning forward, he studied the information on the screen. Hmm... Now that was interesting. The van, which had taken Kellen, belonged to a company known as Dollar Niche. Dollar

Niche was run by a fellow named Eddie Perini, though he wasn't the owner. Daniel was still working on that. He called out the information over his shoulder.

"Cassandra? My friend confirmed the van that took your friend belongs to Dollar Niche."

She looked up from the pile of dust she was gathering. "Dollar Niche was the name on the promissory note I found in Kellen's pocket. Most likely it's one of those shady loan places where you can get money quickly, and end up repaying for the rest of your life."

"Uh-huh." He tapped the computer screen. "That's basically what Daniel found out. It operates just this side of legal."

Abandoning her cleaning, she came to stand beside him, peering at the screen over his shoulder. Her sweet breath softly caressed the nape of his neck and he struggled to control the shiver of awareness that raced over him.

"Did he find an address for the place? That's probably where that goon took Kellen."

"Only a post office box, but Daniel should have that information in a few minutes."

In his peripheral vision, he saw Cassandra twist the hem of her shirt and nibble on her lip. "When we find out where he is, what will we do? Contact the police?"

He snorted and spun the chair around so he was facing her. "No. Remember what I said earlier? Lycans keep a low profile."

"But Kellen isn't a werewolf and I doubt anyone at Dollar Niche is either."

"Cassandra, the police ask questions. They'll want to know your name. Do you really want them checking into your background?"

Her hands stilled, then her fingers tightened into fists as she shook her head. "So what do we do?"

Rubbing the back of his neck he considered the situation. He could easily take on the two men, knocking them out, but it might lead to questions. The goon might already be wondering

218

what type of creature attacked him at the house. Another attack would definitely put the man on alert.

Lycan Link had been less than amused when he informed them of Cassandra's attack on the man. The Damage Control division had been put on alert for any rumours coming out of the Vegas region and a few Lycans would be deployed to the area just in case. He grimaced as he recalled the tone of the email which basically said Ryne's pack was on the verge of being considered negligent in carrying out its duties as outlined in the Finding clause. If Cassandra wasn't kept in line, there would be serious repercussions. Exactly what that meant, he didn't know and didn't dare ask. Thankfully they'd liked his suggested excuse of an animal escaping from one of the shows; perhaps it would gain him some leniency. He hoped Cassandra didn't do anything else to upset the Lycan establishment. A thought popped into his head.

"Does Kellen know that you're a Lycan?"

"No!" She backed away from him, appearing frightened. "I never told him, I swear! I said I had migraines once a month. He doesn't know anything, honestly! There's no reason to kill him."

Perplexed by her reaction, he stood and took a step towards her, but stopped when she backed up even more, finally running into the wall. He spoke slowly and calmly as if trying to gentle a wild animal. "Relax. I wasn't planning on killing him." As he spoke, his wolf muttered to the contrary, still not pleased that another male had been living with her.

Cassandra interrupted. "I've heard about the Keeping; how you kill anyone who discovers your secret. Kellen knows nothing. I made sure he never found out!" Panic laced her voice and he raised his hands in a placating gesture.

"It's okay. I believe you. I was just wondering what he knew."

"What would you have done with him if he did know?"

He sighed. "I don't know exactly, but since he's sort of like a part of your family," he almost choked on the word, "we'd work something out, I guess."

219

A look of relief washed over her face and she visibly relaxed. He wondered about the depth of her relationship with the man, but before he could inquire, another message from Daniel appeared on the screen. He turned and leaned over the computer, bracing his weight on one arm.

"Way to go, Daniel. We have an address and... Huh! Imagine that!" He straightened and rubbed his chin. "Now this makes things more interesting."

"What?" She stepped closer, obviously curious.

"Dollar Niche is an anagram for Leon Aldrich who is the actual head of the company. And Aldrich is the name of the guy who tried to capture and sell our Alpha's mate."

Cassandra paled. "Leon Aldrich was my uncle's lawyer. I saw a werewolf kill him!"

He snorted in disgust. "*Tried* to kill him, but the bastard didn't die."

"What do you mean? I saw the wolf attack. There was blood everywhere. Mr. Aldrich was gasping for air."

"And then you ran."

She froze. "How do you know that?"

He shrugged. "I told you yesterday, the Lycan was Ryne, my Alpha. He told us what happened that night."

"Oh. Right..." Her voice trailed off. He assumed she'd forgotten that bit of news.

"Anyway, as I said, he was trying to kill Aldrich but at the same time his mate, Mel, was in danger of dying from an ill-timed transformation. While Ryne was saving her, someone found Aldrich and got him to the hospital. Since then, we've never been able to get close enough to the man to finish the job."

"Finish the... That's horrible! How can you say something like that as if...?" She shivered and shook her head, obviously at a loss for words. "I can't imagine killing being part of daily life."

"It isn't part of daily life. It's actually very rare, but I'd advise you not to be so quick to judge until you know all the facts." He narrowed his eyes, not liking the way she viewed his people. Hell, they were her people too, even if she didn't seem to realize that. "Aldrich had no compunction about kidnapping

220

Mel, attacking her friend Lucy or holding both Mel and Ryne at gunpoint. The man had been planning on selling Mel to the highest bidder simply for fame and fortune. Aldrich had no respect for her as person. In his mind, she was an animal to be put in a cage."

"But—"

"Some of our laws might seem harsh to an outsider, but rest assured they aren't enacted without careful consideration and full examination of all the facts. Aldrich's plan would have resulted in the deaths of countless men, women, and children. He would have exposed us to the whole world purely for personal gain. There was no consideration for the lives that would be destroyed, the societal changes, the distrust, or even panic that would erupt because of his actions, because of his greed. Man and Lycan coexist peacefully only because our existence is kept secret. To reveal us to the world would have grave repercussions, not only for shifters, but for humans as well."

She folded her arms, her disbelief audible in her voice. "I don't believe it would be that cataclysmic."

"History repeats itself, Cassandra." He struggled to keep his voice calm in the face of her attitude when in reality he'd like to give her a good shaking. "Lycans have kept their existence secret for millennia and with good cause. In ancient times we were hunted to near extinction. Only by banding together and following a strict set of rules were we able to save ourselves. The Book of the Law was our salvation and we adhere to its tenets. Maybe someday, when humanity is more accepting of those that are different—when there is peace between countries, races, religions, ideologies—then we might come out of the shadows, but not now. Humanity isn't ready for us yet."

Cassandra was frowning, but he could tell she was considering his words. A heartfelt sigh escaped his lips. The girl was suspicious and unaccepting of her own kind. Reminding her that Ryne, the man who would be her Alpha, had attempted to kill someone was not helping him build a case as to the benefits of belonging to his pack.

Deciding to leave the philosophical discussions for a more appropriate time, he concentrated on the matter at hand. Aldrich owned Dollar Niche. He was also the lawyer in charge of the Greyson estate and was searching for Cassandra. Cassandra's boyfriend was being held by Dollar Niche because he owed them money and was willing to use Cassandra to get out of debt.

It was definitely a tangled web and he wondered how much was pure chance and how much, if any, had been engineered. When he had more time, he'd try to figure it out, but right now getting Kellen out of the clutches of Dollar Niche was his main objective. Once the man was safe, he'd stand a better chance of convincing Cassandra to accompany him back to Canada.

"So... We'd better head over to Dollar Niche and check the place out. If your friend is there, I'll get him out. Then we're having a serious talk about Canada, agreed?"

Cassandra nodded, but he questioned the look in her eyes. She was plotting something, he was sure of it.

Chapter 14

Stump River, Ontario, Canada…

Mel leaned against the doorframe that led to Daniel's room, and knocked softly. The man inside was engrossed in his computers, as usual, so she waited patiently for him to acknowledge her. He was aware of her presence—she'd learned long ago that sneaking up on a Lycan was hard to do—but seemed busy with his current task. She amused herself by looking around his bedroom. A few piles of dirty clothes lay on the floor while various items covered the dresser top and bedside table. The bed was rather haphazardly made as well. In all, the room had an air of casual neglect as if the occupant had good intentions to keep things tidy, but kept finding more important things to do. In contrast to the scattered appearance of most of the room, one corner was perfectly organized. Several shelves were covered with a sea of electronic gadgets, only half of which Mel had any understanding.

It was strange how all the current fiction showed Lycans as alpha-types, but no one ever mentioned the intellectuals of the species. She tucked that fact into the back of her brain; she planned to write a story about Lycans someday. Given that she lived in a pack, surrounded by hunky men, she figured she'd be able to create some kind of plausible tale. But that was for some distant time in the future. Right now, she had a more important problem to deal with.

Finally, Daniel rolled his chair back and spun around to face her. "Sorry to keep you waiting, Mel. I'm working on a job for Bryan and had just hacked into a computer system. I needed to ease my way back out before any alarms started to ring."

She nodded, wondering if alarms really rang when a computer system was breached, but decided not to ask. Half the time, Daniel's explanations went way over her head anyway. "I didn't mind waiting. Actually, Bryan was the one who suggested I talk to you."

Mel walked into the room, perched on the edge of his bed and rubbed her hands over her denim clad thighs. Her palms were damp, betraying her nervousness about the topic she was going to broach.

"Really?" He quirked an eyebrow, then glanced at the computer screen and clicked a few buttons before directing his attention back to her. "What about?"

"You lived with Ryne and his old pack in Oregon, right?"

"Uh-huh. I was raised there, but after that whole incident with Marla and Rose, I felt I needed to make a new start."

"Rose was your girlfriend, right?"

He shrugged. "I guess. We were both kind of quiet and into computers so naturally drifted together, but then Marla started in on her, filling her head with nonsense and..." A flash of regret passed over his face before he shrugged again. "It's all old history."

"Old history. Yeah." Mel exhaled slowly and stared down at her hands. "That's sort of what I'm interested in actually. You know, Ryne never mentions his family or growing up. I really don't know that much about him." She hazarded a peek up at Daniel.

He frowned. "His childhood was rough."

Mel leaned forward, eager to learn whatever she could. "Can you tell me about it?"

"Why don't you ask Ryne?" Daniel leaned back in his chair and laced his fingers behind his head.

She shifted uncomfortably. Darn. He was as tight-lipped as the rest of them. Why couldn't he start spouting off what he knew rather than making her beg? "He's not much into reminiscing and with the baby coming, I guess I'm curious." Mel let her voice drift off, not willing to give Daniel the real reason until she had her facts straight.

The Finding

Daniel cocked his head and studied her, possibly sensing her reticence. After a moment he came to some decision and gave her a half smile. "Why not? You have your reasons I'm sure. And Bryan did send you to me, so it must be okay." Reaching to the side, he rifled through a pile of papers and bags to pull out a box of granola bars. He offered her one, but she shook her head; her stomach was too tied up in knots to be interested in food.

Shrugging in a 'more for me' manner, Daniel selected one for himself. After unwrapping it, he took a bite and stared thoughtfully at the ceiling while chewing. "Well, I'm a few years younger than Ryne you know, but I do recall looking up to him and his brother, Kane. They used to come and go from the pack a lot back then. His father was always on the move."

Mel dug her nails into her palm and prepared herself to listen. There were specific questions she needed the answers to, but didn't dare voice them for fear of raising suspicion. Hopefully, she'd be able to slip a few into the conversation.

Bryan stood in the dingy hallway outside the door to Dollar Niche and listened carefully. The sounds of traffic drifted up from the street below, but from the office there was total silence. All the other doors that led from the hallway were locked and equally quiet; he'd checked them as they'd made their way down the corridor, walking as silently as possible. The old floors had creaked under the weight of each step, the faint noise sounding loud to his sensitive ears. Luckily, any humans that might be about probably wouldn't notice.

He inhaled slowly, filtering through the array of scents and wrinkling his nose at the staleness of the air. Smoke, sweat, fried food, perfume. The smells of humanity wafted around him, the only pleasing scent was that of Cassandra; alluring and spicy, it brought a faint smile to his lips.

She stood behind him, pressing close, waiting for him to announce their next move. The warmth of her body felt good against his and he longed to lean back, bringing them into closer contact, stretching out the moment as long as possible. Unfortunately, they had a job to do and with a sigh, he resisted his body's urging. Besides, it wasn't appropriate for him to view the girl as anything other than a packmate at the moment. If his wolf insisted on being attracted to her, it would have to wait until the situation was more settled.

The animal wasn't pleased, but knew better than to kick up a fuss during the hunt for Kellen. Stalking required concentration. Having one's senses addled by outside concerns could be dangerous. A split second break in focus could lead to deadly results. He repeated these well known facts to himself as he tried to ignore the woman behind him. He shook his head. What had he been thinking when he'd allowed Cassandra to come with him?

True, she wasn't *supposed* to be here. As a matter of fact, he'd left her with strict orders to wait in the rental car since he wasn't sure what he'd be walking into. However, he'd gone no more than half a block from where he'd parked when he'd heard her tiptoeing along behind him, trying her best to hide in doorways and behind lamp posts. When he suddenly turned around, she'd been scrambling to conceal herself behind a garbage bin.

Shaking his head, he'd stalked back to confront her, rolling his eyes when she'd innocently claimed she was stretching her legs.

"I specifically said to wait in the car." He'd glowered at her, but there was only the slightest flicker of acquiescence in her eyes before she'd lifted her chin and glared back at him.

"Kellen's my friend. It's only right that I help rescue him."

"Or get yourself killed by being in a situation you can't handle."

"I can handle myself. I nearly took you in your motel room this morning."

For a moment he'd considered telling her that this morning he'd been trying to be gentle, not wanting to hurt her. If he'd really tried, he could have killed her with very little effort. However, the information would likely have scared her and he was trying to build up a degree of trust between them, not push her further away. He'd sighed heavily and stared at her, trying to decide what to do.

The Finding

Part of him had wanted to show her what happened to disobedient wolves, but he'd reined in his temper. As appealing as it might be to leash her with his belt again and lock her in the car, he knew he really couldn't go around treating her like a common pet; besides someone might see him forcing her transformation. There were lots of windows in the buildings on either side of them.

Knowing he'd really had no choice, he gave a quick nod. "All right. I'll let you come along, but you have to follow my orders. If the thug who took your friend is inside, stay back and let me handle him."

Cassandra had nodded solemnly, though he'd been sure he saw a hint of a smile playing over her lips.

They'd made their way into the building without incident, Dollar Niche being located in a less than prestigious building, which didn't appear to have any form of security. After making their way up the stairs, they'd cautiously approached the door at the end of the hallway. Faded wording on the door proclaimed it to be Dollar Niche's head office and the name Edward Perini was listed beneath. A cardboard sign thumb-tacked to the wall said the two chairs placed by the wall constituted the waiting area.

He noticed Cassandra eyeing the nearby bulletin board covered in flyers and advertisements. Was she wondering if that was where her friend had found her picture? It was a likely theory since Aldrich owned Dollar Niche.

"Do you hear anything?" Cassandra brushed his shoulder lightly with her fingers.

The soft touch sent tingles of awareness through him and he closed his eyes enjoying the sensation before answering her question.

"No. What about you?" He looked over his shoulder at her.

"Me? You're the one with the wolf ears."

"Not only me. You're a purebred Lycan, too. You can hear and smell as well as I can, the only difference is that you haven't been trained how to use your senses." Her face clouded as if she wasn't pleased with his pronouncement, but he ignored it. This was a good opportunity to slip in some Lycan training without

227

her being aware of it. "You know Kellen's scent better than I do. I want you to inhale deeply and tell me if you think he's inside."

It appeared she'd like to protest, but then closed her eyes and did as she was told. Obviously, her concern for her friend was sufficient to make her override her aversion to using her natural talents. On the flip side, his dislike of Kellen was growing by leaps and bounds. He bit back a nasty comment about the man not deserving her and focused instead on the rise and fall of her chest as she checked the scents drifting on the air. The sight of the curving flesh had his fingers twitching and he wondered what it would feel like to cup the soft weight.

He gave his head a shake when he realized the direction his thoughts were taking and forced his gaze up to Cassandra's face. Her brow was furrowed in concentration.

Unaware that he'd been ogling her, she opened her eyes and shook her head. "He's not there now. I can smell him, but it's not strong. Not like when he's in the room with me." The reluctance with which she delivered the information was evident.

"See? You use your abilities every day; you just don't realize it." He pointed the fact out quietly and then straightened, ignoring the pout that had appeared on her face. She didn't like being proven wrong, he decided with an inward chuckle, tucking the detail away for future reference. "It would seem that no one is home, so we might as well go inside and do some snooping."

He tested the handle and found it locked. After double checking that no one was about, he hit the wooden panel with his shoulder and it popped open. Cheap construction, he thought to himself, recalling all the renovations he'd completed on the pack house over the past three years. None of the doors he'd installed would have given in this easily.

Easing the door open a crack, he did a visual check for any sign of alarms or sensors. Finding none, he rolled his eyes; Dollar Niche was definitely a two-bit operation. Now why would a man of Leon Aldrich's purported power, keep his fingers in this particular pie? Shrugging, he stepped inside.

Cassandra followed, quietly closing the door behind her. "Should I turn on the lights?"

"Better not. Someone might come by and realize that the office should be empty." He answered distractedly as he looked around the room. It was rather shabby, and furnished with mismatched chairs and old filing cabinets. Definitely not what he'd expect Aldrich to be associated with.

There was a wooden chair in front of the desk, a single drop of blood on the floor beside it. He bent and touched it with his finger. It was still wet so whoever it had spilled from had been here recently. A quick sniff revealed it had come from Kellen. Tightening his jaw, he glanced up at Cassandra knowing the news would upset her. Opening his mouth to tell her, she spoke first from her position near the desk.

"Here's the flyer Kellen had." She held up a piece of creased paper. "And there's a number on the bottom that you're supposed to call if you find me."

"Really?" He rose to his feet, deciding to put off informing her about her friend for a moment. He took the paper and studied it. "Hmm... Maybe we should call the number and see who answers." Taking out his phone, he ensured his number was blocked from display and then dialled. After a few rings, a woman answered.

"Hello. You've reached the office of Leon Aldrich. How may I help you?"

He froze, shock washing over him. He knew that voice.

"Hello? Hello?" The woman's voice sounded irritated as it echoed from the receiver.

He ended the call, his mind swirling with memories of past betrayals.

"Bryan? What's wrong? Who did you end up calling?" Cassandra looked at him, no doubt puzzled by his stillness.

"Um... It was Aldrich's office."

"My uncle's lawyer?" Cassandra raised her brows in surprise. "I suppose it makes sense that he'd be looking for me. My uncle relied on him heavily so he's probably in charge of the estate." She frowned and shook her head. "I still can't believe he's alive."

"He is. We—the Lycan community—keep close tabs on all his activities, though this particular one, Dollar Niche, somehow escaped our notice."

Cassandra swallowed hard. He could tell she was uncomfortable thinking about why they kept tabs on the man. She exhaled slowly, then continued. "Do you think Mr. Aldrich knows that Eddie and the thug have Kellen?"

He shrugged. "Perhaps. Or maybe they intend to collect the reward money anonymously."

She nodded and looked around. "I guess there's nothing else to be gained by staying here. Kellen's obviously not here. I wonder where they might have taken him."

"We haven't checked the phone yet." He picked up the handset off the desk and had it redial the last number called. He listened intently, then hung up.

"Well?"

"It was the airport."

"Airport? But why?"

"My guess is that they're anticipating capturing you and booked a flight back to Chicago. Premature on their part though, seeing as they don't have you yet."

Cassandra scuffed the floor with her toe. "I guess they know I won't abandon Kellen. And they're right. I might be angry with him over the stunt he tried to pull, but he's still my friend and he did a lot for me over the years. I don't want to go back to Chicago, but I will if it's the only way he'll be safe." She shrugged one shoulder and gave a wobbly laugh. "Besides, there are probably a lot worse fates than being an heiress." Her voice belied her mocking words and he cautiously put an arm around her shoulder. When she didn't pull back, he drew her closer to him until she rested her head on his shoulder.

He hugged her lightly. "Hey, it will be okay. I'll get Daniel on their trail. He'll be able to check the airport records and find out what the plan is on that front. I'm sure he can also find out where Eddie lives as well as any other buildings they might rent. Then we can go searching for Kellen." He eased her away a little and lifted her chin with a finger, ducking his head so he could make eye contact as he teased her gently. "We're not giving up and sending you off to a life of luxury without a fight."

She laughed softly just as he'd hoped and pulled away. "Thanks. Being rich would be too hard for me after three years of living on minimum wages. I don't know if I could fall back into my old ways or not."

He dropped his arm to his side, returning her laugh. "Yeah. Being rich must be tough. It's a fate I've often had nightmares about."

She sighed and then shoved her hands in her back pocket looking around the room. "So what do we do now?"

He cleared his throat and rubbed the back of his neck, thinking of a call he had to make; one he didn't want her to overhear. "Listen, I'm going to call Daniel and get him working on the airport records. That way he might have some news for us by the time we're back to your house. Why don't you head down to the car and get it started. I'll be there in a minute."

"Okay." She nodded and left the office.

Once he was sure she was out of hearing range, he called home. "Daniel? I've got another job for you. Check all the flights out of Vegas, even the private planes. Look for the names Eddie Perini or Kellen Anderson. Oh, and Leon Aldrich's name, too ... Yeah, it's the same guy. Thanks, let me know as soon as you have anything."

He ended the call and then dialled Ryne's cell phone.

"Ryne? Bryan here ... What's that? ... Yeah, I've found Cassandra, but there's a complication ... The problem is her...er...boyfriend's been snatched by some loan sharks and we need to rescue him before she'll even consider moving to Canada ... Yeah, it should be simple, but there's a twist I think you'll find interesting." He paused and chose his words carefully. "Apparently Leon Aldrich is involved ... Yeah, I know it's not surprising given that he's the executor of the Greyson estate, but the real surprise is what I heard when I called Aldrich's office. Brace yourself ... Marla answered the phone."

He held the phone away as a string of loud curses reverberated across the airwaves. Gingerly, he brought the device back to his ear. "I know it's crazy, but I swear it was her voice. I've only heard it a couple of times, but I'm sure I'm not mistaken ... Okay, I'll give you the number. You call and judge for yourself, then let me know your plans."

After sharing the number, he ended the call and slipped the phone back into his pocket. As he exited Dollar Niche he pondered what steps Ryne might take if it was indeed Marla.

Smythston, Oregon, USA...

"It's her." Ryne barked the words down the phone line.

"You're sure?" Kane glared out the window, not really seeing his mate and children as they walked across the yard examining the spring bulbs that were poking their heads up.

"Yeah. I called the number twice, to be sure. Marla is definitely working in Aldrich's offices."

"Shit." Kane gripped the phone tighter as he considered the havoc those two could create together. Their two worst enemies had apparently joined forces. Go figure the odds on that happening. "I wonder how they ended up together."

"I've no idea. I'm wondering if they're working together or not."

"They must be. How could they not be aware of each other?" Kane pinched the bridge of his nose. "It makes no sense though. Aldrich was intent on exposing Lycans and here he has one working with him. Why hasn't he said anything?"

"Maybe they struck a deal? Marla would do anything for money. Or maybe she never told him. There'd be no way for him to find out what she really is."

"True. But why didn't the Chicago pack notice her? They claim to have had him under constant surveillance."

"Probably the same trick she used on us in Smythston; that scent masking perfume."

Kane grunted in acknowledgement. "Now that we know, we need to do something."

"Inform Chicago?"

The Finding

"Hell, no. They've messed this whole thing up from the very beginning, starting with not knowing Cassandra Greyson was a Lycan living in their midst, all the way to being unable to eliminate Aldrich after three years of trying. I say we go in ourselves and take care of it."

"Trespass on their territory? We might ruffle some feathers, Kane. That's breaking the rules."

"So? Since when have you cared about rules?" He perched on the edge of his desk, thinking it was curious that he was the one instigating the situation. It was quite a role reversal for the two of them.

"Good point." Ryne chuckled softly. "Being mated must be making me soft."

"It happens, brother. It happens." Kane smiled thinking of how his own mate, Elise, managed to wrap him around her finger.

"So do we barge into Chicago's territory or do you have a cover in mind?"

Kane thought for a minute. "I think we should take our mates on a vacation. Make it sort of a family reunion."

"Good idea. Mel's been acting strange lately. A vacation might be exactly what she needs."

"Do you think we should tell them exactly why we're going to Chicago?" Kane kept his gaze fixed on Elise. She had the baby on her hip and was listening intently to Jacob as he pointed out something to her. Elise had been rather vocal about him keeping his nose out of Chicago, but...

"Do you really think we'd be able to take them to Chicago and not raise their suspicions?"

Kane exhaled loudly. "Good point. Elise will kick up a fuss I expect, but maybe when she learns Marla's involved, she'll feel differently."

"I expect she will. The woman did try to kill her."

Kane chuckled. "Having someone try to kill you does tend to colour your perception of them." He sobered, the moment of levity quickly passing. "So we'll meet in Chicago, do some reconnaissance, and then formulate a plan to get at Marla and Aldrich, agreed?"

"Agreed. I'll see what flights are available and then get back to you."

"Sounds like a plan." Kane paused and then asked cautiously. "Did you say Mel had been acting weird as of late?"

"Yeah. There's something bugging her, but she won't say what. Even has me blocked out of our mental link. Olivia tells me it's all part of her being pregnant."

Kane was silent. It wasn't his place to say anything, though why Mel was holding back he wasn't sure. He rubbed his chin. "Yeah, Olivia is probably right."

Chicago, Illinois, USA…

Marla stared at the phone in disgust. Not only was she stuck working late, but there'd been several prank calls; no one on the other end, only barely audible breathing then the caller hung up. It wasn't even an obscene phone call, just creepy silence. The caller ID was blocked, so she had no way of knowing who it was without doing an elaborate trace.

Her wolf wasn't at ease with the calls either. It sensed something, but couldn't or wouldn't communicate what it sensed, stupid beast. Why she found herself fighting and arguing with the creature, she had no idea. Lycans were supposed to live in accord with their inner animal. It was her luck that her animal had to be so contrary. All it did these days was whine and complain.

Pursing her lips, she tried to concentrate on the last of her work, eager to clear her desk and then meet up with Jeffries for some tooth rattling sex. The man wasn't very bright, but what he could do with his fingers and tongue was amazing.

She shivered in anticipation while trying to keep the phone calls from creeping back into her mind. It was ridiculous to even give them a second thought. People got prank calls all the time. No one was out to get her; at least no one who'd be making a phone call, that is. A dark alley, walking in a park; those were

The Finding

places for concern, not the penthouse suite. Besides, the security that Aldrich had in place ensured the safety of everyone in the building. No one got in or out without a thorough security check and even then their movements were monitored by hidden surveillance cameras.

Finishing the last form, she stacked the papers into a neat pile and began to shut down her computer. Finally, the day was done and now she could have some fun away from paperwork, e-mails, and annoying prank phone calls. Jeffries was waiting for her and she'd spend a sinfully delightful night with him.

Briefly she considered that perhaps she should be spending the evening working on Aldrich, cozying up to him, pandering to his ego. She hadn't done that in a while and men enjoyed such attention, but Jeffries was so much more fun and responsive. Besides, Aldrich was an old stick.

Thus far she'd fondled and cooed over him, presented herself in revealing dresses and displayed her legs, but the man hadn't made a move yet. Could he be gay? No. She'd seen a bit of tenting in his lap when she'd leaned over him on occasion, rubbing the side of her breast against his arm. He had a physical response to her, but chose not to act upon it, damn his self-control! Never before had she been forced to make the first move, but maybe it was time she changed her game plan. Standards were all well and good, but if they kept you from the main prize, then they might need to be altered. But not tonight. Tonight, Jeffries awaited her.

Gathering her things, she stood in the doorway, force of habit having her scenting the air and listening carefully, locating everyone else in the penthouse.

Swanson, the security officer, was in his office, faint clicks and whirs letting her know he was reviewing surveillance tapes. The housekeeper was washing dishes in the kitchen and Aldrich was working in his office, coughing slightly. Sylvia's footsteps could be heard heading towards Aldrich's office. The woman was humming under her breath. A growl escaped Marla's lips as she considered the nurse. Aldrich's lack of interest was partially that woman's fault, as hard as it was to admit.

235

Marla proceeded to the elevator, her stiletto heels clicking on the terrazzo tiles. With more force than necessary, she punched in the security code that would summon the elevator. Over the electronic hum of the elevator, Sylvia's humming could still be heard. It was a damned annoying habit. Getting rid of the woman would have to become a priority. As the elevator doors opened, Marla wondered if it was possible to arrange for Sylvia to fall down the shaft. Hmm... She'd have to research that, but right now, there were more important things to be concerned about. Tossing her hair over her shoulders she entered the compartment and pressed the button for the lowest level.

As the door slid shut, she had the briefest glimpse of Sylvia standing in the shadows watching her. Now why would the woman do that? And what was that strange expression on her face?

"Something's gone wrong." Franklin paced the kitchen of the Greyson estate, running his hands agitatedly through his hair.

"Calm down, just calm down." Mrs. Teasdale murmured the words as she endlessly added pepper to the simmering pot on the stove. "Wearing a hole in the floor and stressing yourself into a heart attack won't help Miss Cassie."

"And adding a whole pot of pepper to the soup won't either." He pointed out what she was doing. Mrs. Teasdale gave a gasp, set the pepper down and turned off the burner under the now ruined soup. "What are we going to do?"

He shook his head. "Meredith sounded so sure this morning that this new young man was one of them and I concurred with her assessment of the situation. Her description of him and his behaviour indicated a strong probability that he was a werewolf. Now it appears there's been a violent struggle in the house. If he's interested in her joining his pack, he would have treated her well."

"Perhaps it wasn't this young fellow who caused the problem. Maybe it was someone else?" Mrs. Teasdale's voice quivered as she offered the vague hope.

The Finding

He pursed his lips. "Or perhaps Mr. Greyson was right to be cautious in approaching a pack. Maybe this pack felt she didn't meet their criteria and decided to do away with her. He always said if he found a pack, he'd have guards on hand to take her to safety in case she wasn't accepted. I thought he was too cautious; that a pack would willingly accept a young female." His voice trailed off and he dropped down into a nearby chair, hunching his shoulders, his hands clasped in front of him. "What if I was wrong? What if my grand scheme leads to her downfall?"

Mrs. Teasdale placed a comforting hand on his shoulder. "It won't. And it wasn't just you. When we found out where she was, we weighed the options together and both agreed on the course of action every step of the way. From letting her live her own life, to sending the anonymous personal ad to that little newspaper in Ontario."

"We tried to lure the pack to her, but were never sure if that worked or not," Franklin mused staring sightlessly at the floor. "Mr. Greyson's private files on that last project only indicated that the reporter was working in the Stump River area, not that the pack was actually there."

"It was all we had to go on at the time and there was no way of verifying their existence without stirring up more trouble."

"But it wasn't enough. Meredith watched her carefully for the next month and nothing unusual happened."

"Short of posting her address or where she worked, I don't know what else we could have done. You've told me over and over that subtlety is important in dealing with these wolves."

He sighed and stared morosely across the room. "We did our best to lure the Ontario pack to her and to the best of our knowledge it didn't work."

"Or the fools found her and rejected her."

He nodded. "That could also be the case. Either way, for two years we've sat twiddling our thumbs."

"Waiting and praying for something to happen." Mrs. Teasdale nodded. "And now when there's finally some hope on the horizon, a new glitch occurs."

Franklin grunted and rubbed his eyes. "So what do we do? Do I call in some old favours and send in a team to rescue her? I'm sure I could think up a plausible story without giving her true heritage away."

"Or do we trust in fate? Meredith Mitchell didn't know for sure who had been struggling in the house. When she peeked in the window, no one was about. Perhaps Miss Cassie wasn't involved. Perhaps it was that Kellen fellow who was in trouble."

Franklin gave a short, dry laugh. "A few hours ago, I was the one reassuring you."

She patted his shoulder. "That's what friends are for, Franklin. I say we wait a bit, let Meredith do some more snooping around before we act. If we jump in too soon, we may inadvertently ruin Miss Cassie's chances of bonding with a suitable young man."

Reluctantly, he nodded. "All right. We'll wait for Meredith's next report. I just hope nothing happens to Miss Cassie because we waited too long to act."

Chapter 15

Las Vegas, Nevada, USA…

Cassie paced her living room. She had to do something. Inaction was killing her. She wrapped her arms around her body, her fingers digging into her flesh. At least the pain took her mind off her mental turmoil over this new twist.

After leaving Dollar Niche, they'd driven back to the house. Bryan had been quiet, seemingly lost in thought and she wondered what he was thinking about. The man didn't know Kellen, so it was unlikely he'd be that perturbed over the abduction. Something else was bothering him and she was sure it had to do with the phone call he'd made to the number on the poster.

But whatever it was, he hadn't been inclined to share. After a few unsuccessful attempts at starting a conversation, she'd stayed silent and had begun to plot her next move. Bryan's friend Daniel might come up with something, but just in case, she wanted to be ready.

She'd been in the middle of listing steps in her head—finish packing her bag, withdraw the cost of the airfare from her savings account—when the car pulled into the driveway. Bryan had jerked it to a stop and started swearing, leaving the vehicle before she even had time to register what was going on.

When she finally got out and made her way to the front door, he had tried to block her view of something, but it was her home and she wasn't about to let him tell her what to do. Pushing him aside, she'd taken one look and gasped, stepping back in shock. A picture of Kellen had been taped to the front door.

He was badly beaten; his lip split, his eye swollen shut; she'd wanted to cry. A note had accompanied the picture as well. Kellen was being held for ransom and she had to go to Chicago if she wanted him set free. There was a phone number to call for further instructions, once she arrived.

Terrified, she'd suggested they go to the authorities, but Bryan had been adamant. Involving 'humans' would endanger werewolves. She'd argued against him, but he'd been unyielding on the point, assuring her they could take care of the matter on their own.

Exactly how this was going to happen, she didn't know. Surely it would be better to send the police after the perpetrators? It was a fact that Eddie Perini and his thug had taken Kellen and left what was basically a ransom note. Wouldn't that be enough information to cause the police to act?

Bryan had murmured that Leon Aldrich was involved, as if that mattered. Whether the man was paying a finder's fee to Eddie for bringing her in, or whether he was masterminding the whole situation, she didn't know. Nor did she really care. So what if the man was involved? The police could sort the whole mess out, including whatever part Mr. Aldrich was playing.

She hadn't thought much about Mr. Aldrich over the past few years, or rather when she did think of him, it was to recall his horrific death. Only, he wasn't dead and that fact seemed to give her freedom to recall other things about the man. She'd never formally met him despite the fact he was often at the house meeting with her uncle. Sometimes, she'd sneak downstairs and spy on them, her back pressed against the smooth panelling or crouched under a draped table. While she'd never really understood what was being discussed, she'd enjoyed the grand trick she was playing on the adults.

Looking back now, she recalled how the man had always made her uncomfortable. He'd been obsequious to her uncle; outwardly subservient and yet she suspected it was all an act, that he secretly held her uncle in contempt. And now the man was in charge of her uncle's estate. In fact, when she returned to her proper place as the Greyson heiress, she'd have to work closely with him. The idea made her feel ill; she didn't trust the man at all, but she pushed that aside. Returning to her life as Cassandra Greyson and dealing with the likes of Mr. Aldrich was a small price to pay for Kellen's life.

Her arguments had fallen on deaf ears; Bryan was in a foul mood, actually snarling at her when she mentioned yet again that Kellen's safety was her only priority.

"You'll not risk yourself for him or for anyone." His eyes had glowed with an inner power that had her quaking in her shoes and she'd even seen a flash of his canines. The very thought of what those sharp teeth could do had been enough to still her protests.

She'd clamped her mouth tightly shut and he'd turned away, his displeasure palpable. If she didn't know better, she'd have said he was jealous of Kellen, which was ridiculous. They'd just met. Bryan hardly knew her.

She settled in a chair, watching Bryan warily out of the corner of her eye. That snarl had shocked her. For long periods of time she was actually forgetting he was a werewolf, but the fact had been brought abruptly home moments earlier. He might appear civilized, but underneath, he was still an animal with an animal's instincts. There was no doubt about it; Bryan could be dangerous. She clasped her hands tightly together and wondered why that fact was oddly thrilling.

He was on the computer again, re-checking flights to Chicago, searching for better seats. His friend, Daniel, had confirmed that a private plane had been chartered by Mr. Aldrich and had flown out of McCarran International Airport headed for Chicago. She was anxious to follow, but the earliest flight they could get was tomorrow morning.

It was nerve wracking having to wait around. She wanted to distract herself, but there was nothing to do. The house was clean, her bag was packed. Seeking to occupy her mind, she began studying Bryan.

At first glance, he appeared normal enough, but there was something about him; a certain aura that set her whole equilibrium off balance. It wasn't just the fact that he was good looking. It was the way he carried himself; ease and self-assurance shining through. If he was in a room with well dressed, high-powered business men, he'd be perfectly confident in his casual attire of jeans and shirt.

His shirt—was it only a few hours ago that she'd been forced to wear it?—clung to his muscular body, highlighting his shoulders and back. She remembered the feel of those muscles shifting beneath her hand as she clung to him in the park, his body pressed to hers, his arousal evident against her belly. The memory had her shifting uncomfortably at the thought of how abandoned the beast inside her had acted. It had revelled in his touch, rubbing against him, whimpering in pleasure.

The animal stirred and she forced it back down, shifting her gaze from his body. She wasn't letting the creature get the upper hand again. Who knew what might happen next time?

A ray of sunlight fell across the room and she concentrated on it instead. Tiny motes of dust floated in the air, creating an elaborate dance that led across the room. Her eyes traced the path they took, the beam of light eventually shining on the back of Bryan's head, highlighting the strands of his hair. It was a sandy brown with a hint of a wave and had felt thick and silky against her fingers. She gave a silent gasp when she realized what was happening; she was back to thinking about him again.

Resignedly, she admitted that the man did interest her, but it was nothing more than an appreciation of male beauty, she assured herself. Any woman would react to his physical charms. Thus reassured, she allowed her eyes to wander over his profile, drinking in each feature. Light brown hair hung over his forehead and he occasionally frowned and brushed it back as he stared at the screen. His brows and lashes were darker than his hair and accented his hazel eyes perfectly. A straight nose and strong chin. His lips were firm, the lower one slightly full. She recalled how he had an almost boyish look about him when he grinned. Right now his mouth was anything but grinning. It was firmly closed as something on the screen obviously annoyed him.

Mmm... His lips had felt wonderful when they had moved against her own. Would she ever have cause to kiss him again?

The Finding

Not likely, she decided with a small pout then forced herself to assume an air of indifference. Once Kellen was free, she'd find a way to send Bryan packing; he meant nothing to her, after all. So what if there was some law that said she had to go with him? Being a rich heiress would surely afford her some immunity from werewolf laws, wouldn't it? He'd head back to Canada and she'd never have to set eyes on him again.

The thought of never seeing him again had her frowning, which was ridiculous. She gave herself a mental scolding. He was a werewolf, for heaven sake; nothing more than a filthy animal.

And yet, isn't that exactly what we are? A voice inside queried. Part of her wanted to immediately reject the idea, but she forced herself to look at it.

Yes, she was a werewolf. She couldn't deny the fact, but that didn't mean she had to act like it. Attacking people, giving in to an animal wildness once a month wasn't for her. No, she was stronger than that. It wasn't easy, but she'd managed thus far and she would continue to do so.

But it's getting harder each month, the voice reminded her.

The pills were losing their effectiveness, she acknowledged reluctantly and increasing the dosage might prove dangerous.

Wouldn't it be better to learn from other werewolves how to handle our existence, rather than fighting to subdue it?

Her stomach quivered at the very idea, yet it was intriguing too. Hadn't she spent hours on the internet researching, wishing she understood, wishing she knew what was fact and what was fiction?

Being a werewolf might be exciting and freeing in a way we could never imagine; there could be joys and wonders in the lifestyle too fantastic to be denied.

She licked her lips nervously and eyed Bryan. There was one thing that might be interesting to explore... But, what if once she started to learn about werewolves and her inner beast, she became too caught up in them and lost herself? She could end up like Kellen, constantly fighting the inner demons that made him gamble.

But, the voice pressed its case, *what if instead of losing ourself, we find ourself? What if the lost, lonely feeling that's plagued us all our life, is finally replaced with a sense of peace, of belonging? Are we willing to turn our back on the chance, now that the opportunity has finally arisen?*

"What are you doing?"

She startled, realizing that while she'd been lost in thought, Bryan had moved and now was standing in front of her.

"Just thinking."

"From your expression I'd say they were pretty deep thoughts."

She pulled her legs up to her chest and clasped her arms around her knees. "They were."

Bryan sat down on the sofa beside her, seeming to be in a better mood now. The cushions sank under his weight causing her to slide sideways until their hips were touching. With assumed casualness, she eased herself away and placed a hand on the arm of the chair, hanging on to prevent herself from sliding back against him.

He didn't appear to notice. "Our flight is early tomorrow morning; it's the best I could get. Ryne is flying in to Chicago and so is Kane. He's Ryne's brother and the Alpha of another pack. Their mates are coming along too, so you'll be able to meet some female Lycans."

She gave him a half smile, not really sure if she wanted to meet more of her kind or not. The conversation she'd had with herself—such a strange concept really, to be talking to another living thing inside you—had made her reconsider her outright denial of anything werewolf related. Bryan was nice enough when he wasn't snarling at her, but she still wasn't too sure about the others. Ryne was the one she'd seen attacking Mr. Aldrich, after all. The Alpha probably didn't have a kind bone in his body. She pitied his poor mate.

She picked at an invisible piece of lint. "Is it typical for so many werewolves to get involved when a problem arises?"

"It depends on the problem. Usually, enacting the Finding clause is pretty simple. You find a wolf, bring it home, and

244

integrate it into the pack. Unfortunately, in your case there are a few more issues involved."

"Issues?" She flicked a glance in his direction.

"Kellen." He made a face when he said the name. "And some other old business that the Alphas have to deal with."

She nodded and then stood up, still uncomfortably aware of his body so close to hers. "It's late. Would you like something to eat?"

"Sure." He followed her into the kitchen and leaned against the counter, watching her pull some hamburgers from the freezer and put them in the microwave to thaw.

"I'm not a great cook. Being a *rich heiress*, there was never a need to learn, but I can manage burgers and a salad, I think." She gave a self-deprecating laugh.

"I'm not too bad in the kitchen." He moved to the fridge and took out some lettuce. "Ryne, Daniel, and I lived on our own for a while and learned to make do. Then, when Mel mated Ryne, she wasn't much into cooking either, except for making gourmet coffees. So we still all took our shifts at the stove."

As they continued to prepare the food, she found herself smiling while listening to Bryan share small tidbits from his life. If it wasn't for the fact that they were werewolves, she'd think he lived in a large extended family. She paused in the middle of flipping a burger. Was that what a pack was? A large extended family? Previously she'd envisioned them living in primitive conditions, roaming the woods and taking down elk for food. But Bryan was adept in the kitchen; and he talked about their media room and how everyone fought for control of the TV. It didn't match her preconceived notions at all.

During dinner, Bryan announced he'd be spending the night. She opened her mouth to argue, but the look on his face made her give in. Angrily, she chewed on her burger realizing this would interfere with her half-formed plans to head to the airport tonight and to wait there in the hopes of getting a standby seat. She didn't need Bryan's help to rescue Kellen. And it would be a perfect opportunity to escape his crazy plan of taking her back to Canada with him.

Had Bryan known this? She eyed him speculatively, but he gave no indication that he was gloating over thwarting her plans. Sighing, she decided it was probably a coincidence.

After dinner, they wandered outside to watch the sunset. Bryan had been boasting of the beautiful northern lights that filled the Canadian skies; streaks of dancing light in every colour of the rainbow, shooting across the evening sky in undulating waves. She had to admit it sounded amazing, but she wanted him to see a desert sunset before deciding which celestial event was the most spectacular.

They leaned against the railing that encircled the small backyard deck, watching the light slowly fade and give way to fiery washes of orange and red. The colours slowly grew and spread, intensifying until the entire sky was ablaze.

"Impressive." Bryan murmured the words, his shoulder brushing hers, his eyes fixed on the sky. She smiled as she cast him a sideways look.

"Not everything in Canada is better." She boasted, tongue in cheek.

He slanted a look at her. "Not better. Just different."

She turned to face him suddenly feeling playful. "I hear it can get pretty cold."

"Uh-huh. In the winter it does." He shrugged, but kept his eyes fixed to the sky.

"So I guess you don't mind the snow and the ice?" She twirled her glass of ice water in her hands. The evening was proving to be exceptionally warm and cold drinks had sounded more suitable than coffee after dinner.

"Not really. You get used to it."

"Good." She giggled and quickly grabbed an ice cube from her glass, dumping it down the back of his shirt.

"Hey!"

His shout of surprise was ample reward for her efforts and she managed to lob another ice cube at him while he tried to fish the first one out of his shirt. He growled and stepped towards her, but she quickly turned, running down the steps to the ground level, laughing at his expression.

The Finding

Unfortunately, her reflexes were slower than his for she'd barely taken half a dozen strides when he caught hold of her arm.

"Cassandra!" She tried to break free, but he spun her around and held her tight to his body while he reached back to extract the ice cube from his shirt.

"I'm the pack Beta, little girl. You're not supposed to mess with me." He spoke sternly, but the corners of his mouth twitched upward and the twinkle in his eye gave him away.

"Oh yeah?"

"Yeah." He held the dripping ice cube up. "You deserve a taste of your own medicine." And with that he hooked a finger into the neckline of her shirt and popped the ice down her top.

"Bryan!" She screeched as the cold came in contact with her skin, and tried to grab at it, but he caught hold of her other hand, locking her arms behind her back. She squirmed trying to avoid the ice, but there was no escape. It was trapped between her body and his, slowly melting and dripping freezing water down her stomach.

"So how do you like it?" He chuckled down at her and she looked up ready to give a cutting retort when their eyes locked and the comment died in her throat.

In that moment she was all too aware of the fact that they were pressed together from knee to chest, that his strong hands were holding her delicate wrists, that his mouth was mere inches from hers.

The moment stretched out between them. Light from the setting sun cast shadows on his face, showing his features in relief. She could see the flecks of gold and green in his eyes, the brown lashes framing them, the faint stubble on his chin. He inhaled and of its own volition the tip of her tongue darted out, wetting her lips.

Slowly he leaned closer, releasing her hands and sliding his fingers gently up her arms. Anticipation grew. She held her breath, her eyelids lowering. Then, just when she had begun to raise herself up on her toes, sure he was going to kiss her, he gripped her elbows and stepped back.

With a thump, she came back to awareness of the fact that she was in the middle of her backyard with a man she barely knew and that she'd almost kissed him. What had come over her? Why had she started to tease him like that? And the kiss—well, the almost kiss—he probably thought she was coming on to him. She felt her cheeks flush with embarrassment. How could she have... A whimper sounded inside her head and she halted her racing thoughts, then frowned darkly. No doubt it was the animal's fault.

Clearing her throat, she looked around awkwardly, no longer caring about the ice melting inside her shirt. Should she explain that it wasn't her? Apologize for the beast's behaviour? "Um..."

Bryan spoke at the same moment. "I didn't get much sleep last night. I think I'm going to turn in. Our flight leaves early."

"Right. Good idea." She grasped onto the idea, as if it were a lifeline and she were drowning.

She led the way inside and prepared for bed, still mulling over what had occurred. The scene had been so unexpected, yet so *normal*, as if she were a regular young woman entertaining her boyfriend. And it had been fun to play with him, to act young and carefree for a change. If Bryan wasn't a werewolf, she could find her human self attracted to him. But that wasn't going to happen. No werewolf boyfriends for her!

But who else would you be attracted to? The annoying voice inside her asked. *You're a werewolf too. You tried to have a relationship with Kellen, but he wasn't our kind. You'll never find a human who you can truly be yourself with. Any relationship you try to build will be based on lies and deception as you hide your real self.*

She curled up in her bed, glumly considering the fact that the voice was right. She could never foist this burden on someone else. And sharing her secret was forbidden. Her life stretched ahead of her, long and lonely. She closed her eyes. At least she'd be rich and lonely, if that was any consolation.

She drifted into a restless sleep, werewolves still uppermost in her mind. The image of a large house filled with fellow werewolves formed. It was a happy home, children laughing and playing on the floor, men and women lounging in front of the

The Finding

TV. She was there too, curled up at Bryan's side, but totally unaware of what was on the screen. His arm was around her shoulder, his fingers rubbing circles on her skin while her own hand rested on his stomach.

It was nice. Comfortable. He pressed a kiss to her forehead and she snuggled in closer, breathing in his scent and absorbing the warmth of his body. She felt his hand drift down and cup her breast, his thumb gently stroking the tip. It pebbled in response and she shifted, feeling herself moisten in anticipation.

Slowly she worked a finger between the buttons of his shirt and stroked the skin of his abdomen. His muscles flinched at her touch and she giggled, repeating the gesture, teasing his navel. A low growl reverberated in his chest and before she knew what was happening, he scooped her up and carried her to bed, the rest of the room's occupants barely glancing up as they passed by, too absorbed in their television show to care about the antics of young lovers.

As he lowered her onto the mattress, Cassie laced her fingers behind Bryan's neck, pulling his head down until her lips met his. He braced himself over her so that only their lips touched. It was the briefest of connections, but electricity zinged between them, tingling deliciously. She exhaled softly, allowing her breath to feather over his face and mix with his own. A feeling of rightness filled her; this was where she was meant to be.

Their lips brushed, retreated, then brushed again, teasing, before finally settling on each other. Gentle pressure, tender nips. Angling her head, she captured his mouth, pulling on his lower lip before sealing her mouth to his. His tongue traced her lips and she opened wider for him; his tongue dipping in and stroking hers. She reciprocated the gesture, savouring his taste.

He brushed her cheek with the back of his hand then threaded his fingers into her hair, tugging lightly. She loved the feel of the gentle pull and murmured appreciatively, splaying her fingers over his cheekbones, tracing the shape of his ears, the slant of his jaw. Evening stubble roughened his skin and she revelled in the feel of it against her palms.

249

Heat built between them and soon the tender caresses weren't enough. She wanted to feel him pressed against her and pulled at his shoulders, whimpering in need. Bryan responded, lowering himself onto her, pinning her to the mattress. Eagerly, she let her hands roam his back, tracing the indent of his spine to his waistband and then back up again. Spreading her fingers, she gently raked his skin with her nails.

He groaned in approval and pressed his hips closer to hers. Instinctively, she spread her thighs so she could cradle him closer and was rewarded by a ridge of flesh grinding against her apex. A rush of warmth and an accompanying ache had her pushing up towards him.

Bryan broke from the kiss and trailed his lips over her jaw, down her neck to the sweet spot where it joined her shoulder. He nuzzled the area, then licked and grazed it with his teeth. Her breathing hitched as shivers of excitement coursed through her body.

"Bryan." She exhaled his name and pulled her hands free from his shirt to clutch his head, burying her fingers in his hair.

"You're so beautiful." He breathed the words into her ear and warmth flooded her heart. Had anyone ever said those words to her with such conviction, such feeling?

"So are you." She exhaled the words, eyes half-closed, tracing his face with her fingertips. His every feature was precious to her; the curve of his brow, the slant of his nose. He nipped her finger as it brushed his mouth, then sucked on it, slowly, sensually while sliding his hand down to cup her breast; the heat of his palm burning through the layers of material.

Suddenly she was desperate to feel his lips on more of her flesh and tried to guide his head down to her breast. He resisted, torturing her by slowly trailing his lips over her throat, licking the hollow at its base then nipping her collar bone. Finally, he moved lower to the V-neck of her t-shirt, and then latched onto her nipple through the cloth. The material was soon damp and abraded her skin. She arched her back, wanting more sensation, more heat, more Bryan.

The Finding

Bryan worked his hands under the hem of her shirt and eased it upwards, all the while suckling her through the cloth. When he finally broke away to finish removing her shirt, she nearly cried out from the loss.

The shirt was tossed aside and he reared back to stare down at her, his gaze hot, his chest heaving. Suddenly, she felt shy and her face heated. She was unsure what to do and stiffened. Desire that had flamed so hot moments before banked and she looked up at him through her lashes, fighting the need to cover herself.

Somehow, he seemed to know for his features softened, the hot needy look faded. Now he leaned forward slowly, gently. Tenderly, he cupped her face and pressed a kiss to her forehead before shifting so he lay beside her. He gathered her close and gently stroked her body, playing his fingers over her ribs, fingering the band of her bra then retreating down to cup her hip.

Gradually, she relaxed and the heat of desire returned. She snuggled in closer, subtly arching her back in encouragement and he picked up on her hint. His hand moved up to cup her breast through the lacy material then slid to the front clasp of her bra.

He gave her a questioning look and she bit her lip, but nodded. The material released and her breasts spilled free. Bryan hissed as he stared down at her bared flesh, then his hands covered them, kneading and tweaking, sending spasms of desire to her core. When he dipped his head to flick his tongue over one tip, she thought she'd die from the feeling. First one side, then the other, he paid homage to her breasts until she was nothing but a panting bundle of need.

She pulled his shirt free from his pants and slid her hands under the material. His skin was hot and smooth. She allowed her hands to roam; over his ribs, his back, down to his waistband and then back up to bury in his hair, tugging lightly on the silken locks. Bryan shuddered in appreciation and then sat up, abruptly pulling his shirt off, before leaning over her again, kissing her cheekbones, her nose, her forehead.

With trembling fingers, she rubbed his chest, caressing his stomach then tracing the border of his waistband. Her fingers fumbled as she undid the button and slid down his zipper. Then, with a trembling hand she slid beneath the material, exploring the thatch of body hair she encountered there. A source of heat was just beyond her finger tips and she steeled herself to reach lower. How would it feel to touch a man so intimately? Her palm tingled in anticipation.

"Yes! Touch me. I need to feel you holding me." He whispered the words, his hips undulating gently and she moved to comply, but something held her back.

Was she ready for this? Part of her screamed yes, but another part hesitated. You don't really know him. He's a werewolf. What are you getting yourself into?

"Cassie, please. Now. I can't wait much longer." There was desperation in his voice and she felt tears begin to form. She wanted to please him, but... "You did it for him. For Kellen." He spat the word out and she winced, shamed at the truth.

"I'm sorry. I didn't mean to. It was an accident. I'll...I'll make it up to you!" Taking a deep breath, she tried to move her hand lower, but Bryan was fading away. "No. Don't go! I...I can be what you need. Please give me a chance!"

But he didn't listen and in an instant she awoke in her bed, weeping from rejection. Hot tears streamed down her face as she reached out her hand to touch the pillow and sheets beside her. The other side of the bed was empty and cold. She was alone; always alone.

Bryan woke with a start, his heart pounding, his skin covered in sweat. He was on the couch in Cassandra Greyson's living room, having refused her offer of sleeping in Kellen's room. It wasn't the other guy's fault exactly, but he had taken a dislike to the man and anything associated with him. True, Kellen had cared for Cassandra and had been her support during a time when he hadn't been around, but it still felt as if the other man had trespassed. His wolf was intent on claiming Cassandra and he wasn't sure if he'd ever be able to talk the creature out of its fixation with the girl.

The Finding

Throwing back the light blanket that covered him, he grimaced, realizing he'd found release during the incredibly erotic dream he'd just had. He hadn't done that since his early teenage years. Rubbing his face with his hand, he peered at the clock; four-thirty. They had to be up in another hour and he wasn't feeling sleepy anymore.

With a sigh he stood and grabbed yesterday's clothes, heading to the bathroom to get cleaned up. He hadn't gone back to his hotel the previous night, not completely trusting Cassandra. Exactly what she might do on her own, he wasn't sure, but he wasn't taking any chances. He wouldn't put it past her to try to travel to Chicago without him; perhaps heading to the airport and hoping to get a standby flight. The look of dismay in her face when he announced he was staying led him to believe he wasn't too far off the mark.

He shook his head. There was a headstrong streak in her that would get her into trouble one of these days. As her Beta, he intended to be around to pull her out of whatever mess she landed in.

By time he was done showering, a light was showing under Cassandra's door. Good. She was up. They could head back to his motel to pick up his things and then grab a fast food breakfast on the way to the airport. Knocking lightly on her door, he relayed the plan to her and then headed back to the living room to wait.

He hoped everything would go according to plan in Chicago. If it did, they'd find Kellen and set him free, deal with Eddie and his associate then get tickets back to Canada. Ryne and Kane could take care of Aldrich and Marla and by tomorrow, everyone would be heading back home.

He rolled his eyes and snorted. Yeah. Right. When did things ever go that smoothly for him?

Chapter 16

Chicago, Illinois, USA…

Mel stretched and yawned, tired of travelling. The flight to Chicago had been unremarkable, the only real issue being that they'd had to leave Stump River in the middle of the night to drive to Toronto. Beyond that, time was spent waiting to go through security checks, waiting to board, waiting to disembark, waiting to find their luggage; all the typical tedious tasks of travel.

Ryne had blatantly used his good looks and commanding presence to hurry their own passage through the system. Crowds parted when he walked by, a look had others letting him in line while the female employees hurried to do his bidding when he graced them with his slow, sexy smile. Finally, they were climbing into a taxi bound for the motel where they were all planning to meet.

As the taxi pulled away from the curb, Mel hit him in the stomach.

He grunted and looked at her in surprise. "What was that for?"

"You basically bullied your way through the airport. No one dared say no to you."

"So? You didn't want to spend all that time waiting, did you? And it wasn't bullying. I never said anything threatening."

"No. But it wasn't really fair to the other passengers to use your Alpha status on them."

He shrugged. "If you've got it, why not use it."

Mel rolled her eyes. Her mate was arrogant to the extreme at times and could be unremorsefully rude. Still, it had paved their way through the airport. She rubbed the curve of her stomach and shifted to a more comfortable position. The baby had to be lying on her bladder.

"Are you all right?" Ryne's attitude melted away and he was suddenly all care and concern; brushing her hair from her face, putting an arm around her shoulders.

"I'm fine." She smiled at him and then looked away, feeling guilty. Even after her standoffishness this week, he was still looking out for her. She knew she'd been weepy and irritable, that he found her behaviour inexplicable. The fact that she'd even blocked the mental connection afforded by their blood bond had hurt him. Yet, in her own defence, she hadn't known what else to do.

The news she'd received had thrown her completely off kilter; the possible implications had made her shudder. However, now that Daniel had reassured her and helped her sort out the mess with Lycan Link, she wasn't sure how to broach the topic with Ryne. Last night, she'd just gathered her courage when this surprise trip to Chicago was announced. Packing, gathering passports, rushing to the airport. She shook her head; it had left no time for intimate conversation.

Hopefully, this business with Aldrich could be taken care of quickly. Mel wasn't sure what the brothers had planned but sometimes ignorance was bliss. And then there was this woman, Marla, who had apparently wreaked havoc with the pack long before she'd met Ryne.

Mel knew part of the story; murder, attempted murder, theft, betrayal; the list of sins went on and on. From the look in Ryne's eyes when he mentioned the woman... Well, Mel was just glad she wasn't Marla.

The cab pulled up to the motel and Ryne helped her out of the back seat. Their rooms were pre-booked and supposedly across the hall from Bryan and Cassandra's. Her lips quirked mischievously as she contemplated the fact that the two were sharing. Bryan's obsessive interest in the girl over the past three years hadn't gone unnoticed. She was curious to find out if their face to face meeting had lived up to his subconscious expectations. If the room booking was any indication, it must have!

Kane and Elise had a room down the hall. It would be interesting to finally meet Kane in person, Mel mused, especially given her recent discovery. She wondered if Kane was anything like Ryne and how he'd react to meeting her. She was sure she and Elise would get along, but Kane was more aloof, always preoccupied with pack business. Webcam visits were fine, but not the same as seeing the man in the flesh. A number of possible scenarios had played out in her mind during the flight; she wondered which one would become fact.

"Melody?" Ryne spoke her name and she looked up at him, suddenly realizing they were standing in front of the elevator.

"Sorry, I was thinking about meeting Kane and Elise."

He guided her into the elevator and pushed the button for the third floor. "You'll get along fine, I'm sure." He yawned and stretched. "I can't believe we had to catch such an early flight. Kane and Elise aren't due in for another couple of hours, so you have time for a nap if you'd like."

"That would be nice, especially if you join me." She let her hand drift down his back and cup his rear.

"Melody?" He shot her a look full of both surprise and hot arousal. Well, he would be surprised given the cold shoulder she'd been showing him this past week. When he found out the cause though, he'd understand.

Mel smiled up at him wickedly. "We have some lost time to make up for, don't you think?'

Ryne didn't question her sudden about-face. Instead, he growled and pulled her closer, nuzzling her neck, then grazing her mating mark with his teeth. Excitement shot straight to her core. How had she done without this for so long?

She felt him probing her mentally and hesitated before pushing on his shoulders until he eased back.

"Melody?" His look was questioning, hurt.

Mel looked down, not sure what to say, how to broach the subject. She'd never thought herself a coward, but she wasn't sure of Ryne's reaction.

Ryne sighed heavily, then wrapped his arms around her and pulled her close, tucking her head under his chin. "It's okay. Whatever's going on, whenever you're ready to tell me, know I'll be here for you."

"I love you, Ryne." She kissed an exposed spot at the base of his neck and spread her hands over his chest.

"I know. I love you, too." He swept her up into his arms and kissed her thoroughly. "Let me show you how much." The words were whispered against her lips and she melted into him not even noticing the elevator door sliding open as they arrived at their floor.

Mmm. Maybe if she were lucky, Kane and Elise's flight would be delayed.

Las Vegas, Nevada, USA...

Cassie nibbled her lip and cast yet another sidelong glance at Bryan. He sat beside her reading a magazine and hadn't spoken a dozen words to her since they'd boarded the plane. She turned to look out the window, but since it was overcast there was really nothing to see. Flying in a cloud could be so boring. The magazine in her own lap lay there unopened; gossip about celebrities held no interest for her.

She exhaled softly and continued contemplating Bryan's sudden reticence. It wasn't as if he was a chatter box, but at least yesterday he'd been relaxed around her, talking casually. Now he was so formal and uptight. Was he angry? Had she done something wrong? Made some strange werewolf faux pas?

In her mind, she went over the events of the morning, but found nothing unusual. He'd been showering when she got up. She packed a small bag of essentials, some of which were already in her carryall from her planned escape the previous day. Then they'd gone to his motel to collect his things and he'd checked out of his room. At the drive-thru they'd ordered breakfast sandwiches and ate them at the airport while awaiting their flight. She shook her head; it all seemed ordinary enough.

The Finding

At first, she'd been happy not to talk. Her dream last night had been both erotic and confusing; the memory leaving her embarrassed to face him. After all, it wasn't every day that she dreamed of having her hands down the pants of a man she'd just met. And then, at the end when she'd suddenly froze. What was that all about? Her past was just that, her past.

It had been bad enough when her nocturnal imaginings were about being a wolf and meeting another wolf in the forest, but now that wolf was being replaced by a human.

Her train of thought stuttered to a halt. Wait a minute. The wolf in her dreams? Could it be Bryan? She had only a vague recollection of what he'd looked like as a wolf when he'd chased her down in the park, but surely it was the same creature! Suddenly, she had to know.

"Bryan?"

"Hmm?" He answered vaguely and didn't look up from his magazine. Had he even really heard her? She suppressed the need to hit him and sighed.

Maybe it was easier if he wasn't looking at her. His eyes always seemed to be seeing right into her mind, as if he knew her very thoughts and these definitely were not thoughts she wanted to share with him. If she asked in an idle manner, he'd never have to know. After a moment's debate, she decided to try again.

"Bryan? What do you look like? When you're a wolf, I mean?" She kept her eyes averted as she tried to casually whisper her question, conscious of the passengers around them.

Out of the corner of her eye she saw him close his magazine and look at her quizzically. "Most wolves have similar colouring to their human form, though not all. I'm a light brown with hazel eyes. Why do you want to know?"

She gulped. That was the wolf in her dreams! Struggling to appear nonchalant, she shrugged. "No real reason. Just curious. You want me to show an interest in werewolves, so I'm trying to do my part."

"Lycans."

"I beg your pardon?"

"Lycans. It's the politically correct term for a werewolf."

259

"Oh. I'll try to remember that."

"So why do you want to know about the colour of wolves?"

She shrugged. "Like I said. No reason. Idle curiosity."

"No. There's more. I can sense you're holding something back." He half turned to face her, folding his arms and giving her an unwavering stare.

She shifted nervously, feeling the weight of his gaze, the command in his eyes. It was hard to defy. The animal inside her whimpered, urging her to speak. She licked her lips, shot him a quick glance, and then looked away again. There was a subtle power about him that forced the words from her. "I...I have...dreams."

"Dreams? Really?" Bryan shifted in his seat, his whole demeanour suddenly watchful, wary. He cleared his throat and looked away. "What kind of dreams?"

"Well..." She felt embarrassed sharing the memory but something was driving her onward as if revealing this information was of the utmost importance. "I...I dream that I'm in the woods, being chased by this light brown wolf with hazel eyes. He runs after me, catches me and...and pins me down. Then, he...er...bites my neck."

As she spoke, her voice grew quieter until she was almost whispering, her awareness of the man beside her increasing by the moment. She could feel the heat generating off his body; was aware of the tempo of his breathing, the way their arms almost touched on the armrest. "I...I guess that's sort of a typical werewolf...er...Lycan type of dream, right?" She gave a nervous laugh and looked up at him through her lashes.

Bryan was staring at her, a shocked expression on his face. Then he blinked and looked away. "Uh...no. Actually it isn't." He cleared his throat again and answered slowly. "Lycans have normal dreams, like people do."

"Really?" She furrowed her brow. "So, why do I have that particular dream? It's happened over and over again for years."

"Well..." He exhaled heavily, then glanced around as if to make sure no one was listening in. Most of the other passengers were dozing or watching a movie. Even so, he shifted closer to her and slid down lower in his seat. She did as well, leaning closer to hear his hesitant words. "The funny thing is I...er...have a dream sort of like that, too."

She turned to look at him face on and found herself staring directly into his eyes. He was closer than she'd thought. She could feel his breath against her face and somehow his fingers had become tangled with hers. Did he realize that? She suspected the answer was no.

"I know. I said most don't, but a few do." Bryan looked down at where he was holding her hand and let go. He leaned away and ran his now free hand through his hair, looking ill at ease. "I...I've been told it signifies the fact that your inner wolf knows who will be its mate. The two wolf spirits are meeting on some other level of consciousness."

Her heart started to beat heavily in her chest and she hardly dared ask the next question, but knew she had to. "So... What does your dream she-wolf look like?"

"She's chocolate brown with green eyes." He spoke the words reluctantly, as if he were anxious as to how she'd take the news, then shot her a nervous look. "Just like you."

"Like me?" Abruptly, she sat up straight, speaking louder than she intended, her voice squeaking. Several of the passengers turned to look their way and she smiled weakly then sank down low in her seat again. Finally, they turned away. After clearing her throat, she whispered earnestly to him. "But... There must be lots of chocolate brown wolves in the world, right? And lots of light brown hazel-eyed wolves, too. Right?"

"Um...sure." Bryan's eyes locked with hers. She searched his, staring deeply, sensing another presence, a primitive wildness within him. It called to her, beckoning her, daring her, and an answering response arose within her. Her heart thumped heavily, like an ancient drum creating a rhythm that surrounded her, mesmerized her, pulsed through her very being until she couldn't separate herself from it.

Electricity zinged back and forth between them. She licked her dry lips and inhaled deeply, intensely aware of his masculine scent. Bryan did the same thing, half closing his eyes. The moment stretched between them, the surroundings fading into the background. Images from her dream flashed before her eyes; Bryan half naked leaning over her, his hands on her bare flesh, caressing, bringing every nerve ending to awareness. How she longed to feel that way again.

Bryan reached forward and touched her cheek with his fingertips. She closed her eyes, concentrating on the sensation, exhaling slowly as his thumb stroked her lower lip. Half-opening her eyes she saw him drawing closer. His nose brushed her jaw line and then her ear lobe; she could feel him inhale.

"Our flight will be arriving in Chicago at..." The sound of the pilot's voice crackling over the speakers broke the spell under which she'd fallen and she jerked back.

Her cheekbone struck Bryan's nose and he gave a muffled cry, clamping his hand over the injured member. The pilot continued talking, though she had no idea what he was saying. She was too busy staring in shock at Bryan. At least he appeared equally surprised. He swallowed hard, touched his nose gingerly and then gruffly mumbled something about the bathroom.

Staring at his retreating form, she cursed herself for bringing up the topic of dream wolves; she wasn't ready for this...whatever it was...that had just happened between them. If she'd understood him correctly, Bryan could be her...mate.

She shivered, hardly able to make her mind form the word. It didn't matter that he was the hottest man she'd been around in ages, or that she turned into a puddle of desire around him. Mates sounded so animal-like. Her stomach churned. There had to be some other explanation!

For a while she tried to occupy her mind with her magazine, flipping the pages, looking for something worth reading. Bryan returned and sat down beside her but made no effort to start a conversation. Silence stretched between them and she replayed what had happened over and over in her mind. He'd said a *few* wolves dreamed of their mates but he hadn't said *all*. Perhaps there was a mistake. She needed more information.

Staring down at her hands, she picked at her fingernail and gathered her courage. She cleared her throat and tried to sound casual, indifferent. "You said that only some wolves have dreams of their mates. Why is that?"

At first she didn't think he was going to answer; he seemed lost in thought.

"Bryan?" She looked over at him and touched his arm gently.

"Hmm? Oh, sorry." He gave his head a shake and started to explain. "I'm not an expert on the phenomenon, but a friend of mine knows quite a bit about the old ways. Marco—he's a pack member by the way—said that it's mostly only royal or blue-blooded Lycans that can do this. There aren't many of those around anymore; Marco claims a few of the European packs have practised selective breeding to ensure the trait isn't lost."

Royal. Blue-blooded. She repeated the words to herself thinking of the information she'd read on the internet. "Er...what else can these blue-blooded werewolves do?"

Bryan relaxed, obviously more comfortable with this conversation than their previous one. "Naturally they can magick their clothes on and off when they shift, but a lot of us still have that ability. Um...telekinesis—that's moving objects with your mind—and teleportation—disappearing and appearing somewhere else. There's probably other stuff too, but like I said, I don't really know much about it. It's sort of a cool trick, if in fact it's true."

A funny feeling was growing inside her. It was part dread as the reality that she was indeed a werewolf became more and more apparent, but part of it was anticipation as if she were on the verge of some monumental discovery. "Can you tell me more about this teleporting?"

He shrugged. "I guess it's hard to do and to control. It involves thinking of a place you've been or at least seen in a picture, similar to imagining how you look when you resume your human form. Then somehow you molecularize your body as if shifting, but then transfer the energy across space and you appear in another location."

"You just appear there." She squeezed her hands together tightly and forced the needed words from her mouth. "Bryan, I can do that." She glanced at him nervously, wondering how he'd take the news.

"Do what?"

"What you said. Disappear and appear somewhere else. Teleport."

"You what..?" He looked at her sceptically. "I thought you said you've never even changed into a wolf until yesterday."

"I know. I've kept from changing by drugging myself and locking myself in my bedroom. But sometimes, when it's a full moon, I'll wake up someplace else. In the park or the grocery store." She looked at him earnestly. "That's how I ended up in Vegas. The night my uncle died, I ran away. I was scared the werewolf would get me because I'd witnessed him killing Mr. Aldrich and knew the secret of werewolf existence."

She flushed, feeling embarrassed saying that to him despite the truth of the statement. "Anyway, I got as far as Kansas that first night and took a motel room. It was a full moon and I was feeling really strange. I took one of my pills and lay down on the bed trying to think of someplace fun, trying to take my mind off things. For some reason Vegas popped into my head. I started to feel really weird and the next thing I knew, I woke up in an alleyway in downtown Las Vegas."

For a moment, Bryan said nothing and she wondered if he believed her or not. Then he shook his head, a deep, rich chuckle rumbling in his chest. "Damn, but Ryne does know how to pick 'em."

"What do you mean?" She was affronted that he was laughing after her great revelation.

"I mean, lots of packs have found stray wolves, but Ryne goes and finds a rare blue-blooded Lycan who is also an heiress worth millions of dollars. Damn, but the other packs are going to be jealous now!"

She looked at him askance. "That's all you have to say? Bryan, I can appear and disappear!"

"I heard you. It's a neat trick and we'll have to teach you how to control it, but in the grand scheme of things, it isn't that important." He chuckled again, shaking his head.

"Oh." Her shoulders drooped, feeling deflated by his nonchalant acceptance of her ability. She wasn't sure why she cared. It wasn't like she even wanted to be a werewolf, let alone a blue-blooded one. Hmm... Blue-blooded or royal. "So, who do you think my parents might be?"

"You mean, you don't know?"

She shook her head. "My mother's name was Luisa, but my uncle never mentioned my father. I believe my mom was from Spain."

"With your colouring that makes sense." He eyed her, taking in her hair, his gaze skimming over her features. His eyes grew darker, heavy-lidded, and she could feel the pull beginning between them again. She was starting to lean closer, when he blinked and shook his head, breaking the connection. She felt disappointed for some reason but struggled not to show it.

Bryan continued speaking. "Spain? Marco came from Spain three years ago. When we get back to Canada, he might be able to help out. There aren't that many royal Lycans around. I'm sure he'll know something."

The prospect of learning more about her parents was exciting, even if they were werewolves...er...Lycans. She had always known her uncle wasn't really her uncle, but had sensed she shouldn't query her background. She wondered who they might've been, what they had looked like and if she had any cousins. After years of being alone, the idea of having relatives seemed almost unreal.

Leaning back in her seat, she closed her eyes and contemplated all that she'd just learned. She was possibly a royal Lycan with the ability to teleport, she might have family back in Spain, and—she peered at Bryan through her lashes—she might be sitting beside her future mate!

Chicago, Illinois, USA...

Marla leaned against the headboard, running her fingers through Jeffries' hair. He sighed and rolled over, then rubbed his eyes.

"Hello, lover." She cooed the words and watched the satisfied smile that spread over his face.

"Morning." Jeffries stretched and yawned. "You tired me out last night."

"Mmm... But it was a good tired, wasn't it?"

"Oh yeah. The best."

"I'm glad." She trailed her hand across his chest and then followed the arrow of hair to his navel. "Do you remember what we talked about last night?"

"No. Oh! The elevator? You weren't serious, were you?" He rolled onto his side to face her and propped himself up on his elbow.

"Of course I was. It's a joke on Sylvia, that's all. She was teasing me about being afraid of spiders and actually put one on my desk! I know she's afraid of heights, so if the elevator doors open and there's this big black chasm, she'll be scared spitless."

"That's kind of dangerous. I mean, what if she isn't watching and actually steps ahead, thinking the elevator is there?"

"Don't worry. I'll make sure I'm there to grab her or I'll string a bunch of bungee cords inside the door. It will be harmless prank, that's all."

"I still don't know, Marla."

She gently pushed him onto his back and slid her fingers lower, caressing his manhood. It sprang to life and he groaned in appreciation. "Please? For me?"

"I should have never told you that I used to do elevator maintenance." Jeffries spoke the words through gritted teeth.

"I promise I'll make it worth your while." She leaned forward, her bare breasts brushing against his chest. Her lips trailed over his face and her hand worked his shaft causing it to grow harder.

"Well...I suppose. As long as you promise to make sure she doesn't get hurt."

Marla traced his lips with her tongue. "I promise to be right there to make sure it works perfectly."

"When..." His breathing hitched as she slid on top of him and nibbled his chest. "When do you want to do this?"

"As soon as possible. Maybe this evening? Or tomorrow morning?" She worked her way down his body, dipping her tongue into his belly button.

"Okay. What about Swanson's security?"

"Don't worry. He's not as diligent as people think. If need be, I'll distract him." Marla pressed a kiss to Jeffries thigh. Her wolf whined and whimpered but she ignored it and concentrated on the man before her.

"Make sure you have the doorway secured so she can't fall." Jeffries threw his head back and bit his lip, his body arching in obvious pleasure.

"Don't worry. Everything will be ready on my end. Everything."

Kellen slowly drifted back to consciousness and tried to open his eyes. They felt gritty and the lids were partially stuck shut. He tried to raise his hand to wipe them, but found his arms wouldn't respond. Or rather, they were trying to respond, but were stuck. He shook his head and forced his eyes open, squinting as his pupils adjusted to the brightness.

His neck twinged as he lifted his head, protesting the movement. Apparently he'd fallen asleep sitting up, but where? Looking around the room, nothing was familiar. He furrowed his brow, trying to recall recent events.

He hissed as his memory kicked in, his whole body suddenly alert. He'd been kidnapped by Hugh and taken to Dollar Niche. Eddie wanted to turn Sandy over to whoever it was that was looking for her in exchange for a hefty reward.

Eddie had talked on the phone to someone—Kellen struggled to recall the name, but it wouldn't come to him—then Hugh had slapped him around. Last thing he recalled was being injected with something.

Was he still in Dollar Niche? No, this place was classier. Thick carpet on the floors, fancy window treatments. No furniture though, except of course for the chair he was tied to. It was plain wood without an ounce of cushioning and his body was letting him know that fact loud and clear. He shifted his weight, trying to ease some of the strain and pressure on his back and upper legs.

Without warning, the door swung open and Hugh walked in. The blond giant looked rested and ready for another game of beat-up-Kellen. There were bandages on his neck and Kellen recalled the strange, but well-timed dog attack that had occurred. It had given Sandy a chance to escape. He hoped she was okay, wherever she was.

"You're awake."

"Brilliant deduction, Sherlock." Kellen mentally kicked himself as soon as the words left his mouth. Being rude to the people who held you captive probably wasn't a good idea, but then again, dumb ideas seemed to be his forte lately.

Hugh grumbled and Kellen made a half-hearted effort to apologize. Irritating the man wouldn't help his cause any. "Sorry. I'm not a morning person."

He peered behind Hugh to see a long hallway lined with doors. It gave no clue as to where he was. "So, where's your sidekick?"

"Eddie? He's gone; he doesn't like the rough stuff. Drove us to the airport and then took off."

"But you decided to stick around."

Hugh shrugged. "Sure. This is the type of work I've always wanted to do."

"Being a thug was your career goal?"

"Hey, we all have our own aspirations." Hugh folded his arms and looked at him belligerently.

Kellen sighed. If he'd ever harboured any hopes that Hugh might be a friendly jailor who could be persuaded to let him go, they quickly died.

Another man appeared in the doorway and Hugh stepped aside to let him in. The newcomer was probably in his late fifties, well dressed with a silk scarf wrapped pretentiously around his neck. Kellen raised his eyebrows at the sight of the scarf, but said nothing.

"Good morning, Mr. Anderson." The man's voice was raspy, almost forced. He walked around Kellen making tsking sounds. "I apologize for your accommodations last night, but it couldn't be helped. The same with your appearance. If you'd been more cooperative, Hugh wouldn't have had to get quite so physical with you."

Kellen recalled Hugh grabbing him by the collar and taking a swing at him, but beyond that, nothing. How had he been uncooperative if he'd been unconscious? Or had Hugh only used that as an excuse to deliver a few more blows than needed? Deciding that knowing the truth wouldn't make any difference, Kellen focused on watching this new player in the game. An icy coldness oozed from the man's pores as if his heart had quit beating years ago.

"Who are you?" The words slipped past Kellen's lips before he could stop them.

A shadow of a smile passed over the man's lips, the corners barely turning before it became impassive again. "*Who* I am is none of your concern. What I *want* is. And that is simply to restore that poor child, Cassandra Greyson, to her rightful place as heiress of the Greyson estate."

"Sorry," Kellen shook his head. "She gave me the distinct impression that she didn't want to come back. She wasn't happy in her old life. Even if I knew where she was right now, I wouldn't tell you."

Chuckling the man stood in front of Kellen, his hands clasped behind his back. "Thankfully, that isn't necessary any longer. You are merely the bait now. I have it on good authority that she left Las Vegas on a flight here a few hours ago and should be landing about now." The man reached towards Kellen and he jerked back expecting another blow. Instead the man smiled and patted his cheek. "You sit here like a good boy. As soon as we have the girl, we'll let you go."

Hugh snorted as if he knew some inside joke and held the door open for the other man. As they left, Kellen was sure he heard Hugh address the fellow as Mr. Aldrich. Not that it mattered. The name meant nothing to him.

He pulled on the ropes that bound his arms. He didn't believe them when they said he'd be free to go once Sandy—

Cassandra—arrived. He'd seen their faces and could report them to the authorities. But would anyone believe him, even if he did make it out alive?

Kellen Anderson was just another gambling addict. Besides, he had his own murky past. It was only petty theft as a teen, but still... He clenched his jaw and shook his head. The cops wouldn't believe him. They'd run his background first, question his own involvement in the whole affair, and probably think he was disgruntled because he didn't get his cut of the reward money.

But Sandy would vouch for him, wouldn't she? His spirits perked up, hope swelling in him before plummeting like a popped balloon. Unless she was too angry about him selling her out. His stomach clenched and he felt sick thinking how Sandy probably perceived him at the moment. For three years now she'd trusted him, believed in him, and now...

Swallowing hard, he tried to reassure himself of his true intentions. He hadn't really been going to call that number, at least not after he'd thought it through and talked to Sandy. It was an impulsive idea, but he'd never have carried it through once he knew her true feelings on returning home. Surely she'd know that.

He licked his lips, the nauseous feeling growing inside him again. If Sandy lost faith in him—if he lost her—he'd have no one. Even if she didn't love him the way he hoped, she was still there for him, still someone he could call his own. Without her, there'd be no reason to keep going.

Damn, but he wished he'd never seen that flyer, never borrowed money from Dollar Niche, never even gone gambling with his supposed 'friends'. Why couldn't he say no to the clawing need that rose up inside him? Why was he so weak that he couldn't resist the thrill of the game, the adrenaline rush that came from teetering on the edge of winning or losing a fortune? It was a sickness that left him shaking and light-headed, yet had him returning over and over for just one more game, one more deal of the cards or roll of the dice. Even now he could imagine how it would feel to be at a gaming table; his heart would be pounding, his brain racing as he calculated the odds.

He let his head drop forward and cursed himself. His addiction had already taken so much from him and now it was going to destroy the only good thing left in his miserable life.

Chapter 17

Bryan and Cassie spent the rest of the flight in large blocks of silence interspersed with brief moments of overly polite banal conversation. Recent revelations, especially the fact Bryan might be her predestined mate...er...husband were extremely unsettling. Her human half told her that it couldn't possibly be true; you didn't meet people in your dreams. Another part of her seemed to sit up, eagerly wagging its tail at the very idea. She scolded that part of herself, telling it to try and show some self-restraint while ensuring her human half didn't dwell too much on Bryan's very appealing attributes.

Of course, a union between them would be totally unacceptable. Once Kellen was free, she planned on escaping. There had to be a way to contain the animal within her and live a quiet, normal life. Her brief excitement over being royalty and having the ability to teleport had faded. The dangers involved were now looming over her. She'd have to be even more on guard now, watching her thoughts carefully, especially around a full moon. Thus far, she'd been lucky, but one of these days she might teleport into a group of humans or suddenly appear someplace dangerous, like the middle of a highway. Clenching her fists, her nails dug into her palms; the burden of her new found 'talent' weighed heavily on her.

Feeling wearier than ever, a soft sigh escaped her. Her life kept getting more and more complicated; would things ever be simple again? She turned her head to stare at Bryan. Mates. She wondered how he really felt about the possibility of them being connected by destiny. He'd been quiet, lost in thought for most of the flight. Did he find the idea of her as a mate repulsive? Or maybe he was just tired? He had been up early and sleeping on the couch couldn't have been comfortable.

Nibbling on her lip, she turned back to watch the clouds skimming by the window, still wondering what the man beside her was thinking, but too nervous to ask him in case the answer wasn't to her liking. Why she even cared, she didn't know. Just because he was good looking, and a bit of a knight in shining armour who was willing to help her rescue Kellen, wasn't any reason to be concerned about his opinion of her.

Besides, he had those flashes of bossiness, like he thought he was in charge and assumed she'd fall in with his plans. So what if it was sort of hot when he stared at her with that implacable look of his. She was used to a gentler approach, like Kellen, and that was what she preferred, wasn't it? True, Kellen's indecisiveness drove her to distraction at times whereas Bryan seemed to know exactly what he wanted. She flicked a glance at him out of the corner of her eye and sighed at the pointless speculation. She had no business being interested in Bryan, or anyone else for that matter. Her future was sealed; she knew what she had to do. Glumly, she propped her chin in her hand and stared out the window, dully waiting for the flight to be over.

It was only as they arrived in Chicago and exited the plane that she and Bryan really began to talk again and then it was concerning their next course of action.

She hefted her bag off the luggage carousel, slung the strap over her shoulder, and started walking towards the exit. "As soon as we're outside where it's quieter, I'll call the kidnappers. The number they gave is different than the one that was on the poster of me."

"No way. We'll head to the motel and meet up with Ryne and Kane. Quite likely they have a plan already in the works." Bryan attempted to negate her idea as they stepped out of the airport. He headed towards the line of people who were waiting for a taxi, his hand in the small of her back.

"No." She shook her head decisively. Twisting away, she resisted his attempts to herd her along beside him. "We need to call the number we were given. I'll let them know I'm here so Kellen can be set free as soon as possible."

"Not on your life. We don't know what we might be walking into. It's too dangerous. They could snatch you and, without having done any reconnoitring, I'd have no idea what I was up against. We need to approach the situation cautiously, with a calm rational course of action in mind." Bryan glared at her, clearly annoyed.

"Who put you in charge of all the decisions?" She turned to walk away, but he grabbed her arm, spinning her around and pulling her close so they were almost nose-to-nose.

"Ryne put me in charge, that's who. Our Alpha said no contact until we come up with a plan. As Beta I enforce his rules. We're going to the motel." He started to pull her along, but she dug in her heels.

"No."

He turned around and they stared at each other in a battle of wills. Tension crackled in the air.

"Cassandra." His eyes were flashing with temper and she could hear his teeth grinding together as he delivered the warning. A shiver ran over her, but was it fear or excitement at seeing the fire in his eyes, the carefully controlled temper? There was a certain thrill in defying him and something made her continue to push. How far could she go before he made her comply?

She tossed her hair, her ponytail swishing over her shoulder. "It's my life. My choice. Kellen's in this mess because of me."

"Your friend's in this mess because he was going to hand you over in exchange for saving his own butt." He snapped the words at her. She could feel his fingers clenching around her arm.

Cassie pulled her arm free and glared at him. "That might have been his initial, impulsive plan, but I'm sure he changed his mind. He said as much at the house before that thug grabbed at me."

"And he might have reversed that decision just as quickly, once the pressure was put on him." Bryan pointed out, slashing the air with his hand.

"You don't know that! You know nothing about Kellen, nothing at all!" She took a step towards him, entering his personal space and poking him in the chest. Something flared in his eyes that had her suddenly freezing in place. A feeling of nervousness washed over her, as if she'd crossed some invisible barrier.

"I'd tread carefully if I were you, Cassandra." The words were delivered in a whisper yet the warning they carried reverberated within her, sending a shiver of fear over her. This was a side of Bryan she hadn't seen yet. It was more than being bossy, there was an edge of barely controlled danger about him.

She swallowed and stepped back. He inclined his head as if acknowledging her acquiescence and his whole demeanour relaxed. The fear left her, but now she was left confused. What had just happened? Some wolf dominance thing?

Making an exasperated sound, she turned around and started marching down the sidewalk. Behind her she could hear Bryan giving an equally exasperated huff before following her. She made her way to a bench and sat down, pulling out her cell phone.

Bryan clamped his hand over it. "Cassandra, you are not making that phone call."

She snatched her hand away. "Quit calling me Cassandra. People only use that name when I'm in trouble. It's Cassie or Sandy."

"All right. *Cassie.*" Bryan spoke in measured tones and she had a feeling that he was barely holding on to his patience. "Put the phone down and we'll discuss this reasonably."

"By reasonable, you mean I have to do what you tell me to do. You'll do that weird Beta thing that makes me have to obey you." She kept her face averted, her jaw stuck out defiantly.

"No. We'll *talk* about it. I only do the 'weird Beta thing' when you're totally out of line." He sat down beside her, his thigh pressed against hers on the narrow bench. The warmth of it seeped into her, making her all too aware of his presence.

They sat for a moment, another silent battle of wills going on. She stared straight ahead. Out of the corner of her eye, she noted how the muscle in his jaw flexed in and out and she idly wondered if he was counting to ten, trying to manage his temper.

A twinge of guilt stabbed her. She shouldn't be giving him such a hard time. He was here to help her set Kellen free, even when he'd never met the man before. And rushing blindly into the abductor's nest probably wasn't a good idea. Slowly, she put her phone down.

Bryan exhaled loudly and ran his hands through his hair before turning to look at her. When he spoke his tone was calmer. "I realize you're concerned about your friend, and I am too. But if we rush in doing whatever they say, we have no guarantee that they won't grab you and still keep Kellen or, worse yet, do him further harm."

She flicked a glance at him and then fiddled with her cell phone, turning it over and over in her hand. She studied the ground, noticing the dark marks from abandoned gum, cigarette butts, and a few small scraps of miscellaneous litter. Begrudgingly, she acknowledged the truth of his statement, knowing it was childish to hold onto her anger when he was doing his best to meet her halfway rather than forcing his will on her.

"I know. It's just that I feel responsible for this. If I hadn't hidden who I was from Kellen all these years, if I hadn't told him I wouldn't help him out of debt again, if I'd only—"

"Shh..." Bryan laid a comforting hand on her thigh. "Playing 'if only' won't help anything. Quite likely everyone is partially to blame, but we can't live in the past. We need to focus on the best way to help Kellen and that means keeping the kidnappers guessing by dangling you—the figurative carrot—in front of their noses. They want you, so they have to give us some concessions. If we play our cards right, we can get them to give Kellen back and still keep you free."

She stared down at Bryan's hand, noting his blunt nails, the calluses that showed he'd done manual labour before. It was a strong, capable hand and she liked how the warmth from it seeped into her leg. It was comforting. For a moment she wished she could explore his hands, feel them touching her bare skin. Then she gave her head an imperceptible shake and jerked her attention back to the current problem. "How are we going to outwit the kidnappers?"

"For one thing, we can check out where they're holding Kellen. Daniel tells me he can use mobile phone tracking technology to determine where a call comes from. I'll give Daniel the number, and he'll figure out where the goon is that has Kellen and we'll check out the area."

"But the phone's owner will wonder why Daniel is calling."

Bryan snorted. "Daniel's a pro at stuff like this. He'll block his number, pretend to be a telemarketer and get a fix on the guy in no time. We can grab a bite to eat and he'll have a location for us before our burgers have even cooled."

"Tacos."

"Tacos?"

"Yeah. I want tacos, not burgers." She smiled mischievously at Bryan in lieu of an apology. She was pleased he hadn't gone all 'he-man' on her over the whole 'rush to save Kellen' thing. Yes, he *had* asserted his authority but she was being a tad brat-ish. And truth be told, while she wanted to save Kellen, she wasn't overly keen on handing herself over to Eddie and his muscle-bound friend.

Bryan grinned at her, obviously not the type to hold a grudge if you dared disagree with him. She found that rather endearing, especially since Kellen was prone to pouting when things didn't immediately go his way. "Tacos it is. Just let me call Daniel first."

Stump River, Ontario, Canada…

Daniel wandered out of the kitchen, a thick ham sandwich in his hand. Intently checking his cell phone for messages, he didn't realize someone was walking down the hall until he stepped into their path. Bodies collided. His sandwich landed on the floor and a very feminine 'damn' was whispered as a load of laundry spilled onto the floor.

Tessa stood in front of him, an exasperated expression on her face, though it quickly disappeared when she realized he was looking at her.

"Sorry, Tessa. I wasn't watching where I was going." He gave her a crooked smile then gestured at the laundry. "Was it clean?"

"Yes, but don't worry. I'll get it." She spoke softly, bending down quickly, her long brown hair hiding her face.

"It's my fault. I'll help." Daniel crouched as well and began picking up the bits of clothing. Some lace panties appeared when he picked up a pillowcase, but they were quickly snatched from his view. From what he could see of her face, Tessa was blushing. If it had been Mel, he would have teased her good naturedly, but with Tessa... She was different. Fragile.

He closed his mouth and said nothing, merely shoving the items in the laundry basket then grabbing it and standing up. Handing it over to Tessa, he apologized again. "I'm sorry about all your clean clothes ending up on the floor. If you'd like, I'll rewash them for you."

"No. It's all right." She flashed him a panic-stricken look and began to back away only to stop suddenly and glance down.

Daniel followed the path of her gaze and saw that she was standing on his sandwich. The mustard was oozing out under her foot. He looked back up, ready to brush the incident off with a gentle quip, but the words stuck in his throat as he saw the tears welling in her eyes.

"I...I'm sorry, Daniel. I'm really, really sorry." The words barely made it passed her trembling lips before she spun on her heel and ran down the hall. Something fell from the laundry basket, but she didn't stop, merely racing out the back door.

A heavy sigh escaped him. He'd hoped, now that the Loberos were living in the main house instead of in town, Tessa might start to relax around him. Unfortunately, if anything it was getting worse. She'd been living with her brother Marco, his wife Olivia and their two children in the north wing of the house for almost six months now.

"You'd think she'd be used to me," he muttered under his breath. "They've been part of the pack for almost three years." Bending he picked up the fallen clothes and then gave an ironic laugh. It was the white lace panties and pillowcase of a moment ago. His fingers rubbed over the lace and he wistfully stared out the door to where he could see her hanging her things on the line. "This is probably as close as I'll ever get to her panties, too."

"What's that?" Olivia spoke from behind him and he jumped, then felt his face grow warm.

She laughed and shook her head. "Daniel, I was young once, too. No need to be embarrassed about what your mind is thinking."

He grinned sheepishly, but then sobered. "Do you think she'll ever...?" He didn't need to finish the sentence.

Olivia shrugged. "I don't know. The experience she had back in Spain made her wary of men."

"Yeah." Handing the laundry to Olivia, he sighed heavily. "Here. If I give it to her, she'll likely burn it or faint dead away." Picking up the remains of his sandwich he dumped it in the garbage and then went to his room, no longer hungry. Unrequited love played havoc with his appetite.

Sitting down at his desk, he glanced longingly out the window one more time before beginning to work on the latest task Bryan had given him. They needed to know where the thug was who had kidnapped Cassandra Greyson's friend, Kellen.

Daniel smirked and shook his head at the ease of the task. Tracking the location of a cell phone user was child's play. He'd find the dude and get the address of the building where he was holed up, then send the information back to Bryan. While Bryan checked the outside of the building, an internet search should turn up a floor plan for said building. If the girl's friend was being held there, they'd need a map to aid in whatever rescue plan was concocted. Maybe he'd even check the building's security. If he could find the company that was in charge, he could research the systems they favoured using and see if any weaknesses existed. Shutting off a few alarms here and there might make Bryan's job easier.

Hunching over his computer, Daniel's fingers flew over the keyboard. Tackling problems such as the ones Bryan had been giving him, always gave him an adrenaline rush. Today, it had the added side benefit of taking his mind off a certain other problem. He forced himself not to glance out the window again and frowned fiercely at the lines of print appearing on the screen. It was amazing what you could find on the internet if you knew where to look.

Chicago, Illinois, USA…

Mrs. Teasdale impatiently waited for Franklin to get off the phone. She'd been eavesdropping on his half of the conversation, but whenever she'd prodded him for information, he'd shushed her indicating he was listening and not to bother him. Pursing her lips, she twisted her fingers nervously, wondering what news Meredith Mitchell was delivering. Franklin's face was always so deadpan—darn his perfect, butler countenance—it was hard to determine if the information was good or bad.

When he finally said goodbye and hung up, she had to keep herself from pouncing on the man. As it was she bombarded him with questions as he walked across the room and sat down at the large wooden table that dominated one corner of the kitchen.

"Well? What did Meredith say? Is Miss Cassie all right? Was she involved in the scuffle at the house? Is that other werewolf still with her?"

"Give me a chance to answer, will you." Franklin groused at her and waved for her to sit down.

She complied and clasped her hands tightly in front of her, holding back the other questions that threatened to spout from her lips. Miss Cassie was like a grandchild to her and the thought that some harm had come to her was more than she could bear.

Mrs. Teasdale blinked back a tear and sniffled; she was scared for the girl and not afraid to admit it.

"Meredith has kept a close eye on Cassie's house and from all appearances our girl is fine."

"Thank the Lord," she breathed out and closed her eyes in silent prayer, her shoulders slumping with relief.

"The young fellow is still with her."

"That sounds promising." She opened her eyes and stared at Franklin, her spirits perking up at the news.

"But it seems Anderson is in a pickle with some loan sharks and Miss Cassie is set on saving him."

"Cassie does have the money."

"It's more complicated than simply paying off a debt. The long and short of it is, Aldrich is using Anderson and his debt as bait to get Cassie to come back to Chicago. As a matter of fact, she and the young man—the one we think is a werewolf—are on their way here right now."

"She is?" Mrs. Teasdale beamed for a moment at the news of Cassie's imminent arrival, then frowned. "Wait a minute. What's Aldrich's plan for her?"

"I'm not sure, but it can't be good or he wouldn't be using blackmail to get her to come back."

"But the werewolf is still with her? He hasn't abandoned her over this?" She sought reassurance that Cassie wasn't facing this alone.

"Apparently not. His interest in her must be greater than his need for privacy. If the media ever got a hold of this, the whole werewolf thing could explode around all of us."

"But it won't, will it? I mean, these wolves must be experienced at operating under the radar. They wouldn't do anything foolish."

"If it were only wolves, I'm sure everything would be fine, but there's an estate worth millions involved, a missing heiress, Aldrich and don't forget Kellen. The boy has some feelings for Cassie, but he's unstable and possibly desperate." Franklin outlined all the possible pitfalls and Mrs. Teasdale began twisting her fingers nervously again.

The Finding

"Please let Cassie be safe and find a place where she can belong," she whispered to the powers that be. "Please."

Bryan scanned the lobby of the motel as he walked in and noted two familiar looking figures standing near the elevator. One looked just like Ryne from the back and the other was a petite woman with long brown hair. He sniffed the air, a smile breaking out on his face. It was Elise; he'd remember her scent anywhere.

The two of them had grown up together in the same pack. At one time, he'd even fancied himself in love with her and she with him. Unfortunately, a political alliance had gotten in the way of their youthful plans. She'd been forced to move to a new pack and mate with Kane, a fact that had been hard to deal with at the time. Eventually, he had come to realize his attachment for Elise had been based on familiarity and proximity rather than a deep abiding love. He was still fond of her in a brotherly way, but that was all.

From the way Kane had his arm protectively wrapped around Elise, it was easy to see the two were still besotted with each other. Everything had worked out for the best, he mused. They were happy and so was he.

His wolf rumbled and he qualified his statement. *Mostly* happy. Sure a few things could improve, but living in Canada, being Beta, helping forge a new pack; none of that would have been possible if he'd stayed in his old life.

And Cassie, his wolf added.

He rolled his eyes; the creature really was obsessed. He wasn't sure what to make of the situation. Could his wolf be right? Was Cassie the Lycan of his dreams or was it pure coincidence? While he'd like to think that was the case—the idea of predestination controlling his life irked—he couldn't deny facts. Their wolves were attracted and seemed to know each other, and Cassie wasn't exactly unappealing to his human side. Actually, she was more than a little appealing. The heat that had grown between them on the plane had been undeniable.

A pinging sound caught his attention. The elevator door was opening and his old friend was about to disappear. He called out her name.

"Elise!"

Elise stopped mid-step and spun around. Their eyes locked across the distance of the lobby and then she waved, a wide smile spreading over her face. Kane looked at her, then followed the direction of her gaze. He knew the instant Kane realized who had caught Elise's attention. A glower formed on the Alpha's face before he schooled his features and nodded in recognition.

"I'll talk to you upstairs." Elise called out the words as Kane pulled her back into the elevator just before the doors slid shut.

He chuckled to himself. Obviously Kane hadn't forgotten the past completely. It might be amusing to tease the man.

"Who was that?" Cassie tugged at his arm and he looked down at her, having momentarily forgotten she was there.

"That was Elise. We grew up together."

"Oh." She nodded. "She seemed awfully pleased to see you."

He shrugged. "I suppose. We haven't seen each other in three years."

"Hmm." She made a non-committal noise, then rubbed her hands up and down her arms. He could see faint goose bumps raised on her skin. "The man with her looked familiar."

"That's Kane Sinclair, Elise's mate."

"I'm sure I've seen him before." She scrunched up her face as if trying to find a memory.

Realizing they were almost blocking the door, he urged her towards the front desk. "I don't know where you might have encountered him. As far as I know he's never been to Vegas or Chicago, at least not in the past few years."

He dealt with procuring their room, while Cassie stood beside him obviously still puzzling over Kane. As he bent to pick up their bags, she suddenly grabbed his arm and whispered to him urgently.

"I know where I saw him! Kane looks exactly like the guy I saw the night my uncle died. I mean, it was getting dark and the fellow was covered in mud, but I'm sure it was him." She shivered, a look of remembered fear in her eyes.

"Kane looks almost exactly like Ryne. It was Ryne you saw, but people often mistake them for each other."

"Oh." She bit her lip and looked around. Waves of anxiety washed off her. "So this Ryne, your...er...Alpha, he's upstairs right now?"

"Yep. I'll introduce you as soon as we get settled." He walked toward the elevator, talking to her over his shoulder. "And Ryne's not just my Alpha, you know. He's yours too. You're a member of the pack now."

"Not if I can help it." The words were probably supposed to be muttered under her breath, but he heard them all the same.

As they stood side by side in the elevator, he sighed. Her resistance was starting to get on his nerves. Thankfully other people were on the elevator so it was impossible to continue the conversation. Otherwise he might say something he'd later regret.

The elevator stopped at their floor and he found their room, unlocked the door and gestured for Cassie to enter. She did, then looked at him askance when he stepped inside as well and shut the door.

"You don't have to come in. I can unpack on my own, you know." She dropped her bag on one of the beds.

"I'm sure you can, but this is my room too."

"Excuse me?" Her eyebrows shot upward.

He spread his arms out in a placating manner. "No ulterior lecherous motives, I promise. The full moon is only two days away. It's not safe to leave you by yourself."

"I've survived full moons by myself for three years. I don't need a babysitter. You can leave." She crossed her arms and stuck out her chin.

"I'm not leaving and from what you've told me, you survived them by drugging yourself. That's no way to live and as your Beta, I'm not going to allow you to continue hurting your wolf that way. Not only that, but what are the side effects of those drugs for your human half? You don't take something that powerful for years and years without some damage being done." He had stepped closer with each word and was now in her personal space.

She shrugged, looking to the side. After a moment, she stepped back conceding to his dominance. "I haven't noticed any ill-effects."

"Maybe not yet, but in time." He studied her, puzzled by her stubbornness. Finally, he exhaled slowly. "This is a pointless conversation. I'm staying. We're sharing this room. End of story. Now unpack and I'll introduce you to the others."

"No thanks. I'll wait here." She sat on the bed and traced the pattern on the bedspread.

He had bent to pick up his bag, but turned back to face her. "Why don't you want to meet the others?"

She gave another shrug. "I just don't." He continued to stare at her and she squirmed under his gaze before explaining further. "They're werewolves."

He quirked a brow at her terminology. "Pardon?"

Sighing, she corrected herself. "I mean Lycans."

"So?"

"I don't feel comfortable around them." She looked up at him guiltily, before averting her gaze. "I keep expecting them to jump and attack."

He barely managed not to roll his eyes at her statement. "You've been around me for a couple of days. Aside from our rather 'unusual' meetings," he paused and laughed softly at the memory, "I haven't attacked, have I?"

"No."

"Does the fact that I'm a Lycan make you nervous?"

She paused before answering. "I'm not worried that you're a Lycan. Not anymore. You're just you. But Kane is different. Just seeing him made me quake in my boots."

Bryan grunted in acknowledgement. "That's the Alpha in him. He's a pretty powerful one, especially given the fact that he isn't that old. Your wolf recognizes him as a dominant from another pack and she's unsure what to do."

The Finding

"Well, whatever the case, he bothers me and I'd prefer to keep my distance." She averted her face and Bryan shook his head, looking exasperated.

"Cassie, this is ridiculous. You're prejudiced against Lycans all because of one incident when you saw Ryne at his worst." He paced the length of the room then turned and looked at her. "Are you scared of American servicemen or police officers?"

"No, not really." She answered slowly, obviously puzzled by his sudden change of topic.

"But they carry weapons. They might have to fire at someone, even kill, if that person was endangering the lives of innocent victims."

"True. But that's their job. They're protecting—"

"Exactly!" He cut her off before she could finish her thought. "And Ryne was protecting his mate. The only difference is that his weapon wasn't a gun."

She was silent for a moment, absorbing the idea. "I suppose."

He hunkered down in front of her and took her hands. That same electrical current flowed between them where they touched and he rubbed his thumbs over the backs of her hands, taking a moment to notice the soft, smooth skin. In such close quarters, her scent wrapped itself around him and he inhaled deeply, enjoying the pleasurable stirring it caused inside him.

Looking into her eyes, he spoke softly. "Cassie, Lycans aren't monsters. We're living creatures with hopes and dreams and aspirations. We love, have families and are fiercely loyal to our packmates. You don't need to be afraid of us, or afraid of yourself."

His last comment must have hit home. Her eyes turned a deeper green and a watery sheen appeared. Her pain was palpable.

"That's it, isn't it?" He cocked his head and studied her. "You're afraid of yourself, aren't you?"

Cassie pressed her lips tightly together. She appeared to wage an internal war before finally speaking. "The only werewolf I'd ever seen was your Ryne. My uncle had just announced that I

287

was a werewolf and was talking about how they have this law that requires killing people who discover their existence. Then this awful savage creature appeared and attacked for no reason, or at least I thought it was for no reason." She pulled her hand away and wiped at a stray tear, sniffling. "I'm scared that's what will happen to me if I ever allow myself to transform."

Reaching out, he tucked her hair behind her ear, and then cupped her cheek. "That won't happen to you, Cassie. You have nothing to be afraid of. For the most part, a person's wolf has the same characteristics as their human half. Not always, but those are rare cases. When you turn, you'll still be you, just furrier and more in tune with your natural instincts. The wolf won't do anything that you would find inherently wrong."

"Really?" She gave him a disbelieving look. "I don't think I would have thrown myself at a complete stranger in a public park and started kissing him."

He chuckled at the memory. "Your wolf seems to think it already knows my wolf from those dreams, remember?"

"Right." She shifted on the bed and looked away, a blush staining her cheeks.

He decided not to press the topic further, though it was one that weighed heavily on his mind. He and Cassie as mates. Now that he was over the initial shock, he found the idea more and more intriguing. Exploring a relationship with her might be fun, but now was not the time. Instead he stood up and tugged her to her feet. "Come on. The others are probably wondering what we're doing."

Chapter 18

Bryan tapped on the door to Ryne's room. It was ajar so he let himself in. The Alpha had taken a small suite of rooms. This particular one featured a table and chairs, a small couch, TV and bar fridge. Two doors led off the one wall, probably to a bathroom and bedroom. There was no sign of Mel or Elise, but Kane and Ryne looked up from the laptop they were gathered around. Pulling Cassie in after him, he shut the door and then gestured towards the computer screen where a map was displayed. "What's that?"

Ryne answered. "Daniel sent us a blueprint of Aldrich's penthouse."

"And the security schemata." Kane added.

The two brothers were almost identical. Equal in height, Kane was more heavily muscled with glowing amber eyes while Ryne was on the leaner side, with obvious whipcord strength and bright, piercing blue eyes. Little wonder, Cassie confused one for the other. Unless they were side by side looking at you, it was hard to tell them apart. He drew her forward to his side from where she'd been standing behind him.

"Ryne, Kane. This is Cassandra Greyson." He could feel her tremors and squeezed her hand in assurance before stepping away. It was important that she meet her Alpha on her own.

She cast a 'why did you abandon me look' at him then visibly swallowed before giving a ghost of a smile and quietly offering an unenthusiastic greeting. "Hi."

"Cassandra." Kane nodded his head, but seemed to be more concerned with Bryan than the newcomer. The fact that the Alpha was still jealous after all these years, amused Bryan, and if he hadn't been concerned with Cassie, he might have teased

Kane by mentioning Elise. As it was, he ignored the man's steady stare in favour of the other two occupants of the room.

Ryne was circling around Cassie; as the Alpha of the pack, it was instinct for him to check out the newest member. With narrowed eyes, he took her measure, inhaling deeply, learning her scent. His body brushed against Cassie's as he moved around her, invading her personal space and testing her nerve. She trembled, but held her ground.

After a moment of studying her, Ryne lifted one corner of his mouth and spoke teasingly, a twinkle in his eye. "So this is the one who's causing all the problems?"

She visibly cringed and took a half step back. Bryan winced. Bad move. Up until then, she'd been doing so well, too. While wolves were subservient to the Alpha, they needed to show some spine or they'd end up in the Omega position.

Ryne stilled at her retreat and stared down at her, no doubt assessing her level of fear. She seemed to wilt even further. Bryan was sure he could almost hear her knees knocking together. Her hands were clenched tight at her side and her lower lip trembled. Most likely she was reliving the night she'd seen Ryne for the first time. Poor kid; that was no way to feel on your first presentation to the Alpha.

Even though it broke all protocol, his protective instincts sprang to life in the face of her obvious discomfort. He stepped in front of her, blocking her from Ryne's view. "Yes, this is Cassie, but she's hardly causing a problem."

"No?" Ryne quirked an eyebrow at him, a smirk on his face as if he knew something Bryan didn't and found it extremely amusing. "She's got a Beta and two Alphas all converging illegally in the Chicago pack's territory. I'd say that's stirring up trouble."

"Hardly her fault. You and Kane are here because of Marla and Aldrich, not because of her friend. If anything, she's done us a favour since the situation unexpectedly revealed where Marla's been hiding and gives us a reason to go after Aldrich ourselves."

"True." Ryne folded his arms and cocked his head. "Bryan, if I didn't know better, I'd say you were overly attached to Miss

Greyson. I don't think I've ever seen you leap to the defence of someone quite that quickly."

"Quite telling, isn't it?" Kane looked smug and relaxed as if a weight had been lifted from his shoulders. "I think Miss Greyson is getting some preferential treatment from your Beta, Ryne."

Bryan shrugged feeling embarrassed and struggling not to show it. There'd been no need to defend Cassie from Ryne, he should have known that, but something had come over him. "Yeah, well she's new to the whole Lycan thing and didn't realize you were teasing." He tried to bluff his way out of the situation.

"Hmm." Ryne stared at Bryan a moment longer before turning his attention back to Cassie, holding out his hand. "I apologize. I didn't intend to upset you at our first meeting. Instincts take over sometimes. I'm Ryne Taylor and this is my brother, Kane Sinclair. Welcome to the pack."

Kane must have noticed how she furrowed her brow at the different last names. "Half-brothers. Same mother, different fathers."

She nodded in understanding as she shook hands before shoving them in her back pockets. She looked at the two men, then dropped her gaze in obvious discomfort at still being the centre of attention. Bryan cleared his throat and everyone looked at him.

"So where are Elise and Mel?"

"Melody's having a nap." Ryne supplied with a bit of a grin. "She's tired from the long trip.

"And Elise is on the phone talking to Helen and checking on the children."

Bryan nodded. "Okay, then I'll fill you two in on what Cassie and I found out so far." They all sat down and he began. "Daniel found the address where they're holding Kellen Anderson, Cassie's...er...friend. It's Aldrich's place; a high rise. We checked the building out before coming here. The front door has a controlled entry plus a security guard and the underground parking is only accessible with a key card."

"So we can't just walk in." Kane folded his arms and leaned back in his chair.

"Nope. And we need proof that Anderson is actually in the building. Just because the goon said he's there, doesn't mean the information is good."

"Or that he's even still alive." Ryne added.

She gave a gasp, her gaze flying to Bryan's. Bryan grimaced at Ryne's lack of tact, but knew it was a fact they had to face. He nodded slowly. "So we need some proof."

"Have them send a picture via cell phone. It has to show Anderson and today's paper." Ryne smirked. "Isn't that how they do it in the movies?"

"Good idea." Bryan pulled out his cell phone.

She grabbed his arm. "Let me call. I'm the one they want."

He hesitated, but then nodded knowing she probably needed to feel as if she were doing something for her friend. As he watched her dial the number, he wondered yet again exactly what her relationship with Kellen was.

"See Leon? It was no trouble at all." Sylvia smiled warmly as she patted his hand. Aldrich smiled back and adjusted the silk scarf that covered his breathing tube. He closed his eyes briefly as she laid her hand on his brow.

"You're a trifle warm, Leon. Are you feeling well?" She inquired, a look of concern in her eyes.

"Yes, just excited. A certain business project that is finally coming together. No need to fuss." The chastisement was delivered gently and he boldly reached out and patted her hand.

"That's why I'm here. To fuss over you." Sylvia put away her equipment, then slowly wiped the counter down with a disinfectant.

He watched her work, not rushing off as he usually did. There was something soothing about being with Sylvia.

"Leon, have you thought any more about going for a walk with me one day? The weather's quite lovely, but the forecast says it won't last." She stared at the counter she was wiping as if too shy to actually look at him. He found it refreshing after the bold advances of Miss Matthews.

"Ah, Sylvia." He sighed and responded regretfully. "It's not that I don't want to go for a walk with you."

She turned to face him, the cloth clutched in her hands. "Leon, I know I'm probably out of line talking to you like this, but it isn't good for you to be inside all the time. You're pale and look stressed. Some fresh air and sunshine would do wonders for you."

"Sylvia, the world isn't a safe place—"

"Pshaw! That's an excuse and you know it. Lots of handsome, wealthy men stroll about freely. You need to realize that you're letting your wealth and position make you a prisoner. What good is it, if you never get out to enjoy life?"

He stared at her impassioned face. Her eyes sparkled and her cheeks glowed becomingly. "Well, perhaps..."

A smile spread across her face. "We could go for a walk together through the park. There's a lovely cafe I know that serves tea. Or perhaps you'd come to my home to see my garden? I make a wonderful lemon loaf that we could share on the back patio."

He chuckled over her enthusiastic response, but his laughter stopped at the sound of a snort from behind him.

"Really, Sylvia. Mr. Aldrich is much too busy to spend his time cavorting through your garden and eating mediocre pastry out of doors. He has several important meetings and a slew of paperwork to deal with." Miss Matthews stood in the doorway looking down her nose at Sylvia, a sneer twisting her blood-red lips.

"Oh." Sylvia wilted under the condemning look. The sparkle left her eyes and her shoulders slumped. "Of course. How foolish of me." She twisted the cloth in her hands and then turned back to the counter. "I'll finish up here and let you get back to work then."

"No!" He reached out and touched Sylvia's arm. "She's wrong." He glared at his personal assistant. "Miss Matthews, I am well aware of my schedule. If I choose to cancel a meeting and spend time otherwise occupied, it is none of your concern. I will talk to you later. You're dismissed."

Miss Matthews' jaw dropped in surprise then snapped shut. She pivoted on her stiletto heels and marched out of the room her whole bearing betraying her disapproval.

Turning, he addressed Sylvia who was looking at him with obvious confusion. "Sylvia, there is nothing I'd like better than to go for a walk with you. How about tomorrow morning around ten-thirty?"

"Really? Leon, that would be splendid!" She beamed up at him and he tentatively reached out to take her hand.

"Perhaps I could even take you out for lunch?"

Marla stomped into her office, barely resisting the urge to slam the door. How could Aldrich even consider spending time with that woman? And he was taking Sylvia out to lunch! In three years the man had never so much as bought her, his very own personal assistant, a cup of coffee!

She ran her hands through her hair and gave a silent scream of fury. It was ridiculous, preposterous even, that Aldrich was attracted to Sylvia Robinson and not her. For three years she'd all but thrown herself at the man and gotten nowhere. But Sylvia... All she had to do was suction up some mucous and the man was salivating over her.

Looking around the room she wished she had something to throw or break to ease the anger and frustration inside her. Of course, everything in the room was too expensive to destroy so she resorted to dumping the recycling bin and tossing balled up pieces of paper about the room. It wasn't nearly as satisfying as the crashing sound of breaking glass, but it was all she dared allow herself.

She couldn't let Aldrich or Sylvia know how upset she really was. That would never do. She took a deep breath and forced herself to calm down. Plopping down in her desk chair, she turned to pick up the phone, then blinked in surprise as she noticed the shadowy reflection of her wolf on the blank computer screen. It was a pitiful creature, a dull grey colour that she'd never liked. Snorting derisively, she shook her head. It had been such a disappointment the first time she'd transformed. Honestly, why couldn't she at least have had a wolf that suited her image.

A cold heartless image, her wolf reminded her.

"So?" She snapped back at the wolf annoyed with its comment.

Is that how you want to be seen? Little wonder you had few friends in the pack.

"I didn't need friends in the pack. Besides, they were all dull. Happy to be stuck in a hick town, living lives that went nowhere."

You had a few friends and you could have had more, if you'd tried. Instead you pushed everyone away.

She shrugged. "They weren't worth the effort. Besides, I didn't want to stay there. I wanted to make something of my life."

Make something of your life? Like what? You work all alone in a luxurious apartment with no friends. You go home to an empty apartment. The man you've been trying to catch shows more interest in a middle-aged woman than he does in you.

"No! That's not true. I have a lovely apartment. I spend time with Jeffries."

Who only wants you for sex.

She ignored the interjection and continued on. "And I'm getting rid of Sylvia. Then Aldrich will notice me."

I won't be a part of it this time, the wolf warned.

"As if you have a choice. You'll do as I say." She glared at the computer screen, seeing her own face again. It was contorted, ugly red blotches on her cheeks. She schooled her features into their usual calm, unflappable expression, smoothed her hair, and then folded her hands neatly on the desktop to consider the situation in a rational manner.

Aldrich has been busy all morning on some project in the back rooms of the penthouse. It was the one area to which he refused to give her unsupervised access. She suspected he kept private records back there and she'd tried on various occasions to get in, but like certain computer files, she remained locked out. The entrance was fingerprint activated and she hadn't figured out how to get past it. Plus, Swanson's office was the first door down the hallway and the man was always in there reviewing security tapes and checking codes.

She knew something big was going on. There were people in the back rooms now, something that had never happened before. Aldrich had let two new persons into his sanctuary. She could detect their scents; both were males, one was injured. The coppery scent of blood tinged the air, but it wasn't a serious injury. A drug was being used too, probably a sedative.

She'd spent part of the morning straining to hear what was going on, trying various rooms, standing by ventilation ducts, but to no avail. The rooms were well secured and she had no idea what was going on. It bothered her greatly that Aldrich hadn't mentioned anything to her and was probably one of the reasons she'd snapped at Sylvia like that.

Her reaction had been a strategic error, but what was done was done and now she'd have to deal with the consequences. Picking up the phone, she called Jeffries.

"Jeffries? ... Marla here ... Yes, I miss you too ... Remember our conversation this morning? ... Uh-huh. ... I still want to play that trick on Sylvia. Any idea when you could be ready?" She frowned listening to him making excuses. "No. I haven't changed my mind and you'd better not either. Not if you want any more of what I gave you this morning ... It works both ways, Jeffries. I make your 'elevator' go up and you ... Uh-huh. Now you get the idea ... Good. I really need to do this by tomorrow morning ... Thank you. I'll give you a big reward tomorrow night if this works." She blew a kiss down the phone and then hung up, a satisfied smile on her face.

Cassie stared at the picture of Kellen as it appeared on the tiny screen of her cell phone. The kidnappers had sent it, as requested, when she said she'd turn herself over to them tomorrow, but only if she had proof that Kellen was alive. Well, he was alive, but his eyes were unfocused as if he'd been drugged.

The Finding

At least the swelling of his eye and lip were less than in the picture she'd found pinned to her front door. She bit her lip, holding back the sympathetic tears that threatened to fall and studied the picture again. Someone was beside Kellen though she could only see the person's fingertips. They were holding a newspaper that showed today's date.

She supposed she should be glad that at least he was still alive, but a numbness was coming over her. This couldn't really be happening, not to her, not to Kellen. Things like this happened to famous people, important people. Well, she supposed being an heiress she did fit into that category, but she'd never seen herself as anyone special. The only thing special about her was that she was a werewolf and this didn't even have anything to do with that fact!

Bryan plucked the phone from her unresisting fingers and squinted at the picture, then wordlessly passed it to the other men in the room.

"That confirms it." Ryne tossed the phone on the table and ran his hands through his hair. "The Anderson kid is there. Now how do we go about getting him out?"

"And how do we get in to find Marla and Aldrich?" Kane grumbled from the window where he was observing the view. "The Chicago pack reports that he hardly ever leaves the building and when he does it's in a limo. Damn thing is built like a tank apparently."

Bryan paced the room. "The front door is guarded and we can't take the doorman out. It's too public. There'd be too many questions."

"There's probably a closed circuit TV as well. If we go in the front it will give Marla and Aldrich too much warning. Quite likely Aldrich has a backup escape plan, given how paranoid he is." Ryne stood up and went to the small bar fridge and took out a beer. After taking a swig, he sat on the edge of the dresser, one leg languidly swinging back and forth. "We need to sneak in some way. But how?"

Cassie remained where she was, curled up in a chair in the corner, watching the men warily. For all that Bryan had tried to ease some of her fears, she was still extremely aware of the fact that she was surrounded by three werewolves. Er…Lycans. The Alphas especially exuded a sense of dominating strength that had the wolf inside her tucking its tail between its legs. For once, she was in total concordance with the creature. She could sense the men were angry and frustrated and even though she knew it wasn't directed at her, it didn't make her any less uneasy.

Cautiously, trying not to draw attention to herself, she reached for her cell phone and stared at the picture of Kellen. At present it was zoomed in on his face. She reversed the zoom, easing the picture back, taking in his whole self. The poor man was tied to a hard wooden chair. It was as if the kidnappers were taunting him, seeing as how he was surrounded by soft carpeting and expensive art work. Even the curtains were of a high quality. As she scanned the picture of the room, an idea began to form.

It was crazy, but... She frowned and considered the idea again. It might work, but could she really do it? Perhaps. She stared at Kellen's slumped figure and realized she had no choice. It was probably the only way.

"I can do it." She said the words aloud while staring at the picture. The conversation in the room stopped and she looked up to find the three men staring at her.

"Do what, Cassie?" Bryan looked at her puzzled.

She licked her lips nervously, but then stood up and said it again. "I can get in to the penthouse and then let the rest of you in."

Kane gave her a condescending smile and shook his head while Ryne outright laughed. "Bryan, did you overstate the abilities of Lycans to her?" He chuckled again. "It's nice of you to offer sweetie, but—"

She cut off the man's comment. "I mean it. I can get in there by... What did you call it, Bryan? Tele-something?"

"Teleporting." Bryan supplied the word, but shook his head. "Uh-uh. No way. You aren't popping into a viper's den by yourself. Besides you can't control it. You've never done it at will." His words held a certain finality as if he thought he had the

298

final say as to what she could or couldn't do. She bit back an instinctive retort at his high-handed manner.

"What the hell are you two talking about?" Ryne looked between the two of them, obviously not understanding what they were referring to.

"Teleporting, Ryne." Kane walked closer, staring at Cassie as he addressed his brother. "Don't you remember the lessons we had on the ancient ones? Or was that another of the classes you skipped?"

"Ha, ha. I remember, but..." Ryne also walked closer to Cassie and she took an involuntary step backwards. He turned to look at Bryan. "How does she know about teleporting? I told you to bring her up to speed on Lycans, but that's not the first topic I would have picked."

Bryan rubbed his neck and chuckled. "Me either. Um... I haven't had time to tell you all about our newest pack member, Ryne, but it seems she's no run of the mill lone wolf."

Ryne raised his brows. "How so?"

"Cassie says that she's had a few rather odd experiences during the full moon. Experiences where she's apparently disappeared from her locked bedroom and reappeared in another location."

"Damn, I don't believe it." Ryne stared at her in obvious surprise, then ran his hand through his thick black hair. He shook his head and whistled. "If it's true, this is some stray we've found."

She bristled at the term stray. "I'm not some lost dog, you know."

"He didn't mean it that way," Kane spoke softly. "My brother's not known for his flowery phrases, but he is right. If you can indeed teleport, you are an exceptional Lycan." He turned to look at Bryan. "Has she reported any other signs?"

Bryan shifted uncomfortably. "She says she's had constant dreams of a certain wolf. Always the same wolf."

Kane nodded. "It fits. Her wolf knows its mate and has already formed a blood bond without even having met." He hooked his thumbs in his belt loops and rocked back on his heels. "Congratulations, Ryne. You're probably the only Alpha on the continent with a royal-blooded wolf in your pack."

The three men all gazed at Cassie speculatively and she gave them a hesitant smile, not at all liking being the centre of attention. "So...um...do any of you know how to teleport or have any pointers for me?"

"No." Bryan gave his head a shake. "No I don't have any 'pointers', and no I don't think it's a good idea."

"But why? None of you have come up with a better idea yet." She warmed to her idea in the face of Bryan's outright dismissal. He was trying to tell her what to do again and she wasn't about to put up with it. Jutting her chin, she frowned at him and he glared right back. The tension grew between them and Bryan issued a low growl from his throat. Startled, she blinked, instinctively looking away only to encounter the gaze of the two Alphas. They were studying the interaction with expressions of mild interest. Suddenly, she felt incredibly ill at ease. Here she was surrounded by werewolves and what was she doing? Showing attitude. Looking at the floor, she hoped she hadn't been too insubordinate.

Bryan muttered something under his breath and turned away to look out the window, but the other two seemed interested in her idea.

"She's right, you know." Ryne nodded. "There's no obvious way for us to get in. Aldrich has made his own fortress."

"It might work." Kane concurred. He nodded towards the cell phone in her hand. "She has an image of the room to focus on so she'd know where she was going. It's not a complete stab in the dark."

She stood straighter, pleased that they liked her idea.

"But she's only done it a few times and has no idea how to control it." Bryan faced the room again, a frown on his face.

"We could practise here in the motel. I could go from room to room." She clutched the phone in her hand and looked anxiously at the men.

Kane cocked his head. "You realize it could be dangerous, don't you? When you suddenly appear in Aldrich's penthouse, you'll be by yourself and there's no guarantee that the room will be empty."

She gave a half shrug putting on a show of bravado. "I...I guess I'll just have to hope for the best. And I won't be alone for long. Kellen will be there."

"Sweetheart, your friend doesn't look like he'll be much help. My best guess is that they've got him pretty doped up to keep him quiet." Ryne gave her a small apologetic smile as if he were sorry for bursting her bubble.

"Oh." She did feel rather deflated for a moment, but then she squared her shoulders. "Then, I guess I'll have to find a way of letting you guys in, won't I?" She walked over to the laptop and stared at the screen. "Your friend Daniel sent you the floor plans, right? And the security system. If we look at this picture of Kellen, it seems he's in a corner room. See how the windows are situated?"

The men gathered around her and she pointed to where she was looking. "So Kellen must be in one of these corner rooms. And if we look at the security system, this appears to be the main hub and that's..." she frowned at the screen for a moment, "down the hall from this room here which is one of the possible locations they're holding Kellen."

Bryan rubbed his chin. "It would make sense to hold a prisoner near the main security room." He gave her an approving nod.

She felt a glow of pride over Bryan's comment and struggled to keep from beaming. "So once I get in, I can zip down the hall, turn off whatever alarms there are and then you guys come up and help me get Kellen out."

"And deal with Marla and Aldrich." Kane added darkly.

Bryan exhaled loudly and shoved his hands in his pockets. "I still don't like it, but I don't have another solution." He pressed his lips tightly together then nodded. "Okay, let's head to our room. If Mel's sleeping, we don't want to wake her. We'll start practising teleporting a short distance and see how it goes."

She nodded trying to ignore the acrobatics her stomach was suddenly performing as she contemplated what she'd agreed to do. Wiping her sweaty palms on her pant legs she reminded herself she was doing it for Kellen. The knowledge did little to ease her worries.

Chapter 19

Bryan watched Cassie try, yet again, to teleport from one side of the room to the other. They'd been at it for over two hours and this attempt was as unsuccessful as the previous ten attempts had been. The air shimmered around her, but that was as far as she got. He could tell she was getting frustrated; the flush along her cheekbones, the tightness around her mouth told the story.

Ryne lounged languidly against the door frame, his thumbs hooked in his belt loops, looking totally bored while Kane paced the room, giving orders in what was probably supposed to be a helpful manner. Bryan suspected it was making Cassie even more tense because it certainly was doing that to him. He gritted his teeth and clenched his fists, biting back the comment that hovered on the tip of his tongue.

"Cassandra you need to concentrate and stay focused. Build a clear mental picture in your mind of the far side of the room. Picture the lamp, the texture of the wall paper, the feel of the carpeting beneath your feet. Gather your personal energy into a ball inside you, then let it expand and reach out into the space around you." Kane's voice droned on and on.

Bryan closed his eyes and tried to ignore the dull throbbing in his head. Each word Kane spoke was like a hammer beating against his brain over and over and over. He inhaled deeply and tried counting to ten.

"Dammit, I've done that so many times, I think I'm going to puke. It isn't working. Now will you please just shut up!" Cassie threw her hands up in despair and glared at Kane. The Alpha frozen, an expression of stunned surprise on his face.

For a moment the whole room was silent, even Cassie appearing shocked at her outburst before the outrage drained from her body and she seemed to shrink into herself. The flush left her cheeks, leaving her face pale; her eyes dark orbs staring at the powerful man before her. She pushed her hair from her face, then tucked her hands in her back pockets. Giving an apologetic shrug, she licked her lips in a nervous fashion and dropped her gaze to the floor before speaking.

"I...I'm sorry."

A slow clapping came from Ryne's direction and they all looked towards him. He'd pushed himself away from the door and walked towards Cassie with a crooked grin on his face. "Good for you, girl. If you hadn't said it, I was going to." He gave her a playful punch on the shoulder before sauntering over to grab a handful of peanuts from the selection of snacks on the small table in the corner.

She appeared flabbergasted by the comment and looked at Bryan obviously uncertain what to do. In some strange way, he found it incredibly easy to interpret what she was feeling. She was surprised at her own actions and Ryne's as well, and on some level her wolf was berating her for having mouthed off to an Alpha. That was a definite no-no in wolf society and retribution would normally be swift and severe.

He walked over to her while struggling to keep his face bland, his own feelings about what had just happened firmly in check. As Beta, his job was to enforce, support, and protect. While Cassie likely didn't need protecting—Kane might be ticked off, but he'd not attack the girl—she definitely needed support. Putting a hand on her shoulder, he whispered words of encouragement to her. "You impressed your new Alpha and let me tell you Ryne is hard to impress. Way to go."

Kane glowered at all three of them and opened his mouth, most likely to protest, but the door opened at that moment and Elise walked into the room.

"Hi! How's it going?" She'd stopped by earlier to see what they were up to, but then had left to visit with Mel.

"We're still trying to teach Cassie to teleport." Kane answered stiffly.

"Except your mate is being a pain in the ass and acting like he's an expert." Ryne added, a devilish glint in his eye.

Elise raised her eyebrows and seemed to be biting back a smile. "So what else is new?" She casually walked over to Kane and kissed his cheek.

"Elise, you're developing an attitude." Kane growled a warning.

"Oh hush. I know how you can get sometimes. You mean well, but you can be so stuffy." Elise patted his shoulder and turned to Cassie. "From the emotional atmosphere in the room, I'm assuming Kane is irritating everyone, isn't he?"

"Well..." She blinked and shifted her weight from one foot to the other. "He *was* trying to help."

"You don't need to defend him, Cassie," Ryne leaned against the dresser and stuck his legs out crossing them at the ankle. He appeared immensely pleased with the turn of events.

Kane's face darkened for a minute, then he sighed and pushed his fingers through his hair. "Was I getting that bad?" He looked around somewhat sheepishly.

"Yes." Bryan decided it was time to call a spade a spade. "Repeating the same instruction to her twenty times isn't going to help. You're making Cassie more nervous and that increases the level of difficulty. From what you said she needs to be relaxed in order to be successful."

Kane grunted in acknowledgement. "Okay. I get your point." He looked at Cassie and gave a crooked smile. "Sorry."

She visibly relaxed and smiled back. "It wasn't all a waste of time. The instructions were helpful. The first time you said them."

"The first time, hmm?" Kane cocked his head and studied Cassie. "But not the next nineteen?"

She shook her head and flushed. Everyone chuckled.

"Okay. I guess I've done my part then."

Elise grabbed Kane's arm, tugging lightly on it. "Good. If you're done here, we can spend some quality time together; that was supposed to be one of the reasons for this trip after all, wasn't it? Oh, and John's phoned twice, and Jacob wants to tell you about his loose tooth."

Kane looked down at her, frowning. "This is supposed to be a vacation for you, but this is the second time you've been on the phone talking to the kids."

"And you haven't snuck in a call to John about pack business? That's not the story he was telling me a few minutes ago when I talked to him." A flush appeared on Elise's cheeks as if her temper was starting to rise.

A muscle worked in Kane's jaw and his lips tightened into a flat line. Bryan frowned sensing an undercurrent between the two of them. Was there trouble in paradise?

Kane put his hand in the small of Elise's back, but she stepped away and left the room. With a sigh, he followed. The room was silent after they left, no doubt everyone trying to interpret what they'd just witnessed.

Finally, Ryne broke the silence. "That was an interesting exchange, wasn't it? Still, it did my heart good to see Cassie take Kane down a peg. He can get too full of himself sometimes."

Bryan compressed his lips and resisted saying that the same thing applied to Ryne. It was one of the hazards of being an Alpha, he supposed. Everyone was always turning to you for advice, expecting you to make all the major decisions; it was natural to start to think you were omnipotent. At least Ryne wasn't as inclined to that failing, as some pack leaders were.

"So what should I try next?" Cassie brought Bryan's attention back to the main problem; teaching her to teleport on command.

"Perhaps this isn't a good idea." He began to express his doubts again. "You're still too new to all of this and—"

"At the moment it's our only course of action." Ryne cut off his protests. He frowned and stared around the room. "I'm no expert on this, but teleporting across a small room isn't necessarily the best way to start. On some level her brain is probably telling her it's a dumb idea; why waste energy teleporting when you could walk over there in two seconds?"

306

The Finding

"That makes sense." Cassie's face brightened. "I was sort of feeling that way. Um...what if I tried going from this room to the bathroom?

Bryan nodded. "And we'll lock the door so you can't just walk in."

"Sounds like a plan." Ryne straightened from his perch on the edge of the dresser. "One more thing. I'm leaving. Cassie doesn't know me that well and I sense some tension coming towards me." He paused and looked at Cassie, his brow quirked.

She flushed and stared at the floor, but said nothing. Bryan looked between the two, rather impressed that Ryne had picked up on that; he wasn't always the most sensitive of men. And it was true, Cassie still associated Ryne with the savage creature she'd first encountered. A few hours in his company wouldn't change a three-year belief.

"Okay." Bryan nodded. "It makes sense to me. She needs to be relaxed for this to work. Once she has the basics down, I'll give you a call and you can come back. Then we can practise having her teleport in less ideal conditions."

"Sounds like a plan. I'll go check on Melody and see how she's feeling." He walked across the room, pausing briefly as he passed by Cassie to give her hair a gentle tug. "You can do it, kid." With that he moved to the door, then stopped one more time. "And Bryan, if she needs to be relaxed, sex might help." He gave Bryan a wink and shut the door.

She looked at Bryan, her mouth hanging open.

"See?" He shrugged. "I told you he wasn't such a bad guy."

"Not such a..." She sputtered. "He just suggested we..." Apparently she was incapable of finishing her sentences.

He grinned at her impishly, suddenly pulling her close, wrapping his arms around her and nuzzling her neck. "He's right, you know. Sex can be very relaxing."

She gave a shiver and he leaned back, watching her face, keeping his own expression casually teasing. He was curious as to how she'd respond. Twice now they'd almost kissed, but then stopped. Last night in her backyard he'd let his scruples take over; they'd just met and he was in a position of authority over

307

her; it hadn't seemed right. And then this morning on the plane, having learned they might already be connected, he'd been curious, but the pilot had interrupted and he'd remembered they were in public.

But now, they were alone. How did Cassie really feel? His hands rested lightly on her back and he gently stroked her. A flash of hunger passed over her, her eyes darkening, pupils widening. He could feel her heart rate accelerate, her breathing hitch and his own responded in kind. She pressed her hands against his chest, her fingers spreading, caressing, testing the feel of him. Biting his lip, he stifled a groan; the heat from her palms burned into him. There was stirring in his groin as his own body reacted. He'd meant this as an experiment, a bit of joke, but...

Her mouth opened fractionally and the tip of her tongue snuck out, wetting her lips. He felt himself leaning closer, sensed she was lifting herself onto her toes, her chin tilting upward as if reaching for him and then... She stopped.

Instead of caressing his chest, she was now pushing away. He loosened his arms and she stepped back clearing her throat. "I...um...I think I should keep practising my teleporting."

He kept his own disappointment in check and nodded, keeping his arms limp at his side despite the fact that they ached to grab her and draw her close once again. She kept her gaze fixed on him as she backed towards the bathroom.

"I'll just...um...lock myself in here and see if I can pop myself back into this room." Her back was now pressed against the bathroom door. She fumbled with the handle and then slipped inside. He heard the lock snick into place and exhaled loudly, not realizing he'd been holding his breath.

Sinking down onto the bed, he propped himself against the headboard and contemplated what had happened. Ryne had been teasing—sort of—when he suggested they have sex. And he had been teasing as well when he grabbed Cassie just now. Well, perhaps his wolf hadn't been teasing, but that was a different matter.

What was curious was Cassie's reaction. She'd wanted him and it hadn't only been the animal inside her. This time her eyes had been clear; she was aware of what was going on. It excited him to think she returned his interest and he *was* interested, he couldn't deny the fact any longer. Lying to oneself was a pointless exercise.

He rubbed the back of his neck and considered his new packmate. She had an exotic look about her with her warm skin tones and long dark hair. Her full red lips begged to be kissed and he remembered his own sliding over hers at the park, tasting, nibbling. Swallowing hard, he thought of how expressive her eyes could be; heavy lidded with desire, clouded with fear and doubt, sparkling with mischief.

A smile crept over his face as he recalled how she'd inadvertently put Kane in his place. He suspected once she relaxed a bit, she'd be a fire-cracker. The girl hadn't had much chance for fun over the past few years. Basically living hand to mouth, dealing with Kellen; it would likely try the patience of a saint when his addiction got the better of him. Yep, Cassie's life hadn't been easy since she fled the Greyson Estate. She wasn't whining and snivelling like a spoilt little rich girl, though. She'd found a way to survive. And even now, when her only real friend—her 'packmate' as Kellen seemed to be—was messing around with her life, she was still loyal to him.

He sighed and crossed his arms behind his head. She'd be a great addition to the pack and he'd enjoy tutoring her in the ways of their people. A mischievous grin spread over his face as he contemplated how their 'lessons' might turn out. If she was indeed his predestined mate, there really wasn't anything he could do about it but accept his fate. It wouldn't be such a hardship, being mated to her.

A faint disturbance in the air around him caught his attention and he sat up expectantly staring at a spot near the bed. For a moment, he could almost see Cassie standing beside him, but then the image faded. He held his breath, holding back the impulse to call out her name, to go see how she was. Breaking her concentration at this time wouldn't help.

Seconds ticked by. A minute passed and then another. His muscles were clenched as he kept himself tightly in check.

Finally, the air shimmered again and in the blink of an eye she stood before him.

"Cassie! You did it!" He jumped off the bed and pulled her into his arms and swung her around in a circle before setting her down. Leaning back, he looked at her face and frowned. She seemed to be in shock. For a moment she stood stiffly in the circle of his arms and then her whole body slumped, sobs wracking her frame. "Shh! It's okay. You're fine." He rocked her back and forth, stroking her hair, her back, whispering assurances as she wept.

When her crying eased, he released his tight grip and eased her back in his arms. Keeping one arm around her, he brought his other hand up and cupped her face, wiping the tears from her cheek with his thumb. "Hey, you should be happy. You teleported at will! Why all the tears?"

She sniffed and clenched her hand against his shirt, the material bunching in her fingers. "Because I did it. It worked and that means..." She looked away, blinking rapidly.

"It means what?" He queried, studying her face intently, trying to interpret the range of emotions that passed over it. Emotional pain radiated from her and he winced, feeling the hurt himself.

"It means I really am a werewolf." She buried her face against his chest as she whispered her answer.

"So?" He frowned, puzzled at what she was trying to convey. "You knew that already."

"I know." She flicked a glance up at him, before averting her eyes. "It's crazy, but even though I knew it, I didn't really believe it. I kept thinking—hoping—that my uncle was wrong. Even when I was a wolf in the park yesterday, I kept praying that it was some weird hallucination, but now..." She sighed heavily. "I can't deny it any longer. I'm not human."

"No..." He responded slowly, not really able to grasp why it mattered, but trying his best to understand. "You're not. You're a Lycan like me and all my friends and family. Is that really so bad?"

She shrugged yet again. "I guess not. It's just that after years of believing you're a werewolf, someone told you that you weren't. That you were human. While you know they're right and there's evidence to prove it, a part of you doesn't want to give up your original belief. Sort of like learning there's no Santa Claus."

"Okay." He supposed he sort of understood what she meant. "So being able to teleport made it 'real' to you."

"Uh-huh. Even though I suggested the idea, I think a part of me was hoping it wouldn't work because then it might mean some big mistake had been made. I was still a normal human girl living a boringly normal life with a poorly paying job, a messed up boyfriend and too many bills." She laughed lightly through her tears. "Why I'd want to hang on to that I don't know. Lots of girls would think being a werewolf was more exciting."

"I think it is. Pack life is nothing like what you're used to. There's always someone around. You don't have to worry about bills. We all help each other out." He ducked his head to look her in the eye. "I think you'll like it, once you give it a chance."

"Maybe." She gave him a faint smile then stepped away, wiping her face. Inhaling deeply, she squared her shoulders. "So I managed to teleport once. I guess I should try it again, right?"

He reached out and ran a finger down her cheek. "Sure. And I'll be right here waiting for you."

By the time evening arrived, Cassie had a better grip on her emotions, deciding to deal with them at a later date. Right now, she had to concentrate on mastering teleporting so she could rescue Kellen. Once she got the hang of it, it wasn't too difficult to do. In fact, she was feeling rather pleased with herself. She'd managed to teleport from one suite to another several times and had even gone from the lobby to the fifth floor where their rooms were located by strategically hiding behind a potted plant while Bryan watched to ensure no one noticed her disappearing act. She'd wanted to try going from the parking garage to the rooftop restaurant, but Bryan had vetoed it saying she was too tired and needed to rest for tomorrow.

He was right, but she hadn't liked to admit her weakness, especially not in front of the others. The teleporting—converting her molecules into energy and then sending them through space—was exhausting. Her head pounded, her legs felt like cooked noodles and her entire body ached.

Still she'd tried to project a strong image when they'd reported to Ryne. Bryan had said she'd impressed him earlier with her rant against Kane. She didn't want to change his opinion. If things progressed the way Bryan planned, Ryne would be the equivalent of her 'boss' in the near future. She wasn't too keen on the idea and still hoped to find a way out, but just in case, she'd better hedge her bets.

"So, Cassie, how do you feel about moving to Canada?" Mel sat beside her at the table in the restaurant and had kept up a stream of idle chatter throughout the meal. Ryne and Bryan had indulged in conversation related to pack business as near as Cassie could determine; something to do with renovations to one of the wings of the main house. She hadn't really paid too much attention; it had taken all of her concentration to keep her eyes open and her head from falling forward in her plate.

"I've never been to Canada." She gave a vague answer and looked at Elise who sat across the table from her. "Have you?"

"No. Kane keeps talking about flying north to visit Ryne, but there is always some mini-crisis occurring that keeps him tied to Smythston. I'm surprised he managed to tear himself away long enough to come here." Elise smiled, but there was a certain bitterness underlying her words and Cassie wondered what was going on. Kane and Elise had seemed on edge with each other earlier on and now Kane wasn't eating dinner with them. Apparently another call from his Beta had come in. In fact, except for a brief conversation when Bryan announced the success of her teleporting, she hadn't seen him since her outburst about his over-zealous help.

"I'm glad our pack is still small." Mel said. "Ryne is busy, but he still has time for himself, too."

Elise sighed looking repentant about her earlier words. "Kane tries, he really does, but the pack is so big."

312

The Finding

"Would it ever subdivide and become two smaller packs?" Cassie was pleased the conversation no longer focused on her.

"Kane's mentioned it, but we'd need to find another territory and then see which families would be willing to move." Elise picked up her wine glass and took a sip. "Whether it will ever happen remains to be seen."

"Are you ladies finished?" Ryne interrupted the conversation, pushing his chair back from the table. "We're done eating and Kane hasn't made an appearance yet so there's no point in waiting any longer."

"I'll have room service bring him up a plate." Elise said as they walked to the elevator. "You know Mel, you haven't even seen Kane face to face, yet."

"I know. Maybe tomorrow after all the excitement." Mel sighed and rubbed her rounded belly. "It should be interesting to finally meet him." A faint worried frown appeared on her brow.

Ryne chuckled and put his arm around her shoulder. "Once we get this mess cleared up, there'll be plenty of time for visiting."

"I wish you'd let me go along, Ryne." Mel looked at her mate and ran her hand over his chest.

"Nice try, Melody, but you're carrying my pup and I'm not risking either of you being near Marla or Aldrich."

"I could wait in the car. Please?" She batted her eyelashes at him, but he laughed.

"Tell you what, you can spend the night trying to convince me." He grinned down at her. "But in the morning, don't be surprised if I haven't changed my mind."

Mel made a face, but seemed resigned to her fate.

They all parted ways in the hallway and headed to their respective rooms. Cassie approached the door to her...their...room with trepidation. She'd temporarily forgotten that she and Bryan were sleeping in the same room. True, there were two double beds, but it still seemed intimate. Behind her, she could feel the warmth generating from his body as he waited for her to open the door. Her wolf murmured happily over the situation, but Cassie's stomach clenched nervously.

313

She stared at the door knob, not wanting to touch it, trying to put off the inevitable as long as possible. Her breathing grew rapid, and she felt almost lightheaded as she contemplated the night ahead.

"Come on, Cassie. I'm tired."

Obviously growing impatient, Bryan reached around her, plucking the key card from her hand and opening the door himself. His arm brushed against her breast and her whole body flushed with awareness. Oh God, how was she going to get through this?

"Are you sure, Meredith?" Franklin gripped the phone tightly, nodding as his old partner repeated her message. "All right." He rubbed his forehead thinking quickly. "Okay, I'll need you here. Get the first flight you can, let me know your arrival time and I'll pick you up at the airport. By then, everything should be in place. See you then."

He hung up the phone and stared thoughtfully across the kitchen, not really seeing the old plaster walls and aged wooden beams. His eyes stopped at the large fireplace that usually had a cheery fire burning within, giving the Estate kitchen a warm, homey feel. The hearth was cold and empty now, just as the Estate was. It needed a family to fill it, children running up and down the halls, being shooed away from the fire and scolded for sneaking bits of cookie batter like Miss Cassie used to do. At one time he'd thought Cassie's children might help fill the rooms and bring life back to the rambling old building, but now that seemed doubtful.

Rubbing his hands over his face, he turned to face Mrs. Teasdale, knowing she was anxious to hear the latest information.

"It's bad news, isn't it, Franklin?" She tried to keep her voice calm, but Franklin could see the trembling of her chin.

"I'm afraid so. Meredith saw a report on the news. A dead body was found in a dumpster in Las Vegas."

"Not Miss Cassie's friend, Kellen?" Mrs. Teasdale grabbed the back of a nearby chair.

314

"No." Franklin sighed heavily. "It's Eddie Perini. He was shot last night and left to bleed to death."

"Perini? Who's that?"

"He managed Dollar Niche, the company that lent Kellen Anderson money. And Dollar Niche is owned by Aldrich which was how Miss Cassie was blackmailed into returning to Chicago." He shook his head. "I don't know if this is related or not, but the Dollar Niche office was trashed. Police report that it appears someone was going through the files and they're speculating that Perini walked in on the individual. A fight ensued. Perini was shot, thrown in the dumpster and left to die.

"Do you think it was made to look like a break-in gone wrong to throw off suspicion? Perhaps Aldrich ordered Eddie Perini killed to keep him quiet about his plan?" She quirked a brow, obviously trying to make sense of the situation. While Mrs. Teasdale had never been a part of the Service, her late husband had, and she'd picked up quite a bit over the years.

"Perhaps. Maybe Perini was going to turn the tables on Aldrich and try to blackmail him." Franklin frowned and rubbed his chin. "Usually any death associated with Aldrich isn't ever called a death at all. Aldrich makes people disappear without a trace. This doesn't have Aldrich's touch to it."

"Could someone have a grudge against Perini or possibly be trying to make points with Aldrich by getting rid of someone they thought was a threat to him?"

"From what Meredith has been able to find out, Perini didn't operate in the most exulted of circles but he was mostly bluster with very little action. Killing him was probably unnecessary."

"Interesting, but what does this mean for us?"

Franklin paced the room and rubbed the back of his neck. He hated to give in when they were so close to Cassie finding a real home, but he'd promised Anthony Greyson that if anything ever happened, he'd keep the girl safe. "If someone is starting to kill people over this, it's getting more dangerous than I ever expected. I think it's time we pulled Miss Cassie out."

Mrs. Teasdale looked troubled. "You're probably right, but it will interfere with her chances of becoming part of the pack the young man represents."

"Possibly." He shook his head, regretful at this turn of events. "But at least she'll be alive to try again."

Squaring her shoulders, Mrs. Teasdale straightened to her full height, or at least what there was of it. "What do you want me to do?"

"First of all, we need to find where Cassie is staying. Call around to all the motels within the city and see what you can find out."

"She might not be registered under her own name."

"Right. Meredith found out the name of the young fellow she's met up with by tracing his rental car. It's Cooper. Bryan Cooper. Try his name as well."

"Done. Anything else?" The woman's cheeks flushed at the excitement and Franklin smiled. Life had been dull around the Estate with just the two of them and a few occasional maintenance workers. It was good to have something happening though different circumstances would have been preferable.

"Meredith is flying in first thing in the morning. She'll need a suit. Make it something suitable for a government official. Oh, and perhaps a brief case."

"I'll see what I can find."

"And I'll need you to watch Netty." Despite the seriousness of the situation, Franklin had to bite back a smile at Mrs. Teasdale's expression. Ever since the fat little dachshund had absconded with one of her roasted chickens, she'd proclaimed the dog was a menace.

Despite her animosity, the cook nodded. "What's your plan?"

Franklin grinned, feeling the old adrenaline rush he used to experience when he was still on active duty. "We'll try bluffing our way in to see her. Claim to be IRS and we've tracked her down for tax evasion. People usually don't question the IRS when they show up asking for information."

"If she's with a werewolf though," Mrs. Teasdale frowned, "do they pay taxes?"

"They do now." Franklin nodded emphatically, hoping his crazy plan would work.

Chapter 20

"I'll...um... get ready for bed." Cassie stood in the middle of the room nervously shifting from foot to foot, not sure what to do with herself. She'd shared a home with Kellen for three years and had never felt this unsettled in his presence. Why was sharing with Bryan so different?

Because he's hot and sexy and has a delicious edge about him; not enough to make him obnoxious, just interesting.

She inhaled ready to scold the wolf inside her, then realized those were her own thoughts, not the animal's. She clamped her mouth tightly shut, exasperated with herself.

Bryan grunted in response, his eyes fixed on the TV screen while he absentmindedly took a swig of soda from a can. He swallowed and then responded. "Sure. I'll use the bathroom after you." He was flopped on the bed, with several pillows propping him up and a bag of pretzels at his side. His interest in her activities registered at a zero.

Sparing the briefest of glances to admire his exposed muscular chest—he'd removed his shirt and thrown it on the back of a chair before lying down—Cassie grabbed her bag and headed to the bathroom.

Once inside, she pressed her hands to her face, chagrined to feel the heat coming off her cheeks. She hoped Bryan hadn't noticed she was behaving like some virginal teenager. She sucked in a deep lungful of air and let it out slowly, before giving herself a pep talk. First of all, she wasn't a teenager and secondly she wasn't a virgin. Well, barely not a virgin. Her one time with Kellen hardly qualified her as an expert, but in an official sense she wasn't pure as the driven snow.

That thought made her frown and the animal inside whined pitifully. Would it matter to Bryan that she'd been with Kellen? Perhaps. She worried her lip. Werewolves were supposedly old fashioned about that sort of thing. Wait a minute! Why was she even concerned how he'd react? Sleeping with Bryan wasn't part of the programme. Yes, he was sexy and yes she liked him, but once this adventure was over, they'd part ways, right?

She began to nod then paused and amended the idea. They'd part ways unless she decided to stick around for a few days. She'd never known any others of her kind and it might be nice to talk with Mel and Elise a bit more. Learning more about herself would be like research and, if in the course of that research she ended up spending more time with Bryan, it was just coincidental, right? It had nothing to do with predestined mates. The course of her life wasn't going to be directed by a recurring dream and old werewolf folklore. When the time came—a time of her choosing—she'd bid farewell to Bryan and the others and head out somewhere.

Staring sightlessly at the mirror, she wondered how Bryan would react to her leaving. His wolf was drawn to hers; not that the wants of the animals inside really counted for much, she added. But Bryan—the human Bryan—did seem to be physically attracted to her. Hadn't she felt his arousal pressed against her?

The memory had a rush of warmth developing low down in her belly and she shifted uncomfortably, hoping he wouldn't scent her interest in him when she left the bathroom.

Cassie quickly turned on the taps and splashed cool water on her face, trying to douse the fire that threatened to grow within her. Pulling off her clothes, she changed into a t-shirt and sleep pants. Bryan was older and likely an experienced male. He wasn't going to jump her simply because she was sharing a room with him. It was utterly juvenile to think that way. He might notice she was reasonably attractive, but he wouldn't act on it.

That fact should have been comforting, but it wasn't. She pursed her lips and wondered why. Perhaps because of the whole 'mates' thing, she expected more attention from him? But that was ridiculous because she didn't want to be his mate, did she?

Yes, we do, the wolf inside her insisted.

No we don't, she argued back. If anything, I want a nice normal man of my own choosing, a house in the suburbs, a white picket fence, and a few kids.

We can have that with him!

Could she? She forced herself to think about it while she brushed her teeth. Bryan wasn't normal, he was a pack Beta. From everything she'd read in her research that meant he was second in command, powerful but level-headed, strict but protective. Hmm, that made a normal male sound rather dull, didn't it?

She slowed her brushing for a moment and considered the point. Bryan was anything but dull; she recalled how they'd butted heads during the course of their brief acquaintance. A thrill had coursed through whenever she challenged his authority and felt the force of his personality or, sensed he had latent power that was carefully leashed. Okay, scratch normal from her list of what she wanted. But it should still be her own choice, shouldn't it? Not because of some predestination.

And what about her house in the suburbs and the white picket fence? She began to brush vigorously again. From the way Bryan spoke there was a pack house which housed several wolves; definitely not her dream house in the suburbs. And as for a white picket fence, hadn't she overheard Ryne and Bryan discussing a security fence with video cameras? She pulled a face. That sounded more like a prison camp than a home.

And don't forget children, she reminded herself. Would she give birth to a litter? She thought of Mel's swollen stomach and wondered how far along she was. Was there one—what had Ryne called it?—*pup* inside, or more? Frowning, she recalled the other female she'd met—Elise—only had two children and they were a few years apart, so perhaps werewolves didn't emulate their animal cousins when it came to reproduction. Her shoulders slumped in relief over that fact. The idea of a litter of children seemed overwhelming.

"Are you all right?" Bryan knocked loudly on the bathroom door and Cassie gave a start. She'd been lost in thought much longer than she realized.

"Yes!" She called out, rinsing her mouth and quickly stuffing her possessions back in her bag. In her haste, she knocked over her bottle of pills and they rattled noisily against the plastic side of the container as it rolled off the counter and onto the ground. Bending over to pick it up, the door burst open and Bryan stood staring down at her, fists clenched, a frown on his face.

"What are you doing with those?" His tone was accusatory and she automatically responded in kind.

"What does it look like I'm doing? I'm picking them up."

He reached down and snatched the bottle from the floor just as she was reaching for it. Reading the label, he snorted. "You're not taking these any longer. I don't care if it is almost a full moon. They're dangerous to you and your wolf."

"They're my pills so you can't tell me what to do!" She tried to grab the bottle back, but he held it out of reach.

"They're illegal; little better than common street drugs in my book. And I'm your Beta. I *can* tell you what to do and I'm doing so right now. You aren't taking any more of these. It's time for you to come to grips with the wolf inside you instead of hiding."

"I'm not *hiding*. I'm *surviving* in a world that doesn't even know our kind exists." She reached for the bottle, but he held it higher.

"Funny, I didn't take you for a coward."

"Coward?" She gaped at him. "Where do you get off calling me a coward?"

"What else do you call it when someone is afraid of reality? Afraid of themselves?"

"I'm not afraid of myself." She folded her arms and stared at him belligerently.

"That's not what you said earlier today. And if you aren't afraid of yourself, of the animal inside, then why do you still have these pills?"

"I'm. Not. Afraid." She punctuated each word by poking him in the chest, then brushed past him. "I was merely safeguarding everyone around me." She dumped her bag on the floor and climbed into bed, drawing the covers up around her and turning her back to him.

From the bathroom she could hear the sounds of something being dumped in the toilet and then a flushing noise. She clenched her fists and bit her lip. For all her bravado, she was terrified at the idea of facing a full moon without her medication. Not that she'd been planning on taking the pills tonight; she knew she needed a clear head for tomorrow's rescue of Kellen. Tomorrow night, once the excitement was all over, was another matter. Now she had no choice but to stick around and hope Bryan would be able to control the animal within her. It would be too dangerous to the human population for her to be on her own.

Bryan walked out of the bathroom. She could hear him moving about the room, material rustling, lights being flicked off. The room darkened, only the light from her bedside lamp providing illumination.

Even though she was facing the wall, Cassie sensed Bryan coming closer, standing by her bed, staring down at her. The air fairly hummed with his presence.

"Cassie?"

She didn't respond, trying to keep her breathing even. Maybe he'd think she was asleep.

"I know you're awake."

Damn! She really didn't want to talk to him and considered not answering but then gave in. "So?" Her voice was filled with attitude in the hopes he'd leave her alone.

He exhaled loudly and she felt the edge of the bed dip down as he sat beside her. His hand brushed the top of her head, gently stroking. "I'm sorry. I didn't mean it when I said you were a coward. It's just that the thought of you taking those pills, knowing how dangerous they are, came out as anger. I know it's been hard for you to survive on your own, but the way you've been dealing with it has to change."

She curled her palm over the edge of the pillow, feeling its softness. He'd been worried about her. The idea helped melt away her own anger. "I wasn't going to take them tonight. They fell out by accident when I was gathering up my things." She whispered the words into the pillow not wanting to look at him, but for some reason feeling the need to explain herself, to redeem herself in his eyes.

"I'm glad to hear that." He moved his hand down the back of her head, his fingers trailing through her hair, in a soothing motion. She felt herself beginning to relax when he asked the damning question. "But what were your plans for tomorrow night?"

She shrugged trying to sound blasé. "That's really none of your business."

"Yes, it is. According to the Finding clause, I'm responsible for you. That means not only keeping you out of trouble, but also caring for your wellbeing."

Strangely enough, it hurt that the only reason he was concerned for her was because of some clause in an ancient law. She felt her throat tighten and tried to hide her feelings with an airy attitude. "I'm sorry some silly clause has left you stuck with me. After Kellen is safe, if you just close your eyes for a minute, I'll slip away and be one less thing for you to be responsible for."

"You will *not* slip away." He growled the words at her and took her by the shoulder, forcing her to roll over and face him. "I won't be taking my eyes off you, so don't even bother to try."

For a moment she was stunned by how close he was, her entire field of vision filled with him. The light from the bedside lamp highlighted his form, showing off his well-toned body and smooth skin. She couldn't stop the downward path of her eyes and she noted his firm abs and trim waist, the way his pyjama pants hung low on his hips, revealing the merest hint of body hair. She jerked her eyes back up to his face and concentrated on what he was saying.

The passion in his voice startled her. "Cassie, whether you like it or not, you're part of my pack, so quit fighting it. Pack is everything to a wolf. We live for the pack, die for the pack.

324

Every member is important, almost like a part of our own body. Pack means home, security, friends, family." He shook her gently. "I can't turn my back on you. You're like a part of me now."

She wasn't sure what to think about that. In a way it made her feel warm and wanted, but in another way, she felt hollow inside, too. Yes, Bryan felt she was part of his pack and he would care for her just like he'd cared for any other member, but a piece of her wanted him to see her as special and unique. She frowned and searched his face looking for some sign that she meant more, all the while questioning why it mattered. God, but her thinking was messed up when it came to him!

Bryan must have noticed her expression, but interpreted it to mean something else. "Don't worry. You'll be fine without the pills. I'll help you every step of the way. You need to learn to deal with what you are and the animal inside is a part of you." He paused, and laced their fingers together. "The full moon won't be so bad. I'll stay right beside you, helping you deal with the feelings that come over you."

She absorbed the warmth of his palm against her own, enjoying the brush of skin on skin. A tingle raced up her arm, causing a hitch in her breathing. Her earlier pique dissolved and she shifted on the mattress into a more comfortable position.

Her hip pressed against his thigh and one of his hands rested on the pillow near her head. When she inhaled, his masculine scent filled her. It both excited and calmed her, making her aware of him, yet feeling safe and protected, too. A light smile ghosted over his face as he stared down at her and she responded in kind.

Enjoying the easy atmosphere between them, she let some of her curiosity free. "What's it like when you shift? Do you retain any of your human self or are you totally an animal during a full moon?"

"When you're new at it, it can be hard to rein the animal in. It's so excited to finally be free, which is why having other wolves around is helpful. They guide the new wolf, allow it to enjoy the experience while keeping it out of trouble." His gaze wandered over her features as he spoke and she wondered what he was thinking; did he find her appearance pleasing?

She licked her lips before speaking, hesitant to bring up her first transformation, yet wanting to understand. "The first time I changed—when we met in the park—I had absolutely no idea what was going on. I was shocked to find myself there."

"Very typical for a first timer." He gave her a crooked smile and twirled a lock of her hair around his finger. She almost hummed at the pleasant feel of his gentle tugs.

"But later, when we were back at the house, there were times when the wolf took over and other times when I managed to be in charge."

"Uh-huh. The older you get and the more you communicate with your wolf, the easier it is to maintain control. For the first few shifts, it's almost a power struggle. Eventually though, the animal learns to trust you, to know it doesn't have to fight to be heard, to exist, and it accepts your leadership. In time, you and your wolf will think and act almost as one, complimenting each other's strengths. But you have to get to know each other first, just like any relationship."

"We talk—the wolf and I—sort of. I hear its voice in my head." She made the confession through lowered lashes, feeling embarrassed at the admission.

"That's a good start. I talk to my wolf all the time. I think it's similar to how humans talk to themselves."

She plucked at the covers with her free hand. "My...um...my wolf likes you." She peeked up at him through her lashes wondering why she felt the need to confess that to him or if it was even her idea. Perhaps the wolf had put her up to it?

"Really?" He smiled at her. "My wolf likes you too."

She gave a soft laugh. "Silly beasts."

"Yeah." He tucked the lock of hair he'd been playing with behind her ear, then slowly trailed his fingertips across the side of her face. "There's no accounting for taste."

She closed her eyes at the feel of his hand brushing over her skin, leaning into his touch.

"Cassie?"

"Hmm?"

"I like you, too."

"Really?" Her eyes flew open and a joyous feeling swept over her. Bryan liked her! She looked up into his eyes, unable to hold back the smile that broke out on her face. Was it her imagination, or was he leaning closer to her?

"Uh huh. Would you mind if I kissed you?"

Her throat suddenly felt tight and it was hard to breathe. She studied his features, noting his hot, heavy-lidded gaze, the way his hair fell on his forehead, the fullness of his lower lip. "I think I'd like that."

Slowly, oh so slowly, he leaned forward until their mouths were but a hair's width apart. For an interminable moment he hesitated, his eyes locked with hers. Then his lashes lowered and... Her eyes drifted shut as his lips brushed over hers, the merest whisper of a contact. A sigh escaped her at the butterfly softness of the touch. It was like this was her very first kiss, erasing all previous memories. A happy feeling bloomed inside her and she curled her fingers and toes as feelings she'd never known existed flooded her.

Softly, gently, he moved his lips over hers with utmost care. It felt so sweet, so tender, as if he were worshipping her mouth. She could easily lose herself forever in the feeling of his lips stroking hers, the light sliding motion mesmerising. When he pulled back, she had to force her eyes to open, reluctantly leaving the blissful world she'd found herself in.

Bryan was smiling down at her. "Was that okay?"

She nodded unable to speak for a moment. "A lot different than in the park." As soon as the words left her mouth, she flushed wishing she hadn't brought the incident up.

"Mmm... That was intense." He traced her features with his fingertip, the light touch causing her to shiver. "Our wolves know each other. But you and I..." He shook his head. "I think we're just starting our journey."

Slowly, he eased over onto his back and pulled her close. She rested her head on his chest and bravely placed her hand on his bare skin. His stomach muscles flinched at her touch but then stilled. Exhaling slowly, she relaxed into the warmth of his embrace.

"This is nice." Bryan whispered the words. "Being together and not butting heads."

"Yeah." She nestled her head more securely against his chest and they fell into a comfortable silence.

After a while Bryan spoke again. "Are you worried about tomorrow?"

"A little, but I'll be fine." She spoke positively, ignoring the faint fluttering in her stomach.

Bryan eased back from her. "You know if you don't feel up to this we can—"

"We can what? None of us came up with an alternate plan."

"I know. It's just that I worry about you."

"That's sweet of you. I'm usually the one doing the worrying."

"Cassie, I'm a Beta. I'm not sweet." He groaned and shook his head.

She chuckled softly then lifted her head, quickly pecked him on the mouth and then made a show of licking her lips. "Sorry, you're sweet."

He pressed an equally fast kiss to her lips. "But you're sweeter."

She rolled her eyes. "Bryan!"

He laughed softly, then suddenly stopped, his expression sobering. Rolling over, he braced a hand on each side of her and lowered his head again, this time kissing her properly. His tongue traced the seam of her mouth. She parted her lips slightly and moved them against his, marvelling at the feelings that were coming to life inside her. It was as if she were melting from the inside out.

A low moan came from Bryan, and he pressed closer, working a hand under her shoulder while the other cupped the back of her head. He traced her lower lip with his tongue and she sighed into him, opening wider, welcoming his questing tongue as it slowly explored her mouth. His tongue stroked hers then teased her sensitive upper palate. The feeling had her pressing closer and opening wider, eager for more.

The taste and scent of Bryan filled her and yet it wasn't enough. She wanted to experience every inch of him and ran her hands up his arms to his shoulders. Warm, smooth skin over muscle and bone. So strong. So male. She squeezed and stroked his biceps and shoulders. It was exhilarating to be with a man this way. To touch him, to discover his body.

She slid her arms around him to explore his back. It was broad and equally strong, his muscles moving fluidly under her hands. Moving lower, she traced his ribs then slipped to his narrow waist.

"Bryan..." She said the word on a sigh. It was so right to be with him, to have him close. Snaking her arms around his torso, she pulled him down so that he was on top of her. A shiver of excitement coursed through her as his weight settled over her. This...this feeling of a man's body pressing down the full length of hers.

She drew a shuddering breath, sure her heart was going to pound out of her chest, and the whole time, Bryan continued to rain kisses down on her, exploring her face, nipping her chin, tugging on her earlobe. He inched lower, dragging his teeth down the side of her neck, then biting gently on the sweet spot where her shoulder began.

A pleasure-filled moan escaped her and she drew one leg up to cradle his hips while sliding her hands up his back to bury her fingers in his hair. It was thick and silky and she bunched it in her hands, her nails lightly raking his scalp. Bryan responded, shifting on top of her, his hips flexing. She could feel a firm ridge of flesh pressing against her and she shivered in response. It both excited and frightened her, doubts suddenly popping into her head. What did Bryan expect of her? Where was this going?

Perhaps sensing the change in her, he slid over so he was beside her. He kissed her jaw, then lifted his head so he could stare into her eyes.

"Cassie?"

She tried to duck her head, but he caught her chin, forcing her to look at him.

"What's wrong?"

"Nothing." She shrugged and tugged to free her chin, but he was having none of it.

"Don't lie to me. Tell me what's wrong."

Her eyes seemed trapped by his and she couldn't break free. Nervously she licked her lips. "I was wondering what you expected out of this."

A frown marred his brow. "Out of what?"

"This. You and me." She swallowed hard, taking in his red, swollen lips, the flush on his cheekbones. "We're in bed together and you're obviously..." She paused unable to finish and waved vaguely towards his waist, feeling herself blush.

He gave a crooked grin. "Yeah, I'm *obviously*." Leaning forward he kissed the tip of her nose. "Is that a problem?"

She took a deep breath. As much as she'd like this to continue, she felt she had to tell him the truth. "You see, Kellen and I—"

A low growl escaped him and he stiffened, his face clouding. "You don't have to tell me about you and Anderson. You were together for three years."

"But that's just it. We shared the house for three years, but we never..." She paused, thinking of that one damning time. It wasn't something she could hide. Bryan would find out.

"Cassie, you can't expect me to believe that a man could live with someone who looks like you and never make a move on you." Bryan rolled over onto his back and stared at the ceiling. A space now separated their bodies and Cassie frowned at the loss of contact.

"I'm not saying Kellen didn't. He tried, but it never felt right."

"You never had sex with him?" Bryan turned his head to face her, a disbelieving look on his face.

"Just once." She spoke in a burst of words, feeling tears of shame pricking her eyes. "About two years ago, right around this time. It was a full moon and I was almost out of my pills, trying to make them last as long as I could. I guess I let the drug get too low in my system or something." She shrugged and sniffed before continuing. "Anyway, I woke up one night, desperate, aching. I don't know what came over me, but I suddenly felt I'd die if I didn't have sex with someone. Kellen was there and I basically attacked him. He even tried to stop me, to get me to think, but something was driving me. I couldn't stop myself. Afterwards, I felt awful. Like I'd made a terrible mistake."

"Cassie..."

She could hear the doubt in his voice. "It's true. I'm not making it up. That's why this..." She stumbled in her explanation, but forged on, desperate to make him understand. "I'm sort of scared. I don't really know what to do. That other time, I wasn't in control."

Bryan pushed himself up on his elbow and looked down at her. "So you've never really...?"

"No." She answered in small voice, staring down at the covers.

"Ah, Cassie..." He exhaled slowly then gathered her close, tucking her head under his chin. "I'm sorry. I assumed you and Kellen were together."

She shook her head.

"I never should have started anything with you." He started to loosen his grip on her. "Listen, you have a big day ahead of you tomorrow; so maybe you should go to sleep."

"No!" She blurted out her protest more loudly than planned.

"Pardon?"

"I don't want you to stop. I just didn't want you to expect too much. I might not be any good."

Bryan burst out laughing, flopping onto his back.

"What's so funny?" She felt her face heating with embarrassed indignation.

"You are." He hugged her tight and rested his head beside hers on the pillow. "Having sex isn't a competition where you get rated afterwards. It's two people sharing themselves, giving each other pleasure, telling what they like and don't like. And you were doing a very good job."

"I was?"

"Uh-huh. You were making these great whimpering noises that let me know—"

"I was not whimpering!" She paused. "Was I?"

"Yep. I bet I can make you do it again, too." He turned his head so he was looking directly at her. "Want me to try?"

Did she? A minute ago that was what she thought she wanted but now that the heat of the moment was over she wasn't sure she was ready to have sex with Bryan. There was this connection, this pull between them, but they'd only just met.

Yes! Say yes! He is ours. We've waited all this time. The wolf inside was pressuring her.

"I think so." She gave a nervous laugh. "The wolf is saying yes."

"But the human isn't so sure?"

She searched his face and found no judgement, no condemnation. Just understanding. Reaching up she cupped his face. "I really, really like you Bryan, but so much is going on right now."

He kissed her gently. "I understand and when we finally make love, I want both you and your wolf to be in full agreement. How about I help you relax a bit?"

Relaxing sounded good. Her muscles were as tight as proverbial fiddle strings. "Okay."

"And whenever you want me to stop you just say so, all right?"

She nodded and he eased the pillows out from under her head.

"On your stomach." When she complied he knelt astride her, gathering her hair up and moving it out of the way. Then he settled himself lightly on top of her rear end and began to massage her shoulders.

"Mmm... That feels so good." She groaned into the mattress as his fingers worked their magic on her back.

"See?" He leaned forward and whispered in her ear. "I *can* make you whimper again."

She giggled. "That's not a whimper."

"Sorry. I stand corrected. I can make you moan in delight."

She laughed again. "Okay, I guess you're right."

"Good. Remember that and keep saying it to yourself. Bryan is always right."

"I didn't say *always*," she protested.

"I'm sure you meant to," he answered cockily, then leaned forward to quickly kiss her cheek before sitting up again.

In silence, he worked on her neck, her shoulders, down the middle of her back; rubbing and pressing. His hands moved sideways, the tips of his fingers barely brushing against the sides of her breasts. She bit back a moan, not wanting him to know exactly how arousing she found this to be. What would it be like to have his hands actually cupping her breasts? His thumbs playing over the tips? His hot mouth suckling.

"Cassie..." Bryan's voice sounded deeper and she became aware of the fact that a certain part of his anatomy was waking up, pressing into her backside from his perch on top of her.

She cleared her throat, anxious to return to neutral ground. With faked casualness, she began to ask him questions about his life. "So, besides bossing people around, what exactly does a Beta do?"

He was silent for a moment, his hands still, possibly wondering what she was thinking. Then he started the massage again, his voice a normal tone as he began to explain his duties, then moved on to life in the pack and the townsfolk in Stump River.

She fell asleep under the rhythmic movement of his hands and the soothing sound of his voice.

Chapter 21

The next morning Marla drove to work feeling tired and irritable. Her dreams had been troubled, her wolf dragging her from scene to scene as she revisited her life. Strange how she'd forgotten how happy she'd been as a young pup. It was only as she had become older and begun to sense subtle undercurrents that her discontent had begun. She hadn't thought about it in years, mind you. The arguing; how her mother, a half-breed, never felt totally accepted. How her father sneered at her.

She remembered how scared she'd been the first time she'd had to transform. What if she were more like her mother than her father? What if she had difficulty changing? Thankfully she hadn't and her father had begun to plan great things for her. He'd wanted her to mate an Alpha, or at least a Beta; to regain some status for his family. Status lost due to her mother.

She hadn't understood why it mattered that she was only three-quarters Lycan, but her father had drummed it into her head to keep it a secret. Just as he had kept her mother away from the pack as much as possible. Her father had been a proud man and bitter that a youthful folly had left him saddled with a half-breed mate.

Of course, her father's plans weren't hers. She had her own dreams. Dreams that didn't include living in a pokey town in the middle of nowhere, being mated, or spending part of her life as wolf. Of course, the stupid animal inside her didn't agree; it was loyal to the pack, to their Alpha. The creature rejected her desire for worldly status, her need to leave pack life and set out on her own. That was when the struggle inside of her had begun; the constant conversations in her head, the battle of wills. For years now, she'd been fighting to maintain supremacy over the wolf, but lately... She shook her head and tightened her jaw. No. It wasn't true. She was still in charge, no matter what the creature might say.

She was more human than wolf, but the animal wouldn't listen. It chastised her for her actions, blaming her for the steps she'd been forced to take in life. Well, she didn't care. If people were in her way, they had to be dealt with, by whatever means necessary. It was as simple as that. The wolf could do and say whatever it wanted, but it couldn't force her to listen.

As she arrived at the building that housed Aldrich's penthouse, she lowered the car window and pulled out her security card to open the entrance of the underground parking garage. The usual smells of exhaust and oil greeted her, but another scent lingered too. Carefully, she sniffed again.

Her wolf rose to alert as the scent of other Lycans reached her nostrils. She stiffened and scanned the area, but could see no one about. Another sniff and the scent was gone. Had the wind shifted directions? Or perhaps the creature inside her was playing games with her again. It was so recalcitrant lately; she wouldn't put it past the beast. Irritation marred her face as she examined the quiet street one more time, then put the car back in gear and drove inside. There was nothing about; it was her over-tired mind playing tricks on her.

After parking her car, she went in search of Jeffries. Aldrich had a private area cordoned off in the underground lot for his own use. It included a small room where Jeffries kept his tools, completed maintenance logs, and bided his time when he wasn't needed. She walked over to the room, the clicking of her heels creating an uneven staccato on the cement floor and echoing throughout the cavernous space of the parking garage. She rubbed her side; it was aching from the dampness this morning, making her limp more pronounced and further deepening her dark mood.

As she approached Jeffries' room, her acute hearing picked up faint sounds from outside; the outdoor traffic, the whir of exhaust fans that kept the air in the underground space breathable. A scratching sound caught her attention as well and she cocked her head, giving a satisfied smile when she identified it.

Jeffries was addicted to the various word and number puzzles that came in the daily paper. As she approached the room where he worked, the sound became louder until she stood in the doorway and watched him scribbling away on a bit of paper, obviously trying to figure out an answer.

"Jeffries?"

He gave a start and looked up, a welcoming smile spreading across his face. "Marla? You usually don't come down here at this time of day." Setting the paper aside, he stood up and walked to where she leaned against the doorframe. He placed his hands on her shoulders and gave her a kiss. "Why are you here?"

She studied his face. So handsome. It was a shame he'd likely be blamed for the accident. Oh well, it couldn't be helped. "I was wondering if everything was in place for our little joke today."

The smile left the man's face. "Yeah, but I still don't think it's a good idea."

"Relax. Nothing will go wrong. We'll get together this afternoon in the sauna and I'll tell you all about it."

Jeffries opened his mouth as if to protest, then shut it and nodded. She rewarded him with a warm, wet kiss. As he wrapped his arms around her and pulled her close, an unexpected growl rumbled in her chest.

Embarrassed, she pushed him away and tried to cover up the sound with coughing. Inwardly, she frowned. What was going on? Her wolf had no business judging her taste in men.

"Are you getting sick, Marla? That's a nasty sounding cough." Jeffries peered at her, concern etched on his face.

"Perhaps. Don't fuss. I'll be fine. I'll head upstairs and get something warm to drink. Give me a call when you have the elevator ready."

"All right. But remember what I told you. Once the elevator's been disabled, you're stuck up there for the next few hours until someone comes to fix it.

"Why can't you fix it yourself?" She queried.

"I can't do it myself or it would implicate me in the prank. If Mr. Aldrich finds out, I could be out of a job."

"Of course, how silly of me not to think of that." She patted his cheek and he caught her hand and nipped playfully at her fingers. "See you later, Jeffries."

As she walked to the elevator, she decided she'd miss the man.

Bryan held onto one of Kane's arms and Ryne gripped the other. The man had quit straining against them, but they weren't taking any chances. When Marla had driven up to the entrance of the parking garage, Kane had been all for taking her right there. It had required some fast talking and physical restraint to hold the man back.

"If you attack her out in the open, people will see. And undoubtedly there's a security camera mounted by the garage door." Bryan explained.

Kane growled and tried to pull his arms free again. "Let me go. I won't do anything stupid. It was just the sight of her after all these years. I flashed back to how she'd tried to kill Elise." He continued to growl, but his body relaxed.

Bryan and Ryne exchanged looks, silently agreeing to let Kane go. Once free of their restraint, the man shoved his hands through his hair and began pacing back and forth in the small alleyway where they hid.

"It's a good thing you managed to convince Elise to stay back with Mel and keep her company." Ryne quipped. "She'd have your hide for the fool stunt you almost pulled."

"I know. I know. You don't have to rub it in. But once I get my hands on Marla..." Kane paused and exhaled slowly. "I hope I can restrain myself until we get her to the High Council."

"High Council?" Cassie queried. Bryan glanced over to where she stood huddled by the wall. It was a miserably cold morning, even for early spring in Chicago. The wind was whipping down the alley, stirring up dirt and debris. Being used to Las Vegas temperatures for the past three years, Cassie likely found this a shocking change.

She brushed a few stray hairs from her face and he watched the motion of her hands, noting their jerky movement, the faint lines of tension on her face. He could sense her worry over the plan they were about to undertake and knew she was trying to distract herself. "High Council is where a Lycan who has committed crimes against a pack is judged. It's our version of going to court except there are no lawyers," he explained.

"Oh. I thought you were going to...er...deal with her yourselves." She shrugged and gave a nervous half-smile.

"That's always an option, especially since she's guilty of crimes against an Alpha, but High Council is better. It's more objective and prevents other wolves—family members of the accused for example—from claiming bias or saying we were acting as vigilantes."

She nodded and shoved her hands in her coat pockets, her shoulders hunching against the cold. Bryan moved closer to her and slipped an arm around her shoulder, sharing his body heat. Almost automatically she relaxed against him, a contented sigh escaping her lips.

Ryne noticed the move. Bryan saw how his eyes narrowed and assessed them, but the Alpha said nothing about it, instead returning to the business at hand. "So, when are we going to start this operation?"

"I would imagine Marla's upstairs by now, so I suppose anytime Cassie's ready." Kane looked at Cassie and she straightened, nodding.

"I'll try to teleport into the parking garage and open the door from the inside so you guys can get in. Then I'll teleport upstairs to the room Kellen is in, shut off the security, send a message to Daniel to start purging Aldrich's computer and then I'll hide until you arrive." She checked off the steps of the plan they'd devised.

"I still don't like her teleporting into the parking garage." Bryan frowned, a lead-weighted ball of worry building in his stomach. "She's never seen inside so she doesn't really know where to aim for."

"A parking garage is a parking garage." She huffed, rolling her eyes.

"Yeah, but you don't know where the ramps are or the cement pillars. What if you teleport into one? Or suddenly appear in front of a surveillance camera?"

Cassie bit her lip and shrugged. "I guess we'll just have to hope for the best."

Both Kane and Ryne frowned, neither liking the idea. Bryan started pacing back and forth, shooting considering glances across the street at the entrance to the underground parking garage. He examined the area on either side of the metal door and then looked at the position of the security camera. "Okay, what about this? If I change into my wolf form, I can hide in the bushes beside the entrance. When the next car goes in, I can sneak in beside it. Once I'm in, I'll change back, disable the surveillance cameras, and then open the door for you."

Ryne nodded slowly. "It might work, but I'll do it."

Bryan shook his head. "No. If Aldrich is watching the security cameras, you and Kane are too recognizable. I'm sure he hasn't forgotten that it was a black wolf that attacked him. My light brown fur lets me pass myself off as a dog much more easily. Besides, he's never seen me as a wolf. Neither has Marla."

Kane concurred. "He's right. Okay, we'll wait here with Cassie. Once you're inside, she'll teleport directly upstairs to the room Anderson is being held in. While we make our way to the elevator, she can be disarming the security so we can sneak upstairs undetected."

They all nodded in agreement.

Bryan stepped away to begin changing forms, then paused and turned to face Cassie. He took her in his arms and stared into her eyes. "You be careful, okay?"

"I will." She smiled up at him, her eyes searching his. Then she stood on tiptoe and kissed him gently. "You be careful, too."

"I will." He cupped the back of her head and pulled her back in so he could kiss her slowly, tracing her lips with the tip of his tongue. She moaned, opening to him and he slid his tongue inside to take one last taste of her. Memories of the previous night filled him, of her sleeping in his arms, her dark lashes fanned over her cheeks, her lips parted. His heart thumped heavily and he pulled her even closer, crushing her mouth to his. She responded, clutching his back, rubbing herself against him. It just felt so right to be with her.

Bryan wrenched his mouth away, breathing hard. He rested his forehead against hers, their breath intermixing. "Don't take any risks. If you run into Marla or Aldrich, be very, very careful. I don't want to lose you. Understand?" He stared deeply into her eyes, searching for some sign that she felt as he did. There was a stirring in the depths; was it her or her wolf?

"Yeah."

He gave her one final look and then a quick kiss before stepping away. Inhaling deeply, he focused his energy and concentrated on the change. The air shimmered, a burst of pleasure, so intense it was almost painful, filled him, and suddenly he was on all fours. Giving the people gathered around him a final glance, he stepped out of the alley and trotted across the road.

Marla exited the private elevator that led to Aldrich's penthouse thinking fondly of how it would soon relieve her of an unwanted source of stress, namely Sylvia Robinson. Her wolf protested the plan, whining inside her, the sound making her wince. She rubbed her forehead, her head was throbbing and she wished the creature would be silent for a change.

She left her purse in her office, and walked down the hallway to Aldrich's office for their usual morning meeting. A brief knock on the door let him know she was there and he summoned her in. Functioning on autopilot, she made note of the jobs he wanted her to deal with. The words washed over her, but had little meaning. Her wolf was pacing, restless. It sensed the approaching full moon, but this month it wasn't responding well to being suppressed. Giving her head a shake, she struggled to focus on what Aldrich was saying.

"Before anything else, I need you to contact Dr. Mason." Aldrich flipped through a file in front of him, not even looking at her. "The lead on the Greyson girl means we need to be ready to act."

"Lead?" She snapped her head up from the device on which she'd been making notes.

"Yes, lead." Aldrich looked at her, annoyance written on his face. "Weren't you listening to what I said?"

"Of course I was. I just..." She stumbled to think of an excuse, but he brushed her words aside.

"Never mind. Contact Mason and tell him to be ready with the papers. As soon as Cassandra Greyson is secured, he can sign them and I'll file them with the courts."

"What are you planning on doing?" Her curiosity got the better of her.

Aldrich stared at her and she was sure he'd tell her it was none of her business, but then he sat back and tapped his finger thoughtfully against his lips. "I'm torn between two options, though I'm strongly leaning towards one in particular. Cassandra has certain 'qualifications' that will serve me well."

She puzzled over his words, but wasn't sure what he was alluding to. What qualifications besides wealth could the girl possibly possess? As she debated asking for further clarification, the phone rang.

Aldrich picked up the phone and listened with a deepening frown. "I'll be right there." He stood up and rounded the desk. "I have a situation to deal with in the back rooms. Tell Sylvia I'll meet her in an hour for our walk."

She grimaced as she watched the man leave. Damn. Just when he seemed to be on the verge of confiding in her, there was an interruption. And when he was finished doing whatever he was doing, he'd be off with Sylvia.

She drummed her fingers on the arm of her chair as she thought of the plump nurse. At least Sylvia was one problem she'd be rid of by the end of the day.

Standing up, she intended to head back to her office and check with Jeffries on his progress when she noted that Aldrich had uncharacteristically left his computer on. She glanced at the security cameras and noted they hadn't been moved yet. If she did some snooping, no one would be any the wiser.

The Finding

Idly, she walked to the window as if intent on checking the view, then once out of camera range, turned so she faced the computer screen. It was the Greene file! Excitement almost had her leaning forward, but she caught herself just in time. Keeping one eye on the security camera, she reached her hand towards the mouse and began to scroll down.

As she read, she felt the colour begin to drain from her face. The file outlined how Anthony Greyson had put Aldrich in charge of overseeing a search for Lycans. He'd hired a young woman named Melody Greene to contact a photographer named Ryne Taylor!

Her throat constricted. Her heart began to pound and her hand trembled as she forced herself to continue reading. Greyson had purchased a wolf picture taken by Taylor and had concluded the wolf was a Lycan. Greene had found Taylor, made contact and then—

"What do you think you are doing, Miss Matthews?"

Aldrich's voice sounded cold as he spoke behind her. She whirled around in surprise, so caught up in what she was reading that she hadn't heard him approach. "Mr. Aldrich!"

He strode around the desk and turned the monitor, scanned the information displayed there and then turned to her. His face was a mixture of anger and apprehension. "Miss Matthews—"

She interrupted him. "I quit. I know it's short notice, but I quit." Her voice was trembling, she knew it, but at this moment appearances didn't really matter. If Ryne was in some way connected with Aldrich, she knew she had to leave.

Her words apparently stunned Aldrich. "You're what? Quitting? Ridiculous. You can't quit today of all days! I have too much work for you. All my plans are finally coming together!"

She shook her head and started to back away, but he reached out and grabbed her arm. She stared at his hand in surprise. His grip was surprisingly strong.

"It's because of them, isn't it?" Aldrich pulled her closer, searching her face. When he spoke again, it was in an insistent whisper. "You're a believer, aren't you?" He gave her arm a shake.

"A...a what?" She pulled against his grip, trying to free herself.

"A believer in werewolves." His voice became louder, more assured. "I can see it in your face."

"Werewolves?" She licked her lips and stared at him. His eyes seemed overly bright.

"Yes! I can tell you know they're real, but you've been afraid to mention it, haven't you? Like me, you know the dangers; that people would scoff and think you're crazy. But not anymore. I have proof!"

"Proof! What proof?" Her voice squeaked in surprise. Surely he didn't mean her? There was no way he could know, was there? She glanced at the computer screen wondering what else the file contained. Had she slipped up in some manner?

"Cassandra Greyson! She's one of them."

"Cassandra Greyson? But..." She realized she sounded like a parrot, but didn't really care. What was Aldrich babbling about?

"Yes! Just before he died, Anthony Greyson revealed the truth. He'd been searching for a pack so the girl would have a home and hired a journalist, Melody Greene, to help. Greene tracked down a photographer who had taken pictures of one of the beasts. Then it turned out that Greene was a werewolf herself. She almost transformed in front of me. I knew then that I could make a fortune if I captured a real live werewolf, but the plan went awry. A male of the species, a big black brute, ended up attacking me."

"The wild dog." She stared at his throat and almost laughed as all the pieces finally fell into place. Once she'd speculated that the damage could have been done by a Lycan, but had dismissed the idea as preposterous. And the Lycan had been black. It was Ryne; it had to have been! "Oh God!"

"Exactly. Since then I've lived like a prisoner, knowing they were out there. They know I'm here and they're waiting for me to make a mistake. But now I'll have the Greyson girl. She's one of them. I can prove werewolves exist and then they will become the hunted instead of me!"

By now Aldrich's grip on her arm had become painful. She tried once again to pull away, wishing she'd inherited the superior strength Lycans were noted for. She hadn't though; it was yet another of her failings.

"Mr. Aldrich, sir, I—"

Aldrich must have finally noticed he still had a hold of her, for he let go of her abruptly. She stumbled backwards before regaining her balance. "My apologies, Miss Matthews, but as you are well aware, this is an exciting day for those of us who know about werewolves. Please contact Dr. Mason immediately. I expect to have possession of the Greyson girl by the end of the day. We need to immediately sedate her and keep her locked up."

She nodded while backing towards the door. She didn't give a damn about Aldrich's plans. Escape was more important. His revelations explained why she constantly sensed the presence of Lycans. They were watching him, not her. But that would soon change. Once Cassandra Greyson arrived, Ryne would; surely he must have the place under surveillance. He'd follow the Finding clause and try to claim the girl. And if Ryne came for Cassandra, it was only a matter of time before he figured out another Lycan was present in the building.

How her own presence hadn't been discovered yet was a mystery, but then again no one was expecting her to be here. Everyone was watching for Cassandra, thank heaven. It was undoubtedly the only thing that had saved her all these years.

Thankfully Aldrich didn't seem to notice that his personal assistant was acting strangely. He was staring at the computer screen actually looking gleeful. "Don't forget to tell Sylvia I'll be with her shortly."

As fast as she could, she walked to her office. She couldn't run down the halls; it would draw unwanted questions from the other staff, but she needed to get away as quickly as possible. If Cassandra Greyson was arriving sometime today, then Ryne wouldn't be far behind, she was sure of it.

Just as she reached her office the sound of humming reached her ears. Sylvia. Damn! She suddenly remembered that Jeffries was rigging the elevator and it would be out of commission for some time afterwards.

Realizing she'd be trapped, she grabbed the phone and called downstairs, her toe tapping impatiently on the floor as she listened to the unanswered ringing. Finally, the chauffeur picked up the phone.

"Jeffries? Don't touch the elevator, I've changed my mind... What do you mean it's too late?" She ran her fingers through her hair agitatedly. This couldn't be happening. "Reverse it! Fix it! Do whatever you have to do! ... Fine." She slammed the phone down and began to pace the room. What was she going to do? The stairs? It was possible, though the thought of running down forty storeys was daunting. And then there was the matter of the security alarms set to go off whenever the stairs were used.

She pressed the heels of her hands to her temples. Her head was pounding; her wolf was fighting to get out. Its voice was echoing through her head. She couldn't think clearly; her legs were trembling. Reaching backwards, she felt for a chair and lowered herself into it.

Kellen blinked and tried to force his eyes to focus, but they wouldn't cooperate. Hugh had hit him quite hard and then injected him with something. His brain felt sluggish, his whole body heavy. A faint moan escaped his lips. His arm muscles ached from his hands being tied behind his back for so long. Initially he'd kept tugging and twisting, trying to free himself, but eventually he'd given up. The duct tape that bound him resisted all his attempts.

The knowledge that he wasn't going to escape filled him with despair. He had no illusions that he'd be let go. Once they had their hands on Sandy, he'd become superfluous, a loose end to be eliminated. Regret filled him as he realized his life was likely coming to an end. Twenty-five years of life, all wasted. Helping Sandy was about the only decent thing he'd done in his life and now even that was going to be for nothing.

The Finding

He'd overheard Hugh and Aldrich talking. They planned on having Sandy declared mentally unfit and were going to lock her up. Once she was out of the way, Aldrich said he'd be in charge of her fortune and then eventually he'd reveal her to the whole world for what she was.

That part hadn't made sense to him, but he was drifting in and out, so probably he'd missed something. Poor Sandy. She had been the one who'd been content with their simple life while he'd always wanted more. Now, she was going to end up paying for his greed. If only he hadn't gambled, none of this would have happened. Kellen sniffed, feeling sorry for her, for himself.

There was nothing he could do. He'd tried that a while ago, kicking Hugh when he'd been given one of his twice a day breaks to use the washroom. Hugh hadn't liked that and had shoved him into the wall. Kellen winced, still recalling the burst of pain when he'd slid down the wall, his skull hitting the edge of the marble bathroom counter. After that, he'd passed out.

Kellen wasn't sure how long he'd been unconscious, but when he came to, he was back in the chair listening to his captors talk about Sandy. Once they realized he was awake, Aldrich had berated his foolish escape attempt, pointing out that he was forty storeys up in a secured building. The news had quashed his few remaining hopes. He was trapped. He was going to die here and Sandy... Well, if Aldrich managed to capture her, her life would be a misery and she'd be as good as dead too.

With a sigh, he let his head fall forward and his eyes close, the drugs Hugh had given him taking effect.

Somewhere near the Mexican border...

Nate Graham wiped a shaking hand over his upper lip trying to remove the accumulated sweat. It was fear rather than the temperature that was the problem. Last night, he'd killed a man and now... He swallowed hard.

It hadn't been planned. He'd been at Dollar Niche, trying to find more files that matched the copies of the ones Hugh had given him the night before. Supposedly Eddie Perini was on his way to Chicago with Hugh, so Nate had let his guard down.

When Eddie walked in, he'd reacted instinctively, pulling his gun. A fight ensued and he'd ended up shooting Perini. That was when he'd panicked. He'd dragged Eddie down the stairs and dropped him in a dumpster before running. It had been a stupid move, but it was too late for regrets.

Damn! He'd really hoped to impress Aldie with this job. The man was moving steadily upward and he'd thought to secure a place within Aldie's organization by thoroughly investigating Dollar Niche. Now he didn't know what to do. Aldie didn't like messy endings and a dead body was messy.

Once Nate realized this, he'd gone back thinking to remove Perini from the dumpster and dropping the body in the middle of the desert, but the cops were already there, the alley filled with flashing lights, people swarming all over. How they'd found the body he didn't know. Had someone seen him dumping Eddie or heard the fight? The building and alley had appeared deserted but you never knew. All it took was one person peering out between the slats of a blind.

"Here's your drink." The bartender set a shot of whiskey in front of him. "Anything else?"

"No." Nate shoved some money at the man, keeping his head ducked down. "Keep the change."

"Thanks." The man walked away and Nate hazarded a look around. It was a small bar; not too seedy, but not too fancy either. Just an ordinary bar where people might stop by for a quick drink. No one was paying him any attention and he intended to keep it that way.

Nate tried to steady his hand as he picked up his whiskey and gulped the drink. It burned as it slid down his throat and settled in his belly. A little alcohol induced courage, that's what he needed to help him plan his next move.

When he'd seen all the commotion outside Dollar Niche, he'd driven away, functioning on autopilot; his only thought had been to put as much room as possible between himself and the crime scene. As a matter of fact, he'd driven for hours and now found himself in a little town on the Mexican border.

He knew he should call Aldie and tell him what had happened, but he hesitated not wanting to face the man's wrath. He could almost hear the man's voice, so cold and raspy, even more chilling since that freak dog attack.

"A dead body is a messy ending, Nate, and you know I don't like messy endings. Nor do I like dead bodies. They tell too many tales and lead straight back to their killers. This is not good, Nate. I'm seriously displeased."

Oh God, what a mess. Damn Perini for coming back early! One slip up and 'Nate Graham, P.I.'s' whole career was down the tubes. He pushed back his hair then held his head up with his hand, the other clenching and unclenching around the shot of whiskey. What was worse? The police discovering he'd committed murder or being on Aldie's black list? Neither choice was appealing.

He peered around the room again. Everything was quiet. The bartender was wiping glasses. Several locals sat around a table near the window laughing. Outside, people walked down the sidewalks, their arms laden with purchases. Normal life.

Perhaps he should head to Mexico. There was still some money in his account and more due to him; Aldie was supposed to be forwarding it and he could live on the sum for a while.

Nate took another gulp of whiskey and set the glass down carefully. Okay that was his plan. He'd get his money and then disappear into Mexico. When things calmed down he'd head back home.

Chapter 22

Franklin stared out the window barely noting the scenery that flashed by. He was too busy wondering what might be happening at Aldrich's penthouse. The thought of Miss Cassie in the hands of that man gave him the chills. He knew all too well what the lawyer was capable of, having done his research on the man over the past three years. Learning everything you could about your enemy had always been rule number one.

"I can't believe we missed them." Meredith grumbled from her seat beside him in the back of the taxi, her knuckles white from the tight grip she had on the edge of the seat. The vehicle was weaving back and forth as the driver changed lanes rapidly, having taken the instruction to 'step on it' to heart.

"These things happen," Franklin soothed, his fingers beating a rapid pattern on the armrest and belying his outward calm. "We simply have to change our plans a little. At least we know where Cassie was headed."

"It was a stroke of luck to overhear those two women in the lobby talking about a 'Cassie' and a 'Bryan'. Odds on it being another couple are pretty slim." Meredith preened, obviously pleased that she'd been the one to find that clue.

"And the fact that they mentioned Aldrich's penthouse was a dead giveaway." Franklin added in a dry tone, suppressing a chuckle as Meredith shot him a dirty look. Teasing her was second nature. He was the practical one and she leaned towards flighty, always needing to be restrained from rushing into situations. That's probably why they'd been such good partners, playing off each other's strengths.

"We'll reconnoitre the area first and see if we can find any evidence that Cassie is somewhere near the building." Meredith stated their first move, her whole body appearing tense and ready for action.

Franklin nodded. "And if not, we'll go inside and find her."

"Will we still use the IRS cover?"

He rubbed his chin. "Perhaps. Or I could go in as myself. There have been a few occasions when I've had cause to visit Aldrich there, though I've never dropped in. The man might be suspicious. We'll have to play it by ear. Assess the situation and then when we see an opportunity, run with it."

Meredith nodded and settled back against the seats. Franklin only half listened as she chatted away, knowing it was her way of relieving stress. The familiar rise and fall of her voice soothed him as well. This was what was missing from retirement; the adrenaline rush of working a case, making split-second decisions, living by one's wits. He smiled at the memories, then sighed. He was too old to go back in the business full time, but life at the Estate was too quiet. Perhaps once Miss Cassie was back, things would be different. His thoughts were interrupted by Meredith's elbow jabbing him in the ribs.

"Are you listening to me, Franklin?"

"Of course." He lied glibly.

"Then what was I saying?"

"Um..."

She swatted him lightly. "I was talking about Netty's arthritis and how much better it is lately. As a matter of fact, once we've rescued Miss Cassie, I'm considering moving back here."

"Really?" Franklin folded his arms and considered the possibility. Maybe he and Meredith could start their own business. He chuckled at the frivolous thought. They'd be lucky if they survived their upcoming encounter with Aldrich. Time enough to ponder the future once this mission was over.

Air shimmered around her as Cassie began to teleport from the alley to the room she'd seen in the photograph of Kellen. She'd been picturing it in her head over and over again, nervous at the idea of travelling so far simply using the power of thought.

The Finding

While her head knew she'd be able to do it, a small bit of doubt had lingered, making her insides quiver and her palms sweat as she waited for the right moment to act. Sure, she'd put on a pretty good show for the others, but the truth was, inside she was a mess. What if there was someone in the room besides Kellen when she got there? Ryne said if that was the case, she was to leave immediately, but would she be able to teleport twice in such a short time? It was a physically and mentally draining process, though she hadn't shared that fact with the others.

Thankfully, if the Alphas sensed her discomfort, they hadn't said anything. She instinctively knew Bryan was aware of the state she was in; that strange connection that linked them together appeared to be working overtime lately. He was concerned for her, but at the same time confident that she could do the job. His kiss had provided further comfort, letting her know he cared about her.

The feel of his lips moving over hers, his tongue stroking hers, had filled her with warmth and desire. She loved the sensation of his hands on her, pressing their bodies closer together. To know that someone wanted her, all of her—including the wolf inside—was a heady thing given the fact that she'd envisioned a life alone. When she was with Bryan she felt secure and had a sense of belonging such as she'd never experienced before. It had been all she could do to let him go and not throw herself after him. Instead, she'd gathered some self-restraint and allowed him to leave while the wolf inside her had whined plaintively.

Knowing she had a job to do, she pushed the encounter aside and focused on teleporting. Kane's instructions from the previous day, while irritating when repeated ad nauseam, were helpful and she went through the steps he'd suggested until the energy inside her began to coalesce and shift, filling her with a strange vibrating sensation, as if every molecule of her body were alive. A buzzing sound filled her ears and then the alley disappeared.

Now that she was actually doing it—teleporting across a distance—a thrill rushed over her followed by an enormous crashing sensation as she seemed to thump down onto the ground as if dropped from a height of a few feet or so.

The shock of the sudden stop and change of venue almost had her crumpling to the ground. Vaguely she was aware of the room around her, the fact that she was no longer outside in the cold, but mostly she was focused on her rubbery knees and swimming head. Putting out her hand, she steadied herself against the wall while waiting for the room to right itself.

It was only a small moment of weakness, but Cassie cursed herself for it anyway. What if someone had been in the room? In the time she took to recuperate, they could have grabbed her! She tightened her jaw and resolved that, if she survived this escapade, she'd practise until teleporting was as natural as walking.

Once she felt more stable, she started scanning her surroundings. With a sigh of relief, she noted the room was indeed empty except for a figure slumped in a chair. Kellen! Pushing off from the wall, Cassie made her way over to him, prepared to tell him to be quiet, however it wasn't necessary. His eyes were closed and his face was pale; he seemed to be unconscious.

She crouched beside him and covered his mouth with her hand just in case, then gave his shoulder a gentle shake. He mumbled, his lashes fluttered, but that was all the response she managed to induce.

She bit her lip, her heart pounding, her stomach clenching. Something was wrong with him, but what? She scanned him visually then pulled his sleeves up. Needle marks were evident on his arm and a chemical smell permeated the room. Damn, he'd been drugged; there'd be no help from him if things took a turn for the worse.

His face looked better than it had in the original picture she'd seen of him, but that wasn't saying much. Gently she ran her hands over his body then his skull, biting back a whimper of fear when she encountered a large damp lump on the side of his head. As she withdrew her hand from his hair, her fingers were red and sticky with blood.

The Finding

Oh God. A long ago scene flashed before her eyes; her uncle lying on the ground with a trickle of blood easing across his forehead; Mr. Aldrich gasping for breath as blood gushed from his throat. She shook her head and forced down the bile that rose in her throat. Kellen's injury might not be that serious; head wounds were notorious for bleeding. The thought brought her little comfort when he was slumped and unresponsive beside her. Frantically, she looked around the room, wishing she could call for help, but knowing it wasn't an option. There was no phone in the room, of course, and the only people in the penthouse were likely those responsible for the damage to begin with.

Taking a deep steadying breath, she wiped the blood from her hand on her pant leg, then cupped Kellen's face in what she hoped was a comforting gesture. She whispered to him urgently.

"Hang on, Kellen. I'll get help for you as soon as I can. My pack...er...friends are waiting downstairs. As soon as they get here, I'll call for help."

She waited a moment, but Kellen made no response. Fighting off a feeling of despair, she straightened and headed for the door, opening it a crack and peering out. All was quiet. Mentally going over the map of the penthouse that Daniel had provided, she slipped out of the room, and began to move down the hallway.

This particular area of the penthouse seemed extremely cool and quiet, almost tomb-like, she thought, the thick carpeting muffling the sound of her footsteps. Pale off-white walls created a clinical atmosphere while a few modern paintings hung at evenly spaced intervals added jarring splashes of colour. She was sure it was all very upscale but far from welcoming. How could anyone live in such a sterile atmosphere?

Three doors down, she was at what was supposed to be the main security room. She pressed herself against the wall, her heart pounding with the fear of being discovered, but at the same time filled with a strange sense of déjà-vu. This was so like what she'd done as a youngster, sneaking around her uncle's house, spying on him and the servants. In a way it was thrilling to feel the adrenaline rush, the hint of danger. For so long her life had been dull and mundane that she'd forgotten what it was like to feel alive.

Forcing herself to breathe calmly, she slowed the thundering of her heart and tried to listen carefully, scenting the air as Bryan had done. The faintest of mechanical whirring met her ears and she identified it as probably a computer. The scents however... She frowned, trying to sort through them. A myriad of them drifted past; food, cleaning products, leather. Several humans were in the apartment and one werewolf, too. That must be Marla, she thought to herself.

Unable to gather any more information, she resorted to her tried and true human techniques, crouching down to press an eye to the gap between the door and the frame. What she could see of the room was filled with gadgets; banks of surveillance screens, buttons and switches. Definitely the main security room, just as Daniel's plans had indicated. Unfortunately, there was a man inside the room, too. Damn! She'd have to get him out of the room or distract him. Hmm... He seemed intent on studying the computer screen. She scanned the hallway, noting a small nook a few feet away in which was nestled a large floor vase filled with decorative grasses. Hmm… It had worked on Bryan.

Without a sound, she removed the vase's contents and laid them on the ground. Then she picked up the vase and pushed the security room's door open with the tip of her toe. It creaked lightly as it swung inward, the sound seeming as loud as a gunshot in the quiet hallway.

Her muscles tensed as she readied for whatever might happen. Seconds ticked by and she held her breath, ears straining to catch the sound of the man approaching the door to investigate what had caused it to move. Nerves made her palms wet with sweat and she held the vase even tighter, worried it might slip from her hands. More time passed and still nothing.

Exhaling slowly, she frowned in puzzlement, having expected the man to come bursting out of the room. Lowering her arms, she cautiously looked inside again. The man hadn't moved. He was still intent on the computer screen! What held his attention so raptly? She squinted trying to get a closer look, then bit back a gasp. A porno flick?

She rolled her eyes in disgust and shook her head. So much for the fear of being discovered! Taking a deep breath, she adjusted her grip on the vase and walked boldly into the room. Giving the man no time to react, or even turn around, she brought the vase down on his head. It made a satisfying crashing sound and the man slumped over in his chair with only the slightest cry.

Realizing the noise might have alerted someone, she pushed the man out of the way and went to work on the keyboard. Following the instructions given her, she turned off the security system and established a link with Daniel's computer so he could purge Aldrich's files of anything related to Lycans. In seconds a message appeared on the screen. Daniel would call Ryne and inform him the security was deactivated, then start working his way through Aldrich's computer system.

Feeling relieved that her part was done, Cassie turned and hurried back to the room where Kellen was. She'd agreed to wait there until the others had taken care of Marla and Aldrich. A smile spread across her face. It should be smooth sailing now.

Bryan sat huddled beside a minivan, trying to relax his clenched muscles. He'd managed to make his way into the parking garage by sneaking in alongside a car. Then once inside, he'd located the surveillance cameras that were pointed at the entrance and put them out of commission. Finally, he'd jimmied open a side door to the parking garage, allowing Ryne and Kane inside. The entire time, he'd been expecting someone to notice the cameras at the entrance weren't working, but as the minutes ticked by and no one arrived to investigate, he breathed a sigh of relief.

Thankfully, despite Aldrich's purported vigilance, not everyone was on the ball. Now hidden, the three of them awaited a call from Daniel telling them the security had been deactivated. Once that happened they'd use the elevator and invade the penthouse.

The waiting was killing him; knowing Cassie was upstairs by herself. What if she encountered Aldrich or Marla? She'd have no defences against either of them. He paused, frowning, then changed his line of thought. Actually, when he'd been grappling with her in his motel room in Vegas, she'd done pretty well for a supposed 'poor, little rich girl'. If he wasn't a Lycan, he'd still have a lump on his head and tender muscles from where she'd kicked him. So perhaps she wasn't completely defenceless, but he'd still feel better once he was in the penthouse watching over her.

A faint buzzing interrupted his musings. Ryne checked his cell phone, murmured a greeting, grunted in approval, and then quickly hung up.

"She's done it." Ryne's crooked grin conveyed his approval of Cassie and Bryan felt a flash of pride that she'd not only completed her part of the job, but managed to impress his Alpha as well.

Kane slowly raised himself up and peered around the garage. "No one's about. Let's head to the elevator."

Silently, keeping low and darting from car to car, they made their way to the private elevator that serviced the penthouse. A faint noise was coming from that direction and Kane put out his hand, gesturing for them to stay back. A quick peek revealed the cover was off the control panel and someone was working on it.

The three men shot each other looks of dismay and frustration.

"What the hell's going on?" Ryne hissed the question as he hunkered down behind a limo.

"I don't know, but I'll take care of it." Kane moved to leave, but Ryne stayed him with a hand on his arm.

"Better let me. You haven't done this type of thing in a while." Ryne started to stand, but Kane glared at him."

"No. I said I'd take care of it."

Bryan rolled his eyes. "I don't care who takes care of that joker. Let's just get it over and done with." He stood up. "I'll distract the guy while one of you—and I don't care who—sneaks around behind him." Without waiting, Bryan strolled out of their hiding spot. There was a brief pause behind him, then the sound of movement. He gave a nod, thankful personalities hadn't got in the way, and then moved ahead.

"Excuse me." Bryan stepped up to the man working on the elevator, using a faintly accusatory tone of voice. Always act like you belong, even if you don't; he repeated the rule to himself and raised his chin, ensuring his stance was wide and authoritative. "What's going on here?"

The man jerked back, banged his head on the panel door, swore, and dropped the tool he'd been using on the ground. A metallic ring echoed through the parking garage. Turning around, he looked at Bryan, the scent of nervousness wafting out of him. "Um... I was trying to fix the elevator. I had a report that it was malfunctioning."

"Let me see your work order." Bryan held out his hand and raised an eyebrow, his look demanding compliance. The guy was definitely feeling guilty about something and Bryan planned to use the fact to his advantage.

"Work order? I..." The man stammered and shifted uneasily, darting his eyes around as if searching for an answer. "You see... I was just doing this as a favour for the guy who owns the penthouse."

"A favour? Do you realize the servicing of an elevator can only be done by a qualified repairman? You shouldn't even be opening the panel. What's your name?" Bryan pulled out his cell phone as if he was going to call in a report.

"It's Jeffries, but...?" The fellow huffed and threw his hands out to his side. "Listen, I don't want any trouble."

"Too bad, because trouble just found you." Bryan looked pointedly over Jeffries' shoulder. Jeffries turned...and met Kane's fist. The man slid to the ground in an unconscious heap.

Shaking his hand as if trying to remove the sting, Kane grinned. "Damn, but that felt good. It's been ages since I've had a chance to hit someone."

A chuckle came from the side and they both turned to see Ryne lounging against the wall, one ankle crossed over the other, his thumbs hooked in his belt loops. "Nice to see that parenthood hasn't turned you into a complete wuss." He smirked before pushing off from the wall and wandering over.

Kane growled. "Wait until you're faced with your first dirty diaper, bro. I want to be there to see that."

Bryan interrupted before they could start with the barbed comments again. "I'll drag this guy into that little room over there and take his wallet. It'll look like a mugging. You two take care of the elevator."

Ryne raised his eyebrow and Bryan realized he was stepping out of line, ordering two Alphas around. His concern for Cassie was making him forget protocol.

"If you wouldn't mind, that is." He added a qualifier to his earlier demand and Ryne nodded in acknowledgement of his implicit apology.

Rubbing his chin, Ryne studied the control panel. "I don't know, Bryan. I work on cars, not elevators."

"What's the matter, Ryne?" Kane asked with mock innocence. "Been stuck in Stump River so long that you can't handle a machine fancier than an old farm pickup?"

"Me? This thing is full of electronics. Aren't you the one that studied that?" Ryne glared at his brother.

Bryan sighed, in no mood for sibling rivalry. "Please, just see what you can do." He hefted the man over his shoulder, leaving the two Alphas to stare at the elevator and the open control panel.

Cassie had managed to free Kellen and ease him to the ground. She'd have liked to have placed him somewhere more comfortable, but the room was devoid of other furniture. At least he looked more comfortable than he had with his arms bound behind him.

Sighing, she brushed his hair from his forehead and stared at his face. Her exact feelings for him were mixed. He'd been a good friend to her at a time when she'd had no one and for that reason, she hoped he'd be okay. But the stunt he'd pulled— planning to hand her over in exchange for money, even if he hadn't really meant to carry it through—had damaged her faith in him. While she still cared for him, it was with a certain wariness now. Kellen might not be able to control his addiction to gambling and she felt sorry for him, but he was accountable for his actions. If they were ever lucky enough to get out of this, she was giving him an ultimatum. What he chose to do with it... Well, that would tell the story, wouldn't it?

Glancing up, she checked the door again. She'd jammed the chair under the handle, not thinking it would stop anyone who was really determined to get in, but it might slow them down. Exactly what the benefit of that was, she didn't know. It wasn't as if she had a means of escape. Well she could teleport out, but that would mean leaving Kellen behind which sort of defeated the whole purpose of the plan in the first place.

Sitting on the floor, she leaned her back against the wall, keeping one hand on Kellen's shoulder, just in case he could sense her presence. She leaned her head back as well, and then began contemplating what might happen in the next few weeks, if she managed to survive today. Originally she'd planned on rescuing Kellen and then disappearing, but now she wasn't so sure. Did she really want to leave Bryan behind and never see him again?

The wolf inside her whined at the very idea and for once she was in agreement with the animal. Strange, but it was sort of nice to be on the same wavelength for a change. Tentatively, she connected to the creature, allowing its emotions to flow and mingle with her own as she thought about Bryan.

Her breath caught in her throat at the depth of feeling the creature had for Bryan's wolf. The poor thing was devastated by the thought of being separated from its mate. She felt a tear prick her eye as the animal's emotions became clearer to her. Sorrow, despair, frustration.

For years her wolf had felt rejected and alone, rather like a puppy that just wanted its owner to notice and give approval. The silly thing was thumping its tail with joy over the fact that she was now actually giving it the time of day. A smile spread over her face at the excitement she felt growing within her, a sense of unity as if a missing part had suddenly been found.

A soft laugh escaped her. The wolf wanted out to play. In her mind's eye, she could see it with its front end down and its rear end up, tongue lolling out of the corner of its mouth as it quivered in anticipation of being set free for a good romp. She felt a faint thrill herself at the idea. She hadn't played or had any real fun in ages. Perhaps, when this was all over, they could find a park somewhere and...

The sound of the door handle turning caught her attention and both she, and the wolf within, stiffened, alert to the possible approach of danger. It could be Bryan here to rescue her. She sniffed, trying to search the air for a familiar scent. She wasn't too good at this yet, but it didn't appear that Bryan was anywhere nearby; she was sure she'd be able to detect him if he was. She shifted her feet under her so that she was crouched, ready to move.

Whoever was trying to get in, pushed at the door, then murmured something in an angry tone. There was a pause and then a loud bang as something—possibly a shoulder?—hit the door. The wooden panel reverberated, but held strong. Another strike and then a splintering sound filled the room.

She leapt to her feet and started to back up, her heart pounding, her eyes fixed on the door. What should she do? Leave Kellen and save herself? She shook her head; there was no way she could do that, but what other course of action did she have? Quickly she scanned the room, but it was bare of anything that even vaguely resembled a weapon. Whoever was responsible for holding Kellen here knew what they were doing.

Another hit shook the door and the frame pulled free. Beefy finger tips appeared around the edge, gripped the wood and then the door was moved out of the way to admit the thug from Vegas and a middle aged man who looked familiar.

She frowned and then gasped. It was Mr. Aldrich, her uncle's lawyer! Bryan had been right; Ryne hadn't killed him. She eyed the silk scarf tied around his throat and thought back to the gaping wound she'd seen there three years earlier. What scars might that cloth be hiding?

362

The Finding

"Ah, Miss Cassandra. How nice to finally meet face to face, though I must admit your presence here is a trifle puzzling." Aldrich looked curiously around the room then back down the hallway. "Hugh, go find Swanson and see if you can figure out how she managed to breach my security."

Hugh, as Mr. Aldrich had called the thug, left without a sound. Mr. Aldrich put his hands behind his back, rocking on his heels as he looked her up and down. "I must say, you haven't changed much over the years. Of course, I only know you through a picture we found at the Estate. It was strange that your uncle never introduced us despite all the occasions that I was at the house." He cocked his head. "Any idea why Mr. Greyson was so cautious about revealing your existence?"

She shook her head, unsure where the conversation was leading.

"I've theorized over the fact. Would you mind if I share my musings?" He quirked an eyebrow, but when she didn't respond, he continued. "I think it's because he was hiding you from the world."

"Perhaps." She shrugged and forced herself to leave her hands still at her side rather than twisting them nervously.

Pursing his lips, Mr. Aldrich shook his head. "But it doesn't quite fit. I know the rich do take extreme precautions with their children, but Mr. Greyson seemed to go above and beyond. I think there was an added reason, don't you?"

Cassie swallowed nervously. There was something about the man that gave her the creeps. His eyes were too cold, his voice too smooth. She took a half-step backwards.

"Still not talking? Well, I'll tell you my theory. Greyson hid you because you're a werewolf."

Her eyes flared wide, despite her best intentions to remain calm. Aldrich chuckled.

"You're surprised that I know? You shouldn't be. I was there that night. I heard him tell the other werewolf about you just before I was attacked."

"I...I thought you'd died that night." Why she felt compelled to share that tidbit of information, she didn't know.

363

"I almost did." He reached up and loosened the scarf around his neck, then undid his collar and pulled his shirt open. Some type of breathing tube came into view, but that wasn't what drew the gasp from her lips. It was the appearance of the skin around it; horribly disfigured with scars from numerous stitches crisscrossing his jaw and disappearing down towards his chest.

"I...I'm sorry." The words passed through her numb lips. She knew Ryne had attacked him, but the fact that Aldrich had lived had lessened the event in her mind. Now it all came rushing back to her; the growling, the blood, Aldrich's screams as long sharp teeth ripped at his flesh. The damage inflicted had been severe. She grimaced as the reality of how fierce a werewolf could be came into shocking clarity once again. When she was around Bryan, she forgot that. Frowning, she considered the point.

Aldrich inclined his head. "Thank you. If it wasn't for Franklin—"

"Franklin was there?" She looked up in surprise, his words jolting her from her dark thoughts.

Aldrich narrowed his eyes and studied her for a moment before he replied. "Why, yes. Yes he was. He came looking for your uncle. Unfortunately, it was too late for Mr. Greyson, but Franklin summoned help and saved me. I'm very grateful to the man and tell him so whenever I see him."

"He's still alive? Do you see him often?" She was eager for news about the man who had been more of a family member to her than a servant.

"Yes. And the cook—Mrs. Teasdale, I believe—is still there as well. They'll be delighted to have you back home to fuss over."

For a moment, Cassie forgot everything else that was going on as memories of the two servants flooded her mind; making Christmas cookies in the vast Estate kitchen, finding Easter eggs with Franklin at her side holding the basket, birthday parties where they'd all worn silly hats, picnics at the beach. She blinked, tears threatening at the thought of seeing Franklin and Cook again. They were still alive! She could picture them moving about the house, cooking and fussing.

"I'll take you to them right now if you want." Aldrich smiled at her and extended his hand. "My secretary, Miss Matthews, will summon my chauffeur and we can be on our way in a matter of minutes."

Chapter 23

Mel and Elise peered out of the taxi window at the high rise across the street. It was an impressive structure, rising some forty floors, rivalled by few other buildings in the area.

"Wow! Aldrich has really moved up in the world." Mel said as she fished some money out of her purse and handed it to the driver. "His law office was impressive, but this place is amazing. It must have cost him a fortune."

"Are you sure we should do this?" Elise pursed her lips and looked at her, a frown marring her brow.

"Yes, we most definitely should do this. We're not sitting at the motel twiddling our thumbs. Our men are up there and they might need us." She nudged Elise to get her to open the door and climb out. Mel followed and the taxi drove off, leaving them on the busy sidewalk.

Elise looked around at all the people hurrying up and down the sidewalk. She was jostled to one side by an impatient businessman who was talking on his cell phone and obviously not watching where he was heading. "Where is everyone going in such a hurry?"

Mel grabbed her arm and pulled her to stand by a mailbox. It offered some semblance of safety as the crowds parted to walk around it. "To work, to appointments, who knows? Chicago is a lot different than Smythston or Stump River."

"You can say that again. I'm not used to so many people in one place." She swivelled her head around once more to stare at the crowd. "So, should we stay here and wait for the men to appear? Or try to find someplace to hide? We'll be kind of conspicuous if we stay by this mailbox very long."

"True." Mel glanced around and then grinned. "Ah-ha! I thought I remembered one being in this neighbourhood."

"One what?"

"A coffee shop! It's my favourite chain. We'll sit there and keep an eye on what's happening over here. If the boys need us, we're close at hand."

Elise winced. "Kane will be furious if he finds out I'm here."

"And Ryne will be royally pissed off, too." Mel giggled.

"You like making him angry?"

"Not exactly. But the making up part is well worth it." She winked and grinned.

Elise stifled a laugh, her eyes dancing merrily. "Sounds like fun." She sighed quietly and sobered. "Kane and I don't have too many disagreements. Lately, it's usually me trying to cajole him out of a mood, when pack business gets too intense."

"Our pack's still small, so that hasn't happened yet, thank heaven."

"Lucky you." Elise sounded wistful and Mel looked at her carefully.

"Trouble in paradise?"

Elise shrugged. "Not really. It's like I said at dinner the other night. Kane has a lot of demands on his time. He tries to make sure we have time together, but it's not always possible. And when he's free, I'm often busy with the kids. It's different now that we have a family."

Mel made a noncommittal sound and rubbed her swollen belly, wondering how parenthood might change her relationship with Ryne. She hadn't thought much about it, still caught up with her other recent discovery. "You know, we've been here a whole day and I haven't even met Kane yet." Mel bit her lip. Could it be that Kane was purposely avoiding her? Did he sense the truth? She gave her head an imperceptible shake. No, that couldn't be it, could it?

Elise let out a yelp, then glared over her shoulder at a passerby who had managed to hit her with his briefcase.

The Finding

"Come on; let's find a safer place to talk." Mel grabbed her arm and led her towards the coffee shop. Just the thought of caffeine had her almost floating down the sidewalk.

"You know you can't have any, right?" Elise cautioned as they entered.

Mel pouted and sighed. "Yeah, but at least I can smell it. Ryne's been a regular beast about guarding my caffeine intake. He hardly allows the rest of the pack to make coffee, thinking I'll break down. Poor dears are limited to one pot in the morning and after that it's uptown to Ruth's. That's the diner in Stump River where everyone gathers during the day."

Elise looked intrigued. "I'd like to visit that place someday. It sounds interesting."

"Well, 'interesting' isn't exactly the word I'd use. Quirky would be a better term."

"Quirky can be good." Elise stood in line and scanned the offerings that were listed on the overhead menu. Unexpectedly, she grabbed Mel's arm. "Hey! Look at that. They have a decaffeinated coffee. You could probably drink that."

Mel looked at the sign and then read the explanation underneath. "No caffeine, all natural. Woohoo, that's new since I was last here! I've hit pay dirt." She slung an arm around Elise's shoulders and gave her a hug. "If the guys don't need us, why don't we spend the rest of the day here, bonding as sisters-in-law?"

Cassie stared at Aldrich's outstretched hand, half-tempted by the idea of seeing Franklin and Cook again. Then the image of a gun in that same hand superimposed itself; a gun that had killed her uncle. But that had been an accident, hadn't it? She furrowed her brow trying to recall the events of that night clearly without the clouding effects of emotion.

Mr. Aldrich had been aiming at the werewolf. It was an act of self-defence. The wolf had been going to attack him. Her own wolf growled at the memory of what had happened and Cassie pressed a hand to her forehead, confused by the flood of memories and conflicting viewpoints. Who to believe? Who to trust? Her uncle had been a clever man and he must have trusted Mr. Aldrich, yet Bryan didn't.

The sound of pounding feet drew her attention. Hugh was running down the hallway. Mr. Aldrich heard him as well and spun around.

"The whole security system's been turned off and Swanson is out like a light on the floor. The elevator's out of commission too." The big man panted out the message, obviously unused to moving so quickly.

"Really?" Mr. Aldrich half turned and stared at her over his shoulder, his eyes narrowed. "You've been a busy girl, Cassandra. I can see that you'd tamper with security; how else would you get in. But why did you disable the elevator?"

"I didn't." She was shocked by the news. If the elevator wasn't working, how would Bryan ever get up here? And what had happened to Mr. Aldrich's pleasant tone of voice? She tightened her jaw, glad she hadn't trusted him. Bryan and his friends had been right. The lawyer wasn't what he tried to make himself out to be.

Mr. Aldrich compressed his lips. "Never mind. I'll figure out your motive later." He jerked his head towards Hugh. "Bring her along. I'll have to reset the security myself since no one else knows the code." With that, he headed down the hall. Hugh grabbed Cassie's arm, dragging her along behind.

She stumbled after him, the feel of his thick, warm fingers pressing against her skin making her shudder. At least no one had seemed to remember Kellen was unconscious on the floor so he'd be safe for the moment. Unfortunately, she had no idea how she'd save him or herself with no backup.

Hugh pushed her into the security room, then placed a heavy hand on her shoulder, no doubt as a warning not to try anything. When she attempted to inch away, he dug his fingers into her neck, causing her to freeze in place. The man was big enough to snap her neck without the slightest bit of effort and she strongly suspected he'd enjoy doing it, too. Resigned for the moment, she focused on Mr. Aldrich who was already bent over the computer keyboard. He typed something and a red light started to flash in the corner of the room.

"What's that?" Hugh stared at the array of blinking lights.

"Someone's been tiptoeing through my computer system as well as security. Know a hacker, do you, Cassandra?" Mr. Aldrich looked at her suspiciously.

She said nothing, hoping Daniel had a way to prevent the man from following a trail that led back to his IP address. They didn't need Mr. Aldrich discovering the pack's location. She had a bad feeling that he wasn't the type of person you wanted showing up unexpectedly on your doorstep.

On the floor, the man she'd knocked out earlier groaned. Aldrich nudged him with his foot. "Get up, Swanson. With your training and background, I expected better from you. Explain to me how this chit of a girl took you out."

Swanson slowly got to his feet, rubbing the back of his head and then giving it a shake as if trying to clear his mind. He held on to the side of the desk, frowning and swaying slightly. "Damned if I know. I was viewing security tapes when—"

She couldn't help the snort that escaped her lips and Aldrich shot a look at her. "Something to say, Cassandra?"

She hesitated then shrugged. Creating dissent amongst the enemy was supposed to be a good strategy. "He was watching a porno flick and didn't even notice me coming up behind him."

"Really?" Aldrich swung his gaze back to Swanson. "We'll be having a talk, Swanson, once I've dealt with Miss Greyson."

Swanson paled and opened his mouth, but Hugh interrupted.

"Mr. Aldrich, look at this!" Hugh pointed to one of several screens that apparently broadcast the views from the security cameras. She bit back a gasp. It showed Bryan, Kane, and Ryne running up a set of stairs. "Someone's coming up the interior fire escape route."

By the time Aldrich had moved closer to the small screen, they were gone. He flipped a switch and another camera took over, catching the men as they rounded another flight. Aldrich studied the image for a moment and then swore. "Damn! It's him."

"Who?" Hugh frowned.

"Never mind," Mr. Aldrich touched the scarf around his neck, looking decidedly nervous. "Hugh and Swanson, I need you to slow down our unexpected company."

Swanson made to move, but Hugh didn't budge. Instead he pressed Mr. Aldrich for more information. "I don't go head to head with three men unless I know something about them."

"They're here to take Cassandra."

"Really? And why is that?" Hugh flicked his gaze at Mr. Aldrich and then back to Cassie, turning her so he could see her face.

She bit her lip, wishing she could say they were her pack, but she remembered the Keeping and held back. Damn, she thought, I'm barely a werewolf and already thinking about the rules. "They're my friends. I'm going to give them a cut of my inheritance."

Mr. Aldrich gave an evil smile, seeming to know full well what she longed to say. "See, Hugh? Simply men trying to get their hands on her money."

"So what's my percentage?" Hugh studied Mr. Aldrich again. "I said I'd help you, but you never gave me a number."

The lawyer narrowed his eyes, obviously tiring of the word play. "Once you've dealt with the intruders, we'll talk money."

"If he's getting a raise, I want one too." Swanson spoke up.

"After your earlier performance you'll be lucky to have a job, Swanson. Now both of you go. Get rid of those men before they're knocking on my door."

Hugh nodded. "What do you want me to do with her?" He shook Cassie gently.

"I'll deal with her. Just make sure those men don't reach this floor."

Swanson said nothing, but he gave Cassie a dirty look when he passed by and she shivered at the hatred she saw there. Maybe ratting on him hadn't been a good idea. Hugh left as well, looking too pleased with his job for Cassie's peace of mind. She hoped Bryan and the Alphas would be all right.

Nervously, she brought her gaze back to the screen, wondering what floor the men might be on. Climbing forty storeys would be exhausting; would they have any energy left to fight? And it would be in a stairwell, which seemed a more dangerous venue to her. Images of Bryan falling down several flights of stairs, his limbs twisted and broken, filled her mind.

She fisted her hands, wishing there was something she could do to help him, but what? She was too far away to do anything. There was no way to warn them that Hugh and Swanson were coming. She sighed in frustration. God, she hated standing around like some pathetic character in a romance novel.

Her eyes flashed around the room, looking for something, anything, to do. There was just herself and Aldrich. Hmm... She looked at the man before her. He was an average build, greying... Surely, he couldn't be that strong. And she was a werewolf, wasn't she? That must give her some advantage. She *had* knocked out the security guard and her uncle had enrolled her in several self-defence courses. Maybe it was time to put them to good use. She licked her lips and shifted her weight to the balls of her feet.

"I wouldn't do that if I were you, Cassandra." Aldrich turned slowly to face her and casually withdrew a gun from the pocket of his jacket. "You might be a werewolf, but I think a bullet at this close a range would slow you down considerably, don't you? Oh, and by the way, I'm an excellent shot. Marksman class."

He smiled politely at her and Cassie eased her weight back. Okay, so attacking him wasn't an option.

Aldrich cocked his head to the side and considered her. "You have the look of someone who could be impulsive and we can't have that now, can we?" He opened up another drawer and rummaged around, then pulled out a roll of tape and held it up triumphantly. "Just the thing to keep you line. Turn around please, hands behind your back."

She hesitated and Aldrich tutted in obvious annoyance.

"Come, we don't have much time. If you don't cooperate, I'll be obliged to knock you out. Which would you prefer?" He raised an eyebrow, his face bland, and matter of fact.

Realizing she'd rather be bound than unconscious, Cassie slowly turned, her mind racing. He couldn't tape her hands together with a gun in his hand, could he? As she stood with her back to him, she listened carefully. There was rustling of cloth, then the ripping sound of tape being pulled from a roll. Was the gun in his hand or had he placed it in his pocket or waist band?

She hesitated for a moment then decided to chance it. Kicking backwards, her foot made contact with some portion of his anatomy. He gave a loud 'oomph' and she took off running.

Unfortunately, it was a short run, for as soon as she turned the corner she encountered a security door. She tugged at the handle, growling in frustration when she realized it was palm print activated. Whirling around, she came up short. Aldrich was behind her, looking extremely displeased and holding the gun levelled at her chest.

"Did no one ever teach you how to play nicely?" His raspy voice was deceptively mild as he stepped closer.

She felt her eyes widen as he reached up with his hand. Was he going to strike her? She braced herself to endure the blow, but rather than hitting her, he grabbed her pony tail and used it to twist her around until her neck was bent at an uncomfortable angle.

"Now hold still this time or I *will* use the butt of this gun to knock you out."

She whimpered as he yanked her hair even harder.

"Hands behind your back."

She complied and he thrust a piece of tape into her palm.

"Hold the end."

While she gripped the end of the piece of tape, he wrapped the rest around her wrists using one hand. Once her wrists were secured to his satisfaction, he released her hair. "Very good. It's likely that Swanson and Hugh will only be able to slow them down for so long, so please move along quickly." He reached around her, pressed his hand to the sensor on the door and it swung open. Gesturing with the gun, he urged her ahead of him. "Turn to your left and proceed to the main living room."

She did as she was told, her feet sinking into lush carpeting as she moved deeper into the apartment. She looked around, taking in her surroundings and searching for anything that might help her escape. The decor was as cold and unwelcoming as the back rooms had been; ultra modern, no doubt expensive but lacking in any personal, homey touches. How could someone live in such a sterile environment?

Behind her, she could hear Mr. Aldrich breathing, a faint wheezing sound occurring with each breath he took. He seemed as cold and unemotional as his home. No, that wasn't strictly true. The man was scared, she could smell the fear coming off him. Strange how she was able to identify that; perhaps it was her wolf's doing. Outwardly he gave the appearance of being calmly in control. She supposed that was what made him such a good lawyer and why her uncle had employed him.

She glanced over her shoulder at him, wondering what his plan was.

As if he could read her mind, he answered her question. "I'm prepared for events such as this. If your packmates—and I assume that's who they are—thought to take me by surprise, they're sadly mistaken. In the event of a security breach such as the one they're attempting, there's a silent alarm, which summons a helicopter. It will land on the rooftop patio and whisk me away to safety."

Her stomach dropped. Did Aldrich mean to take her along with him? And if he did, once she was in the helicopter, how would Bryan be able to find her?

Bryan led the way up the stairs, taking two steps at a time. It was quite a climb and he could feel the sweat dampening his body, trickling down the indent of his spine and dampening his waist band. His leg muscles were starting to protest, too. As he reached yet another landing, he looked up, but could only see more and more flights of stairs. There was no end in sight. Behind him, he could hear the panting breaths of the two Alphas.

"How many more floors to go?" Ryne paused for a moment, leaning his back against the wall and then sliding down to sit on the floor.

"I lost count," Kane admitted, also stopping. He bent over and braced his arms on the railing then rested his head on them.

"A few too many hours at the Broken Antler, Ryne?" Bryan teased through his heavy breathing. He was tired as well, but not as much as the Alphas.

Ryne shot him a dirty look. "I can still whip your butt with one hand tied behind my back, pup."

"True." Bryan conceded the point having no wish to challenge Ryne. While he himself might have the physical endurance due to his strict training regimen, Ryne was the strategist whose cunning and quick moves allowed him to out-manoeuvre almost any opponent. Besides, being Alpha wasn't in his plans; he enjoyed his Beta position too much.

"Was that light on before?" Kane had raised his head to watch their good natured sparring, but now his eyes were fixed on a camera mounted in the upper corner of the stairwell.

"Damn!" Bryan started moving even as he spoke. "Someone's turned the security system back on which means Cassie's probably been discovered." He forced himself to move faster, paying no attention to whether or not the Alphas were keeping up. A feeling that something was definitely wrong came over him; Cassie was scared, much more so than she'd been earlier.

He bound up the steps, hopping the railing at each landing, rather than taking the extra steps to walk around. His mate needed him and he wasn't there to defend her!

The sound of their pounding feet bounced off the cement walls and echoed through the cavernous space. It was only by chance that Bryan caught the squeak of a door opening somewhere overhead and then the sound of more footsteps joined the din they were making.

Sparing a glance back, he caught the alert looks on Kane and Ryne's faces. They, too, were aware that other persons were now in the stairwell and heading down towards them. Their expressions were grim as they continued to climb upwards—there was no other option—but now they were prepared for a confrontation as well.

The footsteps were getting closer and he could make out two voices though the exact words were muffled and distorted. Two more flights, possibly three and they'd meet up, he judged, coiling his muscles in readiness.

He rounded the next corner and two large men came barrelling down at him.

"Heads up," Bryan shouted. "Incoming!" He bent low and rammed his shoulder into the gut of the first man, using the man's own momentum to help pitch the fellow over his head.

Behind him, he heard shouts of surprise from Kane and Ryne. Someone was falling; there were grunts and groans, then the unmistakeable sound of flesh hitting flesh. He didn't turn to see what was going on, knowing the two Alphas would easily handle one man between them.

Instead he concentrated on the next fellow. While he'd only had a brief glimpse of him outside Cassie's house, he knew it was the thug from Vegas. Without another thought, he tackled the man. Unfortunately, he didn't have the element of surprise that he did with the first. The thug was ready for him and threw him sideways over the railing.

Air rushed out of his lungs as his body slammed into the stairs, the edges digging into his flesh with bruising force, then raking his skin as he slid down a few steps before being able to gain a hold. Every bone in his back protested the treatment and a string of curses ripped from his throat, followed by a snarl as his wolf threatened to take over. He rolled over and got to his knees only to have his head snap back when a kick landed in his face. It drove him backwards and he hit the wall hard, his head bouncing off the cement bricks. A coppery taste filled his mouth and he spit out blood before wiping his face with the back of his hand. Giving no thought to his throbbing head, he launched himself forwards again.

The thug was in the process of climbing down towards him, when Bryan grabbed him by the knees, knocking the man backwards. They fell as one with the thug on the bottom, providing a cushion from the impact. Bryan's already sore body whispered its thanks. He pushed off the man, and grabbed the railing to steady himself as he attempted to regain his balance. Everything was swimming around him and he blinked trying to clear his eyes. A groan escaped the other man and Bryan turned towards the noise. Two and sometimes three images came in and out of focus before him.

Wasting no time to strategize, Bryan simply staggered forward and grabbed at the middle figure, which luckily enough was the real person. Closing his eyes, he let his other senses lead him, drawing his arm back, and swinging with all his might. He was rewarded with the jarring feeling of his fist connecting with bone and opened his eyes in time to see the man's head snap back, his eyes roll upward, and then his whole body falling limply to the ground.

Bryan flexed his fingers and gave his head another shake, pleased his vision was already clearing. He glanced around to see how the others were doing and saw Kane and Ryne were climbing over the body of the first man. Both looked the worse for wear, but pleased with themselves at the same time.

"You two all right?" His eyes sought Ryne's and then Kane's even as he prepared to start climbing again.

"Piece of cake." Ryne pushed the hair from his eyes, wincing as he touched a large bump on his forehead. "Except for the fact that when you pitched the guy over your shoulder, he hit me like I was a bowling pin in an alley. Knocked me down a whole flight of stairs. A bit more warning would be helpful next time."

"I managed to duck." Kane smirked before his face turned serious again. He jerked his head up towards the next flight of stairs. "Keep moving. Something tells me Aldrich isn't sitting there twiddling his thumbs, waiting for us."

Bryan grunted in acknowledgement, the delay the fight caused upping his concern for Cassie even more. Turning, he started running up the stairs again.

The Finding

Marla opened her eyes, feeling disoriented. What was she doing sitting in her office holding her head? She felt strange, disconnected, as if a part of her was missing. With a shaking hand she pushed her hair from her face and took a deep breath trying to regain her equilibrium and recall what was going on. There was a vague recollection of arguing with her wolf, then nothing.

She got to her feet and carefully walked to her office door. Pulling it open she frowned. Why was there a light flashing in the hallway? Wasn't that part of Aldrich's alert system, if the building's security was ever breached? There wasn't a security test scheduled for today, was there?

Stumbling down the hallway she made her way to Swanson's room, surprised to find the palm print security panel deactivated. She peered down the hallway, but no one was there. She'd only been in the security office a few times and never alone, but she'd studied it carefully enough to understand some of the basic functions. Stepping into the room she looked around, wondering what was going on. All the systems seemed to be activated. Reaching out, she shut off the irritating flashing lights—they were making her head throb—and began to study the monitors.

Movement on one of the surveillance screens caught her attention. It showed Aldrich walking across the living room with someone. She leaned closer to determine who it might be, when out of the periphery of her eye, she caught sight of a familiar face on another screen. Her attention swung that way and she gasped, grabbing the edge of the desk to keep her balance as everything came rushing back to her; Cassandra Greyson, the connection to Ryne, Aldrich's admission of knowing about Lycans, the rigged elevator.

And now, oh God, Kane, Ryne, and Ryne's sidekick, Bryan, were running up the stairwell that led to the penthouse!

She backed away from the screen and out the door unable to take her eyes off the men she'd feared for so long. They were coming and when they found her...

She turned and ran down the hall as quickly as her wobbly legs would take her. Aldrich was in the main living room. He had to have another escape route; the man was too paranoid to rely solely on an elevator and a set of stairs. It all made sense now; his ridiculous security, the fact that he was almost a recluse. If she'd known it was because of Lycans, she'd never have set her sights on him. It was too dangerous. However he was leaving, she was going with him. She couldn't be left behind to face those men. Who knew what they had planned for her?

We should stay and accept the consequences of our misdeeds. The wolf inside her intoned solemnly.

She ignored it and continued to hurry down the hall.

We can't run forever. The creature almost sounded forlorn. *This is not how we were meant to be.*

"Be quiet, you stupid beast. Just shut up." She pressed a hand to her head and tried to force the creature down again, but it was struggling harder than ever before. She rounded the corner and saw Aldrich near the French doors that led to the rooftop terrace. There was a girl—Cassandra Greyson—sitting in a chair close to him. She hated her on sight. The girl was the cause of all this. If she hadn't come back, Ryne wouldn't be here.

She's one of us. Her own wolf proclaimed.

As if I give a damn about that! She hissed back.

"Leon, they're here!" She called out the warning as she crossed the room, holding onto the various pieces of furniture to steady herself. Damn the wolf for interfering; her own legs didn't even want to obey her.

Aldrich spun around, an irritated look on his face. "I know that already, Miss Matthews. Where have you been? Sleeping on the job? Or perhaps watching movies? It *is* the trend today." He looked out the glass doors and seemed to be searching the sky. "The helicopter will be here any moment."

She breathed a sigh of relief. "Good. I'll run and get my purse and then I'll be ready to go."

"Go? Go where? The elevator isn't working." Aldrich swung his head around and quirked an eyebrow.

"With you. In the helicopter." She paused in the act of turning. A bad feeling swept over her. Surely Aldrich didn't intend to leave her? She swallowed nervously.

"Unfortunately, Miss Matthews, there's only room for 3 passengers; myself, Sylvia and Cassandra Greyson." He gestured with his gun towards the silent girl.

"But..." She sputtered, unable to formulate a clear sentence.

Aldrich paid her no mind. "Sylvia!" He called out as loudly as possible.

The woman appeared in the doorway, almost as if she'd been waiting for her cue. "Now, Leon. There's no need to yell. I'm here and all ready for our walk."

"A change of plans, I'm afraid." He smiled gently at the older woman. "We'll be taking a helicopter ride instead."

Sylvia gaped at him. "A helicopter? But what about our walk? I had everything arranged at my house." Her voice trailed off as she stared at the gun in his hand. "Leon? What's wrong?"

"A security breach, my dear. That's why we're taking the helicopter. We have to leave immediately."

"Oh." The woman blinked. "So that's why the lights were flashing? I thought Swanson was running another test, especially when they just turned off after a few minutes."

"Never mind, Sylvia. Come over here and we'll wait together."

"No!" Marla stepped forward, her hand held out. "You can't leave me here! Please, Leon! I mean, Mr. Aldrich. You have no idea what they'll do to me. Leave the Greyson girl. She'll be in no danger."

"Back off, Miss Matthews." Aldrich's soft gentle tones of a moment ago disappeared and his face was an icy mask. He pointed his gun at her. "You've served your purpose. Now it's time for us to part ways." A contemptuous look filled his eyes as he looked her up and down. "Why don't you use your 'charms' on them. That's how you usually operate, isn't it?"

He gave a dry laugh and then flicked a glance at Sylvia, urging her closer. "Sylvia, come here."

"I...I don't know, Leon." The words stuttered from Sylvia's lips and she nervously fumbled with her handbag, clutching it close to her chest.

Marla paid no attention to the nurse. She was frozen in place staring at the gun, her mind racing. Surely this couldn't be how it all ended? There had to be a way out. Sylvia was expendable, so was the Greyson girl. Aldrich had to see that! Perhaps once they were outside, she could push the nurse off the roof.

Chapter 24

Cassie sat in the chair watching the scene that played out before her. Mr. Aldrich had his gun trained on her, but his attention was divided between the woman he called Sylvia and a blonde he called Miss Matthews. She assumed Miss Matthews was Marla. Surreptitiously, she sniffed the air and confirmed her supposition. There was definitely another Lycan in the room, not that it would work to her advantage. From what she'd been told Marla wasn't to be trusted.

Slowly Cassie exhaled, realizing she was on her own. A moment ago, she'd tried to teleport out of the room, but nothing had happened. Kane had said it was important to relax and focus in order to teleport successfully, but that was hard to do when someone was holding you at gun point. Besides, she couldn't form a mental picture of where she wanted to go, since the only place she really wanted to be was with Bryan. He was somewhere in the building; she had a vague sense of him drawing closer, but exactly where that might be she didn't know.

Sighing, she moved on to her second plan. With Mr. Aldrich distracted by the conversation, she began to work on the tape that bound her wrists together. It was the silvery-grey kind with fibres worked into it and didn't come loose easily. Still she twisted and tugged, hoping to make some progress. Anything was better than sitting and waiting for fate to play out the scene.

The wolf inside her wasn't happy with the situation either, disliking the feeling of being captured and bound. She was beginning to find it comforting to have the creature with her; at least she wasn't totally alone in her predicament.

She wondered if it were true that werewolves had superhuman strength. If that were the case, she should be able simply to break through the tape, but unfortunately it didn't seem to be happening. The only result of her struggles was that her wrists hurt from the tape digging into her flesh.

'Why aren't you helping me when I need you?' She inwardly muttered to the wolf but it didn't answer. It was distracted and kept wanting her to look at Marla, though why she didn't know. The woman wasn't doing anything except standing there. In fact, she seemed odd almost as if her body were present, but her mind wasn't. Was Marla busy talking to her own wolf? And if so, what were they saying to each other? It likely wasn't anything good, since her expression wasn't a happy one.

Mentally shrugging, Cassie concentrated on her bound wrists again. The chair she sat in had a wooden arm. She felt the edge with her fingers; it was a nice ninety-degree angle so it might work. Shifting, she began rubbing the tape against the edge trying to keep her movements small and unnoticeable. Her arms protested the unusual motion and awkward position but she persevered.

'Hello? Wolf? Are you there? Can you help me out a bit?' She again tried talking to the animal within, but she only got a distressed whimper followed by a shiver that ran over her. Was the creature trying to channel some energy her way, but didn't know how? Maybe this was another skill she had to tap into and practise, like understanding scents and teleporting. Or maybe it required her to be—what was it that Bryan had called it—at one with her wolf? Perhaps the strength came from the beast and until she integrated with it, the extra muscle power didn't emerge.

Discreetly huffing in frustration, she decided that at this point, it didn't really matter. She was stuck for the time being, so she might as well concentrate on what was going on around her since the werewolf route wasn't going anywhere.

Continuing to work on the tape binding her wrists, she flicked her eyes between the room's occupants. Marla was in a daze, Mr. Aldrich was trying to cajole Sylvia into escaping with him, and Sylvia herself was biting her lip and nervously fumbling with her purse.

"I've never been in a helicopter before, Leon."

Mr. Aldrich smiled, his eyes taking on a gentle expression. "There's nothing to be nervous about, Sylvia. You'll enjoy it."

"Actually, I don't think I will." Suddenly, Sylvia's worried expression was replaced by a ruthless sneer. No longer was she nervously playing with the clasp on her purse. It had dropped to her feet and a gun was in her hand!

She stifled a gasp as she swung her eyes between Sylvia and Mr. Aldrich.

"Sylvia?" Mr. Aldrich blinked rapidly, shock momentarily showing on his face before he schooled his features. "What's this all about?"

"I was hired to carry out a hit on you by the end of the month, but the job is taking too long. You wouldn't leave the building and go for a walk like I initially planned and shooting you here wasn't my first option, too many witnesses, you understand." She snorted inelegantly. "And now that I've finally convinced you to go with me, it's too late! You know, I've found this to be a very frustrating job."

"My apologies for not cooperating sooner." Mr. Aldrich inclined his head, his face expressionless. She wondered what he was feeling. Mere moments ago it had sounded as if he cared for the woman.

"I won't be cheated out of my commission." Sylvia continued. "I'll have to shoot you here and unfortunately, these two ladies as well." She flicked a glance at Cassie and Marla. "Sorry but I can't leave witnesses. The helicopter is a bonus though; it will provide my escape and the people who are presently breaching your security can take the blame for your deaths."

Mr. Aldrich frowned and cocked his head to the side as if trying to figure the woman out. "Who hired you?"

"Anonymous." She answered in clipped tones. "In this business you don't ask for names."

Mr. Aldrich sighed heavily and shook his head. "I actually liked you, Sylvia. Do you know how few people I've ever said that to?"

Sylvia shook her head and spoke with mock regret. "Sorry. I should feel honoured, I'm sure. If it makes you feel any better, I did briefly consider forgoing the hit and staying with you." She glanced around the room. "You're wealthy enough, but after considering the matter I decided you were too unreliable. I know your type. You dispose of 'friends' when the novelty wears off and by then my reputation as an assassin for hire would be ruined." She shrugged and raised her gun. "So unfortunately..."

The quiet yet unmistakeably muffled sound of a bullet fired from a gun with a silencer filled the room. She started at the noise, staring at Mr. Aldrich in dismay. His arm fell limply to the side, his face greying. "You're right, Sylvia. I am the type to dispose of friends." His head fell forward and his shoulders slumped, then he slowly slid down to sit on the arm of a chair. "... and enemies who pretend to be friends."

For a moment the room was silent, expectation heavy in the air. Then he breathed deeply once more and straightened, tightening his grip on his gun. "Goodbye Sylvia. I did...care for you."

Realizing that it hadn't been Mr. Aldrich who was shot, Cassie snapped her head around to look towards where Sylvia had been standing. The woman was now lying on the ground, a red stain showing on her prim white shirt.

"So Cassandra, it's just me and you now." Mr. Aldrich shifted his attention back to her. His face looked worn and tired.

"And me?" Marla suddenly jerked as if coming out of a trance and began wringing her hands, looking nervously behind her, then at the dead body and then back at Mr. Aldrich. She'd been surprisingly quiet throughout the whole dramatic event almost as if she were unaware of what was going on around her.

Mr. Aldrich looked at Sylvia's body, then gave a negligent one shouldered shrug. "Sure, why not? There's an empty seat on the chopper now. And at least I know where I stand with you. You're a conniving bitch, but I won't make the mistake of expecting anything more than that from you." He flicked a glance up and down her body and then barked out a laugh. "It might even be fun availing myself of you after all these years of resisting your attempts to seduce me."

She watched as Marla frowned, her eyes going unfocused, but then the woman gave her head a brief shake and stepped forward. "Whatever you need, Mr. Aldrich. I'll be happy to help."

Using his gun, Mr. Aldrich indicated that Cassie should stand up.

She obeyed, but her vision blurred and there was a buzzing in her ears. She hoped she wouldn't faint. Maybe it was the shock of another person being killed in front of her. Her stomach felt queasy and she swallowed hard to keep from being ill as she cast a final look at the body on the floor.

"What are you going to do to me?" She forced the words passed her numb lips.

"I have big plans for you Cassandra, don't worry." Mr. Aldrich opened the French doors and ushered her out onto the roof top.

The terrace appeared to cover a quarter of the roof. There was a hot tub and several groupings of patio furniture as well as a barbeque with a wet bar beside it. Several lattice screens and some large cement flower boxes surrounded the space, serving to delineate the entertainment area from the rest of the roof. Beyond them, Cassie could just make out the painted markings for a helicopter landing pad and several jutting metal objects that appeared to be air vents or other structures to deal with the internal workings of the building.

"We'll wait here." Mr. Aldrich sat on the edge of the planter, near an opening that allowed access to the rest of the roof. He was seemingly oblivious to the strong cold wind that blew across the open space.

She shivered as the wind buffeted against her body, actually forcing her to take an unplanned step before she steadied herself. At this height the wind was stronger and colder than at ground level. It tugged at her hair, pulling strands free from her pony tail so that they whipped about in her face, stinging her eyes and making it hard to see. She wished her hands were free so she could at least push the hair behind her ears. Tugging and twisting her wrists, she tested the strength of the tape again but it was holding firm.

Marla stood silently beside her, appearing lost in thought again. The woman occasionally brushed the hair from her own face but didn't seem to care that the wind was blowing her skirt scandalously high.

After a moment of studying her, Cassie ignored her, deciding that despite the men's warnings, Marla posed no threat; she was more like a wind-up fashion doll than an evil villain.

A noise in the distance caught her attention and she looked up to see a helicopter approaching. It was like a huge dark bird of prey, waiting to pluck her up and carry her off. The sinking feeling in her stomach grew as she wondered where Mr. Aldrich might be taking her and what his 'big plans' might entail once they arrived.

Desperately, she wished Bryan were there, holding her close as he'd done last night. It had felt so right to be with him, like she'd finally found her home. She cursed herself for not making use of the opportunity to share her feelings. Instead, she'd just absorbed the security of his presence and listened to the rise and fall of his voice as he spoke. Why hadn't she said something more than 'I really like you' when she'd had the chance? 'Like' was so banal. 'Like' was vanilla ice cream or toast with butter. There were lots of things she *liked*, but her feelings for Bryan were so much more. And this morning in the alley, she'd told him to be careful, but something had held her back from saying more. She'd wanted to, but the words wouldn't come.

Swallowing hard, she faced the cold reality that now it might be too late.

They'd finally done it. They'd reached the penthouse. Now, only a door separated him from Cassie. Bryan wiped the sweat from his eyes and grasped the handle only to jerk back swearing.

"What is it?" Ryne was breathing heavily as he pulled himself up the final steps followed by Kane.

The Finding

"The damned door has an electric charge." Bryan growled in frustration as he examined the burn marks on his palm. His skin was already healing, but it still hurt. He shook his arm trying to rid it of the tingling feeling the electrical jolt had caused.

Kane immediately began examining the door. "There's no obvious wiring for us to disconnect."

"What about behind this plate?" Ryne hunkered down by a rectangular piece of metal located beside the door. He tried to work his fingers around the edge and pry it off but couldn't find anything to hold on to. "Anyone have a screwdriver or a knife on them? If we can get inside here, maybe we can short out the system."

"Sorry, didn't think to pack one." Bryan answered distractedly as he stared at a metal grate near the ceiling. "This looks like an air vent." He reached up and worked his fingers between the slats and pulled. There was a screeching sound of metal against metal. Taking a deep breath, he pulled even harder and suddenly he was stumbling backwards as the covering came loose. Setting it down, he grasped the edge of the opening and chinned himself up to peer inside. "Damn! Too small. None of us would fit inside." Dropping to the floor, he ran his hands through his hair in frustration. "How the hell are we supposed to get in? We haven't climbed forty storeys to be stopped by a door." He reached out and grabbed the handle only to jerk back as, once again, it shocked him.

Kane had his hands spread before him and was hovering them over the door's surface. "The charge doesn't seem to be deadly, at least not for me. I think I can drain it or maybe even short circuit it."

"No way. It's too dangerous." Ryne looked up from where he was still trying to loosen the metal plate, a frown on his face.

Bryan shook his head. "I agree with Ryne. We use energy from our surroundings when we transform, but we only absorb the minimal amount required. The energy in the door will come at you in one big jolt. Your body won't know how to handle it."

"I don't think so." Kane was studying the door, his eyes narrowed. "I can almost see the electrical current. I'm sure it's only marginally more than what I use when I change. Besides, without sounding like I'm bragging, I'm a strong Alpha. Controlling a bit of extra input might tire me out, but that's all and it will only be for a moment. If I touch the door and channel the energy into a transformation, it should give you a chance to grab the handle and yank the door open. Once you're in, I'll let go."

Rising to his feet, Ryne nodded slowly. "I hate to say it Kane, but you're on to something. The plan just needs one modification."

Kane quirked his eyebrow. "Such as...?"

Ryne grinned. "We both do it. Two Alphas absorbing the energy are better than one."

Bryan shifted uneasily. The idea of both men risking their lives at the same time didn't sit well with the Beta in him. Protecting the pack, taking the risks; that was his job. Yet he knew he didn't have the mental control needed to channel an external charge of that magnitude.

"You two better be right because I don't want to face Mel and Elise if something happens to either of you." He expressed his concern through a joke.

Ryne clapped him on his back. "It'd be a good experience for you. Who knows, you might be placating an irate mate sooner than you think."

Bryan didn't have an opportunity to respond as suddenly Ryne was all business. The two Alphas stood side by side, hands outstretched ready to touch the door.

Kane looked over his shoulder at Bryan. "As soon as we touch the door, we'll start to transform. It'll be fast and probably won't be pretty, but don't worry about us. The charge in the door will have dropped sufficiently that you'll be able to pull it open safely. Once it's open, we'll let go and the door will recharge so don't brush against it when you go through."

"We might need a minute to recuperate but don't wait for us." Ryne added. "Just get in there and find Cassie. Make sure she's safe before you start to deal with Marla and Aldrich. We should be there to help you by then."

Nodding, Bryan braced himself, his hand held out, ready to grab the door. His teeth were clenched and he felt a muscle throbbing in his jaw. If there was any other way, he'd try to dissuade them, but another solution wasn't apparent. And Cassie was inside and in trouble; he couldn't not do everything possible to get to her. Taking a deep breath, he called out. "Ready."

The brothers looked at each other, their faces grim and then as one leaned into the door.

Immediately they gave loud cries of pain and their bodies went rigid. Wincing, Bryan forced himself not to look and grabbed the handle instead. Only a slight tingling affected his palm as the Alphas absorbed most of the charge. He yanked the door open with all his might, kicked the attached door-stop into place and immediately released the handle. The momentum dislodged the Alpha's hands and they dropped to the ground, writhing as the forced transformation swept through them.

The change happened at an alarming rate. Instead of the usual gradual morph when skin and bone melted and reshaped with fluidity, this appeared to be a sudden agonizing slam with all the grace and finesse of a train wreck. Limbs cracked loudly and reshaped in the blink of an eye, hair tore itself through skin, joints shifted, nerves and muscles spasmed, teeth ripped through gums while muzzles pushed outward grotesquely distorting features. It was like something out of a horror movie, too terrifying to watch yet holding the observer captive with morbid curiosity.

In mere seconds it was over and two black wolves lay unmoving on the floor.

Elise dropped her tea cup on the floor, gasping as pain slammed through her. She gripped the edge of the table, her knuckles white as she fought not to pass out. "Something's wrong."

"What? Oh God!" Liquid sloshed over the table as Mel set her own cup down abruptly. She seemed to be struggling to breathe, her eyes squeezed tightly shut.

Around them patrons turned to stare and Elise forced herself to stay calm, fighting the panic that welled up inside her.

They were in public, surrounded by humans. She couldn't give in, no matter how desperately she wanted to. Leaning forward, she whispered to Mel. "We have to get out of here!"

Mel nodded, her arms wrapped around her abdomen, as she rocked in place. Her lips tightly compressed as if she were fighting to stay in control.

Elise swallowed hard. A sick feeling roiled in her stomach and it was all she could do to keep from bolting from the coffee shop.

"My friend's ill. We...we have to go." She stumbled over an explanation as she gathered her coat and purse, then helped Mel stand up. Holding her arm, she guided her around the server who had come to clean up the spill, then through the maze of crowded tables.

Once outside, Mel collapsed against the wall of the building, turning tortured eyes to Elise. "What?"

Elise shook her head. "I don't know." She pressed her hand to her mouth and stared upward, blinking rapidly. They were on a crowded downtown street; falling apart wasn't an option. She was the senior Alpha female and Mel looked horrible. It was her job to take charge. Duty first, she reminded herself. Wasn't that what Kane always said? Duty first. Trying to purge the emotion from her voice, she cleared her throat. "The baby?"

"It's fine. Don't worry. It jumped when I felt that sudden...whatever it was that we felt...but it's fine now."

"Good." Elise rubbed her forehead and took a deep breath, trying to remain detached. That's how one got through difficult situations, or so she'd been told but it was rather hard to do when it felt like someone had ripped your heart out. "That was intense. I've never felt anything like it before."

"Any idea what happened?"

Pursing her lips, she shrugged. "Kane blocked me out this morning, the silly man." She paused and blinked, struggling for calm before continuing. "He didn't want to worry me while he was on a mission. But just a moment ago, the block vanished with no warning, as if he completely lost control and then...wham!" Elise shook her head again. "Kane doesn't lose control. Not ever. It's one of the frustrating things about him. But he was in pain; intense pain. I think he transformed, but it shouldn't have been like that. It was agonizingly painful." Her eyes filled with tears as emotion began to take over despite her efforts to prevent it. "I can't sense him now. There's nothing there at all; no thoughts, no feelings." Her breathing hitched and she forced herself to take deep breaths, fighting against the feeling of despair that rose inside her. "He can't be..." She clenched her fists, unable to voice the words.

Mel grabbed Elise's hand and held it tightly. Her chin wobbled and it took several tries before she could speak. "It's the same for me. I suddenly had a jolt, almost like he stuck his finger in a socket and his feelings crashed into my brain and then, just as quickly, they were gone." She wiped her eyes. "I feel hollow inside, like a part of me is missing."

Their eyes met and they stared at each other, sharing the pain and emptiness of suddenly losing an integral part of themselves. Even when mates blocked out their mental connection, there was still a sense that the other was there, but now a black void existed on the fringes of their minds where minutes before a living, breathing mate had been.

Elise turned to look down the street, towards Aldrich's building. "It makes no sense though. Who or what could take out two Alphas at exactly the same time?"

Mel turned as well. "I don't know, but we need to find out."

Elise nodded and stuck out her chin. Her despair was fading and her logical mind was taking over. She refused to believe that both Kane and Ryne could be gone. "Come on. We're not going to stand here and wallow in our misery. Something is happening and we need to figure it out."

Mel sniffed and wiped her nose. "I agree. Ryne and Kane are in that building and we need to find them and help them."

They hurried down the street until they stood on the sidewalk in front of the building that housed Aldrich's penthouse.

"What now?" Mel looked at the entrance. A security guard sat in the entry way, his arms folded across his chest and a bored expression on his face. "Do you think he'll let us in?"

Elise peered at the man carefully. "I think he's sleeping."

"Then maybe we can sneak by him."

"No. If we get caught, he'll never let us in." Elise nibbled on her lip then smiled when an idea came to mind. "We're going to try the old 'pregnant woman needs a bathroom' routine." She grabbed Mel's arm and dragged her to the entrance, hissing instructions as they went along. "Look pale and worried. Hop up and down like you really need to pee, too."

Mel rolled her eyes. "You're talking to a pregnant woman, remember? I always have to pee." Nevertheless, she put her hands around her belly to help emphasize its size and tried to look anxiously in need of a washroom.

Elise pushed the door open and smiled at the doorman. "I'm so sorry to bother you but my friend here really needs a bathroom. Is there a public washroom in the lobby that she could use?"

The man took in how Mel was shifting from foot to foot, looked at her swollen stomach and finally her anxious face. He sighed heavily as if moving his eyes had been a huge effort. "Sure. Go to your right. Third door on the left." Slowly, he reached out and pushed the button that released the door then leaned back against the wall as if to resume his nap.

Elise and Mel slipped through the door and turned right as the man had indicated. Sure enough, a washroom sign was ahead.

Mel winced apologetically. "I'm sorry, but thinking about it has made me really have to go."

"That's okay." Elise pointed at herself. "Two kids. I know how you feel. Just try to make it fast."

Mel nodded and slipped inside then moments later returned looking much relieved. "Okay, I'm ready. Which way do you think?"

They looked around, but saw no sign of an elevator beyond the one right across from the front door.

"We can't use that one. That man might wake up and see us." Elise pointed out.

The Finding

Mel nibbled on her thumb nail. "There's a set of stairs just behind us. Oh no!" She grabbed Elise's arm and pulled her behind a potted plant.

"What?"

"Another security guard and he's definitely more awake than the guy at the door!" She looked around then pointed. "This way. There's some kind of patio at the end of the corridor. We'll slip outside until he's gone."

They hurried down the hallway and stepped outside.

"That will be our ride." Mr. Aldrich nodded toward the approaching chopper and stood up. "Miss Matthews, did you contact Dr. Mason?"

"Hmm?" Marla blinked at him.

"Dr. Mason." Mr. Aldrich looked exasperated. "I gave you the instructions less than an hour ago. We need to have Cassandra declared mentally unfit and locked up as soon as possible."

Cassie narrowed her eyes. So that was his plan! She'd spend the rest of her life locked up and most likely drugged out of her mind while Mr. Aldrich controlled the estate! The money didn't concern her, but the idea of being locked up and drugged did!

Already too much of her life had been spent being restrained, one way or another. Kept in a figurative glass cage by her uncle, hiding from werewolves, drugging herself every month. She shook her head. No, she couldn't go through that again. Not now that she'd had a glimpse of what her life could be like. She started to inch away.

Mr. Aldrich continued. "Once I have her out of the way, I'll start to work on the estate funds so that I have complete control of all finances."

Carefully, Cassie edged farther away. She wasn't sure where she was going to go but staying wasn't an option. There were a few roof vents she could hide behind and what looked like a rooftop access to the elevator shaft to the one side. Perhaps she could make it that far. The door might not be locked and once inside, well... She'd figure out that part later.

395

A gust of wind caught her by surprise and she stumbled. The movement attracted Aldrich's attention and he grabbed her arm and dragged her back, his fingers biting into her arm. "Don't even think about it." He pressed the gun's barrel to her side and she winced at the feel of it against her ribs. "You're worth more to me alive, but even dead I can still profit from you. A werewolf corpse should fetch a pretty penny, don't you think Miss Matthews?"

"Corpse?" Marla frowned at the word and shot a glance between Cassie and Mr. Aldrich.

"Yes. Even dead, I'm sure scientists would be interested in studying her." He gave Cassie's arm a shake.

Marla licked her lips, squinting against the wind. "I...I don't think—"

"You're not paid to think, Miss Matthews. And in case you're getting squeamish, let me tell you, I know about the items you've been pilfering from the Estate. Swanson followed you several times. I have dates, amounts. You cross me and I'll see you in jail for stealing."

Marla sputtered in protest.

Mr. Aldrich continued, not listening. His eyes were glazed as he spoke, excitement filling his voice as it rose to be heard over the noise of the approaching helicopter. "So you *will* assist me with Cassandra, Miss Matthews. No more of this foolishness. If all goes as planned, in a few years we'll hand her over to science as a living specimen. It will be a dramatic revelation and turn the table on the damned beasts that have haunted me these past three years."

A specimen? Turned over to scientists? Mr. Aldrich was talking about her as if she wasn't even there! As if she were nothing more than an animal! She gasped, affront and fear filling her. There was no way she'd let herself be stuck in some cage to be poked and prodded like some lab rat. She wasn't a freak; she was just different!

"We need to go." He began walking, one hand gripping her upper arm, the other holding the gun pressed to her side.

The Finding

The natural wind, combined with that created by the helicopter circling the building made walking difficult and Mr. Aldrich bent forward to counteract the force of the moving air. As they drew closer and closer to the landing pad, Cassie became more desperate, digging in her heels, no longer caring that Mr. Aldrich might shoot her. She was *not* getting into that helicopter. There was no way that...

Her vision blurred again. There was a buzzing in her ears, her skin prickled. Was she going to be sick? Was she shifting? Tension built within her. Oh God, it was happening again! Her breathing quickened. She felt like she was hyperventilating, her muscles tightening, straining and then the air shimmered around her.

She had a vague impression of Mr. Aldrich gasping and stepping back, then in an instant he was no longer at eye level. He loomed over her as if she were much shorter than she'd been mere seconds ago. His fingers were no longer holding her arm, the gun no longer pressed to her ribs. Relieved to be free, she started to back away, only to trip when she realized she now had four legs to coordinate instead of two and the remnants of sticky tape around her ankles!

Scrambling, she sought to get her feet under her and shake off the now loose tape. The rough surface of the roof felt strange under her paws, the wind whipping her fur about and whistling past her ears was stimulating yet confusing at the same time as a myriad of scents swirled by. She ignored them though, keeping her eyes fixed on Mr. Aldrich, trying to judge his next move.

He was pale, no doubt as surprised as she was. Then a change came over him as he appeared to recover from the shock of her transformation. His features hardened, his eyes narrowed. Even before his hand moved, she knew what he intended to do.

Letting out a woof, she spun around and began to run. A shot rang out—her hearing was even more acute now and the sound seemed louder than it had been inside the apartment— then a bullet dug into the roof's surface mere inches from where she was.

With a yelp, she jerked to the side as small bits of debris shot up and hit her in the face. Her legs tangled and she fell sideways, skidding across the rough surface. Even through her fur coat, she felt her skin being abraded, her ribs protesting. She rolled over, gained some control, and sprang to her feet again, taking off running once more.

Behind her, the rhythmic thumping of the helicopter blades distorted the sound of pounding feet. Some instinct had her swivelling her ears back, trying to determine how close Mr. Aldrich might be. Her heart was pounding, panic washing over her at the thought of being shot or, even worse, being captured, drugged, and put in a cage.

Her wolf was coming to the foreground. She could feel it taking over, telling her to run in a zigzag pattern that would be harder to hit, to keep low to the ground. Her eyes darted back and forth, searching for cover, a place to hide.

A roof vent was to her right so she veered that way, ducking behind it just in time to avoid the spray kicked up by the next bullet. Spinning around, she crouched low and peeked out. Mr. Aldrich was farther away than she thought he'd be; almost on the other side of the roof.

She couldn't help but grin briefly as she realized how fast she must be in this form. And her wolf was a quick thinker too. In the middle of all her panic, a pleasant feeling washed over her and she knew the animal was pleased with her. Was that her tail thumping behind her? She chanced a quick look and saw that it was. Silly beast, she thought fondly, before returning her attention to the scene before her.

The helicopter was still circling the roof, the pilot leaning out and yelling at Mr. Aldrich. Something about the wind and having difficulty controlling the helicopter. She couldn't make out the words clearly.

Keeping one eye on them, she tried to decide her next move. The rooftop elevator access was a few yards away but as a wolf, she wouldn't be able to open the door to get inside, so that eliminated one possible means of escape. Her next best bet was to circle back to the penthouse. Surely Bryan and the Alphas would have made it past Mr. Aldrich's goons by now. A small frisson of worry swept through her when she thought of the man she'd spent the night with.

She was aware of him—his thoughts and feelings—in some strange way. It wasn't totally clear but she was sure at this moment he was feeling impatient, worried, and angry. And he wasn't hurt—she knew that too and was thankful—but what could be keeping him? It wasn't that she was looking for a knight...er...wolf...to rush in and rescue her but she hadn't expected to handle this all on her own. And what about Kellen? Was he all right? How severe was his injury? A whimper escaped her as she worried about the men in her life.

Mr. Aldrich shouted out an instruction and she pulled her attention back to him again. He was heading her way.

"You go to the right. I'll go left. There's no way for her to escape."

She perked her ears at that statement and then jerked her head around. Damn! She'd forgotten Marla; the woman had been so unresponsive earlier she had dismissed her. Definitely a mistake. Marla was approaching from the rear and Mr. Aldrich was in front.

Getting to her feet, Cassie began to back away from the two people who were approaching her. Exactly what she'd do if they came too close she wasn't sure. When the thug had been hurting Kellen, she'd attacked him but it had been a spur of the moment thing. The wolf had taken over and acted on instinct. This was more premeditated. Did she have it in her to knowingly attack? The very idea of biting and scratching someone, even someone intent on harming her, made her feel sick. But what else could she do? As Mr. Aldrich had said, there was nowhere to go.

She kept her head low and emitted a warning growl.

Chapter 25

Mel and Elise huddled near a grey cement wall in the shelter of potted evergreen. The small patio area they found themselves in likely served as a gathering area for the building's occupants on nice days. Unfortunately, today wasn't a day for sitting around the picnic tables and enjoying the spring flowers. A cold wind whipped around the building, stirring up bits of dirt and garbage that had collected over the winter, making their hiding place less than ideal. However, since there was a security guard lounging just inside the door, they really had very little choice. Discovery would mean being kicked out of the building and putting them even farther away from their mates.

Elise peered through the scented green branches, then ducked back out of sight. "He's still there."

"Why'd the guard have to take a break right by the patio doors? Why isn't he out patrolling the halls on the far side of the building? We need to get upstairs and help our men." Mel grumped.

A sigh escaped Elise's lips. "At least the empty feeling inside me is fading. Sometimes I think I can sense Kane but then other times I wonder if it's wishful thinking. There's a connection, but it feels off." She shook her head. "I can't explain it, other than it's like he's there, but not there. It's frustrating." Leaning her head back against the cement wall, she rolled her shoulders, trying to relax her tense muscles. Being an Alpha's mate was taxing. You spent a lot of time alone worrying, yet knowing you had to let him go and do what he was born to do. There was no solution; you just had to accept it as part of life. It didn't mean she had to like it.

Mel's eyes grew misty and distant, as if she were mentally reaching out, searching for her mate. "I...I think Ryne's tired, like all the energy has been sucked out of him. I don't think I've ever felt him this weak, as if he's drifting along, almost disconnected from his body." She shivered and wrapped her arms around her stomach. "I wish we were with them." Exhaling slowly, she stared up the wall, passed some forty sets of windows to where their mates were. "You know, most penthouses have their own private elevators or at least a special lock on the keypad that only allows certain people to gain access."

"So basically, even if the guard goes on his merry way, there's not much chance of us getting to Aldrich's apartment." Elise concluded.

"Uh-huh. There are too many Lycan rules and laws restricting our movement when we're out in public like this. I hate to say it, but I think the best we can do is wait here." Mel settled herself on the edge of a planter. "It's small comfort, but at least we're close at hand if something does happen."

Elise sat down too and reached over to clasp Mel's hand. She tried to speak positively. "I think if they're really in trouble, our being closer will help. We can send them our support, let them know we love them and we're waiting for them to come back to us."

Blinking back tears, Mel nodded and the two sat in silence for a few minutes, willing their mates to be strong and well.

After a while, Elise frowned. "What's that sound? At first I thought it was the traffic, but it isn't. A helicopter perhaps?"

Mel cocked her head and listened. "You're right." She shaded her eyes and craned her neck, squinting upwards. "I don't see anything. Wait. There it is!" She pointed at the dark belly of a chopper as it momentarily appeared over the edge of the building before circling around and out of sight.

"Is it trying to land on the roof?"

Mel surveyed the L-shaped building; the portion which they were near was lower, perhaps twenty storeys but the tower part rose a full forty. "It's probably headed to the tower. A lot of buildings have landing pads on the roof, but from the way it's moving I'd say the wind is giving the pilot a hard time."

"Then why is he out in this weather?" Elise paused, then stared at Mel wide-eyed as something occurred to her. "That's it! I bet Aldrich is going to escape us again using the chopper!"

Bryan stepped cautiously into the penthouse from the stairwell, his senses on alert for possible danger. Behind him, he could hear Ryne and Kane's laboured breathing, both still in wolf form and trying to recover from the jolt of electricity they'd absorbed. They appeared physically drained, and both were suffering muscles spasms, twitching horribly. He felt guilty leaving them behind unguarded, but their final instructions had been to go ahead without them and, truth be told, the pull to find Cassie was too strong to resist.

He listened for a minute longer, scenting the air and searching the surrounding space for signs of movement. There was no one in close proximity, though he could hear the distant hum of conversation and the clattering of dishes as if people were going about their day, completely unaware of the drama that was probably playing out in one of the other rooms. The scent of cleaning products was overpowering and he growled in frustration when he could detect no sign of Cassie.

With the tips of his fingers, he gently pushed open the door to his right, revealing a washer, dryer and sets of shelves holding detergent, and disinfectants. Apparently the stairs opened up into a service area. Several piles of laundry sat on the floor and an open bottle of bleach was near the sink. He stepped inside and capped the bottle. Little wonder his nostrils burned and he couldn't smell the occupants of the penthouse.

Pulling the door shut, he began to walk cautiously down the hallway, peeking into the various rooms he passed, expecting an attack at any moment. When none came, he frowned. This made no sense. His own security plan for the pack involved several layers of defence. Surely Aldrich, with his supposedly impermeable fortress, didn't rely solely on the two goons in the stairway?

The sound of voices coming his way caught his attention and he ducked into the closest doorway. It opened into a bedroom, which thankfully was unoccupied. Pushing the door partly closed with the toe of his shoe, he pressed himself against the wall. There was a crack where the hinges met the door frame and he peeked into the hallway, curious to know who was coming.

The voices grew louder and shadows appeared on the wall. He tensed, ready to react.

"So then I told him, if he wanted 'dessert' he'd have to take me somewhere fancier than the bowling alley." A woman appeared, possibly mid-twenties, red hair, average appearance. She was dressed in a blue and white uniform and carried an empty laundry basket.

The other woman was of a similar age and build. She laughed. "So where's he taking you tonight?"

"I don't know, but he told me to dress up."

"Sounds like he really wants that dessert. Will you have something juicy to tell me tomorrow?"

"Maybe. He's really cute *and* he has good manners." The woman giggled then glanced towards the door where he was hiding. Did the smile on her face falter? Had she noticed him looking through the crack in the door? He drew back and held his breath. "I'll finish gathering the bedding and you get the towels from the bathrooms."

"Okay. I'll meet you in the laundry room in about ten minutes. Once this load's in the wash we can tackle the floors."

Damn! They'd be heading back to the laundry area. He clenched his fists, wondering how Kane and Ryne were doing. Hopefully they were feeling better by now, or at least would have moved to a hiding place before these two women returned with their loads of laundry. What would the ladies do when they saw the door to the stairs open? Did they know the outside had an electric charge and was part of Aldrich's security or did they think of it as a fire escape that was never used? Would they sound the alarm?

The door he was hiding behind pushed open and a shaft of light illuminated the room. A woman stood quietly in the doorway. He tensed. What would she do?

"Hey, I know you're in here." The woman's voice conveyed a sense of curiosity rather than danger, but he didn't respond. After a moment, she spoke again. "It's okay. I've worked here long enough to know to keep my mouth shut. I'm just going to come in and change the bedding; don't jump me or anything, all right?" She paused again, then turned on the light and moved into the room.

He stepped out from behind the door and the woman cocked her head at him. "You're better looking than the last guy."

"The last guy?" He edged around the door, never taking his eyes off the woman.

"Yeah. The guy who stayed here last night. I think his name was Hugh. Big fellow, no manners, though." The woman smiled at him. "You have good manners?"

"My mother would like to think so."

The woman nodded. "So, why are you hiding in here?"

"I thought you said you knew how to keep your mouth shut. Shouldn't that include not asking questions?"

She shrugged.

"Let's just say my friends and I are conducting a security check of the building, finding its weak spots."

"Ah! So that's why the warning lights were flashing a while ago. I figured it was another test when they went off after a minute. Swanson does that every few weeks; we hardly notice them anymore." She took a step closer looking him up and down. "You're cute."

"Er...thanks? Listen, I'd like to stay and talk, but I'm on a tight schedule. Um... If you see some other guys back near the stairs, they're part of my team."

"Sure." She winked at him. "I won't say anything if you make it worth my while." The woman stepped even closer, her breasts brushing his chest while she walked her fingers up his arm.

He cleared his throat and spoke firmly. "Sorry. No fraternizing with the help; Mr. Aldrich's orders."

The woman huffed, but stepped back. "The old miser; he sucks the fun out of everything!" She immediately clamped her hand over her mouth, her eyes wide. "You won't tell Mr. Aldrich I said that, will you?" She spoke between her fingers.

"Not this time." He forced himself to look stern. "Just continue with your duties and I'll forget all about it."

Nodding, the woman backed up until her legs bumped into the bed then turned and began stripping the sheets. He took that as his chance to escape and ducked out of the room, almost slumping in relief. Talk about bluffing one's way out of trouble!

Anxious to be away before the woman questioned his story, he quickly slipped down the hallway and around a corner. His heart was pounding from the close call and he took a second to lean against the wall to gather his wits about him. That's when the scent hit him; the coppery smell of blood!

It was fresh and entwined with it was Cassie's own unforgettable scent of exotic spices and flowers. Panic flared inside him. He'd sensed Cassie was afraid, but how had he missed this?

Uncaring if he was detected or not, he took off running. Adrenaline pumped through his system, his heart pounding so loudly he could hardly hear or... Was it his heart or was it the sound of a helicopter? Damn it! Understanding dawned. That was Aldrich's second line of defence; a strategic retreat via chopper, not more guards. No wonder he hadn't encountered anyone trying to stop him. Aldrich had a rooftop landing pad and was going to use a helicopter to escape. And he was probably taking Cassie with him, if she wasn't already dead!

He put on a burst of speed. Cassie couldn't be dead; it must be just an injury. That was where the blood was from. He'd sense it if she was dead wouldn't he? That fact provided him with some small comfort but he clung to it like a lifeline. Of course, injured she'd be unable to resist when they tried to put her on the helicopter. And once airborne, there'd be no way to catch them. A chopper could set down anywhere.

The Finding

The idea of never seeing Cassie again filled him with dread. He ran down the hallway, rounded a corner, and suddenly found himself in a large room. The stark white walls and ultra modern furnishing barely registered with his brain. The odour of death and blood did. It was heavy in the air and his vision blurred momentarily, pain squeezing his heart before he realized the scent was off; it was human blood, not Lycan.

A wave of relief passed over him but it was short lived. Cassie was still alive, but where? The sounds of the helicopter were even louder now. He glanced around, saw a set of French doors at the far end of the room, and headed towards them, only to skid to a halt.

A middle-aged woman lay on the ground near the doors, a red blood stain marring her white shirt. He spared her a brief glance, but it was obvious she was dead from the way her unblinking eyes stared up at the ceiling. He had no idea who she was and didn't have time to ponder the fact. Outside he could see a helicopter lowering onto the roof top, its side doors open ready to receive passengers.

Yanking the door open, he hurried outside and scanned the rooftop, trying to figure out what was going on.

The helicopter was situated on the far right of the roof, its whirling blades adding to the already windy atmosphere and stirring up bits of debris. A pilot was looking out towards the far side of the roof. He swung his gaze that way as well. He could make out Aldrich, hurrying away from the landing pad, as quickly as the strong winds would allow. And there, farther to the left and near the edge of the roof, was Marla. But where was Cassie?

She had to be hiding somewhere, it was the only explanation for Aldrich to be running across the roof rather than escaping in the waiting chopper. He tried to scent the air, but with the strong winds it did no good. He scanned the possible places Cassie could have taken shelter; the rooftop elevator access? An exhaust stack? No.

Over there! There was a tiny movement near a roof vent. It had to be her. But, damn, it was the farthest from him and the closest to Marla!

Vaulting over a cement flower box, he landed lightly and took off running. He kept himself as low as possible, but the roof top provided little in the way of cover. Momentarily, he considered shifting. As a wolf he'd move faster and lower to the ground, but the pilot might see him transform. No, he couldn't risk exposing his kind to humanity; his hands were tied by the laws of his people.

Thankfully the others were too intent on what they were doing to notice him. Yet, even as he approached, Cassie stood up from her hiding place, but... She was in her wolf form! His fear spiked even higher. Cassie and her wolf weren't one yet. How would they be able to work together to save themselves? Damn, she must have been terrified to have changed willingly.

Aldrich shouted something. Cassie's wolf looked around wildly from Marla to Aldrich and back to Marla. It began backing up away from the approaching individuals. Bryan opened his mouth to shout a warning; she was nearing the edge of the rooftop; a forty floor fall was only steps away!

Marla's heart was pounding and her vision was blurring even as she approached the Greyson girl. When Aldrich had taken off after the girl, she'd slipped around the other way. Now Cassandra was within her grasp. She could easily subdue her, even if the girl was in wolf form. A new shifter would be no match for her.

Yet even as she planned her next move, a strange prickling sensation was coming over her. It was as if her wolf were trying to transform without her permission. She swallowed hard and clenched her fists, her nails digging into her palms. No! She couldn't do this. Not now! Didn't the stupid beast have any sense?

Go away, she hissed inwardly, flicking a glance around the rooftop. Aldrich was giving instructions and she tried to listen. Something about circling around and capturing the Greyson girl. She forced herself to take one step and then another. They had to grab the girl quickly and get away. Kane and Ryne would be here any minute.

The Finding

No, the creature insisted. Its power swelled, pushing outward. She felt herself starting to tremble with the force of her inner conflict.

She took another step. The Greyson girl. Aldrich would be pleased with her. And once the girl was declared unfit...

Not again. I won't help you bring down another of our kind.

You have no say in the matter. She lifted her chin, her eyes almost shut to block the bits of dirt the wind was blowing about, and took three quick steps before a blinding pain flashed in her head. She bent over cursing, holding her head. Why are you doing this to me? This is my chance to get on Aldrich's good side. To ensure my place.

No. The wolf snarled at her. She could feel its anger at her plans and she let her own emotions escape as well.

Mentally, she screamed at the creature. I hate you. I've always hated you. You're nothing but a stupid, ugly animal. I wish you'd never been a part of me.

I know. Its anger abated and it answered sadly. She froze transfixed, listening to it lament. *The day of our first transformation, I was so excited. I knew you were worried and tried to tell you not to be. I'd been with you for years, watching you grow, waiting for my time. I was anxious for us to finally meet and bond. I was so sure we'd be friends, that you'd be pleased to finally see me. We'd always be there for each other, helping and supporting.*

Instead, you hated me. You didn't like how I looked, how I thought. I tried to please you, I really did! I helped you even when it was wrong; even when you killed our Alpha! There was a break in the animal's voice as if it were recalling something painful. *You never changed, you were never happy with me or our life. I wanted a mate and pups; a place in the pack, nothing special just a home, someplace where I belonged. But you never listened, never cared. In all my years, you've never once welcomed me or shown me any consideration.*

Too bad! She snarled. I didn't want that life. I didn't want to be scorned as a half-breed for the rest of my life. The others laughed at me behind my back, they only pretended to be my friends; I know they did—my father told me. I was never good enough. My very existence was a stain on the family's name. The only way to redeem myself was to choose a worthy mate and I refused to do that. I wasn't giving in to him and the pack's ways, no matter what. I was going to be whatever I wanted to be and you weren't part of the plan. I don't want you. I'll never want you. Just go away!

The wolf paused and then began again, its voice growing steadily stronger. *I'm tired of being pushed aside. Tired of trying to be what I'm not. Tired of hiding, tired of living a half life.*

"No!" She tried to yell the words out loud, but not a sound came out of her mouth. She shook her head violently. The wolf wouldn't win! It couldn't.

She forced herself to move. One step, then another. She was almost close enough to catch her prey. The edge of the building was behind Cassandra, but it didn't matter. Another step. She reached out a hand to grab the young wolf when a spasm of pain stabbed her and she pitched forward onto her knees, falling to the ground beside the large roof top air vent.

Cassie jerked backwards as Marla suddenly lunged for her. Her hind legs stepped over the edge onto thin air and she fell onto her stomach, her front legs scrambling for something to hold onto, her rear end dangling forty floors above the street below. She whimpered in fright as she tried to dig her front nails into the hard roof surface while her hindquarters tried unsuccessfully to find a foothold on the metal flashing that edged the roof.

Oh God, she never realized how much she hated heights. Her heart pounded and her skin prickled. She was slipping backwards and there was nothing she could do about it.

She was going to die. Already her front legs were trembling from the strain of trying to hold herself up, that supposedly superior Lycan strength still missing. She couldn't hold on much longer. Despair filled her. What would happen to Kellen? Would Bryan find him and get him help? And where was Bryan? Perhaps Hugh or Swanson *had* succeeded in ambushing him in the stairwell. In her mind, she called out to him, desperate to know he was all right before she met her end.

The Finding

And then, as if in answer to her prayers, he called out to her! He knew she was in trouble and his voice was ringing in her ears, telling her to hang on, that he was coming. There was a sound in front of her. She looked up expecting to see him, but found herself face to face with a grey wolf instead!

Shocked by its sudden appearance, she stopped struggling for a fatal moment and in that instant quickly began to slide backwards. Too late, she scrambled for a hold, but felt herself going farther and farther over the edge. A panicked yelp escaped her and then the grey wolf lunged forward. It grabbed her by the scruff of the neck and began to pull, attempting to drag her to safety. For a moment they were both sliding closer to the edge, then the grey wolf seemed to gather its strength and gave a mighty tug.

She felt herself moving forward and hope sprang up inside her. She clawed at the roof with all her might, breathing a sigh of relief when her back toes finally found the edge of the building. One more tug and she was able to heave herself up. Collapsing on the roof, she panted heavily, unable to believe she was safe.

Something cold and wet nudged her. Trembling, she raised her head to stare at the other wolf, unsure who it might be. The creature blinked and nudged her again. Cassie knew it wanted her to move away from the edge of the building. She got to her feet and complied, her legs still shaking with reaction.

The grey wolf whined, then licked her muzzle. She almost stepped back in surprise not appreciating the slobber, but her own wolf took over, and licked the other animal in return. The grey's tail swung slowly from side to side as if pleased to meet her and make a new friend, then turned to stand in front of her in a protective gesture, its hackles rising as a low growl sounded from its throat.

She flicked a glance over the wolf's shoulder and tensed her own muscles. Someone—it had to be Mr. Aldrich—was coming, the sound of running feet audible over the wind and chopper noises. Actually, there were two separate sets of footsteps; one from where she'd last seen Mr. Aldrich and another from the direction of the penthouse. Who was the second individual? Another of Mr. Aldrich's guards? Or perhaps...

Bryan! He appeared beside the roof vent and breathed out her name in excited relief. "Cassie!"

Falling to his knees, he pulled her into his arms, burying his face in the fur around her neck. She squirmed, equally happy and relieved to see him and wishing she were in her human form so she could tell him so. As it was she satisfied herself by nuzzling him and licking his face.

With his arms still wrapped around her, he turned to address her new friend. "I saw what you just did, and I have to admit I don't understand. When we have more time you'll have to explain it to me."

The wolf said nothing, but its eyes were haunted and sad before it turned to face the next arrival.

Mr. Aldrich appeared from the other direction, looking less than his usual pristine self. The wind had blown his hair all over, revealing the beginning of a bald spot. His cravat was askew and his shirt rumpled while dusty stains about his knees revealed the fact that he had fallen at least once while traversing the rooftop.

She had to give the lawyer credit. He came to a sudden stop, blinked twice possibly assimilating the situation, and then assumed a posture indicative of supreme confidence as he levelled the gun at them.

"More unexpected guests, I see. Such bad manners, appearing without an invitation." He tutted mockingly. "But then why would I expect anything else considering I'm dealing with filthy abominations." The last word was spat out.

Bryan released his grip on Cassie and rose to his feet. His anger was palpable, but that didn't stop Mr. Aldrich.

He shot a glance at Bryan, a sneer curling his lip. "I see only one of you made it by my guards and the charge in the electric door. That makes two for me and zero for you."

Cassie looked around, suddenly realizing the Alphas were missing. Was Mr. Aldrich right? Had they been killed too? A feeling of loss swept over her; one she didn't really understand.

She barely knew either of the men, but some instinct had acknowledged that Ryne was her Alpha.

"Two for you?" Bryan quirked his brow. "You don't consider your own men of any consequence?"

"Swanson and Hugh? Collateral damage." Mr. Aldrich gave a negligent shrug. "Do you have a name, wolf?"

"Bryan. And you must be Aldrich." Bryan looked the man up and down, as if taking the measure of his opponent.

"That's Mr. Aldrich to you." He gave Bryan a contemptuous look before shifting his attention to the grey wolf. "And Miss Matthews, I presume? For that is the only person I can imagine that you might be. To think I had a viper in my nest all this time." He cocked his head. "I'm curious as to why you never attacked. Certainly there were sufficient opportunities over the past three years." He chuckled darkly. "Not that it matters. Whatever game you were playing, it's backfired hasn't it?"

The grey wolf chose that moment to growl and took a step closer to Mr. Aldrich.

Frowning Cassie studied her wolf companion, understanding dawning. How could she have been so dense? In all the excitement of nearly falling, she'd ignored the fact that Marla had disappeared and been replaced by the grey wolf. But how could that be? From everything she'd heard, Marla would have pitched her off the roof, not saved her. Was it possible that Marla's inner wolf was as nice as the woman was nasty? It was a question she'd have to consider at another time for Mr. Aldrich was talking again.

"Don't come any closer, beast." Mr. Aldrich levelled his gun at the wolf. "I'll have no compunction about killing you. I don't need all of you. One will be sufficient proof for the scientific world."

"Put the weapon down, Aldrich. You won't be shooting anyone." Bryan narrowed his eyes, his fists clenched ready to act. There was such confidence in his voice; was he crazy? Cassie stared at him. Mr. Aldrich had a gun! What was Bryan thinking? Was this his Beta mode he'd been talking about last night?

Mr. Aldrich laughed and swung the gun towards him. "You're hardly in a position to be making demands. There might be three of you, but I'm the one with the weapon and I actually have silver bullets, specially made just in case."

Bryan snorted. "Fallacy. It only causes a mild allergic reaction."

"Really?" Mr. Aldrich nodded. "Thank you for the information. Still, I'm sure a bullet of any form will do some damage at this close range. Perhaps I should test my theory right now?" He cocked the gun and Cassie flinched as did the other two.

Mr. Aldrich laughed darkly. "Point proven. You all reacted so now I know this gun is a satisfactory weapon." He waved the deadly bit of metal negligently at Bryan. "You and Miss Matthews stay put. Miss Greyson, come here. If you cooperate, and get on the helicopter with me, I'll let your friends live."

She hesitated and then took a step towards Mr. Aldrich. She couldn't let anything happen to Bryan, and Marla, regardless of her past sins, had just saved her.

"Cassie, no!" Bryan reached for her and Marla growled, but Mr. Aldrich merely raised his arm and pointed the gun directly at Bryan's heart.

"Cassandra, you will do as you are told or your friends' deaths will be on your head."

She had no question in her mind that Mr. Aldrich meant his words. In fact, she was sure he'd kill them anyway, but at least this bought them a few precious minutes for whatever good it might do. She took another step towards the lawyer.

"Good doggy. Nice to see you won't need obedience school." He chuckled at his own joke and began to back away. "Head towards the helicopter, staying directly at my side. I don't want you attacking me from behind."

Desperately, Cassie tried to think of something to do. Aldrich was right beside her, his thigh level with her mouth. If she bit him, could she throw him sufficiently off balance that his shot wouldn't hit the others? It wasn't much, but it might be their only chance.

The Finding

She flicked a look behind her. Her gaze briefly caught Marla's then Bryan's. Understanding flashed between them.

For a moment, everything seemed to happen in slow motion. She turned her head and opened her mouth wide. Out of the corner of her eye, she saw Mr. Aldrich glance down. His mouth began to open to say something, his face contorting in anger. Her teeth pierced the cloth of his trousers, she could feel the material against her tongue. Bryan gave a cry and launched himself forward at the same time that Marla barked and jumped.

Then time returned to normal. She felt her teeth sinking into flesh and blood spurting into her mouth. The gun cracked down against her skull, pain exploding in her head. With a yelp she let go, and collapsed. Bryan knocked Mr. Aldrich to the ground and Marla had his wrist in her mouth.

The gun hit the ground and a shot rang out. Bryan swore, grabbed his leg, and fell backward. Mr. Aldrich scrambled to his feet. Cassie shook her head, trying to clear her blurred vision, but everything was growing dark. She had a vague impression of the grey wolf circling around before leaping to attack again.

Just as the wolf jumped, Mr. Aldrich kicked out catching the animal in the ribs. It flew through the air, hit the ground, and rolled over the edge of the roof.

"Marla!"

Chapter 26

Mel and Elise stared upward. What was going on in Aldrich's penthouse? The chopper had disappeared from sight, but they could still hear the sound of the blades.

Tired of sitting, Mel stood and began to pace back and forth. "I hate this waiting. I hate not knowing what's going on. I'm an action type of person. I know being pregnant I can't do much right now, but...argh! It's never bothered me before that Lycan society is so male dominated, but this," she swept her hand out to the side, "is driving me crazy!"

Elise frowned. "I've never thought about it; the men being in charge, I mean. That's just the way it is."

"I grew up in human society, with equal rights, women climbing the corporate ladder and all those other 'advanced' ideas. Aren't there ever any female Betas or Alphas?" Mel warmed on her theme, her frustration coming out.

"Well, you and I, being mated to Alphas, wield a certain amount of power because of our mates." Shrugging, she glanced around as if searching for words. "The males are—" She broke off what she was saying and jumped to her feet pointing skyward. "Oh my goodness, I thought I saw people near the edge of the roof!"

Mel turned and looked up, a hand clasped to her mouth. "Do you think it's...?" She couldn't bear to finish the question.

Elise squinted, then shook her head. "Even with Lycan vision, I can't tell for sure from this distance." She flicked a glance at Mel then returned to studying the roofline. "I might have been mistaken."

"I hope so." Mel relaxed, but kept glancing up nervously. "What could be going on up there?"

"Excuse me, ladies. What are you two doing out here?" A voice spoke behind them and they both spun around in surprise. It was the security guard they'd been hiding from earlier. His name tag said Vanderpelt.

"We...er..." Elise shot a panicked look at Mel.

Mel rubbed her hand over her extended abdomen in a circular motion and smiled ruefully at the guard. "I had to use the bathroom and we spotted this cute patio area and thought we'd check it out." She widened her eyes and slowly batted her long lashes in a manner she knew usually distracted the male population.

The guard frowned, but his voice softened. "This is a private building, ladies. You have no business being out here."

"Really? We didn't know that. I'm so sor—" She didn't get a chance to finish what she was saying for Elise suddenly let out a piecing scream.

"Oh my God, someone's falling!"

The words weren't even out of her mouth when a sickening dull thud echoed through the small courtyard. For a moment everyone stood frozen in place, then as one, took off running towards the fallen figure.

The guard was ahead of them and tried to block their view. "You'd better stay back, it's just a dog, but if it isn't dead, it might be vicious. I'd better shoot it just to be sure."

"No!" Mel and Elise spoke as one.

Mel grabbed his arm. "My friend here is a...a...vet. Let her check the...er...dog first."

Relenting, the guard nodded and stepped back muttering to himself. "What the hell was a dog doing up there? This is a no pet building. I'd better call Johnston and see if he knows anything about this." Pulling out his cell phone, he turned his back to place the call.

Mel and Elise clutched each other as they slowly stepped closer, both dreading seeing who it was yet knowing they had to look. As the guard paced back and forth waiting for someone to answer his call, Elise gave a quiet gasp.

The Finding

"Who...?" Mel peeked at the broken body, not recognizing the wolf at all.

"Marla." Elise breathed out the word as she slowly sank to her knees beside the animal. For a moment her hand hovered over the broken body, then with shaking fingers she stretched out her hand to touch the wolf's neck.

"Is she dead?"

A faint whimper came from the wolf in answer. It looked at them blearily and attempted to lick Elise's hand. Then, as the light faded from its eyes, a shuddering breath signalled the end.

"Oh God!" Elise started to cry and Mel crouched down beside her, cradling her in her arms and making soothing sounds.

"It's all right. Shh..."

"She's dead. All these years I've hated her, but now..." Shaking her head, Elise tried to bring her tears under control. "She apologized. Her wolf's last act was an apology. Why?"

"I don't know, Elise. It must have something to do with what's happening up there." Mel glanced up at the roof, wondering what was going on.

"Yes!" Aldrich gave an exultant shout as the wolf, his former assistant, Miss Matthews, disappeared from view. One down, two to go. They might have kept him hiding in fear for three years, but in the end, he was the one who would be triumphant.

He swung around, and scooped up his gun noting in passing that the young wolf, Cassandra, was limp on the ground beside him, a faint trail of blood showing on her head where he'd hit her.

"Aldrich!" The male beast, Bryan, growled at him from where he lay a few feet away. Blood was pooling on the ground around him as he clutched his thigh.

"You thought you were so tough, but you're nothing better than a dog. Perhaps I should put you out of your misery." With a sneer, Aldrich pointed his gun at the man. Surprisingly enough the fellow didn't flinch or cower, instead narrowing his eyes and

419

growling even louder. In fact, the creature seemed to be tensing its muscles as if preparing to attack.

Aldrich quickly calculated the odds. If his bullet didn't kill this Bryan fellow, there could be trouble. It was a noted fact that wounded animals were twice as vicious. And then there were witnesses to consider. The pilot had undoubtedly observed some of the interaction. Self-defence would explain one shot, but a second... Aldrich shook his head. It was better to make a strategic retreat but first...

Without warning, he swung his foot and kicked the man in the ribs.

Even as Bryan yelped and curled over, Aldrich was turning, shoving his gun in his pocket and hefting Cassandra in his arms.

She was a heavy, limp weight and he hoped he hadn't killed her. It suited his plans so much better, if she were alive for a few more years. Either way, he had a specimen to show the world.

He began to run towards the helicopter. His thigh throbbed in protest from where the wolf had bitten him, damn the creature. Clenching his jaw, he ignored the pain in his limb and kept his eyes trained on his means of escape.

Behind him he could hear a horrific growling and pushed himself even harder. His feet pounded across the surface and he fought to pull in air for his starving lungs. Aldrich dared to glance back and saw Bryan struggling to his feet. A movement by the patio doors caught his peripheral vision next. Swivelling his head in that direction he could see two half-naked men barrelling out onto the terrace. Damn, they looked like the men he'd seen in the surveillance video! Now there were three werewolves on his rooftop!

Swinging his gaze back to his goal, Aldrich saw that the chopper was only yards away.

"Get ready! We're taking off now!" He shouted the words at the pilot who was staring in shock at the scene taking place before him. "Move! Don't sit there gaping like an idiot! Move!"

Finally, the pilot seemed to come to his senses and grabbed the controls.

The Finding

The chopper's side door was open and Aldrich threw the wolf inside, then jumped in himself, quickly turning so he could check on his pursuers.

Franklin stood on the sidewalk in front of the building that housed Aldrich's penthouse. It was an impressive structure of steel, glass, and cement. The lower floors appeared to house exclusive businesses. He scanned the list of names noting expensive lawyers and psychiatrists for the wealthy, a jeweller, a few dummy corporations. Nothing for 'off the street' customers, though. Only private clients would get inside. The upper floors were high-priced condominiums. Again, no one could just walk in.

He rubbed his chin thoughtfully before giving a decisive nod. Bluster and bravado might work. Exchanging a glance with Meredith he jerked his head, knowing she'd follow his lead. They worked together like a well-oiled machine.

Lifting his chin, he set his face into an expressionless mask and strode up to the building. He pulled open the door without even a glance at the sleepy security guard posted there.

The man grunted in surprise and stumbled to his feet. "Hey, you can't—"

Franklin didn't break his stride, merely flashing his Service badge. It was outdated, but if no one looked too closely they'd never know. "Government business. Out of the way unless you want to be cited for obstructing justice."

Meredith followed behind elbowing the guard in the stomach when it appeared the man might try to stop her.

"Hey lady! Watch it!" The guard rubbed his stomach and hurried after them, straightening his jacket in what was likely a feeble attempt to look in control. "This is a private building. You can't just walk in."

"What's your security clearance?" Meredith snapped the question at the guard.

"No. Don't waste your time on him." Franklin directed the comment at Meredith, pleased that his skills hadn't tarnished from lack of use. "He's obviously not involved."

"Unless it's a clever ruse. Perhaps we should bring him in for questioning. He might know something." Meredith gave the man a considering look before moving on.

Striding through the lobby as if they had every right to be there, they made their way to the elevators, the guard trailing behind, sputtering questions of who and what and why.

"Penthouse suite, now." Franklin barked out the command, pleased when the man jumped. He smiled inwardly. Damn, but I still have it, he thought to himself.

"I...I'm sorry, sir, but that elevator is out of commission. Er...what branch of the government are you with?"

Franklin and Meredith exchanged looks of concern. How were they going to save Cassie if they couldn't get up to the penthouse?

"Alternate entrance?" Meredith ignored his question and gave him a hard stare. There was no indication of the worry she must be experiencing.

"There's the stairs, but they're only used in case of fire." The man explained apologetically. "It's forty storeys up, you know."

"Johnston!" A voice called from down the hallway. Another security guard was walking towards them. "Why aren't you answering your phone?"

"Sorry, Vanderpelt. I was dealing with these people." He gestured towards Franklin and Meredith then added in a sotto whisper, "Government suits."

Vanderpelt nodded. "Sorry to interrupt. When you're done here Johnston, we have a dead dog in the courtyard. It fell off the roof somehow. Big grey brute; almost looks like a wolf."

"A wolf?" Meredith started and paled.

Franklin struggled to keep his face implacable. "Can we see it? We're dealing with the illegal smuggling of wolves and have reason to believe the occupants of the penthouse are involved."

"Smuggling wolves?" Vanderpelt gave a disbelieving look then shrugged. "Sure. Whatever. As long as I don't have to dispose of the carcass. Follow me." He turned and led the way to the patio.

The Finding

When Franklin stepped outside, he saw two young women standing near a dead animal and fear clenched his chest. Could the wolf be Miss Cassie? Meredith grabbed his arm, obviously looking for support as they walked closer.

Franklin narrowed his eyes. Who were those women? One looked vaguely familiar and he searched his memory. Ah! Her pictures were in Mr. Greyson's files, the ones he had hidden away along with the wolf picture that had started it all. It was Miss Greene, the young reporter. He furrowed his brow in a moment of indecision before deciding to take a chance on her.

He nodded towards the women. "Those are two of our agents. We'll need to talk to them in private about this matter."

Vanderpelt rolled his eyes, but agreed. As he walked away, Franklin could hear the man muttering how his tax dollars were being spent on ridiculous projects like capturing wolf smugglers.

Franklin loosened Meredith's grip on his arm. "I'd better approach alone. If one of them is what I think she is, she'll be leery of strangers." Taking a deep breath, he approached the women. "Excuse me, are you Miss Greene?" He spoke softly and the woman turned as did her companion, looks of shock on both their faces.

"I...Yes, that's me. And you are...?"

"Franklin. I worked for Mr. Greyson and am a friend of Miss Cassie."

Both women gave him a wary look and he tried to reassure them without tipping his hand too much.

"I'm aware of Miss Cassie's...special qualities...and am only concerned for her wellbeing. Might I inquire if..." He swallowed and nodded toward the dead wolf on the ground.

For a moment neither woman spoke, they just studied him carefully, then Miss Greene slowly shook her head. "Miss Cassie isn't here."

"Ah..." He let his relief be seen. "That is exceptionally good news. Do you know where she might be?"

Both women looked up and Franklin followed their line of sight to the rooftop. He tightened his lips and exhaled in frustration.

Bryan gritted his teeth as he pulled himself up, one arm cradling his bruised ribs as he tried to stand on his injured limb. The bullet had gone straight through and he could feel the warmth of blood still trickling down his leg. Nope, silver wasn't deadly to Lycans, only an allergen, but dammit, it hurt and he was more sensitive than most. A stinging burn accompanied the throbbing of the wound, traces of silver left behind as the bullet passed through. It would also slow down the healing process. Shit! He took a hobbling step and exhaled loudly trying to rise above the pain.

Looking up, the sight that met his eyes, drew all thought from his injuries however. Aldrich had tossed Cassie into the helicopter and was now climbing in after her!

Bryan clenched his jaw and began running. It was a slim chance, but maybe...

"Up! Up! I want this thing in the air now!" Aldrich was shrieking instructions, the wind carrying the words towards Bryan.

Damn! He couldn't be too late. If Aldrich got away...

The chopper began to slowly rise, wobbling as the gusting winds battered it. The pilot seemed to be cautious in his manoeuvres, perhaps leery of flying in such conditions or perhaps shocked from what he'd probably witnessed.

Pain rippled through his body with each breath he took and shot up and down his leg with each pounding step, but he didn't falter. Closer, closer...

Hanging on to a safety rope, Aldrich was leaning out, looking down even as the helicopter rose from the rooftop. The man crowed over his success, calling down taunts. "You lost. I won. I'll always win against you. You're nothing but freaks of nature!"

"What's going on?" The pilot could be heard shouting questions back at Aldrich.

"None of your business. Just get us out of here."

"Okay, but strap yourself in and stay away from that door. The winds are strong and we're in for a rough ride."

"Yes, yes. Go!" Aldrich waved his hand dismissively at the pilot and looked out again, no doubt gloating over his escape.

Bryan inhaled deeply and tensed his muscles. The man might think he was getting away, but...

Taking two final running steps, Bryan leapt into the air and grabbed hold of one of the chopper's skids with one hand. His added weight made the helicopter list to the side and the pilot cursed violently. He could hear whimpering coming from inside the chopper; Cassie must be waking up! Gathering his strength Bryan managed to bring his other arm up as well so that he now had a two handed grip.

Above him, he could hear Aldrich shouting directions at the pilot. "Shake him off! Shake him off!" There was terror in the man's voice and well there should be, Bryan thought to himself with a snarl, but first...

"Cassie!" He shouted her name, praying she would hear him. "Cassie, wake up! You have to get out of there!"

He took a brief glance down and gulped when he saw how high up he was; the drop was at least twenty feet to the roof top. If Cassie didn't wake up and jump out in the next few seconds, they'd be too high up and the drop could be deadly.

Out of the corner of his eye, he caught a glimpse of Ryne and Kane as well. They weren't moving quickly, but at least Cassie wouldn't be alone should the worst happen and he didn't make it.

Suddenly, the chopper began to swing from side to side and he snapped his focus back to the skid he was holding onto with all his might. Obviously, Aldrich had persuaded the pilot to follow the command to shake him loose.

Bryan tried to pull himself up enough so he could swing one leg up, but his injured limb refused to cooperate. Cursing, he tried to bring his other leg up, only the chopper swung around in a circle and he missed. His arm muscles were burning, trembling from the strain and his bruised ribs protested being stretched. Fear and pain had his hands sweating. He felt his fingers slipping and sought to tighten his grip, when something smashed against his fingers.

Reflexively, he jerked away and found himself dangling by one hand.

"Ha! Take that!" Aldrich was hanging half out of the helicopter, and had used his foot to stamp on Bryan's fingers.

Suddenly, Cassie's head appeared, peering out the door. "Jump, Cassie!" Bryan issued the command, but her wolf whimpered, instinctively scared of the height. Its front paws shuffled nervously as it looked down. He could see the fear and confusion in her eyes, but there was no time for pretty words. It was leap from the chopper or be carried away by Aldrich to suffer who knew what.

Better the devil you know, he whispered to himself. Praying she'd survive, he growled his instructions. "Now! I'm giving you an order."

For a moment their eyes locked. He saw pure trust and belief shining in them, her faith that he wouldn't lead her astray and then she launched herself from the helicopter, the force of her pushing off causing the machine to sway even more.

"No! That's my werewolf!" Aldrich shouted in fury.

The man's words ruined any chance of hearing Cassie land. Was she safe? He closed his eyes; he'd made the best decision he could, he told himself. Ignoring the sick feeling in his stomach, he was about to turn and look down when Aldrich swore.

"Damn you! You'll pay for this." The man was inching along the skid, intent on stepping on Bryan's other hand.

Bryan clenched his jaw and slowly pulled himself up with one arm until he could swing the other up, grabbing onto Aldrich's ankle.

"No! Let go! Take your filthy hands off me!" Aldrich kicked and jerked, obviously desperate to free himself. Bryan tried to hang on, but knew his strength was almost spent. His fingers slipped a bit more. The wind buffeted the helicopter again and it swung around, Aldrich leaned even further out of the chopper still struggling to shake free of Bryan's hold, only his grip on the safety rope keeping him from falling.

And that's when it happened. Bryan watched the expression on the man's face as it switched from pure rage to terror and then... Aldrich's hand slipped on the safety rope and he screamed, toppling into space. It happened in a split second and before Bryan could think to let go, the lawyer's weight jerked against his arm and he too was pulled down.

There was a sense of air streaming past him, a crowd gathered below, the rooftop and the edge of the building rushing closer and closer and then...nothing.

****

Cassie crouched near Bryan's unconscious body, uncaring of the hard surface beneath her knees or the cold wind that whipped her hair into her face. People were hurrying past her, but she didn't look up to see what they were doing. Instead she kept her eyes glued on Bryan, watching the steady rise and fall of his chest, the pulsing of the vein in his neck. She hadn't dared move him, unsure of what type of injuries he might have sustained. Instead she forced herself to just stroke his hair and press a careful kiss on his forehead.

Ryne had assured her he'd be fine; that Bryan's metabolism would quickly heal any breaks or even a concussion, but she hadn't really believed it until he started to move and murmur.

"Bryan. Bryan?" She stroked his face and grasped his hand. "Please wake up and look at me so I know you're really all right."

Bryan's closed eyes quivered, then he slowly opened them and looked at her blearily. A crooked smile formed on his lips. "Hey. You're okay." He reached up to cup her cheek and she leaned into his caress, sniffling lightly as a few stray tears escaped. "Ah, Cassie, don't cry."

He moved to get up and she jerked her head away, pressing her hands to his chest to keep him on the ground. "Don't you dare! You stay right here until we're sure you haven't damaged anything." She leaned back and called for their Alpha. "Ryne! He's awake. Can you come and check on him?"

Ryne sauntered over, a towel wrapped around his waist. He seemed impervious to the cold temperatures as he hunkered down beside Bryan. "Your mate's worried about you. You okay?"

She shot her Alpha a panicked look at the word 'mate'. What was Ryne talking about? She opened her mouth to protest, but then clamped it shut. Time for that later, it was Bryan who mattered right now.

Bryan moved to sit up again and Ryne didn't stop him so Cassie just bit her lip. Supposedly Alphas knew best. "Yeah, I'm fine. Feel like I've been hit by a truck though."

Ryne nodded wisely. "Falling out of a helicopter will do that to you. Anything permanently damaged?"

Slowly, Bryan moved his limbs, wincing when it came to the leg that had been shot. "Nothing permanent though my leg stings. Aldrich was using damned silver bullets. I'll probably have a rash for weeks."

A crooked smile broke out on Ryne's face and Cassie sensed he'd been more worried than he'd let on. "Maybe Cassie can help you apply some cream." He winked at her roguishly and she felt her face burn with embarrassment. What was it with Ryne and all the sexual innuendo?

Bryan jerked his chin towards Ryne. "A bit cold for sunbathing. Or were you using Aldrich's hot tub?"

Ryne glanced down at his near naked form and chuckled. "Nah, when Kane and I switched forms, we...er...were a little low on energy and had to make some concessions. Luckily two cleaning ladies came along and we persuaded them to lend us some towels." Ryne grinned. "They were very helpful and under the impression that some elaborate security check was going on. You know anything about that?"

"I might. Was one of them concerned about your manners?" Bryan quirked an eyebrow.

"Yep. She preferred Kane and felt I was rude. Can you imagine?"

"Definitely delusional, I'd say." The two men laughed and Cassie could see the friendship they obviously shared.

Ryne got to his feet. "We have quite a mess to clean up here. Concocting a story to cover all of this won't be easy. I've put in a call to Lycan Link to send a Damage Control agent."

The Finding

Bryan slowly got to his feet. A few grimaces passed over his face hinting that he didn't feel quite as fine as he claimed. "I'll be with you in a minute, Ryne. I just need to..." He flicked his eyes towards Cassie and smiled sheepishly, giving a small shrug. "You know."

Ryne glanced between Bryan and Cassie. "Yeah, I know. I just finished with Mel a few minutes ago. Needed to reassure her I wasn't dead. And Kane's still with Elise." He chuckled and walked away.

Inexplicably, Cassie suddenly felt shy. Staring at the ground, she struggled to think of what to say. "I'm glad you're okay." She rolled her eyes and shook her head; that was a dumb thing to say. The man had almost been killed trying to save her.

However, Bryan seemed to have no problem knowing what he wanted. He took her by the shoulders and pulled her close, kissing her soundly before releasing her abruptly. "God, Cassie, I'm so glad you're safe."

"Me? I'm okay. My ankles and wrists hurt a bit from absorbing the shock of landing, but other than that I'm fine. You're the one we were all worried about."

He shook his head then wrapped his arms around her. Rocking her gently, he rested his chin on her head. "I wasn't sure. When I told you to jump, I prayed we weren't too high, that you'd be fine. I didn't know if I was making the right decision, telling you to jump, but I wasn't sure where Aldrich might take you and if I'd be able to track you."

She stopped his ramble of self-doubt by twisting in his arms and kissing him. When she felt him relax, she slowly pulled away. "I trusted you. I knew you'd never tell me to do something I couldn't handle."

"Yeah, well..." He pulled her close again, rubbing his cheek against her hair. She sighed and melted into him, content to stay within the haven of his arms while others dealt with the chaos around them.

All too soon, Bryan sighed heavily and released her, his hands loosely resting on her hips. "I should go help. But first tell me what happened to Aldrich."

"He's dead." She stated the fact plainly feeling no remorse over the man's demise. "You landed on the roof. He didn't."

Bryan winced. "That's going to be hard to explain."

"Not really." Kane strolled up to them in a state of undress equal to that of his brother's. "We have some unexpected help from some friends of yours, Cassie."

"Friends of mine? Who...?"

Kane nodded his head, and Cassie looked in the direction he indicated and gasped, barely able to believe her eyes. "Franklin?"

The man in question was framed in the French doors that led into the penthouse, looking much the same as he always had except he wasn't wearing his butler gear. He took a half step towards her, a smile breaking out on his face and Cassie began to run towards him, barely aware of Bryan's hands releasing her.

"Franklin!" She launched herself at the old man, nearly knocking him over, but he managed to brace himself. His arms wrapped around her, hugging tightly and she buried her face in his shoulder inhaling the long forgotten scents of cologne and peppermint that she'd always associated with him.

Leaning back, she smiled up at him. "I'm so glad to see you, but how...?"

Franklin smiled down at her, his eyes twinkling. His grip tightened, then he slowly let her go and stepped back. Arranging his features into the bland expression she knew so well, he clasped his hands behind his back. "Your uncle charged me with your care if something ever happened to him. I've been using certain resources to keep an eye on you. When it seemed you were in a spot of trouble, I felt it prudent to step in and do what I could."

"What he could!" Ryne barked out a laugh from where he stood nearby. "The man's got everyone involved convinced this is some top secret government case and that they'll be arrested if they breathe a word to anyone. His partner, Meredith, is going around collecting 'affidavits' and having people sign some pretty official-looking papers swearing secrecy."

Franklin lifted an eyebrow and inclined his head. "We do what we can."

"The DC Officer won't have much to do when she arrives." Ryne gave a satisfied nod.

"So you've been watching me all along?" Cassie frowned, still focused on what he'd revealed earlier.

"Not myself, but Meredith Mitchell has been supplying weekly reports."

"Mrs. Mitchell from the grocery store? I thought she was just a nice old lady who took an interest in me!"

"She *is* a nice old lady, as well as my former partner."

"Former partner?"

"I wasn't always a butler, Miss Cassie. Before working for your uncle I led a rather interesting life. In fact, we met through one of my cases. Unfortunately, I'm not at liberty to tell you anything about it though."

"Oh." She stared at the butler, not sure what to say.

He cleared his throat. "I've also taken the liberty of making arrangements for your young man."

"My young man? You mean Bryan?" She swung her head around and saw that he was walking towards them.

"Not that young man, the other one."

"The other...? Kellen! Oh my God, I forgot all about him!" She made to run inside, but Franklin put out his hand to stop her.

"No need to worry. He's on his way to the hospital. I've been assured he'll be fine."

Bryan arrived at her side and slid an arm around her waist. "What's up? You look worried."

"I forgot Kellen!" She shook her head unable to believe her lapse in memory. "And he's the reason we're here." She looked up to see him trying to hide a smile! "What are you looking so pleased about?"

"Me? Nothing." Bryan's face became a study of innocence and she stared at him suspiciously. Was he happy that she'd forgotten an injured friend?

Turning to Franklin, she opened her mouth to ask his opinion, but thought she saw a hastily erased smile on his face as well.

She folded her arms and huffed. "All right. I get it. Neither of you are Kellen fans. I understand, but he was good to me and I feel I owe him some loyalty."

Franklin nodded slowly. "Yes, he helped you when you needed it. But over the years, you've repaid your debt with interest. Supporting your friends is important so long as you don't let it come between you and something even more meaningful."

She bit her lip. Was something even more meaningful standing beside her?

Chapter 27

Bryan lay beside Cassie, his arm curved under his head as he watched her sleep. Her lips were parted and her lashes fanned out over her cheeks. He reached out and brushed a lock of hair from her forehead and she murmured softly, but didn't awaken.

His eyes were heavy and gritty; he knew he needed to get some rest for the day ahead. There was still some clean up to do, if they wanted to keep their involvement in this affair out of the public eye. In only a few hours the alarm would be going off and he'd have to leave, but right now, observing Cassie was more important. Poor thing was worn right out, he thought to himself. The teleporting, the drama at Aldrich's apartment, her reunion with Franklin and Teasdale, and now tonight, her first full moon. He smiled thinking of how the night had played out.

Things had been cleared up at Aldrich's with surprising ease considering the scope of the mess. While the case wasn't closed, Kane had seemed confident that with the help of a DC Officer, the Chicago pack and Franklin could cover up the entire incident, and was planning on contacting the other pack in the morning. With that in mind, they'd returned to the Estate at Franklin's insistence and enjoyed an elaborate meal of all Cassie's favourites, prepared by Mrs. Teasdale, the cook.

Since it would be a full moon, they'd decided to spend the night at the Estate as it gave the wolves lots of room to roam. As the evening had progressed and the skies had darkened, Cassie had become increasingly distraught.

She'd pulled him aside into one of the alcoves off the living room where they'd gathered and whispered desperately to him. "Bryan, I can't do this. I can't let go and allow a wolf to take over my body. I'm scared of what it might do." As she'd spoke, she constantly darted her eyes about as if fearful the others would hear.

He'd laced their fingers together and squeezed her hand. "You don't have to be scared. You've already changed twice. Once at your house and once on the rooftop."

"I know, but... I didn't plan those, they happened because I was scared. Tonight, it will be my choice to change."

"Yes, it will be your choice to embrace who you really are, to accept your whole self. The wolf's been with you for years. You know it, you've talked to it; is it really such a scary creature?"

She had frowned thoughtfully. "I guess not. We actually had a nice talk today and I could sort of see the wolf in my head." She gave a little laugh. "It was like a puppy wanting to play."

"See? Puppies aren't scary." He'd quirked an eyebrow. "I think what you're really worried about is losing control. You, my dear, are a control freak."

"Me?"

"Yes, you. And I can understand why. You've had to be in control to survive; there was Anderson you watched out for, working to support the two of you, maintaining the house, and keeping your wolf under control so you weren't discovered. It was a lot of responsibility to have thrust on you with no training and no one to guide you. But now, you have to realize you aren't alone. You don't have to be in control all the time. I'm here, Ryne's here. We'll keep you safe. Just let go and enjoy the experience."

She'd exhaled a shuddering breath. "I'll try, but my stomach's quivering."

"First time butterflies."

"Butterflies?" She snorted. "They feel more like vultures, if you ask me."

The sky had darkened and it was time to go outside. Kane and Elise had slipped away first. Then Ryne had clapped his hand on Bryan's back and wished him luck before moving on to Cassie. The Alpha had taken her by the shoulders and stared at her intently. "You did a great job today Cassie and you'll do fine tonight. Bryan's my Beta for a reason. He'll take good care of you." He'd then playfully tapped her nose and hugged her before putting his arm around Mel's shoulders and leading her outside. Mel was going to watch the transformation rather than participate since shifting after the first trimester was considered too dangerous. Bryan had watched them leave and thought he overheard Mel whisper something about giving Ryne a belly rub. Given Ryne's throaty chuckle and the way he'd nuzzled Mel's neck, Bryan decided he'd probably overheard correctly.

Alone in the front entrance, Cassie had looked up at him nervously. "Well, this is it." She'd tried to smile, but it had been wobbly and he sensed she was on the verge of tears. "What do I do?"

"Nothing. We'll go outside, sit in the moonlight, and relax. Our wolves will do the rest."

"Just like that?"

"Yep, just like that."

And so they'd sat on the front step, side by side silently watching the sky darken until they were bathed in moonlight. It had been a perfect evening for a first transformation; no clouds to obscure the moon, the air crisp and clear, but not too cold, at least not for him. Cassie had shivered, but whether it was nerves or the temperature he wasn't sure.

He'd pulled her close, an arm around her shoulders and had her rest her head on his chest and close her eyes. She'd snuggled in closer and he felt her breath feathering across the exposed skin at his neck. Rubbing his cheek over the silky smoothness of her hair, he'd kissed the top of her head, then lifted his face to the sky, calling his wolf and setting it free.

His muscles had slowly tightened and his breathing grew more rapid. Tension grew within him and he'd reached for it, embraced it, straining to draw it out as long as possible so that Cassie would be sure to join him. It grew and coiled tighter and tighter until he was teetering on the edge. And then, when he could resist the pull no longer, he'd let it wash over him; the most delicious feeling of release exploding within him as the air shimmered and his body changed form and the wolf appeared.

As he'd planned, Cassie had been drawn along with him. He'd reasoned she was too nervous and too tired after the day's events to go it alone. There'd be time enough for that on the next occasion. Turning to look at his companion, he'd nudged her playfully, snuffling her neck and welcoming her to the pack. The creature had been all aquiver; nervous and excited, eager to explore yet unsure.

He'd led the way, across the lawn and towards the tree line, the wolf at his side gradually relaxing as it came into its own. Their bodies had cast long shadows across the frost covered ground as they'd raced side by side, their breath puffs of vapour in the cool night air. Together they'd explored the small forest, playing tag, jumping over fallen logs, splashing through small streams created by the spring thaw. In a few places, small patches of snow still existed and her wolf had enjoyed burying its muzzle in the cold whiteness, then snuffling and shaking its head when the frosty crystals got up its nose.

The evening had been perfect, though taxing for him. His own wolf was ecstatic to finally have its mate by its side and was determined to stake its claim. Cassie's wolf had shown no restraint either, flipping its tail, giving come-hither looks, nipping playfully then rolling on the ground. It had taken all his willpower to hold the wolf back. In her human form, she wasn't sure if this was what she wanted and so he was determined to respect her wishes even if it half killed him.

It had been nearly dawn when he'd finally convinced her wolf to allow her to transform back. She had been exhausted and disoriented with only the vaguest memories of running across the expansive lawns of the Estate. She'd claimed that after that, everything was a blur. In his own mind, he thought her memory lapse was likely a good thing. Her wolf's wanton behaviour would probably have embarrassed her.

Now they were tucked in bed together in Cassie's old room. Childhood mementos were still scattered about; posters on the wall, a few school books stacked haphazardly on the desk. Apparently, Mrs. Teasdale had insisted that everything be left as it was, convinced that her Miss would come back. He lifted one corner of his mouth. The cook had been correct. Miss Cassie had returned, but would she stay?

He stared at Cassie again. A woman, yet still a child in many ways due to her unusual life. She had so much to learn; how to be a wolf and part of a pack, how to enjoy life without the constant fear of discovery, how to love, how to make love. An ache grew in his heart as he thought of the future. Would she be able to accept him as her mate? Could he overcome her earlier prejudices? He hoped so.

Oh so carefully, he moved to wrap his arm around her and slide her close. He buried his face in her hair, inhaling her unique scent, letting it wrap itself around him. This was home, here with Cassie. He closed his own weary eyes and sighed contentedly before drifting off to sleep.

The two Alphas and their mates lounged comfortably on the leather sofas that flanked the fireplace in the sitting room at the Greyson Estate. A fire burned cheerfully in the hearth, chasing away the morning chill, and a tray of bagels, croissants and various spreads, as well as coffee, tea and juice were set on a low table within easy reach. The heavy velvet curtains had been pulled back, allowing the early spring sun to shine into the room, brightening the rich, dark panelling and highlighting the interesting array of wolf memorabilia that Anthony Greyson had amassed over the years.

They'd all stayed at the Estate last night. It had been a full moon and the grounds had provided ample room for them to enjoy the occasion. Presently, they were waiting for Bryan and Cassie to make an appearance. The young couple had still been out frolicking when the rest of them had gone to bed. To pass the time, they were studying a picture of Kane in his wolf form, Franklin had retrieved it from its hiding place and re-hung it over the mantel where Anthony Greyson had originally displayed it.

"Damned fine picture I took." Ryne mused as he stared at the photo through narrowed eyes.

"You had a good subject to work with." Elise murmured from where she was tucked into Kane's side.

"It's hard to believe that so many events stem from the taking of one picture," Melody mused, her hand on top of Ryne's as he rubbed slow circles on her stomach. His other hand was busy holding a cup of coffee out of her reach.

Kane grunted. "We're lucky everything worked out as neatly as it did. Between Marla and Aldrich, that picture could have led to the destruction of us all."

"But it didn't. And in the end, Marla redeemed herself." Elise had a sad faraway look in her eyes as she spoke, always too tender-hearted.

"Her wolf redeemed itself, but I'll never believe that Marla actually did." Ryne took a swig of his morning brew, his face set in a scowl.

"But aren't they one and the same?" Melody looked puzzled.

"Usually, but not always." Kane sighed regretfully, staring at the contents of his mug. He took a sip and slowly shook his head. "I feel partly responsible. As Alpha I should know what's going on with the members of my pack, but I never realized. Little wonder Marla never wanted to go on a run. I'm guessing she's one of those strange cases where the human half never integrates with the wolf inside. Their personalities weren't compatible. It's sort of like twins. They might look the same, have the same parents, but they turn out totally different from each other."

Melody cleared her throat and sat up straight, looking nervous. "Speaking of parents..."

Kane flashed her a look and smirked, causing Ryne to frown. When Kane smirked it usually meant trouble for him. He dropped his hand from Melody's stomach, set down his coffee and shifted so he could see her face more clearly.

"As you probably know..." She paused and darted her eyes around the room's occupants as if worried about their reception of her statement.

Ryne raised his brows. "Know what, Melody? Spit it out."

"Ryne, leave your mate alone. She'll speak when she's ready." Kane rebuked him softly then settled back and looked at Melody with calm inquiry.

Melody glanced at Kane, flushed and looked down. Ryne felt himself bristle as jealousy shot through him. First Melody blocked their mental link and now she was looking at his brother and blushing! He fought to hold back the rumble that arose inside him and glared at Kane. Kane grinned evilly, but said nothing.

Taking a deep breath, Melody began again. "As you know, Lycan Link has been searching for my father and... They've found him."

Ryne snapped his head back to look at Melody. This was her big news? It was interesting, but... He frowned. Something wasn't right. What was going on?

Elise sat up, smiling broadly. "Mel, that's wonderful news! Isn't it, Kane?" She glanced up at her mate who seemed to be trying to hold back his own smile; the faintest hint of which could be seen in the corners of his mouth.

"And who might the lucky man be, Mel?" Kane asked smoothly, casually folding his arms behind his head.

"It's..." She started to say, then paused to study Kane carefully. Her mouth fell open as she gave an exasperated gasp. "You knew! Here I've been stewing over this for the past few days, not sure how to break the news, and you knew!"

"Knew what?" Ryne and Elise spoke in unison.

"About my father!" Melody stood up, hands on her hips, obviously fuming. "How dare you not tell me?" She glared at Kane.

Kane threw up his hands in mock surrender. "Don't be mad at me. I found out the same time you did, but figured it was your place to share the news."

"Oh." Melody began to calm down. "Well...that's okay then, I guess. Did you know about the mix-up, too?"

"Uh-huh. It gave me a few bad moments before I realized the mistake and moved to have it corrected."

Melody sat down again. "It gave me some bad moments, too. I had almost a week of thinking that…" She paused and shook her head.

"What?" Ryne broke into the conversation unable to wait any longer. "Melody, I swear if you don't tell me what the hell you're talking about this very minute, I'll—"

"Kane's my brother." Melody delivered the news deadpan, her eyes focused on Ryne's face.

Elise could be heard gasping and Kane chuckling, but Ryne barely noticed. He stared at Melody in shock, his entire body tensing as the implications made themselves known. "But he can't be. I mean, he's my brother and you're my mate." Suddenly, he paused and frowned, then slumped back in the sofa as understanding dawned. "Half-brother. He's your half-brother and my half-brother, but we don't share any of those halves."

"Right. Kane and I share a father while you and Kane share a mother. But you and I share absolutely nothing!" Melody beamed at him.

Ryne shook his head and ran his hand over her stomach. "I wouldn't say we share absolutely nothing."

Melody smacked him lightly and then turned to Kane. "Hi, brother!"

"Sis." He nodded at her then grinned. "Are you going to tell Ryne about the part that nearly gave you a nervous breakdown?"

"Oh! Right!" She looked at Ryne sheepishly. "I know I've been a pain in the rear lately, standoffish and—"

"Not letting me touch you." Ryne finished the statement, a scowl on his face.

"I know and I'm sorry." Melody cupped his face and gave him a quick kiss. "But you see, Lycan Link made a mistake and switched you and Kane, so for a period of time I thought you and I shared a father and were half-siblings."

"You and me?" Ryne let out a low whistle. "Now that would have been a complication."

"Damned right." Melody ran her hands through her hair. "I didn't know what to do, who to tell. I tried to talk to Bryan, but he was busy finding Cassie and then he told me to talk to Daniel since Daniel had grown up in the pack with you."

"Why didn't you ask me?" Ryne tried to keep the hurt out of his voice. Why hadn't Melody turned to him?

"Don't you see? I just couldn't because if it were true, then we couldn't be together and then there was the baby..."

A sheen of tears covered her eyes and Ryne pulled her close, pressing a kiss to the top of her head. "I understand. What did Daniel say?"

"Not much at first. Honestly, it's so hard to get information out of you guys. But eventually he started talking about your parents and how your family would come and go. I started to realize that certain things didn't line up with what my mother had told me about my father, so I contacted Lycan Link. I found out they'd discovered the mistake and were correcting their records and now you and I aren't related anymore!"

Elise laughed. "That's quite a tale, Mel. But why was Kane contacted and not Ryne?"

A guilty flush came over Melody's face. "Er...Ryne was, but I kept sneaking into his office and checking his e-mail. When a message came in from Lycan Link, I deleted it."

"Melody! Reading your Alpha's e-mail is not allowed!" Ryne scolded her.

"It's your own fault. Your password is my name. Even I can hack into your account when you make it that simple." Melody rolled her eyes and Ryne tried to growl, but ended up laughing.

He stood up and scooped her into his arms. She squealed rather satisfactorily and he grinned.

"Ryne Taylor, what do you think you're doing?" Melody squirmed in his arms.

"Taking you upstairs to have wild sex with you, of course. And you'll re-establish our mental link first. I miss sharing orgasms with you." He nuzzled her neck and nipped lightly.

"Ryne!" Melody shot an embarrassed look at Elise and Kane.

"Great idea, Ryne." Kane stood up and pulled Elise to her feet leering at her playfully. "Should we emulate them?"

Elise opened her mouth to answer, but Kane's cell phone rang. He checked the number and grunted. "It's the Chicago pack finally getting back to me. Every time I call, I get the Alpha's granddaughter on the phone. And then she says the old man is too busy to talk to me! If Sam Harper tries to put me off one more time..." He growled discontentedly. "Ryne, don't be too long. If we can finally arrange a meeting with the old man, I want to be able to jump on the chance."

Sighing, Elise stuffed her hands in her pockets and moved to stare out the window. Ryne couldn't make out exactly what Elise was saying, but she was definitely muttering angrily under her breath.

Melody nibbled on his neck and he switched his attention back to her, pushing his concerns for his brother and Elise to the back of his mind. Whatever their problem, they'd find a way to work it out.

Cassie walked down the hospital corridor reading the room numbers as she passed each door. Four-forty-six, four-forty-seven, four-forty-eight. There it was, Kellen's room. She paused and took a deep breath, her hand in her pocket touching the papers she had carefully printed off the internet earlier that morning. Blinking her eyes rapidly she held back the threatening tears, damning her raw-edged emotions. What was wrong with her? She'd thought this out carefully; she owed Kellen this much. She reached for the door handle.

Bryan's hand settled over hers, stilling her movement. "I still think you shouldn't see him."

She looked up at him over her shoulder. His face was devoid of emotion, just the flexing of a muscle in his jaw giving away the fact that he was displeased. Bryan felt she shouldn't be visiting Kellen, that she owed the man nothing. Earlier, when she'd tried to explain she wasn't just going out of duty, but out of friendship, he'd turned away, his hands clenching into fists.

The Finding

"I can go by myself," she'd said. "I know you don't care for Kellen. There are several cars in the garage that still have current plates. I'll drive myself."

But Bryan wouldn't hear of her going alone and so they'd driven to the hospital together. It had been a tense ride, the atmosphere thick between them. She hadn't known what to say and Bryan had been moody, almost angry. Any topic she thought of had seemed inappropriate and so she'd said nothing at all, twisting the ends of her scarf in her hands. It was a deep green and matched her eyes, or so her uncle had said. She'd found it in her closet that morning and had ended up crying over it; it was the last thing he'd ever given her. Tracing the tear stains with her finger tip, she'd sighed and leaned her head against the window, staring at the passing scenery…

It was that annoying state just before a rain. The world was dull and grey, the air heavy and damp. Bare, lifeless trees and muddy ground were about all there was to see; the only colour came from bits of garbage that had somehow escaped going to the dump. She noted a scrap of old Christmas wrapping paper caught in a clump of weeds. Its once colourful print now faded and sad, speaking of happier days now long past. Even the snow was depressing. The few remaining patches along the edge of the road were filthy from car exhaust. All in all, it matched her mood perfectly.

Glumly, she thought back to two nights ago and wondered how her relationship with Bryan could have changed so dramatically in such a short period of time. Transforming under the full moon had been one of the most freeing experiences of her life and she'd awoken the next day full of excitement and happy with the world. Bryan hadn't been there, though the indent on her pillow showed that he'd spent the night.

Two nights in a row sleeping in the same bed; she'd giggled, feeling foolishly happy and hugging the pillow to her chest. It seemed like her life was finally turning around. Mr. Aldrich was gone and she was back home. She no longer feared being a Lycan and Bryan was now in her life. A wide smile had spread across her face and she'd flopped back in the bed, hoping he'd return soon.

Of course he hadn't and she eventually went in search of him. Sadly, Mel informed her that he and the two Alphas were still working on 'clean up' getting rid of anything that might link the previous day's events to Lycans. They also had a meeting with the Chicago pack and there was no telling how long it might take.

She'd sighed but had made the best of things, filling the day with other activities. That, of course, didn't mean she forgot Bryan. He was often on her mind and she longed to talk to him about her night as a wolf. Some of her muscles were stiff with overuse and she was curious as to what they'd done. Hopefully nothing embarrassing, she thought, scowling when the wolf inside gave what sounded like an exceptionally contented sigh but refused to reveal any details.

With nothing in particular to do, she'd spent some time on the internet researching an idea she had, soon becoming so engrossed in the topic that she had been surprised when Franklin called her to dinner.

The skies darkened and Bryan still didn't appear. She had consoled herself that Mel and Elise were alone as well and they'd spent a pleasant evening getting acquainted. They'd all stayed up late waiting for the men to return until Ryne finally called around ten o'clock.

Apparently the Chicago pack was less than pleased that their territory had been invaded by two Alphas without first obtaining consent. They wanted compensation and various laws, clauses and precedents were being tossed about almost like weapons.

Ryne confessed that Kane was so upset he was threatening a takeover, which hadn't helped negotiations run smoothly at all. In short, it was going to be a long night and the women would be lucky to see them by morning. On that note, they all said good night, each heading off to their own lonely beds.

Which brought her up to this morning. She'd felt groggy when she'd awoken, having spent a restless night missing Bryan's presence in her bed, but shook off the feeling, knowing he was sure to come back soon. Anxious to finish her project before he arrived, she'd quickly dressed and settled down at the computer.

And that was where Bryan had found her; looking up treatment centres for Kellen to help him learn how to control his gambling addiction. That was when everything started to go downhill.

Dark circles under Bryan's eyes gave evidence that he'd been working hard on little sleep. Lines of tension had tightened his features. Apparently, there'd been some issues with the Chicago pack, but he didn't elaborate on them. In fact, he'd been rather taciturn and disinclined to talk about the situation, more interested in what she was doing and why.

It turned out, Bryan didn't want her looking up information for Kellen; he didn't want her visiting Kellen or even calling him. His demands got her back up and after that, well... Now they were outside Kellen's hospital room, barely speaking to each other.

"Cassie?" Bryan's curt voice brought her out of her reverie.

"I need to see him, Bryan. I know you don't understand, but it's what I feel I have to do."

"Then I'll go in with you." His chin jutted out and she held back her annoyance at his high-handed manner.

"No. This is something I need to do by myself. Go and wait in the lobby. I'll meet you downstairs in fifteen minutes."

Bryan clamped his jaw shut, his displeasure palpable, but he released her hand and stepped away. "Fine. I'll be waiting."

She nodded and watched him walk down the hall hurt by his unfeeling attitude. Her chin quivered but she quashed her feelings and turned to face the door. One deep breath, then another. Okay, she was ready.

She walked into the hospital room and was immediately struck by white. White walls, white curtains, white bedding, and Kellen's white face. His eyes were closed and his hands were lying at his side.

"Kellen?" She whispered his name, wondering if he was awake or not, taken aback that he looked so poorly.

Immediately, his eyes opened and a smile spread across his pale face. "Sandy!"

She walked over to the bed and sat down beside him, the mattress making a soft whooshing noise. "Hey, how are you? You don't look so good." She brushed his hair from his forehead.

"I'm okay, all things considered."

"What did the doctor say?"

He shrugged negligently. "A few bumps and bruises, some residual sedatives in my blood, but I'll be good to go tomorrow."

"I'm glad." She took his hand and he squeezed it.

"And you? How's my Girly?"

She closed her eyes at the endearment, forcing down the emotion that welled up inside her. She swallowed and opened her eyes. "I'm good."

"Then what's this?" He touched her face where a lone tear had escaped.

She sniffed and blinked hard. "Nothing. I'm just happy you're all right."

"Sure you are." He studied her face then dropped his gaze. Silence stretched between them, Kellen plucking at the bedspread, while Cassie studied the floor. It was white, too, with a few flecks of grey.

"Sandy?"

"Yes, Kellen?" She looked up at him warily.

"I'm sorry about Dollar Niche and Eddie and Hugh and—"

"It's okay." She interrupted falling back into her old habit of minimizing his failings.

"No. It's not okay. I was willing to trade you, our relationship, for money to finance my gambling. It was wrong. It was stupid." He pursed his lips and shook his head. "The only thing I can say is that at first I thought you'd be happy to be rich, but then, when I talked to you at the house, I realized you'd left your old life for a reason and I had no right to decide for you if you went back or not."

She smiled sadly. Same old Kellen, always thinking things through after the fact. "I know. You didn't mean to hurt me."

He smiled and looked relieved, pushing himself up a bit in the bed and seeming perkier. His guilt was always short-lived. "So, what happened to all the bad guys? I guess I missed all the excitement."

"Um...Mr. Aldrich was involved in some illegal dealings, but it's all being kept pretty hush-hush. I even had to sign papers swearing I won't talk about it with anyone."

"Whoa! That's serious stuff."

"Yep. They'll probably be around to see you, too. So don't say anything to anyone about what you heard or saw." She put some added sternness in her voice in the hopes that Kellen would realize how serious this was.

"That'll be pretty easy. I was too drugged most of the time to remember anything. Just fuzzy images and bits and pieces of conversations."

"Good! I mean it'll be easier for you this way, not to slip up."

He nodded. "So... After I've been sworn to secrecy and I'm released tomorrow, what are we going to do? Do you want to do some sightseeing in Chicago or fly right back to Vegas?"

She took a fortifying breath. Here came the hard part. "I'm not going back, Kellen."

"Oh." The smile left his face for a moment and then he brightened again. "That makes sense. You're an heiress. Why would you live in a pokey house in Vegas and work at a grocery store? You know, I was thinking a change might do me some good, too. What do you say I move up here and...?" He stopped talking obviously noticing that Cassie was shaking her head no.

"No, Kellen. You aren't moving here with me."

"But I said I was sorry! It was all a big misunderstanding, a mistake..."

"Kellen..."

"...anyone can make a mistake..."

"Kellen..."

"...and I promise I'll never do it again."

"Kellen! Will you please quit talking and listen to me?" She shouted the words at him and he finally stopped, giving her a hurt look.

"All right, I'll stop."

"Thank you." She composed herself for the little speech she'd prepared. "Kellen, I care for you."

"And I care for you."

She continued on, ignoring his interruption, staring at the wall over his shoulder. She knew she'd never get this out if she looked at him. "And for a time, we were good for each other. You helped me when I had no one and I'll never forget you for that."

"I didn't mind. I wanted to help you."

"And I'd like to think I helped you, too."

"You did, Sandy, more than you'll ever know. Without you I'd—"

"But we aren't good for each other anymore." She paused and this time Kellen had nothing to say. Stealing a glance at his face, she saw the shocked disbelief, the denial. He was slowly shaking his head.

She took a shuddering breath and opened her mouth to continue when he finally spoke.

"Sandy, you don't mean that. You and I..." He paused and swallowed hard. A sheen developed on his eyes and hers began to tear in response. "You're all I have. If you give up on me..." Kellen bit his lip and looked down; his hand was clenching the covers.

"I'm not giving up on you, Kellen, but I am moving on. I...I can't take it any longer; the broken promises, the disappointment, the sneaking and lying. We're always in debt."

"I'll stop gambling, Sandy. I promise. Right now on this very spot, I swear."

She reached forward and pressed her hand to his lips. "No, Kellen. We've done this before. You need help. More than I can give you." Pulling back her hand, she dug in her pocket and pulled out a piece of paper and held it out to him. "I found this on the internet. It's a private clinic for gamblers and it's not too far away. I called this morning and they're willing to take you, to help you. I'll pay the entire cost, if you'll go."

Kellen reached out and slowly took the paper from her hand. The room was silent as he read the information. "I don't know, Sandy."

"It's supposed to be one of the best places in the country. The success rate is high. Please, Kellen. Do this for me. For yourself. You're a wonderful man—smart, kind, funny, good-looking—but the gambling is ruining your life. You were lucky this time, but one of these days your luck will run out." She stopped talking and pleading and held her breath, hoping her words were finally making an impression, that he'd accept what she was offering.

"If I go, will you take me back?"

Her heart plummeted. This was the question she'd feared. Would her answer seal his fate? Should she lie? Or put her life on hold for him one more time? "Kellen, I..." Her voice cracked and she could no longer hold back the tears. "I can't. I'm sorry, I wish I could, but I can't. I have to move on; live my own life."

Kellen was crying too, silent tears dripping down his face as he finally realized this was the end. "What are you going to do? Will you stay here?"

"I don't know. I have my uncle's house, but I...I met someone. We've only known each other a few days, but I think...I hope we might have something together."

He wiped his nose on the back of his hand and took a deep breath, staring up at the ceiling. "I'm glad for you and I hope it works. You deserve to be happy."

"Oh, Kellen!" She launched herself at him and held him tight, sobbing against his chest. His arms wrapped around her, his warmth seeping into her, his familiar scent surrounding her. She cried for the loss of his presence in her life, for the dreams she'd had when they first met. She cried for the wasted years, the fights, the good times and happy memories. And she cried for Kellen and his future, hoping he'd make it and knowing it was quite likely she'd never really know. This was it, the end of the line for them. It was time to say goodbye.

She pulled away and wiped her eyes, taking deep breaths to try and compose herself. "There's one more thing, Kellen. I hope you won't be mad, but...I tracked down your parents. I called them and, if you want to talk, they're anxious to hear from you. Your mom...she cried when I said your name. Here's their number."

She fumbled in her pocket and pulled out the second piece of paper and pressed it into his hand. He looked up at her, his face ravaged and shocked. She imagined she looked equally bad with red eyes and a blotchy face. "Call them, please. They still love you." Standing, she backed out of the room, watching him stare blankly at the phone number in his hand. "Goodbye, Kellen. I'll never forget you."

As the door swung shut, she heard him softly call out. "I'll never forget you, either. Goodbye, Girly."

Girly. He'd called her Girly! The tears streamed down her face at the familiar term. Her vision was so blurred, she could hardly see as she made her way to the elevator. "Damn him!"

"Miss, are you all right?" Someone, a woman, placed a hand on her shoulder.

"I'll be fine." Cassie brushed passed the concerned citizen, uncaring that her scarf had fallen from her shoulders and was now in the stranger's hands.

"Miss, you dropped—"

She walked on, trying to hold back her tears. Girly. Why had Kellen said that? It was one of the first words he'd said to her and now it was the last. Looking around, she suddenly realized she was in the lobby. How had she arrived there? She didn't even remember using the elevator. She pressed her hand to her mouth, and tried to calm down, but her mind kept going back to what had happened.

She'd cut her ties to Kellen. It had been the right thing to do, the only way to force him to get help, but now... Oh God, she needed a shoulder to cry on, but where was Bryan? She scanned the room, but there was no sign of him.

She quickly walked around the perimeter of the lobby. He'd been here, she could scent him, but why had he left? Had Ryne or Kane called him with a job? Surely he could have told her he was leaving. Just in case she was mistaken, she peeked in the gift shop and the small cafe that was off to the side. No. He wasn't there. She compressed her lips and blinked hard, tears welling in her eyes again. Had he left her here? He had the other morning after the full moon. Was he going to be like Kane? From what Elise said, Kane worked all the time.

Insecurities filled her. Bryan had been so cold and bossy this morning. And he'd been angry while driving her here, almost as if spending time together was a burden. Had the tenderness merely been a show to lure her into joining the pack? And now that he thought he had her convinced, he was going to ignore her, possibly leave her to fend for herself back in Canada? What proof did she have that pack life was one big happy family, beyond what he'd told her?

Suddenly she felt empty and abandoned. The two most important people in her life were gone; Bryan had left her and she'd just pushed Kellen away. Was this how Kellen had felt when she'd said goodbye? Had it hurt him as badly as the loss of Bryan was doing to her now? Oh God, she had to get out of here before she totally lost control.

She began to walk towards the exit as fast as she could, brushing past other visitors, skirting around a grouping of chairs. The door was in front of her. She had to get outside, had to breathe some fresh air. The doors slid open automatically and she hurried through them.

The sounds of conversation washed around her, but she had no thought other than escaping. She looked around wondering where to go, then noticed a cluster of trees, instinct telling her to head that way. Blindly, she set off for the small green belt, picking up speed, then running, cutting across the parking lot, splashing through puddles, uncaring that it was raining, giving no thought to the traffic. Brakes squealed, profanities yelled, but she didn't stop.

Run, get away. Hide. It was all she could think of. If she ran fast enough surely she'd be able to escape the pain inside.

Chapter 28

Bryan strode down the halls of the hospital, peering into rooms, scanning seating areas. Where the hell was she? When Cassie hadn't appeared after fifteen minutes, he's gone upstairs to get her. He wasn't leaving her with Anderson any longer than necessary. Whatever she had to say to the man should have been over and done with in that period of time. Cassie was his and he didn't want Anderson near her. The man had had his chance and he'd messed up.

But when he'd arrived at Anderson's door, the man had been talking softly on the phone to someone. A quick scan of the room had allowed him to pick up Cassie's scent, but she wasn't there any longer. Thankfully, Anderson had been facing the other way and never even realized someone had popped their head in. He doubted he'd be able to exchange a civil word with the man.

Now he was looking for Cassie. The stench of illness, medicine, antiseptics, and humanity swirled around him as he tried to distinguish her scent. She'd headed to the elevator and then...? Logically, he decided she would have headed back to the lobby. Perhaps their paths had crossed, Cassie coming down while he was going up? He took the stairs, too impatient to wait for the elevator to arrive. As he clattered down the stairwell, he gave a short ironic laugh. With all the stairs he was climbing lately, he didn't have to worry about missing his workouts.

Arriving back in the lobby, he made his way to the middle, looking around expectantly. When Cassie didn't immediately appear, he stopped in the centre of the busy space, turning in a slow circle, studying each grouping of chairs, each huddle of humans. He clenched his jaw; she wasn't there.

He closed his eyes and inhaled deeply, frowning in concentration as he used all his skills to sort through the confusing cacophony that assaulted his keen senses. A smile slowly spread over his face as he detected the faintest trace of her scent. Following it carefully, he made his way through the hospital down one hallway and then the next; where was she headed? Her scent grew stronger and he walked with greater speed. Surely she was just around this next corner. Mentally, he planned the chastisement he'd give her for not meeting him as they'd arranged. He turned the corner and then stopped abruptly. She wasn't there. An older woman was holding Cassie's scarf and handing it over to someone at an information desk.

"...and she didn't stop when I called after her, so I thought I'd leave it here."

He stepped forward. "Excuse me, that's my girlfriend's scarf. I'll take it." He snatched it from the woman's hand, the cool silky material sliding over his fingers; it was as soft and smooth as Cassie's skin. Resisting the urge to bury his nose in the fabric and revel in her scent, he cleared his throat and tried to speak civilly. "Um...where was she heading when she dropped it?"

"Oh! It was near the elevator. Fourth floor. She was upset and crying." The woman flushed and leaned closer. "I don't know if she was referring to you or not, but I'm sure she was saying 'damn him'. You might want to have an apology ready."

"Thank you. I'll do that." He stepped back, guarding his expression to give no indication of the emotional turmoil he was suddenly experiencing. Who had she been cursing? Anderson or him?

Swearing under his breath, he'd moved farther down the hall and then leaned against the wall, closing his eyes. He was so tired he could hardly think straight; he'd barely had three hours sleep in the last few days. Kane was a hard taskmaster at the best of times and then when the Chicago Alpha had sent the granddaughter to the meeting... It had been touch and go if they'd be able to keep Cassie and maintain control of the Estate.

The Finding

While he hadn't cared about the Estate, the idea that another pack wanted control of Cassie had made him almost rabid with rage. Ryne had to order him from the room, to keep him from attacking the Chicago pack's representative. Thankfully, Kane knew the law well enough to ensure everything worked out, but the experience had been draining and had left everyone on edge. In fact, Kane was still muttering about taking over the Chicago territory and running it as a satellite operation.

He rubbed the heels of his hands over his eyes and then gave his head a shake. He needed to find Cassie and she had to be somewhere in the hospital. She wouldn't go wandering off. Would she? And so he began searching floor by floor, even being scolded by irate nurses for poking his nose into places where he wasn't allowed.

Still there was no sign of her. Obstetrics, geriatrics, paediatrics. Fuming, he swallowed his pride and headed back to Anderson's room, determined to beat the man if he didn't reveal where Cassie had gone.

Without knocking, he pushed the door open, startling Anderson who was eating some debatable-looking food.

"I'm here for Cassie. Where is she?" Bryan growled the words and Anderson dropped his fork and inched back in his bed.

"I...I think you have the wrong room. I don't know anyone named... Wait a minute. Do you mean Sandy?"

"Her proper name is Cassandra Greyson, as you well know. Now where is she?" He almost barked the words and Anderson visibly paled.

"Are you with the government? She said you might be coming." Anderson paused and frowned. "Though you don't look the type."

Bryan quickly clued in to what the man was thinking and used it to his advantage. "I'm plain clothes; undercover. Now where is she?"

"I'm not sure. She left half an hour ago. Listen, do I have to sign something for you because if I do I—"

Bryan left before the man finished. Half an hour ago. Where could she have gone? He ran his hand through his hair and tried to quell the fear that twisted in his gut. What had she said the other night? Once Anderson was safe, she'd leave if he took his eyes off her.

Damn. He thought they'd moved beyond that. After all the talking they'd done about belonging to the pack and how he'd take care of her. And then during the full moon when they'd been wolves together. No. It couldn't be true. She wouldn't leave him, not when he'd finally found her.

But what if she had? It would be his own fault. He'd left her alone—with good cause, mind you—but a Lycan's first transformation could leave them feeling off-kilter and vulnerable. And what if she was going into heat? Hormonal surges happened four times a year with the seasons, but given the pills she'd been taking, who knew what her system might be up to. If she was in season, her emotions could be all over the place!

And this morning, God he'd been so tired. And when he'd seen her, she'd been looking up information for Anderson. Without meaning to, he'd snapped, barking orders at her, not listening, not thinking. Little wonder she'd taken off at the first opportunity.

He walked out of the hospital and sniffed the air, hoping to catch Cassie's scent, but the rain was pouring down now, washing the air clean. Shoulders slumped, he sank down on a nearby bench. The rain soaked his hair and shirt, trickling down his face, but he paid no attention; his external discomfort was meaningless now. The pain inside him was all-consuming, there was an aching emptiness where his heart should be.

People walked past. Conversations drifted around him. They barely registered. His brain couldn't process anything beyond the fact that he might never see Cassie again. He propped his elbows on his knees and leaned forward, burying his head in his hands.

How could he have screwed up so badly? Right from the very moment he started looking for her, he'd made one stupid mistake after another. He'd tried his best to make up for their awkward beginning, painting a glowing picture of pack life and how he'd be there for her. Did she really hate the idea of being with him, of being part of his pack, so much that she had to sneak away without even saying goodbye? Apparently so.

He scrubbed his face with his hands. What should he do? Find her again, track her down, and drag her screaming and kicking back to Canada? Or should he admit defeat? She'd protested continually that she didn't want to be a Lycan, but he thought they'd been making real progress. The full moon they'd shared had seemed so special. And the times he'd held her as she slept. He'd been sure he'd found his other half. Obviously, he'd been wrong.

His throat grew tight as a lump formed in it. His eyes burned with suppressed tears. He squeezed them shut and firmed his jaw, willing his chin not to quiver. A pack Beta didn't cry, not even when his heart had been ripped from him. He'd never love another; never find a mate to replace her.

"Bryan?"

God, he could hear her voice as if she were beside him. And her scent. He'd never forget it as long as he lived. It would haunt him in his dreams...

"Bryan, are you okay? Are you sick or something?"

A soft hand touched his hair and then his shoulder and he jerked as an electric zing travelled straight to his heart. Cassie? In a blur of movement, he was standing and holding her in his arms, raining kisses down on whatever part of her he could find.

"Bryan! What's wrong? What's going on? You're holding me too tight, I can't breathe." She pushed against him protesting and he finally let her go, grabbing her shoulders instead.

He held her so he could see her face and shook her gently. "I've been looking all over for you. I thought you'd left. Where the hell did you go?"

"I...I was upset so I went over to that grove of trees to calm down. I looked around the lobby, but you weren't there and for a while I thought you'd left me." She stuttered to a halt and reached up to touch him. He closed his eyes as she brushed the hair from his forehead then cupped his face, running her thumb over his cheekbone. He leaned into the caress, pressing a kiss to her palm, a soft rumble rising from his chest. "Once I calmed down, I realized it was pretty stupid to get so worked up over you not being in the lobby. I'm sorry; I didn't mean to worry you."

Slowly, reluctantly, he straightened and her hand fell to her side. "It's all right. I might have over-reacted a bit." He cleared his throat. "Or maybe a lot."

Cassie stood on tiptoe and pressed a soft kiss to his lips, then looked at him, searching his eyes. "Would it really bother you that much if I left?" She cocked her head to the side, a curious expression on her face.

He closed his eyes and swallowed hard. This was it; the moment of truth. The words in his heart ached to be shared, yet actually saying them, opening himself up to possible rejection had him clenching his fists to hide their trembling.

"Cassie, when I couldn't find you, when I thought you'd run away from me, I nearly died inside. When you're gone, it's like a part of me is missing."

"Really?" A smile slowly broke out on her face.

"Yeah, really." He leaned forward until their foreheads touched. "I love you, Cassandra Greyson."

"Oh, Bryan!" She stared up at him, innocent wonder and love shining from her eyes, then she grabbed his face and kissed him hard. Laughing, she wrapped her arms around him and snuggled in close, rocking him from side to side. He brought his own arms up around her and hugged her tightly. She hadn't said the words, but he could see the love in her eyes and in his heart he knew someday soon, she'd be ready to speak them.

After a few minutes, he loosened his hold. "You're soaking wet, you know."

She gave a careless shrug, apparently content to rest her head against his chest. "So are you."

"Good thing the rain has stopped."

"It has?" Cassie looked around. "Oh yeah, you're right."

"I always am."

She chuckled and pushed him gently. "We should be going."

The Finding

He took her hand and began to lead her to the car. "You're all done visiting with Anderson?"

"Uh-huh."

He gave her a sharp look. Something was wrong, he could tell from her voice. "Did Anderson say something to upset you?"

"Not really." Her steps slowed. "I...I gave him information on that rehab centre I was researching and his parents' phone number and then..." She stopped completely and swallowed. "I said goodbye."

"Goodbye?" He said the word cautiously, not wanting to read more into it than he should.

She nodded slowly. "I told him we weren't good for each other anymore and that I thought..."

"Yes?"

"I thought...maybe...probably..." She stopped and faced him, placing a hand on his chest and looking up at him, her eyes filled with uncertainty and hope. "That I'd found someone else. Someone who was right for me."

He took her hand and brought it up to his mouth, pressing a kiss to it. "I think you have, too." He gave her a crooked grin then pulled her to his side. His heart soared in his chest and at that moment, he was sure he could conquer the world. "Come on, Cassie. Let's go home."

She wrapped her arm around his waist and there was a skip in her step as they continued to walk to the car. "Yeah. Let's go home.

Six months later, in Stump River, Ontario, Canada...

Cassie nervously wiped her hands on her dress and glanced across the room to where Bryan was sitting. Their eyes locked and he grimaced, rolling his eyes before turning away. As was the custom, the two who were to be mated didn't sit together during the meal, only coming together for the bonding ceremony. She thought it a foolish custom. It wasn't like she hadn't met Bryan before—they'd known each other for six months—but Ryne had been inexplicably insistent that the first bonding ceremony to take place in his pack be done properly.

Secretly she wondered if it wasn't fatherhood that had changed him. Ever since baby Grace had been born, he'd been acting different. Melody said it was what happened to all reformed bad boys once they had their own daughter. They suddenly saw the world in a whole different light.

Whatever the case, she couldn't wait for the meal to be over so Ryne could bond them and then—she pressed a hand to her stomach, trying to still the quivering inside—she and Bryan would finally be mates and consummate their union.

Surprisingly enough, since they'd arrived in Stump River, Bryan had behaved like a perfect gentleman, much to her chagrin. Oh they'd kissed, had even made out, but the stubborn man had a will of iron. He claimed he wanted to give her sufficient time to be sure this was what she wanted; that her life had been too full of changes and she needed to adjust first, to become one with her wolf.

It was sweet of him; thoughtful, kind. And at times she'd wanted to bash him over the head with his good intentions, especially when she'd gone into heat. Thank heaven for the Lycan form of birth control! Even with its help, she and her wolf had spent many a night bemoaning their fate, pacing restlessly, wishing for their mates.

Someone reached in front of her and she gave a start. They were removing her plate and she'd barely eaten a thing. With dinner over, the ceremony would be soon. A few of the guests were getting up and starting to mingle. She watched Bryan stand up and step towards her only to be intercepted by Levi and Marco who steered him in another direction. He cast a helpless look at her and she gave him a tiny wave, sighing as he was whisked out of sight.

"This is lovely, Cassie. I can't believe how beautiful Stump River is in the fall." Elise sat down beside her, looking out the window at the trees. She followed the direction of her gaze, taking in the amazing array of colours; deep reds, burnt oranges, leaves so golden they looked like drops of sunshine against the dark tree trunks. Warm days and cool nights had created the perfect conditions for an amazing display of fall colours.

"Thanks. Mel said September was the perfect time for a bonding."

"And a naming ceremony, too." Mel sat down on her other side, cradling the baby in her arms. "Where are Jacob and Leah? It's almost time for the ceremony and they won't want to miss it."

Elise surveyed the room, scanning the tables still overladen with food, the tall pots of dried grasses and fall flowers, the groups of visiting guests. "Hmm, Kane's outside with Leah, and Jacob was supposed to be with Daniel."

"Ah! Then they'll be playing computer games in Daniel's room." She nodded wisely, having come to know the pack 'computer geek' quite well over the past few months.

Elise made to get up. "Oh, I'd better get Jacob then. It isn't fair that Daniel misses all the fun because he's babysitting."

Mel chuckled. "Relax. He's happy to have a reason to hide. Ever since Cassie snagged Bryan, Becky and Emily—they're the teens in the pack—have set their sights on Daniel. The man spends half his time hiding nowadays."

"Poor fellow." Elise frowned.

"Not really. It's made Tessa come out of her shell a bit. She was always so shy and nervous around Daniel, despite the fact that he obviously liked her. But now that the girls are after Daniel she's showing signs of feeling territorial." Mel gave a satisfied smile which quickly faded as an undeniable odour wafted up from the baby. "Uh-oh. Time to find Daddy."

"Ryne?" Elise raised her brows and gave a disbelieving laugh.

"Yep. It's amazing what a man will agree to do when he watches you give birth." Mel stood up, and holding the baby gingerly went in search of her mate.

Elise turned back to Cassie. "So, how are you holding up?"

"Fine." She gave a self-deprecating laugh. "Actually, nervous as hell."

"Bryan will be a fine mate."

"I know. It just seems like such a big step."

Elise gave a reminiscent smile. "It is, but it's worth it."

"You and Kane... You're happy together?" She was hesitant to ask, but she'd sensed undercurrents between the two of them when they were in Chicago and was curious to know how it had worked out. They certainly seemed happy enough now.

"Uh-huh. We have our moments, but we manage to work out our problems. For example, back in Chicago. Kane had been working too much and I was spending too much time with the kids. We had a long talk and came up with a solution we hope will work." She frowned as if uncertain.

"What's the solution?"

"Kane wants to split the pack. It's getting too big for one person to manage. He has his eye on a territory that's under-populated with wolves and, in his opinion, poorly managed. There's something in the works, but he's being pretty close-lipped about it until he has all the facts. Damien—he's a friend of Kane and Ryne's—is going to do some preliminary scouting." She shrugged. "If it works, Kane should have a lot more free time."

"When will this all take place?" She asked, trying to distract herself from her growing nerves.

"If everything goes well, Kane's hoping to have a report by the time we get back." Elise glanced over at her mate. "He has a lot of confidence in Damien."

Chicago, Illinois, USA…

Sam Harper tapped the table with a pen, eyes narrowed, mouth clamped shut in a straight line. Six months ago a meeting with Kane Sinclair had raised everyone's hackles and the memory still rankled. The arrogant son of a bitch had dared to claim the Chicago pack was inefficient and mismanaged. Ha! As if he knew anything about what went on in this city. The man had no idea; absolutely none!

And then there was the brother. Ryne Taylor had stolen from the Chicago pack; Cassandra Greyson had been a potential packmate. Both her land and money would have gone far to assist their beleaguered resources.

But instead of being grateful that the Chicago pack wasn't pressing charges against them, Kane, Ryne, and the Beta, Bryan—another pain in the ass—had pulled out the Book of the Law, using it to claim what wasn't theirs. And then Sinclair had the gall to leave mumbling about a takeover!

Well, it wasn't going to happen. The pack had met and agreed on a course of action. It wasn't ideal—they all knew it— but sometimes necessity drove you to take actions you never thought you would. For example, hiring 'Sylvia,' or whoever she was, to kill Leon Aldrich. It had gone against the grain to go to outsiders for help, but that damned Sinclair wouldn't leave them alone; constantly demanding reports and updates.

Sam snorted. Well, Aldrich was gone and at least they hadn't had to pay Sylvia. It was a small thing, but some days you took what you could get in the way of good news.

With the money saved, they could afford to buy some more help for the next problem looming on the horizon. Rumour had it Sinclair was sending someone in to check the pack out, but the intruder would have a surprise waiting for him. Sam took a swig of beer and leaned back against the wall, one lip curled.

There was a small faction of Lycans that were true loners or rogues. They were usually tough, mean and as deadly as they came, but they were also for hire. A meeting had been set up with one of them for tonight. On the off chance Sinclair's 'spy' came around, the Chicago pack would have the rogue in their back pocket and whip the intruder's butt, sending him back to Oregon with his tail between his legs.

A glance at the clock let Sam know it was almost time. A final swig of beer; a glance around the smoky, crowded bar… Yep, the usual crowd looking to start something. Good luck with that you losers, Sam thought. I don't take crap from anyone.

Shoulders back, chin up; look each person straight in the eye until they're compelled to look away. Sam smirked. I'm an Alpha, buddy. You don't stand a chance.

Almost to the door and… There it was, a hand on the shoulder. Some jerk always had to try his luck.

"Hey, baby. You got a cute ass." The man's liquor-soaked breath was offensive as was the stench coming off his sweaty body. He tried to pull her backwards. "Wanna share—"

She jerked her arm back, elbowing the idiot in the stomach. As he bent forward, clutching his mid-section, she ground her stiletto heel into his foot, then pivoted around to deliver an uppercut to his chin. In less than a second, the man was an unconscious heap on the ground.

"Anyone else?" Hands on her hips, she surveyed the men who were gathering around her. The assault was nothing new. She frequented quite a few bars and the human males always thought she'd be an easy target, not knowing what she lacked in size, she made up for with skill and speed.

When no one answered, she sniffed and turned, walking slowly towards the doors; no hurried exit for her. She could see her reflection in the glass doors as she approached. Short, black hair spiked on top with a longer fringe almost hiding her eyes. She'd used black kohl liner to take further attention away from her eye colour. They were violet, a rare shade in humans and even rarer in wolves. Sam despised the colour; it was too girly for the image she tried to portray. Now, her black jeans and T-shirt, complete with leather jacket—that gave off the right vibes. Her heels were her only concession to femininity since they gave her some much-needed height.

She was at the exit now. No one had made a move to follow her, not that she expected them to. As the door started to swing shut behind her, she could hear the murmur of voices and allowed herself a tight smile.

"Did you see that?"

"She flattened Phil in two seconds!"

"Just a mite of a thing, too."

"Hey, Phil! You okay, buddy?"

The sound of the voices faded as she walked down the street, carefully assessing the shadowed doorways. Pools of brightness from the street lights brightened select areas giving a false sense that the street was safe, but Sam knew better.

Someone was following her. Not someone from the bar. This person had been waiting outside. Her rogue perhaps? She wouldn't put it past the unpredictable beasts. If he thought to get the better of her, he had another think coming.

The man was good, she'd give him that. His pace matched hers perfectly, but a prickling on the back of her neck, and the faintest shuffling sound gave him away. He had a slight limp. Odd. Wolves usually healed completely unless they neglected the injury. She'd ask him once she was done taking him down a peg or two for tailing her.

It wasn't that she needed help against Sinclair's spy, she was sure she could take whoever the bastard sent, but a male always seemed to impress other wolves more than a female and creating an illusion was what this was all about. Smoke and mirrors. She'd been using it successfully for the past three years, it would work again—a faint frown passed over her features and she bit her lip—it had to.

Sam reached the corner and walked around it, then ducked into the first doorway she came to. This was the corner she was supposed to meet the rogue at. She chuckled thinking that this meeting wouldn't go quite as the man had planned.
The sound of his footsteps grew closer, but the tempo had changed. The man suspected something. Sam twisted her lips, impressed, but not ready to let the man off. Muscles tensed, senses alert, adrenaline rushed through her as she prepared for a fight.

Damien paused in the shadows and assessed the situation. He'd been standing outside the bar, looking in through the windows, and had seen the little she-wolf sitting in the corner acting as if she owned the place. Her chair had been set at an angle to maximize her view of the room and prevent anyone from creeping up on her. It was a smart move, especially given the fact that she was nearly daring every red-blooded male in the joint to approach her.

She'd negligently rested her ankle on her knee, pulling the already tight jeans even tighter against her shapely legs. And her t-shirt, while conservatively cut, showed off her curves; not overblown but definitely present and well-toned. Yes, she had the type of body that haunted every man's dreams but what really attracted attention—at least his—was her attitude. The cocky tilt of her chin, the narrowed eyes—were they really violet or just a trick of the light? And then there was the arrogant half-smile that played over her full red lips; it all but screamed a challenge.

He'd love to take her on, but he had a job to do. Damien snorted at the word 'job'. It was a make work project dreamed up by Kane, but he'd taken it to humour his old friend. What was supposed to be a short visit with Kane's pack had turned into two months. Every time Damien made noises about leaving, Kane had another 'job' for him to do.

Kane and his cute little mate, Elise, were trying to save his soul, Damien was sure of it. Not that he had a soul left to save, but with no real plans of his own, he'd let himself be drawn into their various schemes.

Which was how he found himself in Chicago, watching this girl with the purpose of gathering intelligence about her pack. Were they really vulnerable to a takeover or was Kane overstepping himself? So far he'd only encountered the girl, but no doubt other pack members were about the city. Damien gave a brief chuckle. He really shouldn't call the female a little girl. While her height was lacking, she was supposedly in her early twenties.

Sighing, he tried hard to recall being that young. He'd just turned thirty and felt twice that old. And when he looked in the mirror each morning, the bleakness in his eyes and the haggard lines of his face told the tale of a life lived too hard for too long. Not that it mattered to him what he looked like. In fact, nothing really mattered anymore. He was just going through the motions of living.

When the girl finally stood up, she'd strolled across the bar and was promptly accosted by a middle-aged man unable to say no to the challenge she presented. Damien took half a step forward, ready to act—old instincts hadn't died after all—but stopped himself. He had to see if she was as tough as she pretended to be. If things got really bad, then he'd step in.

Of course, his chivalry hadn't been required. She'd flattened the man with a few smooth moves that gave no indication she was a Lycan before strutting out of the bar. Observers would think she was a star student from some local self-defence class.

Now she was walking down the street as casual as could be. Only the stiffness of her shoulders gave any indication she was aware someone was following her. Most wouldn't even notice the change in the set of her shoulders, but fine points like that always stood out to him; one of the many 'talents' he'd acquired over the course of his misspent life.

Well, he was here to learn about the Chicago pack. Using Samantha Harper seemed as good a way as any of getting up close and personal. With any luck, he'd have the information he'd need in no time and be sending it back to Kane.

If the Alpha decided to go with a takeover, it would eventually lessen the man's workload. Part of the pack could move to Chicago and function under the direction of a strong Beta appointed by Kane. With half as many wolves to watch over, in theory Kane would have more family time. It was a wise move. In the short time Damien had been there, he'd seen how much time the pack took, how the hours spent on pack business carved lines of stress in Kane's face and took away time from his personal life.

Yeah, he'd do this for Kane and his family. Family was important; they were with you for so short a time. Damien blinked and swallowed past the lump that suddenly appeared in his throat. No, it didn't pay to think of the past. There was only today. No past. No future. Just...today.

His skin prickled, the hairs on his arm rising as his instincts warned him of upcoming danger. Narrowing his eyes, he inhaled slowly and gently so no one could hear him testing the air. Picking through the scents, he drew out the salient information, then assessed the shadows again for any new movement. He cocked his head and listened. The she-wolf was poised, ready for action. He'd discreetly followed her progress down the street. Now he wondered what she'd be like against one of her own species.

This is for you, Kane, he thought to himself. I hope your idea works.

Holding his arms loosely at his side, ready for what might come, he stepped forward.

Chapter 29

Stump River, Ontario, Canada…

Time dragged by. Cassie smiled politely, made small talk, and tried to stop checking her watch every few minutes. Where was Bryan? When was the ceremony? Did it really take this long to clear the tables? She clenched her fists and tried not to scream in frustration.

Mel came bustling up and pulled Cassie to her feet, leading her to the back of the room. "It's almost time. Let me look at you." She began to adjust Cassie's dress and smooth her hair.

"Mel, stop fussing. She looks fine and you're going to make her nervous," Elise appeared with a glass of water and Cassie took it thankfully, enjoying the feel of the cool liquid sliding down her throat.

"I'm living vicariously through her—I never had a bonding ceremony—so leave me alone." Mel continued on with her poking and prodding, but Cassie frowned.

"You and Ryne never officially bonded?" She looked at the Alpha female in surprise.

Mel's hands stilled for a moment and then she continued. "No. Ryne was too unconventional back then and I was too new at being a Lycan to even know bonding ceremonies existed. And there was no Alpha around to perform the ceremony, so…" She let her voice drift off and shrugged.

Elise frowned. "I'll be back in a minute." She hurried off and a minute later could be seen talking earnestly to Kane.

"I wonder what that was all about?" She stood on her tiptoes to see over the crowds, squinting as she tried to determine what was being said.

"Who knows?" Mel gave the dress a final twitch then stood back looking satisfied. "There, all set and just in time. Here comes Ryne and Grace."

She watched Ryne proudly carrying his daughter. The baby was now dressed in a frilly pink dress with a lace headband complete with a big flower. Her eyes were already deep brown and framed by long lashes reminiscent of her mother's. "Here's our princess, all clean and ready to go." He tenderly kissed the baby before passing her to Mel.

Elise must have finished her conversation with Kane, for he strolled up and nodded at Ryne, smirking. "All done with your diaper duty, daddy?"

"Yep, all done." Ryne eyed his brother with a 'want-to-make-something-of-it' type of expression.

Kane grinned and hit his brother playfully on the shoulder. "Welcome to the club, bro."

"If you men are done, we have a bonding ceremony and then a naming ceremony to perform. The moon's rising. We can't wait much longer." Mel raised her brows, her toe tapping impatiently.

"In a minute, sis. I—" His cell phone rang and he cast an apologetic look at Mel before answering the call. "Kane here ... Damien? Do you have something to report already?"

She listened with interest to the one sided conversation. From the sounds of things this Damien person had been in some sort of a scuffle but was fine, just a bit bruised.

"All right. Keep me posted. Oh, and Damien? Good luck with Sam." Kane chuckled then flipped his phone shut.

Ryne raised his brows. "You didn't warn him about Sam Harper?"

"Naw. The surprise was exactly what Damien needed to pique his interest." Kane smirked as he put the phone away then looked Ryne up and down. "You and I, we need to talk."

"What about?" Ryne eyed his brother warily, but Kane just grabbed his arm and dragged him away.

Mel sputtered. "Kane! You bring him right back. We need to start the ceremony!"

Kane waved at her negligently and Mel folded her arms, obviously fuming.

Thankfully, Olivia and Marco passed by and offered some distraction. Both praised Mel for her planning of the event and then brushed kisses over Cassie's cheek. "You look so lovely, dear." Olivia's eyes misted over.

"Just like the pictures of her mother," Marco nodded taking Olivia by the arm. "Come, we need to find our seats."

Elise returned, holding Leah. "What was that about Cassie's mother?"

"Marco's done some discreet research and discovered he knew of Cassie's mother. As we suspected she was from one of the royal families and quite well known."

"So how did Cassie end up in Chicago with Anthony Greyson?" Elise pulled her necklace out of Leah's mouth and shifted her to the other hip.

Cassie only half listened to the explanation as she scanned the crowd wondering where Bryan might be. She already knew the story by heart.

Luisa, her mother, was supposed to mate another royal Lycan since apparently they were big on keeping royal blood in the family. But her mother fell in love with another were—no one knows for sure exactly who since it was covered up right away—and she ran off with him. When it was discovered, her lover was killed and Luisa was almost beaten to death for defying a royal edict. Somehow Anthony Greyson found her and whisked her away to America where Cassie was born. Unfortunately, Luisa eventually grew homesick and wanted to return to her pack to see her family, not knowing there was now a price on her head for sullying the blood line. She was killed hours after stepping into the country.

When the tale was finished, Elise looked at Cassie with sympathy in her eyes. "Oh, Cassie, I'm so sorry to hear that."

"Thank you. It's strange, though. I'd like to have known my parents, but I have no memory of them so it's more like a story than something that really happened, if you know what I mean."

Elise patted her arm. "I think I understand."

"Oh look!" Mel interrupted. "Ryne's heading to the front. Elise, we have to go."

Cassie leaned forward to accept Mel's kiss, then Elise's and then, finally, she was alone. She slumped back against the wall, already exhausted, her face hurting from the smile she'd been maintaining for hours.

From her alcove at the back of the room, she could survey the crowd. The whole pack was there as well as Kane and his family and some of Bryan's as well. She'd met his parents briefly and they seemed like nice people.

Franklin, Mrs. Teasdale, and Mrs. Mitchell had been invited, but had declined feeling it might be too dangerous and draw unwanted attention to their connection with Stump River. Instead, they were back at Greyson Estate. Cassie had decided to open it up as a getaway for members of both packs. Franklin, Mrs. Teasdale, and Mrs. Mitchell were considered her 'family' and being in on the secret of Lycan existence, now had the status of unofficial pack members. They took care of the Estate and made sure it was ready for any visitors. Mrs. Mitchell was especially proficient at ensuring there were no inexplicable wolf sightings and arranging cover-ups if any vacationers got careless. Even Netty was happy, once the poor dog got over the shock of being surrounded by wolves.

Cassie understood their reasoning for not attending, but still missed them. The pack might be her new family, but sometimes she still felt alone.

Not for long, her wolf whispered. *Soon we will be joined with our mate.*

That's true. She nodded, shaking off her moment of melancholy. Soon she and Bryan would be as one. She squared her shoulders and lifted her chin. The signal came. The ceremony had begun.

It passed in a blur of faces and words. She couldn't recall what she'd said, let alone anyone else. Ryne stood before Bryan and herself. He tied their wrists together with a finely braided leather rope while reading the ancient words outlined in the Book of the Law. Then, before she knew it, it was over.

The Finding

Bryan was leading her from the room and they were officially mates. As they stepped outside, she could hear the crowd clapping and then shouts of laughter. She paused and looked at Bryan. "What's going on? I didn't think Grace's naming ceremony would be that funny."

"Didn't you hear? Elise and Kane ganged up on Ryne. They told him that since he's a father now, he'd better be officially bonded with Mel. There was no excuse not to since Kane's an Alpha, so he can perform the ceremony. Funny thing is, Ryne didn't even balk at the idea. I guess becoming a father has made him see things differently."

"So they're being bonded right now?" She turned and looked back at the house. "Can we go and watch?"

Bryan shook his head. "No, they'll do the bonding tomorrow. Elise said Mel needed time to get ready and everything is in place for Grace's naming."

"I wish we could see the naming ceremony. I've never been to one." She affected a pout.

"Sorry. The bonded couple isn't allowed to return until the next day."

She sighed. "Surely, they could have bent the rules a bit?"

Bryan shrugged. "Some of the traditions are pretty rigid. Bonding ceremonies have to be conducted before naming ceremonies if they're held on the same day. It's strange to us, but the ancient ones must have had their reasons."

Gently tugging on their bound wrists, Bryan led her towards the woods. He'd been busy the past few months building a small guest cabin, but for a while it would be their home. Newlyweds, he said, needed more privacy than the main house provided.

She didn't mind, in fact she was thankful that no one would accidentally overhear them. Consummating their relationship was exciting, but at the same time she was nervous. She'd read about it and knew the mechanics, but the real thing... It seemed overwhelming. Biting Bryan and drawing blood; him biting her. A shiver ran over her.

"Cold?" Bryan tucked her closer to his side. "We're almost there. I had Daniel light a fire so it will be warm.

473

"Thanks." Suddenly she felt tongue-tied which made no sense. She and Bryan talked all the time, but now it seemed...different.

Clutching Bryan's hand, she stared up at the sky. The moon was high overhead now; a golden orb on a midnight blue canopy dotted with sparkling stars. Its light filtered down through the still remaining leaves, casting interesting patterns on the pathway they walked along. A faint mist was forming near the ground as the cooler night air met the sun-warmed earth. It swirled around their ankles making the familiar woods seem new and mystical.

They rounded a bend and there in front of them was the cottage. She found herself slowing her pace as she neared the small building, climbing the two steps even slower, and then staring at the door as Bryan pushed it open.

Suddenly he tugged her close, their bound wrists between them and, snaking his free arm around her waist, picked her up and twirled her around twice. She squealed in surprise. "Bryan! What do you think you're doing?"

"Ancient human custom; carrying the bride over the threshold. I think it had something to do with warding off evil spirits or pretending that the female was being taken against her will." He shrugged and spun her around again before kissing the tip of her nose and setting her down inside. "I thought it would be fun to do."

She regained her balance and giggled. "It was sort of fun, once I caught my breath."

"Do you feel better now? Less nervous?" Bryan looked at her tenderly and she wondered how he knew. He cupped her face and rubbed his thumb over her cheekbone. "I always know how you feel. In my heart, in my head, we're connected already and it's only grown stronger these past few months. It's not as clear as a full blood bond, but I know."

"Why don't I have that yet?"

"You do. You just don't listen to it as carefully as I do and you still rely on your human senses more than your Lycan ones. But after tonight, we'll be on equal footing."

She looked at the floor and then peeked up at him through her lashes. "Will it hurt? When I bite you, I mean."

He laughed softly. "I sincerely doubt that I'll notice. I think there'll be a lot of other things on my mind. And you likely won't feel me biting you, at least not in a painful sense."

"That's good." She inhaled deeply and licked her lips, not sure what to do next.

"This leather binding has to go. I have some scissors on the counter." Bryan moved to get them, but she stopped him.

"Don't cut it! I want to save it as a memento of today. Let me try to untie it."

"We can't do that. It's bad luck and signifies the couple's bond isn't strong enough. Cutting it off is the only way to remove it. It shows that only death can ever separate us now." Bryan stared into her eyes as he spoke and she felt herself being drawn to him as never before.

He took their bound hands and pressed them to his heart. "Nothing will ever separate us, Cassie. I won't allow it. Not time or space. We might disagree and argue, but we'll always be together. The fates predestined our bonding. Our wolves knew each other even before we met and when we leave this world, we'll still be together."

"Bonded for eternity?"

He nodded and raised her hand to his mouth, pressing a kiss to it. "I will always love you, Cassie Greyson. No matter what. For Eternity."

With tears in her eyes, she twisted their wrists and pulled his hand to her mouth, so she could repeat the gesture. "And I will always love you, Bryan Cooper. No matter what. For Eternity."

Epilogue

Through half open eyes, Cassie watched the sunlight filter across the bedroom floor and onto the dresser. She could see the leather rope that had bound them together. It was coiled in a circle and she planned to tie it with a ribbon later on today and put it in her memory chest. Not that she'd need anything to help her remember yesterday. Her blood bond with Bryan had been spectacular.

She sighed contentedly. Bryan's head pressed to her chest and she lazily ran her fingers through his hair as she recalled the previous night.

The minute Bryan freed their wrists, she had felt her senses inexplicably heighten. The scent of new lumber and burning wood, the flickering light from the fire, the faint sound of chirping crickets outside the door; all came at her with increased clarity. Her own breathing, Bryan's, the thudding of her heart, the rustle of material as he stepped closer.

He'd slid his fingers into her hair, tipping her head up so he could stare deeply into her eyes. A faint smile had played over his lips, a look of wonder on his face as he lowered his head to kiss her, pausing when only a breath had separated them. "I love you, Cassandra Greyson."

The words had been whispered against her lips before he reverently kissed her. His lips had been soft and gentle, making her feel as if she were fragile and precious. He'd brushed his mouth over hers, back and forth, back and forth, until she was sure she'd die if he didn't stop and kiss her properly.

She'd whimpered and grasped his head, pulling him closer, pressing her lips to his and it seemed to have been the signal he was waiting for. Suddenly, the kiss became hotter, more passionate; his fingers clenched in her hair, and his tongue probed her mouth.

Her heart had begun to beat harder as Bryan slid his hands down her neck to her shoulders, her back. He'd nibbled on her lower lip, then slid his mouth along her jaw to her earlobe. Vaguely, she was aware of the zipper sliding down her back, of the cool air hitting her skin as the strapless gown pooled at her feet. Bryan's hands had felt hot on her skin, burning into her, stoking a fire inside her.

He'd eased her away from him and she'd opened her eyes lazily, her lips still parted and moist from his kiss. Why had he stopped? She'd wrinkled her brow then realized he was staring at her and that she was naked, except for her thong. Instinctively she'd moved to cover herself, but he'd caught her wrists and held her arms out to her sides.

"No. Let me see you, all of you." Bryan had breathed out the words and she'd trembled as his hot gaze seemed to devour her. The moment had stretched out and she'd felt her cheeks heating with embarrassment. "Cassie, you're so beautiful." He'd looked up at her and she'd seen the wonder in his eyes. He'd truly believed his words and she'd relaxed, basking in the glow of his praise. "Can I touch you?"

She'd swallowed and nodded, feeling overwhelmed by the enormity of the moment.

He'd let go of her wrists and reverently reached out to stroke her with one hand, sliding the back of his knuckles along the outer swell of her breast, down her side to her hips and back up again. Then, as if warming to the task, he'd used both hands skimming his knuckles down along the same path, turning his wrists when he reached her waist so his palms were touching her skin. Oh so slowly he'd stroked her, his fingers spread, encasing her hips, playing over her ribs, and then, finally cupping her breasts.

She recalled inhaling quickly as his warm hands had lifted her breasts, testing their weight, squeezing gently before he gently rubbed his thumbs over her nipples. She'd bitten back a cry that rose in her throat, but he'd known and stroked the sensitive tips again. Pleasure had shot through her and she'd grasped his arms to steady herself, almost falling when he replaced his thumb with his mouth.

"Bryan... Oh, Bryan..." She'd arched her back, thrusting her breasts closer, revelling in the feel of his mouth on her sensitive flesh; licking and sucking, tugging gently. Warmth had pooled between her legs and she'd squirmed wanting to rub herself against him, to feel his bare skin along hers.

Again, he'd seemed to know what she needed for suddenly she'd found herself being carried to the bed, and gently set upon it. As she'd sunk into the soft mattress, Bryan had stood beside the bed and stripped off his clothes.

She had been mesmerised as more and more of his body was revealed. She'd seen him shirtless and in gym shorts before, but Bryan at her bedside with the light of the fire playing on his shifting muscles—it had been more erotic than she could have believed.

When he'd finally skimmed off his briefs, her breath had caught in her throat. His manhood had stood out proudly from his body, long and thick, the head flared. She'd wondered what it would feel like to touch it with her hand, to feel it against her body, in her body...

Bryan had given her no time to think. He'd hooked his fingers into the waistband of her thong and drawn it down her legs. She had fought off the embarrassment as her last barrier disappeared, but soon forgot when he'd begun caressing her legs.

"I love your legs. They're so long and slender." He'd slid his hands up and down her calf and then moved to her thighs, stroking and squeezing, raining down random kisses. "The way they look in jeans should be considered sinful." His hands had slid under her to cup her rear. "And watching your butt wiggle when you walk almost brings me to my knees."

"No it doesn't." She'd giggled, suddenly finding his enumeration of her attributes funny.

Bryan had leaned forward and kissed her hip, before sliding his lips across her belly to lap at her navel. "Mmm... It does so, but you don't know it because if I'm looking at your ass, you're walking away from me. Just check over your shoulder sometime and then you'll see." He'd moved so they were face to face and smiled down at her.

She'd smiled back and reached her hands up, so she could explore his chest. "Your chest does the same thing to me. When I watch you working out in the gym and you're all sweaty. It's so sexy I want to rub my hands all over you." She'd accompanied her words with action and felt a rumble reverberate through his chest.

"Really?"

"Uh-huh. And I've longed to lick the sweat from you." She'd lifted her head and flicked her tongue over his brown nipples, giving them the same treatment he'd given hers. He'd closed his eyes and groaned again. Pleased to be affecting him as he did her, she'd begun to feel bolder and had moved her hands to his hips, her fingertips stroking his lower cheeks. "And for the record, I like your butt, too."

"Any other part of me you like?" Bryan had slid so that he was on his side, his arm propping him up. He'd gently brushed the hair from her face.

"Well..." She had touched his shoulder and then his chest. Sensing his invitation to explore his body more intimately, she'd moved her hand down his torso, noting how his stomach jumped when she trailed the tip of her finger around his navel and then traced a path lower still. Hesitantly, she'd stroked his shaft with her finger and watched it bob in response. "I don't know for sure, but rumour has it I'll really like this part of you." She'd peeked up at him through her lashes, smiling shyly.

"It likes you already." One side of his mouth had curled up.

"So I see." Feeling braver she'd wrapped her hand around him, marvelling at the rigid flesh. The skin had been warm and satiny smooth, pulsing beneath her fingers. She'd explored his length, tentatively squeezing, flicking glances up at his face to judge his reaction.

Bryan's eyes had closed, but a pleasure-filled groan had escaped him, so she'd continued. She'd held him firmly in her hand and stroked him towards the tip and back down. On her next upward stroke, she'd caressed the tip with her thumb and he'd jerked in her hand.

"Ah, Cassie, that's so good."

"I'm glad. I want to make you happy." She'd whispered the words breathily, her heart pounding with excitement.

"You could never do anything but make me happy." He'd opened his eyes and pulled her closer, giving her an open-mouthed kiss. His tongue had explored her mouth, and their tongues had duelled. Wet lips had slid over wet lips. The kiss had grown hotter, deeper. It'd been as if they were trying to consume each other.

Bryan's hand had roamed over her back, cupping and kneading her buttocks while he'd gently thrust his hips in response to her ministrations. The dampness between her legs had grown and she'd wanted to feel more of him. She'd drawn her leg up over his hip and guided his rigid flesh so it rubbed against her most sensitive parts.

"Not yet, Cassie. Not yet." Bryan had dropped his head back on the pillow, gasping the words as he'd pulled away from her.

She'd whimpered in discontent. There was a yearning for more at her very centre. "Soon? I want to feel you Bryan, all of you."

"I know, I know. Me, too." He'd flipped them over and trailed his hand down her body while nibbling on her neck. She'd felt his fingers playing with her lower curls, and then delving into her folds.

For a moment she'd stiffened, but it had felt so good, so right, she'd soon relaxed. She'd let her head drop back on the pillow, biting her lip, becoming lost in the feelings Bryan created. He'd stroked her sensitive flesh until she was writhing, so lost in need she couldn't think straight. And when a finger probed her and slipped inside, she was sure she might die from the joy, but it was only the beginning.

Bryan had known just where to stroke, where to press. A feeling had grown inside her and she'd found herself flexing her hips against his hand, rubbing against him, wanting more, needing more... Unexpectedly, a warm wave and a shiver washed over her and her body had tightened on his hand.

It had been nice, good. Her body had relaxed a bit, but then... Oh damn! Was that it? Had she climaxed too soon? Before she could formulate the words, Bryan had stroked her again, sucking on her breasts, gently biting, the tiny hurt excitingly erotic. The tension had begun to build again, faster this time.

She'd burned for him, her heart pounding, the blood thrumming through her veins. An aching void had grown within her again and she'd pressed closer, knowing only he could ease the discomfort.

"Please." She'd begged her request, no longer really knowing what she wanted, consumed with need.

Finally, he'd heeded her request. His fingers had slid out; he'd risen above her and parted her thighs. He'd paused at her entrance.

"Cassie, look at me."

She'd forced her eyes open and he'd smiled tenderly, grabbing her hand, pressing a kiss to her palm. "I love you."

"I love you, too." Tears had pricked her eyes at the expression on his face.

Then, lacing their fingers, he'd pressed her hand to the bed beside her head and slowly, oh so slowly, guided his flesh into hers.

She hadn't been a virgin, but it had still felt...strange. A tightness and fullness. He'd pressed in deeper, withdrawn, and pressed again. She had tried to relax, her breathing shallow, her heart pounding at the enormity of the moment. They were going to blood bond if she could just survive this...impalement.

When he'd filled her completely, he'd stilled. He'd leaned his forehead on hers, his breath shuddering. She had stared up at his face, his jaw had been clenched, his eyes squeezed tightly shut.

She'd worked her hand free and stroked his face. "Bryan?"

He'd opened his eyes and stared into hers. "You're perfect, Cassie. Hot and tight and perfect." He'd lifted his head to kiss her and had then begun to move.

The Finding

The first stroke had had her gasping as a bolt of sensation shot through her, then another and yet another followed. They'd grown within her, expanding with each stroke until she'd thought the pleasure couldn't get any better and then... Then everything had begun to tighten. Tension had coiled within her; Bryan's strokes had grown more rapid. Her own desperate need to respond could no longer be controlled and she'd thrust upward.

She recalled tossing her head on the pillow, needing more. Bryan's body had been pounding into hers. It had been hard to breathe, hard to see, hard to think. She'd clenched the bed sheets in her hand, sure she couldn't handle it, knowing she had to do something, she had to, had to...

Her body had started to tremble; the air had shimmered. She'd been panting, her lips dry. A drink, she'd needed a drink, but where...? There'd been a rushing sound, a thrumming. Right in front of her, she'd seen Bryan's neck, the vein pulsing, blood rushing beneath the surface of his skin.

Bite. We need to bite.

She'd blinked, trying to clear her thinking, vaguely aware of Bryan's hot mouth on her neck, his tongue licking, his teeth grazing.

Now, it must be now. Our mate is waiting. We'll be joined forever. Don't hold back. Now, now!

With a cry, she'd given in to her wolf's demands, her teeth sinking into his flesh. Warm, rich liquid had spilt into her mouth and she'd began to suck and lap, digging her fingers into his shoulders while his body still thrust into hers, harder and deeper, almost erasing the pinpricking feeling on her own neck.

Lights had begun to dance before her eyes. A voice—not her wolf, but another voice—had echoed faintly in her head.

Mine, my mate, my Cassie.

It had been Bryan. The blood bond was taking effect!

Voices, thoughts, and feelings had begun to knit a mental pathway, snippets of ideas and sensations flowing between them, increasing their mutual pleasure...

So good, so good. Her body had arched as her muscles tightened.

Can't hold on... Bryan's fingers had dug into her flesh.

More, faster, harder... She'd strained and reached...

I have to release... He'd plunged into her one more time.

She'd thrust upwards taking him as deep as she could and then...

Yes! Yes!

"Yes!" They'd both cried out in unison as the world exploded around them forging a link that would connect them forever.

She smiled as the memory played out. Bryan shifted against her and made a contented sound. Was he experiencing her thoughts even in his sleep? Recalling their bonding last night? Could they meet each other in their dreams? It was a curious idea and one she'd have to explore. With a happy sigh, she closed her eyes and opened her mind to the wonder of their new life together.

The dark brown wolf stirred and lifted its head to stare about through half closed eyes. The forest was silent, the light of early dawn creeping between the trees casting long shadows on the ground. Birds twittered overhead, but it wasn't their noise that had awoken her.

She got to her feet, yawning and stretching out her muscles in preparation for a run. He was here; she could sense his presence. Slowly, she began to move, the leaf strewn forest floor making silence impossible, but she wasn't worried. This time she wanted him to find her. For too long they'd been playing an elaborate game of hide and seek; living in the shadows, meeting in secret, not daring to reveal too much. But now those days were over. They were free to be as they were meant to be. There'd be no more denial. No more waiting.

A sound to the side caught her attention and she paused, one foot suspended in the air. She lifted her muzzle and sniffed, nostrils flaring as she took in the myriad of scents that drifted by on the light breeze, but there was only one that interested her.

He was there; his masculine musk had her quivering. She searched the shadows for movement and gave a soft woof of relief when she finally found him. Thick light brown fur covered his massive body, muscles rippling as he shifted his stance and raised his head in challenge. His hazel eyes narrowed and she dipped her head under the force of his gaze. As always his beauty and power took her breath away but now there was no need to run.

As one, they both moved, approaching each other, watching carefully. Noses touched and their tails began to slowly wag. She licked his muzzle and he returned the gesture, nipping lightly. He rubbed his fur the length of her body, marking her with his scent. Eagerly, she submitted to his attention, pleased they were finally one. For too long they'd been forced to stay apart, but now... A deep contentment filled her.

Soon, he was nudging her side. It was time to go, time to run. She followed his lead as they moved deeper into the forest, across streams, over fallen logs, around outcroppings of rock. The sun rose in the sky and leaves, heavy with morning dew, began to fall about them in a shower of red, orange and gold.

The air was crisp and cool, filling her lungs with its freshness. She gave an excited yip and her mate glanced back at her, his tongue lolling out the side of his mouth. He was happy, too. This was how they were meant to be. Running wild and free. Together. Forever.

~FIN~

A Message from Nicky

Hi!

Thank you for reading my book. I hope you enjoyed the story. If you did, please consider leaving some feedback at a book review site, or email me; I love hearing from my readers!

This series started as a one chapter short story which turned into a novel, a trilogy and eventually a whole series. With each book I write, the Lycan universe I've created seems to expand, new characters appearing and demanding their story be told. At this point, I can foresee this series continuing for some time.

~ Nicky

Connect with Me:

Email me at
nicky@nickycharles.com
Or nicky.charles@live.ca

Visit my website:
http://www.nickycharles.com

Follow me on Facebook:
https://www.facebook.com/NickyCharles/

Books by Nicky Charles

Forever In Time

The Law of the Lycans Series
The Mating
The Keeping
The Finding
Bonded
Betrayed: Days of the Rogue
Betrayed: Book 2 – The Road to Redemption
For the Good of All
Deceit can be Deadly
Kane: I am Alpha

Hearts & Halos series
(Written with Jan Gordon)
In The Cards
Untried Hearts

523 Central Avenue

MAR 2020

$18.98

Massapequa Public Library
523 Central Avenue
Massapequa, NY 11758
(516) 798-4607

CPSIA information can be obtained
at www.ICGtesting.com
Printed in the USA
BVHW091131030220
571274BV00006B/100

9 781989 058152